INTO THE FIRE

The incoming hurricane of flying steel pounding into the SEAL positions grew with each passing moment. Bullets whined and cracked through the air around the Americans, some clipping the taller blades of grass. It was obvious to everyone that the enemy had night vision equipment and was well prepared to deal with sneak attacks; especially those that happened during the hours of darkness. But like the SEALs, this evening's violence made it impossible for them to deliver accurate fire.

Brannigan knew the tiger was now tested; and he was tough, efficient and professional. Now was the time to break contact. The Skipper thought quickly, almost instinctively reaching the decision to withdraw fire teams from the ends first to leave the center of his battle line as strong as possible. He once more grabbed the radio handset. "Fire Team Delta, this is Brigand. Break contact and withdraw a hundred meters to the rear. For God's sake keep your heads down! The incoming fire is as thick as swarms of hornets . . ."

SEALS
GUERRILLA WARFARE

JACK TERRAL

JOVE BOOKS, NEW YORK

THE BERKLEY PUBLISHING GROUP
Published by the Penguin Group
Penguin Group (USA) Inc.
375 Hudson Street, New York, New York 10014, USA
Penguin Group (Canada), 90 Eglinton Avenue East, Suite 700, Toronto, Ontario M4P 2Y3, Canada
(a division of Pearson Penguin Canada Inc.)
Penguin Books Ltd., 80 Strand, London WC2R 0RL, England
Penguin Group Ireland, 25 St. Stephen's Green, Dublin 2, Ireland (a division of Penguin Books Ltd.)
Penguin Group (Australia), 250 Camberwell Road, Camberwell, Victoria 3124, Australia
(a division of Pearson Australia Group Pty. Ltd.)
Penguin Books India Pvt. Ltd., 11 Community Centre, Panchsheel Park, New Delhi—110 017, India
Penguin Group (NZ), Cnr. Airborne and Rosedale Roads, Albany, Auckland 1310, New Zealand
(a division of Pearson New Zealand Ltd.)
Penguin Books (South Africa) (Pty.) Ltd., 24 Sturdee Avenue, Rosebank, Johannesburg 2196, South Africa

Penguin Books Ltd., Registered Offices: 80 Strand, London WC2R 0RL, England

This is a work of fiction. Names, characters, places, and incidents either are the product of the author's imagination or are used fictitiously, and any resemblance to actual persons, living or dead, business establishments, events, or locales is entirely coincidental. The publisher does not have any control over and does not assume any responsibility for author or third-party websites or their content.

SEALS: GUERRILLA WARFARE

A Jove Book / published by arrangement with the author.

PRINTING HISTORY
Jove mass market edition / April 2006

Copyright © 2006 by The Berkley Publishing Group.
Cover design by George Long.
Cover illustration by Larry Rostant.
Text design by Kristin del Rosario.

ISBN: 0-515-14120-8

JOVE®
Jove Books are published by The Berkley Publishing Group,
a division of Penguin Group (USA) Inc.,
375 Hudson Street, New York, New York 10014.
JOVE is a registered trademark of Penguin Group (USA) Inc.
The "J" design is a trademark belonging to Penguin Group (USA) Inc.

PRINTED IN THE UNITED STATES OF AMERICA

10 9 8 7 6 5 4 3 2 1

To Mark Roberts
Caballero Valeroso de los Gatos de Oro
and discriminating patron of
la Cantina Bajo el Cielo de México

Special Acknowledgment to
Patrick E. Andrews
82nd Airborne Division and 12th Special Forces Group
(Airborne)

NOTE: Enlisted personnel in this book are identified by their ranks (petty officer third class, chief petty officer, master chief petty officer, etc.) rather than their ratings (boatswain's mate, yeoman, etc.) for clarification of status and position within the chain of command.

TABLE OF ORGANIZATION
BRANNIGAN'S BRIGANDS

COMMAND ELEMENT

Lieutenant William "Wild Bill" Brannigan
(Commanding Officer)

PO2C Mikael "Mike" Assad
(Rifleman/Scout)

PO2C Francisco "Frank" Gomez
(Rifleman/Commo Chief)

PO2C David "Dave" Leibowitz
(Rifleman/Scout)

PO3C James Bradley
(Rifleman/Hospital Corpsman)

FIRST ASSAULT SECTION

Lieutenant (J.G.) James Cruiser
(Section Commander)

PO2C Bruno Puglisi
(SAW Gunner)

ALPHA FIRE TEAM

CPO Matthew "Matt" Gunnarson
(Fire Team Leader)

PO2C Garth Redhawk
(Rifleman)

PO3C Chadwick "Chad" Murchison
(Rifleman)

BRAVO FIRE TEAM

PO1C Michael "Connie" Concord
(Fire Team Leader)

PO2C Lamar Taylor
(Rifleman)

PO3C Paulo Cinzento
(Rifleman)

SECOND ASSAULT SECTION

SCPO Buford Dawkins
(Section Commander)

PO2C Josef "Joe" Miskoski
(SAW Gunner)

CHARLIE FIRE TEAM

PO1C Michael "Milly" Mills
(Fire Team Leader)

PO2C Wesley "Wes" Ferguson
(Rifleman)

PO2C Reynauld "Pech" Pecheur
(Rifleman)

DELTA FIRE TEAM

PO1C Guttorm "Gutsy" Olson
(Fire Team Leader)

PO2C Andrei "Andy" Malachenko
(Rifleman)

PO3C Guy Devereaux
(Rifleman)

Falange: Spanish word for "phalanx," a military combat formation of ancient times in which foot soldiers formed a tight square with shields and spears overlapping. Also a fascist political party organized in Spain in the 1930s that was instrumental in overthrowing the Republicans in the Spanish Civil War. This was the only official party allowed in Spain under the regime of Generalissimo Francisco Franco, who ruled the nation from 1939 until his death in 1975.

RANKS OF THE FALANGIST ARMY—
EL EJÉRCITO FALANGÍSTA

Generalísimo
(Commander-in-Chief)

Mariscal
(Marshal)

General
(General)

Coronel
(Colonel)

Comandante
(Commandant)

Capitán
(Captain)

Subalterno
(Subaltern)

Suboficial
(Warrant Officer)

Sargento-Mayor
(Sergeant Major)

Sargento
(Sergeant)

Cabo
(Corporal)

Soldado
(Soldier)

Excerpt from Sun Tzu's *The Art of War* as paraphrased by Petty Officer 2nd Class Bruno Puglisi of Brannigan's Brigands:

When you're in enemy territory and they don't know you're there, just play it cool and stay laid back. Then, when the time is right, you hit the rat bastards with everything you got while they've still got their heads up their keisters.

PROLOGUE

ARTURO Sanchez of Bolivia, Patricio Ludendorff of Chile and Luis Bonicelli of Argentina were special envoys from their respective governments to the United States. They had been brought together through a most unusual agreement and sent north to the land of the *yanquis* on a mission of extreme sensitivity and confidentiality.

The three South American diplomats were given a covert but warm welcome to Washington upon their arrival and provided with quarters at a safe house in Georgetown. Now, after cooling their heels for forty hours, they sat in sullen silence at one end of a large conference table located in an out-of-the-way State Department meeting room. The trio, a trifle irritated, waited impatiently for their American contact to appear.

These gentlemen were specialists in the complicated environment of international diplomacy. They participated in clandestine segments of unique proceedings that only a few insiders knew about. Their duties required them to perform their surreptitious tasks in the strictest secrecy, and that particular day's activities were no exception. The subject to be discussed could absolutely not be revealed to the outside world, particularly to the populations of the emissaries' home countries. Revelations of the conference would cause untold embarrassment to all concerned, not to mention instigating the bloodiest revolution in the history of Latin Americà.

In short, it would make a bad situation worse.

The door to the room opened, and the South Americans snapped their eyes over in that direction. Carl Joplin, PhD, an American undersecretary of state walked in with a friendly smile, taking a seat at the head of the table. The African-American superdiplomat displayed a warm smile. "Good morning, gentlemen. Or should I say, *Buenos días, caballeros*?"

The three visitors smiled slightly in a subdued manner of greeting.

"I was most surprised to hear from all three of you at the same time," Joplin said. "It is hard to imagine what sort of crisis would have brought Argentina, Chile and Bolivia together in what appears to be a common cause."

"Then you realize that only the gravest of circumstances would have brought about this event that you find so electrifying," Ludendorff of Chile said.

"Frankly," Joplin said, "I must admit that at this moment I am more than just a little apprehensive. Your grim demeanors do nothing to allay my uneasiness." He leaned back in his chair. "I believe it is obvious that since I know nothing of your mission, I am unable to officially open this diplomatic session in which no agenda has been introduced." He smiled again. "Would one of you gentleman kindly do the honors?"

The Argentine Bonicelli spoke up in the realization that he and his two companions would have to start the ball rolling. "It begins with a fascist Spanish Army officer by the name of Jose Maria de Castillo y Plato."

"Ah!" Joplin exclaimed. "The Far Right enters the picture, hey? I am very familiar with *el coronel* Castillo and his service in the notorious Spanish Foreign Legion. His dossier also emphasizes a rather malevolent political background. Thus, it appears you are having problems with neo-Nazis in your particular necks of the woods. Is this the case?"

"Not neo-Nazis in the conventional interpretation of the term," Sanchez of Bolivia said. "In this case it is Falangists, Dr. Joplin. Castillo is from an old, established and extremely wealthy industrial family. His kinsmen are dedicated followers of traditional Spanish right-wing philosophies that strongly purport the reestablishment of a dictatorship in that country. We believe this potential regime would be even more draconian than that of *el generalísimo* Francisco Franco."

"A moment please," Joplin said. "As I recall the Falange was the political party that ran Spain under Franco."

"The same," Ludendorff said. "And since Castillo cannot realize his dream in Spain, he has chosen South America as the locale to establish a new fascist country. To be more precise, he wishes to do this in an area where Argentina, Bolivia and Paraguay come together. We are not in the least appreciative of this dubious honor."

"I am confused," Joplin said. "I see a representative from Chile here, but nobody from Paraguay."

"Paraguay is not involved," the Bolivian Sanchez said. "The war we had with them precludes any hope of cooperation between our two nations' armed forces."

"You are speaking, of course, of the Gran Chaco War, *Señor* Sanchez," Joplin said. "But all that happened between 1928 and 1935. Don't tell me that there is still bitterness about a conflict that occurred over three-quarters of a century ago."

"I assure you such animosity is alive and well to this day," Sanchez said. "At any rate, Colonel Castillo believes Chile has more strategic importance, because of its availability to the Andes mountains and the Pacific Ocean to the west. Consequently, he is ignoring Paraguay."

"Argentina," Bonicelli interjected, "offers access to the Atlantic Ocean, and thus is included in Castillo's ambitions."

Joplin shrugged. "Please, gentlemen, this is all pretty far-fetched, is it not? The whole concept is preposterous."

Sanchez shook his head. "I beg to strongly disagree, sir! Castillo has taken dissident officers and noncommissioned officers of the armed forces of the three countries into his movement. They have looted entire garrisons to get the matériel and weaponry they need. They are now well-equipped, armed and have begun making raids against isolated military posts in the area. These *Falangístas* have hidden camps in the Gran Chaco. As you know, that is an isolated section of South America abounding with swamps and grasslands. There are no roads or rail transportation. Rivers offer the most efficient means of travel. Thus the populations living there are under the Falangists' command and control."

"I would think," Joplin said, "that if you sent the armies of your nations against these rebels, you could easily crush them."

Ludendorff looked at his two companions, then turned a sad expression on Joplin. "The Latin American military has always been fond of political adventuring. Consequently, we do not know who to trust in our armed forces. We require outsiders to rid us of this problem."

"To be more precise," Bonicelli said, "the situation requires *fuerzas especiales*—special forces—to defeat the *Falangístas*."

"Let's speak plainly, gentlemen," Joplin said. "You are requesting American military assistance in battling and destroying these fascist revolutionaries, are you not?"

"Precisely," Ludendorff said.

"Then we should get to the specifics and requirements of the situation," Joplin insisted. "Without a detailed analysis of our adversaries, I cannot forward your request to my government."

"As of the moment," Ludendorff said, "the Falangists are no more than a detachment or two."

"A detachment is an ambiguous military term," Joplin said. "It is impossible to determine the makeup of such an organization."

Sanchez sighed. "We do not know their exact numbers, Dr. Joplin. But they have the potential of growing stronger—*mucho más fuerte!*"

"I see," Joplin said, "In that case, I must insist that you pass on to me all the intelligence you have on these fascists. I cannot possibly bring this matter up with the American secretary of state with no more than sketchy details."

All three South Americans reached under the table for their briefcases crammed with data. Now they could get down to business.

CHAPTER 1

SCPO Buford Dawkins turned off Orange Avenue and into the bar's parking lot. He whipped into a space, braked and cut the engine. His companion, CPO Matt Gunnarson, glanced over at him from the front passenger seat. "Looks like some Thanksgiving and Christmas plans are gonna go completely to hell, huh?"

"Yeah," Dawkins said. "There'll be at least a dozen leaves canceled."

"Well," Matt commented dryly, "it's like they say in the Russian Navy: toughski shitski."

"Tell me about it," Dawkins grumbled.

The two veteran sailors got out of the Accord to stride across the lot toward the entrance to the tavern. Dawkins led the way inside with Matt right on his heels. The Fouled Anchor was a SEAL hangout, and the noisy crowd inside was passing the evening in the riotous good spirits of being with their own kind. The deep camaraderie among the young men getting happily and carelessly drunk had developed through the sharing of ideals, commitment and experiences. These were the three traits that develop élan and discipline among professional fighting men, and outsiders were not be tolerated in their midst.

Senior Chief Dawkins and Chief Gunnarson nodded to a couple of acquaintances while glancing around the room. Moments later they spotted their quarry at the rear of the tavern deep into an evening of serious drinking. Several members of the SEAL platoon known as Brannigan's Brigands sat at a table happily knocking back pitchers of beers with the establishment's owner Salty Donovan, who was a retired SEAL. Salty's wife Dixie was behind the bar drawing some beer into a couple of pitchers when she noticed Dawkins and Gunnarson heading for the back of the tavern.

"Hey!" she called out. "You two hold up and grab these pitchers. They're for your buddies in the back."

"Sorry, Dixie," Dawkins said. "We ain't here to drink. We got important business to conduct."

"Are you collecting bets, or is it Navy doings?" Dixie asked. She was a heavyset woman, built solid like her robust Irish female ancestors.

"Navy," Gunnarson said.

"What the hell am I gonna do with these pitchers?" Dixie asked, exasperated.

"Give 'em to Salty," Buford suggested. "He'll knock 'em all back within five minutes."

"Oh yeah!" Dixie said. "That's just what that old bastard needs: more beer."

The two chief petty officers walked through the other tables of drinkers until reaching the place where the Brigands sat. They all looked up, surprised at the sudden appearance of the senior enlisted men of the platoon. But any happy drunken greetings were squelched by the serious expressions on Dawkins's and Matt's wind-burned faces. This arrival was obviously going to have serious consequences.

Bruno Puglisi, a petty officer second class, winced. "Hey, Chiefs," he greeted them. Then he hopefully added, "What's the good word?"

"Isolation," Dawkins said. "Now."

Salty Donovan, a holder of the Navy Cross won during his third tour in Vietnam, had been happily drunk, not only from the beer but from the enjoyment of being with some of his favorite people. This group had lost two men KIA on their last operation, and now it appeared they were about to go out on yet another. He set his mug down and leaned back in the chair, glancing at the young faces around him. The old vet wished he could go with them. Others in the room also noted what was going on at the rear table and realized something urgent was in the works.

Matt walked over to an old-fashioned pinball machine where PO2C Mike Assad was working flippers as he batted the steel ball under the glass cover. Mike's best pal PO2C Dave Leibowitz, sipping from a mug, silently cheered his buddy on. When he noticed Matt's presence, he nodded a greeting.

Matt nudged Mike, saying, "I hope you ain't winning."

Mike frowned. "Why the hell not, Chief?"

"Because you ain't gonna be able to play any extra games. The platoon has been alerted. Let's go. Immediately if not sooner!"

The two young SEALs looked around and saw Dawkins with Salty and the others. Dave grimaced. "Oh, shit!"

"Yeah," Matt remarked. "Oh, shit." He walked to a table where PO3C Chad Murchison was playing chess with a SEAL from another team. The chief announced, "Checkmate!"

Chad looked up. "Not yet."

"Then stalemate," Matt said. "Move out, Murchison. We've been alerted."

Chad frowned. "How incommodious!"

"Whatever," Matt commented. "Move!"

Brannigan's Brigands walked toward the door as a

group without making any comments. They nodded to Dixie on their way out the tavern, and she gave them a proud smile. Dawkins and Gunnarson followed them through the door into the cool night air.

An impromptu convoy formed as four POVs followed the senior chief's car out of the parking lot and into the street for the short ride down to the base.

NAVAL AMPHIBIOUS BASE
ISOLATION AREA
21 NOVEMBER
0530 HOURS LOCAL

THE sun was on the eastern side of the Laguna Mountains, hidden down near the desert floor, and none of its illumination showed yet on the distant horizon. It would be some time before it rose high enough to light the sundown side of the mountain range. Over near the Isolation Area entrance, a Navy Humvee appeared out of the darkness and came to a stop. Lieutenant Wild Bill Brannigan and his 2IC Lieutenant (J.G.) Jim Cruiser quickly exited the vehicle to walk into the illumination of the light at the gate. The Marine guard on duty knew them both by sight, but he checked their I.D.'s per regulations before he allowed them to enter the compound.

They quickly crossed the short distance to the entrance of the squat building to their direct front. When the two officers entered, they found Brannigan's Brigands just beginning to stir to greet the new duty day. A few were in the head going through their morning *toilette* while others were sluggishly dressing. They still hadn't gotten the word on why they had been so unceremoniously pulled out of the Fouled Anchor the night before.

The appearance of their two officers snapped them out of the early morning doldrums. Senior Chief Buford Dawkins walked in from the head. He immediately bellowed the order to attention. Now the men moved smartly, snapping into the traditional position.

"Good morning, sir!" Dawkins said with a salute as he reported.

"Good morning, Senior Chief," Brannigan said. "Gather the guys around. I've got a couple of items to pass on to them."

"Aye, aye, sir!"

It took Dawkins one more bellow to have the entire platoon assembled within five seconds. Brannigan gave the SEALs permission to make themselves comfortable, and they sat down on racks and footlockers, waiting to learn what the hell was going on.

"The first thing I want to say is that I'm sorry about everybody's plans for the holidays fizzling out. But I'm afraid it couldn't be helped."

Frank Gomez, sitting on a footlocker beside his buddy James Bradley, grinned. "You've probably saved the lives of about two dozen turkeys, sir. The humane society should give you an award."

"It wasn't my idea, believe me," Brannigan said. "Lieutenant Cruiser and I received a preliminary briefing last night. None of it was etched in stone, so we won't get the final word until the N2 and N3 show up with an asset. But right now I have good news, and I have bad news."

Joe Miskoski stood with a towel around his waist, his face still covered with shaving soap. "Give us the good news first, sir."

"Sure," Brannigan said. "The good news is that this mission will be carried out with one foot in the water. In other words, it's an old-fashioned SEAL operation with boats. There're evidently some rivers and creeks involved."

"Excellent!" Connie Concord said. He suddenly sobered. "What's the bad news, sir?"

"It appears we're going to be in the OA for quite a spell," Brannigan said. "Possibly for much longer than the last operation." On their last mission, the platoon had deployed on what was supposed to have been a quick linkup with a defector in Afghanistan, but the situation quickly deteriorated to the point that they were on the mission a bit over five weeks. Two of the Brigands had been killed in action during the ensuing combat. "And one more very important item. Because of the nature of this upcoming little happening, I'm adding seven more guys to the roster. Two are to replace Kevin Albee and Adam Clifford, of course. The other five are going to flesh out the assault sections."

"Assault sections?" Gutsy Olson asked. "What's that all about, sir?"

"It will all be explained later," Brannigan replied. He checked his watch. "All right! Go ahead and finish getting dressed. The briefing is scheduled to start at oh-seven-thirty hours." He nodded to Dawkins. "Take over, Senior Chief."

"Let's go, people!" Dawkins yelled. "We're gonna have company!"

The SEALs turned back to dressing. Thanksgiving and Christmas were completely forgotten with this latest news of going back into harm's way. Most wondered where on the globe they would be headed to put their asses on the line this time.

0730 HOURS LOCAL

THE Brigands were already occupying the seat/desks in the briefing area when the visitors arrived. There were more than just the usual three-man briefing team; seven SEALs, complete with their personal field gear, also came through the front door. These were the replacements and reinforcements Brannigan had mentioned earlier. Chief Matt Gunnarson directed them to the rear of the briefing area where chairs had been arranged for them. All were known by Brannigan's Brigands from other activities within the SEAL teams at the base. Reacquaintances were accomplished with nods and waves.

Commander Thomas Carey, the N3, took the floor, positioning himself behind a battered podium that had held many an OPLAN in the past. "Good morning," he said. "I see that Brannigan's Brigands are ready to go." He gestured to his two companions. "You know Commander Berringer, of course."

Lieutenant Commander Ernest Berringer, the N2, stood up and nodded to the assembled SEALs.

"And this other gentleman with us is our asset," Carey continued. "He'll be known as Alfredo for the time being." A husky, balding Latino sitting next to Berringer made no reaction to being introduced. Cary took a few seconds to arrange his notes on the podium. "Well! Shall we begin the briefing? The first item is the situation. A right-wing organization of rebel military officers of the Chilean, Argentine and Bolivian armed forces has occupied an area of southeastern Bolivia known as the Gran Chaco."

The Brigands began taking notes as Carey explained about the Spanish *generalísimo* Jose Maria de Castillo y Plato and his Falangist political movement. A question and answer period followed the situation briefing, lasting until all the Brigands were thoroughly familiar with the latest information on their potential enemy.

"I do want to emphasize one very important characteristic of these Falangists," Carey said. "These are not haughty Nazis as you would see in old World War II movies. The leader Castillo is a tried and proven officer in the Spanish Foreign Legion. This is an organization noted for brutal discipline. Castillo is also a modern right-wing fascist who has learned one very important lesson from the Communists. He quickly establishes rapport with the common people in the areas he wishes to control."

Chad Murchison, in civilian life a wealthy preppy with intellectual leanings, folded his arms across his chest as he thoughtfully scratched his chin. "Is it possible for us to neutralize this relationship he has established with the indigenous people? I am suggesting that this could effectively be managed if we are provided with the means and commodities to launch our own program of goodwill, i.e., food, clothing, medical support and even outright donatives."

Puglisi looked over at Chad. "Just what the fuck are donatives?"

"Gifts," Chad answered.

Brannigan interrupted, saying, "I've already got that potential under consideration, Murchison. We'll have to play it by ear until we discover the extent of these Falangists' activities in that area."

"This Castillo fellow," Carey continued, "is in fact striving to establish a nation within the Gran Chaco. This country is to be called the *Dictadura Fascista de Falangia*. That translates as the Fascist Dictatorship of Falangia. It's evident that he's making no pretense of forming a democratic government. And, by the way, the nation is referred to by its Spanish acronym DFF."

Joe Miskoski was skeptical. "This all sounds like a bad movie."

Brannigan again interjected, "It's all real, and you had better take it seriously."

"Now the mission," Carey said. "You are to enter the OA and locate the Falangists, engage them in battle, and defeat them. By 'defeat' I do not mean driving them from the Gran Chaco. That will not do—I say again—that will *not* do! They must be killed or captured to break the back of this revolution. If you fail, the result will be one of the bloodiest uprisings in the history of South America. And that's saying a lot."

Brannigan looked up from his notes. "Since the three armies of the affected nations cannot be trusted, who will be our backups?"

"All your support will come through American military and intelligence channels," Carey answered. "And the situation in Iraq puts you on low priority. However, actual deliveries will be made through CIA arrangements. But I'm edging over into Commander Berringer's bailiwick. So I'll turn the intelligence portion of the briefing over to him."

Berringer, a morose man who spoke in a near mono-
tone, replaced Carey at the podium. "The enemy you face
is called the Falangist Army. It is made up of units called
banderas that are similar to battalions in our armed forces.
These *banderas* are further divided into three to six *desta-
camentos* or companies. Each *destacamento* consists of
four *secciónes* each with four *equipos*. Naturally these are
all conventional in that they have infantry, heavy weapons
support, artillery and all the normal organization of military units."

Brannigan got to his feet. "Hold on! You're talking
about battalions here that could have as many as a thousand men each. Take a look around you, Commander. If
you count us, you'll see that we number twenty-one. How
the hell are we supposed to take on a field army or army
corps?"

"As of this time," Berringer explained," the Falangists
are only the cadre of such a unit; that is to say no more than
the nucleus or core. The commanders and staff are all that
make up these *banderas*. Without the rank and file the average of these units will be equal to your detachment's
strength. You'll find lieutenants and sergeants acting as riflemen in squads led by captains and majors."

"That's good news," Brannigan acknowledged. "But
how many *banderas* are we going up against?"

"We don't know," Berringer replied.

"This is getting more and more interesting with each
passing moment," Brannigan growled as he sat back down.

"Sorry I can't give you more information," Berringer
said. "But quite frankly there just isn't that much known
about this revolutionary army. However, as a side note of
interest, in most cases you can tell the nationalities of the
hostile force by their last names. Argentines seem to have
more Italian names, the Chileans are predominantly German, and Bolivians Spanish."

Milly Mills raised his hand. "Is there any cultural
clashes or prejudices between 'em?"

"Well," Berringer said, "the Argentines and Chileans think of themselves as Europeans. They have a tendency to look down on the Bolivians as country bumpkins, since many of them are of Indian ancestry like the Mayas and Aztecs." He stuck his notes back in a manila folder. "At this point, I'm going to let Alfredo continue with the intelligence briefing. He has actually been in your impending OA and knows it well." Berringer began passing out packets of maps and satellite photos of the area.

Alfredo had no notes with him. The man, a CIA operative, got to his feet and ambled over to the podium with his hands in his pockets. "Good morning, gentlemen," he said. Rather than speak in a foreign accent as expected, he had the intonation of southern Florida. "First of all, let me give you the lowdown on the Gran Chaco, since it is not a particularly well-known area. It is widespread, covering northern Argentina, northwestern Paraguay and southeastern Bolivia. You, of course, will not be expected to operate across the entire spread of the place. Your OA is in an area called Desolado."

Dave Leibowitz, one of the platoon scouts, asked, "What's the layout of the terrain?"

"To the west and south is a swamp called Los Perdidos," Alfredo replied. "It's pretty desolate and forbidding. You aren't going to be able to travel through there on foot. Boats are the only means of transportation. To the east and north are the Lozano Grasslands, which is a prairie of sorts. That's where several colonies of settlers are located. This is cattle country, and those people are struggling to establish themselves. You can be sure the Falangists have made friends with them, so you must approach the civilians with caution. In fact, I suggest you avoid them as much as possible until it is to your advantage that they know of your presence in the area."

"You haven't said anything about trees," Mike Assad, Leibowitz's partner in scouting, said.

"There aren't any on the grasslands or in the swamp,"

Alfredo said. "However, to the southeast is the beginning of the Selva Verde Mountains that stretch into Paraguay. That is jungle country in the truest sense of the word. It's almost as forbidding as the Los Perdidos swamp. And I might add it's a good place to hide out if it becomes necessary."

"I was told we'd have one foot in the water," Brannigan said. "What about waterways?"

"All right," Alfredo said. "The biggest river is the Rio Ancho, which flows west to east through the Lozano Grasslands. The smaller Rio Torcido comes down from the Selva Verde Mountains and goes into Los Perdidos Swamp. I might mention there are numerous creeks and tributaries going out of and feeding the two rivers. You can see that in the satellite photos. Unfortunately, not all these are mapped."

Jim Cruiser looked up from the photographs he was studying. "Will boats be provided for us down there, or must we bring our own?"

"I've made arrangements with some people I trust in the Argentine Marine Corps—*la Infantería de Marina*—and you'll be given three rigid raider boats. These are British Royal Navy surplus but are in good shape. They're propelled by one hundred and forty horsepower Johnson outboard motors, and can hit some thirty-five knots. These craft are a little more than five meters long and two meters wide."

"That sounds all fine and dandy," Brannigan said grumpily. "But they're noisy as hell, aren't they?"

"That they are," Alfredo replied. "And I've taken that into consideration. There will also be three civilian piragua wooden boats that are propelled by basic poling. As long as you're quiet when you're using them, there'll be no problems when noise discipline is a must. These are three meters long and will also prove more than adequate in the unhappy event you're forced into the swamp."

"What kind of weather can we expect?" Senior Chief Dawkins asked.

"At this time of year, which by the way is early summer in the Southern Hemisphere, temperatures range from one hundred degrees down to sixty-eight, so it's not all that bad," Alfredo said. "But at times it can become hot and humid. And there is also rainfall to consider. You can expect fifty inches to twenty-five inches. So take your ponchos."

"One foot in the water!" Bruno Puglisi exclaimed. "We're gonna be in up to our asses!"

James Bradley, the hospital corpsman, raised his hand. "What about medevac?"

"You will be able to call in medical evacuation," Alfredo answered. "Helicopters from the Petroleo Colmo Oil Company will respond. Their call signs are Petrol Uno and Petrol Dos."

"What the hell is this oil company all about?" James asked.

"Don't worry," Alfred said. "They can be trusted. You will also have access to an emergency relay station in Colombia that can send your transmissions farther on if that becomes necessary. Information on this is in the very highly classified SOI that you will keep sealed unless you find yourselves up to your necks in shit." He looked around the room. "Any more questions? Fine. Thanks, guys. And good luck."

Commander Carey retook the floor. "That's it, gentlemen. It's sketchy, I'll admit, and you can see that reconnaissance will be your first priority when you get into the OA. We'll be back in about forty-eight hours for the briefback."

The three-man briefing team made a quick, unceremonious exit. Brannigan went to the front of the room. "Okay. First things first. Organization. With the new men making us slightly larger, the platoon will be divided as follows. A command element for overall control, communications, reconnaissance and medical; and two assault sections that will consist of two fire teams each. A SAW gunner will stick with the section commanders during ops. Chief Gunnarson has a roster for each of you. Senior Chief Dawkins will make the briefback assignments."

The senior chief stood up. "Now hear this! The Skipper and Mr. Cruiser will take care of basic tactics, camp locations and other administrative details. Bradley will cover the medical and sanitation aspects of the operation. Concord takes weapons and fire support, while Gomez is in charge of commo. Me and Chief Gunnarson will handle the individual clothing and equipment." He paused and scowled. "Well? What the hell are you waiting for? Get to work!"

23 NOVEMBER

THE days and/or hours following the briefing were taken up by the creation of an OPLAN for the upcoming mission. The men, having now been assigned specific tasks, wrote up their portions of the plan. Lieutenants Brannigan and Cruiser, along with Chiefs Dawkins and Gunnarson, perused the work handed in. After a careful scrutiny, these were either accepted or handed back for additions, deletions and corrections.

When the work was complete, Brannigan took the whole thing off to a corner by himself for further tweaking and finalization. But even then it wasn't etched in stone. Commanders Carey and Berringer would return to have the OPLAN presented to them in a procedure called the briefback. If they approved everything, the document became an OPORD and would be considered the bible for the coming operation.

0645 HOURS LOCAL

THE platoon was assembled and waiting when Carey and Berringer returned to Isolation. At that point they were the audience, and they settled down in a couple of the desk/chairs ready to listen, take notes, and comment on the briefback presentation.

Brannigan, as the commanding officer, led the procedure. "Since the first order of business is reconnaissance, that is exactly what we're going to do. Rather than send the whole detachment out at once, I'm going to commit an assault section at a time to scope out the surrounding area. However, our two scouts Assad and Leibowitz will go on all these patrols. Since the Lozano Grasslands will probably be the scene of most of the action, we'll start there. The sections will take a motorized rigid raider boat, towing the piragua behind it. They will go down the Rio Ancho." He used his laser beam to point at a spot on the enlarged satellite photo mounted on the wall. "It will be the section commander's prerogative which of the creeks extending from the river to explore. They will leave the rigid raider boat hidden, then pole their way along the waterways in the piragua. No contact with the enemy will be made. If such a thing happens, the patrol is to immediately withdraw, engaging the attackers only in self-defense."

Carey wrote in his notebook as he asked. "How many of these recons do you plan to make, Lieutenant?"

"As many as it takes to get enough intelligence to launch active ops against the enemy," Brannigan replied. "That sounds simple at this point, but there's every chance things could get very hairy and complicated right off the bat."

The next speaker was Lieutenant (J.G.) James Cruiser. His topic was the establishment of camps. He swung his laser beam up to a spot on the photograph where the Rio Ancho eased out of the Los Perdidos Swamp. "This will be the location of our base camp for use during the recon phase. If the results of the scouting reveal long distances must be traversed during operations, I plan on having more camps as well as caches for weaponry and equipment. We will need waterproof containers for that. I've already sent in requisitions for a couple of dozen."

"I've seen the paperwork," Carey said. "It's being taken care of."

The next speaker was Hospital Corpsman James Bradley. "Due to the high temperatures, humidity and heavy rainfall in the area, I anticipate problems with rashes and possible heat stroke. I have made sure I'm taking plenty of antifungal ointment, and I plan on making sure precautions are taken to avoid heat exhaustion due to the climate."

"What about mosquitoes, Petty Officer?" Berringer asked.

"I've arranged for a case of insect repellent that should last for a long time," Bradley said. "I also coordinated with Senior Chief Dawkins on hammocks and headgear with netting. There will be plenty for the detachment."

"Have you taken any other medical problems into consideration?" Carey asked.

"Yes, sir. Each man will have an emergency medical kit to carry in his assault vest. These will include bandages, codeine, morphine, sedatives, stimulants and other medicine for illnesses. I will also have my field surgical kit for major trauma."

Petty Officer First Class Connie Concord gave a quick report on the weaponry. "The major new items in our arsenal are a pair of SAWs with one for each assault section. They will provide support fire when needed. I might add that these use the same 5.56-millimeter ammo as our CAR-15s. They are also magazine fed rather than belt fed, and that makes each man a potential ammo bearer. SIG Sauer nine-millimeter automatic pistols will be the hand weapons. We'll also tote some M-67 fragmentation grenades for defensive and ambush situations."

Frank Gomez, the commo chief, reported he was taking in an AN/PSC-5 Shadowfire radio with a spare for long-range commo. "All contacts among the Command Element, assault sections and fire teams will be conducted via AN/PRC-126 radios that have handsets. The detachment scouts will also have one. In addition, LASH radio head-sets would be employed within the assault sections. That way everyone can transmit to their mates via the throat mike that is capable of making even whispers audible."

"Call signs?" Berringer asked.

"The Command Element is Brigand," Frank said. "The First Assault Section is Brigand One and the Second is Brigand Two. All fire teams will use their phonetic alphabet designations. And we will have that emergency relay station in Colombia. That will only be used as directed by the SOI."

Next Chief Matt Gunnarson presented the personal supply picture. "The first-line equipment, that is what the guys will wear, will be lightweight tropical BDUs. Everyone will also tote along an emergency compass, matches, a good Swiss Army knife, a couple of PowerBars and condoms. The rubbers are good to keep things dry as well as keep the dust out of sensitive gear."

"Are you calling for combat vests or LBEs?" Berringer asked.

"The vests will work fine for our second-line equipment," the chief replied. "That'll include a day's MREs, the medical kit, two-quart canteen, frag grenades, binoculars, the GPS and water purification tablets. The third-line Equipment will be carried in the rucksacks. That's a basic load of MREs, entrenching tool, poncho, poncho liner, hammock, mosquito netting, extra socks, water bladder, an extra BDU, and night vision goggles. I checked with Alfredo, and he says there'll be no problem with resupply. It will be brought in by the same oil company we'll use for medevac. So we don't have to hump in two tons of stuff into the OA. Also, on account of security and concealment problems, there's gonna be plenty of FRHs for heating the MREs. It's gonna be rare when we'll be able to enjoy the coziness of fires. That's it!"

That was the end of the briefback, and Carey stood up. "You're ready to go, as far as I'm concerned. You'll be flown to Argentina on different airlines, dressed in civilian clothes. Your equipment will go down through CIA channels, and you'll pick it up down there. Alfredo will work out your infiltration into the OA. Times and places will be given you as soon as it's all firmed up. Good luck guys."

"Be careful out there," Berringer said.

The two staff officers walked out of the briefing area, and Senior Chief Dawkins turned to the detachment. "Okay, people. We've got to get our gear, detachment equipment, and other crap ready for the flight down south. Turn to it!"

The SEALs hurried back to the rear of the building.

CHAPTER 2

THE trucking center was a staging area for all interior shipments from the port of Buenos Aires. This cargo was not only sent to destinations in that country but to freight depots in landlocked Bolivia. The place bustled madly twenty-four hours a day as containers offloaded from merchant ships onto the trucks at the docks were brought in to be put into the transportation mill that would distribute the goods to their destinations. To the casual observer, the place would seem to be in disruptive chaos, moving slowly but inextricably toward its own self-destruction. But somehow the system worked, and the loaded vehicles were sent on their way.

One of the trucking companies was an innocuous outfit set off in a far corner of the shipping yard. This was Estrella Roja Transportes, S.A., which had no more than an office with a small warehouse located behind it. At that moment Lieutenant Wild Bill Brannigan, Lieutenant (J.G.) Jim Cruiser and Senior Chief Petty Officer Buford

Dawkins lounged on worn vinyl furniture off on one side of the establishment's single room. A middle-aged lady named Rita sat at a battered desk that bore no more than a nondescript personal computer, printer and telephone. At that moment she was printing out a manifest for a shipment of goods to be taken to the small city of Los Blancos to the north. Alfredo, the CIA asset, waited patiently for the documents to be spewed out. As soon as the last emerged, he gathered them up and walked over to join the three SEALs.

Alfredo sat down in a battered chair that had seen better days. "These papers will be presented to the authorities at checkpoints along the way," he explained. "Everything has been arranged to ensure they will be accepted by the customs inspectors."

Brannigan, sipping a can of Diet Coke purchased from a vending machine outside the door, asked, "What is this 'everything' that has been arranged?"

"Bribes and other payoffs," Alfredo answered matter-of-factly. "These preparations are not unusual in this part of the world. Normal business could not be conducted efficiently without the payments of what Latin Americans call *la mordida*—the bite—which is a colloquialism for bribes. This is the way official permits are issued in a timely fashion. To follow proper procedures would take days and days. Thus, what we are doing will not attract undue attention."

The phone rang, and Rita picked it up, speaking softly in Spanish. When she hung up, she turned to Alfredo. *"El autobús está a la puerta."*

"Ah!" Alfredo said. "The bus has arrived at the gate. It should be here shortly."

The SEALs exchanged glances of relief. This meant the Command Element and First Assault Section were now in Argentina. They walked to the front window to look for the vehicle to appear through the bustle of the depot. A couple of minutes passed before an ancient bus coughed its way into view, coming to a squeaking halt in front of the office.

Eleven obviously disgruntled travelers disembarked, carrying cheap luggage. They were dressed in clothing that would give the impression they were itinerant laborers going from one low-skilled job to another. From all appearances, they had purchased their garments in flea markets or secondhand stores.

Alfredo opened the door, and they trooped in. The Odd Couple—Mike Assad and Dave Leibowitz—led the way. As the detachment scouts, this was their customary place in any formation. Everyone showed the fatigue of a long, boring trip. They had left San Diego, California, at various times, taking a multitude of airlines through Mexico, Panama, Colombia and Brazil before finally getting together in Montevideo, Uruguay, for the last leg of the trip to Buenos Aires.

"Listen up!" Senior Chief Dawkins said. "We ain't gonna be here long, so don't try to make yourselves too comfortable."

"It don't look like we could if we wanted to," Bruno Puglisi growled as he surveyed the dingy interior of the office.

"Yeah," Connie Concord agreed. "I can't wait to get out into that swamp."

Dawkins snorted a sardonic laugh. "I'll remind you of what you just said after you been out there for a few weeks up to your ass in quicksand. There's a vending machine with soda pop outside. If you need change, see Rita at the desk. But first Alfredo is gonna brief us as to our movement out to the OA."

Alfredo stepped up. "You'll be loading into a couple of semitrailers at the warehouse docks to the rear of this building. All the weapons and your personal equipment have already been put aboard, so you will have whatever comfort items you've packed for yourselves. But we don't want you to change into your BDUs until Lieutenant Brannigan gives you the word."

Frank Gomez searched his pockets for coins to use in the vending machine. "Is my commo gear in there?"

"Affirmative," Alfredo said. "As well as three rigid raider and piragua boats. I'm afraid you're going to be even more disenchanted with this phase of your infiltration. You're going to have to endure a nonstop one thousand two hundred kilometer trip from here to a place called Los Blancos. That's where you'll marry up with your Second Assault Section."

"You say this is nonstop?" Chief Matt Gunnarson remarked. "What about heads?"

Brannigan interjected, "There are Porta Pottis aboard the trailers along with drinking water and MREs. It'll be bleak and harsh as hell, but you guys can tough it out."

"Ah, well," Chad Murchison said. "I suppose we can pass the time reading."

"There're no lights," Brannigan said. "You'll be in the dark, and I don't want you using any batteries up in your flashlights. We don't know how reliable our resupply is going to be until we get a chance to really test it."

"I'll be going to Los Blancos with you," Alfredo said. "When your entire detachment is together, I'll bring you up to date on all the happenings in the OA. I haven't gotten the word from there myself yet. I'll be staying with the Petroleo Colmo Oil Company, so we'll be in contact with you. Any questions? No? In that case, gentlemen, go get yourselves some soda pop, and we'll get into our luxury accommodations for the big journey."

Half the SEALs went to Rita for change while the others hurried outside to the vending machine.

HEADQUARTERS OF *BANDERA* 1
EL EJÉRCITO FALANGÍSTA
2045 HOURS LOCAL

THE camp was so new that it had not yet been named. The commanding officer, *Comandante* Javier Toledo, had only about three dozen men in a unit that would normally have numbered between six hundred and seven hundred troops. This, in actuality, was a cadre waiting for an influx of additional noncommissioned officers and soldiers to flesh out the rosters.

The camp itself was crude, as could be expected, but the buildings were well-constructed and weatherproof. The barracks were airy with plenty of space between the bunks. This was where the noncommissioned officers slept and ate. A small parade ground dominated the center of the garrison, while over on the north side was a headquarters hut—actually a CP—that included the living and mess quarters for the outfit's four officers. A flagpole bearing the DFF banner with three broad stripes of red, black and red of the Falangist movement stood in front of the thatched building. But instead of the traditional yoke and arrow symbol of the Catholic royalty, an insignia of a medieval sword with wings dominated the center of the black area. This represented the warrior archangel Michael, who was the spiritual inspiration for these twenty-first-century fascists.

Comandante Toledo was a ruggedly handsome Spaniard whose deportment and appearance gave strong evidence of having led a tough and demanding life. His physical prowess was backed up by a keen intellect developed through a robust, disciplined lifestyle.

At that moment, he and his immediate subordinates were enjoying their only luxuries of Cuban cigars and Italian brandy. Their meal had consisted of French Army *rations de campagne*. These were preferred over American MREs because of the canned bread, cheese, pâté and powdered soup. Now, after partaking of the *cuisine militaire française*, *Capitánes* Francisco Silber of Chile, Roberto Argento of Argentina and Tomás Platas of Bolivia turned their full attention to the liquor and stogies. All looked forward to the day when they would have a proper officers' mess with silverware, plates, cups and other items needed for fine dining.

Toledo lit his cigar and exhaled contentedly before reaching for his brandy. After a slow, appreciative sip, he sighed. "Well! It was simple fare, but filling, *verdad, caballeros*?"

"I think we should appreciate what we have under these conditions," *Capitán* Silber said. "At any rate, a year from now, we will be dining with beautiful women at a four-star restaurant in a big city."

"Indeed," Toledo said. "And at much higher ranks. By the way, we may have had a close call yesterday." He glanced over at Argento. "Tell us about it, *Capitán*."

"My men on patrol learned of a Bolivian Army unit on the periphery of the Gran Chaco," Argento said. "The people of the village called Novida said they had spotted them while out herding cattle. The *Bolivianos* were obviously making a reconnaissance, but evidently it was a very timid one."

Toledo laughed. "I think the various loyalists sense there will be big changes around here, no?"

"The villagers fully realize that prospect," Silber remarked. "Those gifts of rice and beans we gave them have obviously impressed them quite favorably where our movement is concerned. They are struggling peasants illegally occupying land that is not theirs."

"The Red Chinese figured out how to take advantage of such situations early on," Toledo remarked. "If you have an impoverished populace within your theater of war, they will be easily won over even by the most basic necessities of life."

"That is how the Nazis failed in the Ukraine in World War II," Silber said. "My grandfather told me about it. He was in the *Waffen-SS* at the time and talked about how the excesses of the rear-echelon *Allgemeine-SS* drove many potential supporters to the Soviet partisan units."

"That will *not* happen here!" Toledo exclaimed. "Our men are all well-indoctrinated in the aims and goals of the DFF."

"They are also well-trained," Plata added.

"*Por su puesto,*" Argento agreed. "They are professional soldiers of noncommissioned rank. Unfortunately, some are not in the best physical fitness because of years in staff duties."

"*Suboficial* Punzarron will take care of that," Platas said with a laugh.

"Eventually they will form a superlative nucleus for the Falangist Army," Argento said.

Toledo raised his brandy in toast. "*Viva el Ejército Falangísta!*"

The four snifters were clicked together.

COMANDANTE Javier Toledo was a former officer of the Spanish Foreign Legion, having served for ten years under the *generalísimo* of the Falangists, Jose Maria de Castillo y Plato when he commanded a regiment of the Legion.

This fanatic outfit was made up of soldiers who called themselves the Bridegrooms of Death. Although a "foreign" legion, over 90 percent of the men in the ranks were native-born Spaniards. The basic training of volunteers was short and brutal. Any misconduct or even an honest mistake would result in a severe beating. When the recruit graduated into one of the *tercios* (regiments) he was not much more than an automaton, having to rely on his officers for such things as land navigation, map reading and communications. His weapons training was also rudimentary and far behind that of other modern military units. Harsh discipline would continue through the legionnaire's enlistment, providing a pliant soldiery easily bullied and manipulated by sadistic officers and noncommissioned officers. This leadership cadre was able to get away with cruelties that would not be tolerated in regular Spanish Army units.

Life in the *Legión Extranjera* was lonely for the officers. They were isolated from the enlisted men by tradition and regulation, forcing them to withdraw into an exclusive little group that ventured out only on rare occasions when the regiment drilled or trained as a whole. They lived in genteel poverty—even those from wealthy families had little on which to spend their money—but were waited on by orderlies and stewards in feudal military grandeur. These servants escaped the barbarism in the ranks because of having the right appearance and mannerisms to serve their masters in the monastic atmosphere of the garrisons. This better treatment was also afforded to those rare individuals who had administrative capabilities such as typing along with an ability to read and write better that the average legionnaire.

The officers spent evenings in their mess, which was decorated with flags, photographs and other mementos of the bygone days of Spain's former glory when she was a colonial power. They drank heavily, getting drunk almost nightly as they expounded on their personal philosophies and attitudes.

Javier Toledo fell under the influence of *Coronel* Jose Maria de Castillo y Plato during those discussions. Castillo was the commanding officer of their *tercio,* and the younger Toledo listened and learned as the *coronel* told of his dream of power that could only be realized by a strong fascist leader with a dedicated following. According to Castillo, the present remnants of Falangists out in the civilian world were out of touch, out of date and out of luck, but if the movement were fine-tuned to meet the contemporary political scene, they would eventually rule the world.

Toledo picked up five main points from Castillo's preaching:

1. Spain was destined to regain her former glory.

2. The conflict between the decadent West and the anachronistic Muslims was exactly what the fascists were waiting for.

3. As the West unwisely spent much of its money, building up enormous deficits, and the Islamics squandered the lives of their people, a vacuum would be created in which a strong fascist nation could move in and conquer all.

4. The discouraged and disgusted populace of the West would be willing to give up the weaknesses of democracy for a strong leadership that would rid the world forever of Islam and other inferior societies and cultures.

5. The establishment of the Dictadura Fascista de Falangía would bring about all the above.

Countless hours of discussion brought not only Toledo but other officers into Castillo's elaborate design to reshape the world. When *el coronel* proclaimed himself the *generalísimo* and revealed that he had gained strong financial support from industrialists in Europe and South America, Toledo and his brother officers knew that the establishment of the DFF was only a matter of time.

2330 HOURS LOCAL

COMANDANTE Javier Toledo, the snifter of his sixth brandy of that evening in his hand, stepped out on the veranda of the officers' quarters, gazing out over the darkness of the Gran Chaco. He remembered studying about the *conquistadores* of old Spain who had come to the New World to expand the Spanish empire. Eventually corruption and moral weakness had allowed indigenous revolutionaries to drive the Spanish rulers back across the seas to their native land. But now, in this beginning of the twenty-first century, a new brand of *conquistador* strode across this hemisphere: stronger, more intelligent, more dedicated, and better led than ever before. A new world was in the making.

Toledo put the drink to his lips and drained the snifter.

LOS BLANCOS, ARGENTINA
28 NOVEMBER
1500 HOURS LOCAL

BRANNIGAN'S Brigands were all together now. They celebrated Thanksgiving in a corner of a rat-infested warehouse with MREs and a local brand of beer called *Cristal*. They put on a good show, but in truth the affair fell short. Several members of the detachment would have been back in hometowns with family if it hadn't been for this current operation, and the married men felt especially lonely; even the bachelors would have at least been in a base chow hall enjoying a traditional menu in a holiday atmosphere. But here they were, way down in South America, off by themselves, hiding like escaped convicts in dank surroundings.

Frank Gomez sorely missed his wife and little boy. "Christmas is really going to suck this year."

"Hanukkah ain't exactly gonna be a wingding jubilee," Dave Leibowitz observed.

The sound of the door opening caught their attention, and everyone's eyes turned in that direction, hoping to see something interesting or perhaps encouraging. But it was only Alfredo, coming in.

"Happy Thanksgiving!" he said cheerfully. He noted the lack of response and shrugged. "Anyhow, I have the latest intelligence from the Gran Chaco to pass on to you."

The SEALs stopped eating, giving him their full attention.

"Okay," Alfredo continued, "we know now that a group of the Falangist troops are out there. We don't know how many of them there are, or where they're located, or what their intentions are, or how they're equipped."

Joe Miskoski groaned loudly. "You call *that* intelligence?"

"It's a big, empty country out there," Alfredo said defensively. "Just keep in mind the enemy knows less about you. As far as can be determined, they have absolutely no idea of your existence, much less that you're on your way."

"All right!" Brannigan said loudly. "Let's not start bitching! The fact we're able to make a clandestine infiltration gives us one hell of an advantage. I'm going to do a map reconnaissance this evening and pick out an easily defended area for a base camp. From that point on, we'll start going up and down rivers, creeks, streams, mud puddles and shit holes until we find the sons of bitches. Once we have the intelligence we need, we'll take the appropriate action." He looked around. "Are you listening, Odd Couple?"

"Yes, sir," came Mike Assad's voice from the back of the crowd.

"You and Leibowitz had better rest up while you can," Brannigan said to the pair of detachment scouts. "You two are gonna be running your asses off."

"Right," Dave Leibowitz said under his breath. "Like that's a big surprise."

"What did you say?" Brannigan asked.

Dave grinned weakly. "I said, 'That'll be nice.'"

"Good attitude, Leibowitz," Brannigan said. He turned to Alfredo. "When are we going in?"

"Tomorrow morning," the CIA operative replied. "And again. Happy Thanksgiving."

He walked from the warehouse, and the SEALs turned back to their holiday repast.

CHAPTER 3

**THE GRAN CHACO
SEAL BASE CAMP
30 NOVEMBER**

LIEUTENANT Wild Bill Brannigan chose the site for the permanent base camp after making a close study of a combination of maps and satellite photographs of the OA. The selected area was situated on firm ground where the Lozano Grasslands and Los Perdidos Swamp came together. The farther someone walked from the grassy area westward into the swamp, the softer and wetter the terrain became until the wanderer would be in water that could be anywhere from ankle deep to over his head. To add an attribute of danger to the marshy environment, pools of quicksand lay hidden under the murky depths.

This swamp was definitely not visitor friendly.

The base camp location offered an easily defended position as well as a handy place where supplies and ammunition could be securely cached. The marshland also made it unnecessary to set up a defensive perimeter of 360 degrees. The firing positions were arranged in a horseshoe shape with the open side next to the bog. Not even the most determined enemy would be able to mount an effective attack from that direction. A system of streams that offered enough depth for the raider boats and piraguas ran from the north side of the camp to the nearby Rio Ancho. As far as Brannigan could determine, the river would be the main travel route used in the coming operation against the Falangists.

The Command Element was located to the center rear of the horseshoe, while the First Assault Section covered the center right around to the right flank. The left center and flank were protected by the Second Assault Section. However, there were no trees, and the grass was not high enough to offer much in the way of concealment. This problem was dealt with handily through the use of camouflage netting slung low to the ground. In addition to protecting the fighting positions from sight, the arrangement provided concealment for Brannigan's CP, the supply stockpile watched over by the Odd Couple, Frank Gomez's commo center, and the medical aid station set up by Hospital Corpsman James Bradley. Additionally, a trio of temporary OPs had been put out in front of the perimeter for use when necessary.

The detachment also constructed some small, fortified dugouts to be used as living quarters. The abodes were quickly dubbed "hooches," and were also skillfully camouflaged to blend in naturally with the local surroundings. Most of these earthen domiciles were occupied by two or three SEALs who shared the housekeeping and maintenance chores.

It was from this bucolic headquarters complex sunk into the terrain of the Gran Chaco that Brannigan's Brigands would carry on their campaign against the enigmatic enemy known as Falangists. Even to the pragmatic SEALs, used to operating under austere and perilous circumstances, this latest setup had an eerie, unknown quality about it. It was almost like being on another planet, albeit a hot, steamy mosquito-infested one.

RIO ANCHO
0830 HOURS

IT was raining heavily as the First Assault Section under Lieutenant (J.G.) Jim Cruiser came down the Rio Ancho in a raider boat towing a piragua to use when silent traveling was necessary. The Odd Couple, Mike Assad and Dave Leibowitz, had been attached to the patrol to act in their usual capacity as scouts. After a short twenty-minute run along the waterway, the patrol reached a point where a large creek intersected the river. Cruiser decided to hold up at that location and send the Odd Couple forward in the piragua to see what lay ahead.

The section moved into the cover offered by the vegetation along the banks to wait for the result of the Odd Couple's recon. Chad Murchison and Garth Redhawk were put on outpost duty a dozen meters up the creek. The pair, their ponchos dripping, sloshed through the wet grass to reach the position.

Redhawk, one of the new men in the Brigands, was a Kiowa-Comanche from southwestern Oklahoma. This descendant of two of the fiercest warrior tribes of the American prairie country was the quintessential Native American. The SEAL was dark-skinned with coal-black hair, and his sharp features gave him a rather aggressive countenance when he wasn't smiling. The effect was intensified when he applied camouflage paint to his face. Rather than put on irregular smears like everyone else, he applied a special pattern used by the Comanche warriors of old. The bold stripe over his eyes and the zigzag pattern down his cheeks symbolized thunder and lightning, the plains Indians' representation of war. It was something learned from his grandfather, who was a member of a society dedicated to the study of the culture and history of their ancestors. This elder Redhawk, a retired schoolteacher, was in the finishing stages of writing a Kiowa-English dictionary in a project to preserve the native tongue before it disappeared altogether from use.

It was from his grandfather that Redhawk learned about the tradition of medicine bundles for divine protection in battle. His was a small pouch that contained a hunk of wood from an Oklahoma cottonwood tree that had been struck by lightning. The other item was the original trident badge issued him by the Navy when he qualified as a SEAL. The young Native American would add other charms as his combat experiences multiplied.

Chad Murchison crouched in the grass beside Redhawk as they maintained watch out over the empty rain-swept grasslands to their direct front. The two, who hadn't known each other before Redhawk's arrival in the detachment, had been silent for almost a half hour. Then Redhawk asked, "How come you guys call Assad and Leibowitz the Odd Couple?"

"There's quite a story behind them," Chad said. "You've probably taken note of the fact that they are the best of buddies, have you not?"

"Yeah," Redhawk said with a slight grin. He was slightly amused by Chad's accent and manner of speaking. "I did take note of that."

"What makes that deep friendship so unique is the fact that Mike is an Arab-American and Dave is Jewish," Chad explained. "That's quite a mix when one considers the animosity between the two ethnic groups. You wouldn't think they would be buddies, but they're about as inseparable as twin brothers. Thus, we have dubbed them the Odd Couple. Like the Neil Simon characters in his play. Get it?"

"I get it," Redhawk said. He was not familiar with the play but knew the TV series. "Them two are Felix Unger and Oscar Madison in the real world. But maybe they're both just out of touch with their ancestries."

Chad shook his head. "Mike speaks Arabic and was raised in the Muslim faith. He's from an Arab community near Detroit. Dave's family is far from secular, and he was brought up in that culture. He even has family in Israel."

"Does he speak Hebrew?"

"Just enough to get bar mitzvahed," Chad replied. "The Leibowitz family has evidently been in America for several generations."

"So has the Redhawk family."

"Indeed," Chad remarked.

They fell back into silence, maintaining their vigil over the immediate area. After another half hour passed a single small splashing sound could be heard to the direct front. Immediately a voice came over the LASH headsets.

"This is Mike. Me and Dave are coming back."

A few moments later the piragua appeared, and the two SEAL scouts nodded greetings to Chad and Redhawk as they poled by. It took another minute before they came to the spot near the junction of river and creek where Cruiser and Bruno Puglisi had set up just behind the rest of the section. The wooden boat was taken up to the bank, and the scouts jumped out.

"We didn't find anything, sir," Leibowitz reported. "The grasslands are empty up to where we went. But we determined the creek can give us good penetration farther into that area. It stays wide and goes anywhere from three to maybe five feet deep."

"Good enough," Cruiser said. "We'll tie the piragua to the raider boat and move up a couple of kilometers for another scout." He spoke into his AN/PRC-126 radio handset. "Alpha and Bravo leaders, this is Brigand One. Bring your guys in. We're going to extend this patrol a bit more. Out."

Chief Matt Gunnarson and Connie Concord gathered up their men for the short trek back to the boats.

PIAGGIO P 166 TURBOJET
OVER THE CHILEAN-BOLIVIAN BORDER

THE rainstorm had blown through the Gran Chaco as *Generalísimo* Jose Maria de Castillo y Plato sat in the passenger cabin of the small private jet aircraft, gazing down 2,500 meters to the ground below. He had a special appreciation for what he saw. This was where the *Dictadura Fascista de Falangía* was to be established, and he fully expected the nation to be flourishing well within a year to eighteen months. This flight, his first into the potential domain, was to take overall command of the preliminary military actions to conquer the Gran Chaco. But first he wished to make an inspection of the small, scattered detachments of the Falangist Army.

Teniente-Coronel Jeronimo Busch of the Chilean Army sat dozing beside him. This paratrooper, who was carried on the roster of his parachute infantry battalion as AWOL, was Castillo's main liaison officer when it came to dealing with the mutineers of the Chilean, Argentine and Bolivian armed forces. After months as a military attaché in Madrid, Busch was looking forward to being back in camouflage fatigues to do some real soldiering with a 9-millimeter Star submachine gun in his hands. He'd even taken some time before this trip to get in a couple of parachute jumps with his battalion before taking French leave.

On the other side of the aircraft's aisle, Castillo's personal adjutant, *Suboficial* Ignacio Perez, busily perused the latest logistical figures in one of his many notebooks. The skinny little man looked as if he belonged more in a chess tournament than in a military campaign.

Jose Maria de Castillo y Plato, the supreme leader of the Falangists, was five feet, ten inches tall with a physique of muscular compactness. Long years of service in Morocco in the Spanish Foreign Legion had brought him into middle age in excellent physical condition; additionally, it was during this time that he painstakingly developed his personal political philosophy. He was trapped in a more or less arranged marriage to a grumpy, unattractive wife he had left behind in Madrid. Consequently Castillo had empty hours in the evenings with little to do in the isolated garrison where he had been posted. He could have filled the time with heavy drinking in the mess or fornicating with local slatterns brought in for the officers' collective pleasure, but he preferred to use the time to write a manifesto he had entitled *La Nueva Falange de la España Moderna (The New Falange of Modern Spain)*. He further separated his new brand of fascism from the traditional by placing an accent mark in the name. Thus his followers were known as *Falangístas* rather than *Falangistas*.

It had all been laboriously spelled out in his neat, precise handwriting, and when it came time to have it entered into a word processor, he knew who to turn to. One of the clerk-typists in his *tercio* was a small, clever fellow by the name of Ignacio Perez, who had been convicted of forgery and embezzlement. The judge had given him a choice of fifteen years in the penitentiary or three years in the Foreign Legion, and he had chosen the military option. Unfortunately, Perez was not good soldier material and had been beaten half to death by the noncommissioned officers for his physical ineptness until it was discovered that he had certain office and administrative skills. Such individuals were rare in the *Legión Extranjera,* and the fellow was rescued to an assignment in headquarters, where his expertise in typing and filing could be put to good use. Most legionnaires were pathetic brutes who could barely read and write. Eventually, Castillo pulled Perez from headquarters and put him to work full-time entering his political writings into a word processor.

Castillo's philosophies were more than just a little different from that of the original Falange. He had no devotion to the Catholic Church, considering the modern version of the religion in Spain as too liberal and leftist. Instead, he looked to the archangel Michael for divine guidance and inspiration. After all, *Arcángel Miguel* was the warrior angel who had cast Satan down into hell. Castillo wrote a carefully crafted pamphlet explaining how Archangel Michael would give his followers spiritual guidance if they meditated properly, seeking a mystical rapport with him by drawing off by themselves and concentrating deep enough to turn off external stimuli and distractions.

Castillo designed an insignia of a medieval knight's sword with wings to represent the archangel, placing it on the center of the original Falangist flag design. He further decreed that the DFF would be run from a Center of Supreme Command and Dictates, using corporations to administer the running of the dictatorship. There would be separate corporations for Power (nuclear rather than fossil fuel), Transport (sea, land and air), Medical (including euthanasia of the hopelessly ill as well as the insane and feebleminded), Public Safety (to include the Secret Police), Sports and Recreation, Merchandising, and others as needed. The armed forces, of course, would be kept separate and run personally by the *generalísimo* and his hand-picked staff.

Castillo sincerely felt that this organization would be welcomed by the weary, disappointed populaces of Western democracies who would appreciate a strong leader to take them away from the decadent, disorganized and corrupt society they lived in. Only people of European ancestry would be allowed in the ruling class of the DFF. The darker races would be the laborers and factory workers while Orientals would be employed in the sciences under strict supervision of the Europeans. Semitic people—both Jewish and Arabic—would be eradicated in a carefully applied program of genocide. They would be joined by Gypsies and homosexuals as the new Falangists finished the job the Nazis started in World War II.

When Ignacio Perez finished entering the manifesto in the word processor and printed it out, Castillo took a thirty-day leave to distribute the document. His family members were wealthy industrialists with heavy investments and ownership in manufacturing, and he used these kinsmen to establish contacts not only in Spain but also France, Portugal and Germany to expound on his goals. In almost all cases he met with enthusiastic approval by these people who would be at the top of the heap if this philosophy became an established government. The present political climate in Europe forced them to exercise great clandestineness in their support. However, they were most generous with their secret donations hidden within the enigmatic ledgers where one plus one equaled whatever sum pleased the accountant. Within a short period of time it became apparent there would be absolutely no problem in funding the operation.

The South American side of the great scheme came into being from a Chilean military attaché in that nation's embassy in Madrid. *Teniente-Colonel* Jeronimo Busch was not only fanatic about becoming a follower but had contacts in the right-wing elements of his own army and also those of Argentina and Bolivia. Disaffected officers in all three countries were looking for a way to rid their homelands of what they considered effete, leftist governments.

Thus, like the proverbial snowball rolling down the mountain, the Falangist movement picked up speed, steadily gaining momentum and strength.

HEADQUARTERS, *BANDERA* 1
0930 HOURS

THE forty men of the *bandera* were drawn up in four ranks facing the landing strip that ran along the north side of the garrison. *Comandante* Javier Toledo stood to the direct front, while directly behind him, *Capitánes* Silber, Argento and Platas were spaced evenly across the formation. Not all the sweat that was soaking the creases out of the uniforms was because of the humidity left behind by the recent rains. All were nervous at this auspicious arrival by the *generalísimo* in his move into the theater of war.

The distant sound of a jet aircraft was discerned a few moments before a dot appeared in the western sky. It gradually grew larger until the Piaggio could be clearly seen. The jet banked gracefully and came in for a landing. As soon as the wheels touched down, the four officers marched smartly over to where it would come to a halt. At that point the subalterns and warrant officers took charge of the formations.

When the aircraft braked to a halt, the engines were immediately cut. The door opened, and a crewman stepped out, lowering the steps that slid out from the fuselage. The first man to exit was the *generalísimo,* followed by Busch and Perez.

Toledo stepped forward and saluted sharply. "*Mi generalísimo! Comandante* Toledo of *Bandera* 1 reporting for inspection and review."

Castillo returned the salute and looked around, obviously disappointed. "You know, Toledo," he said with a frown, "we really must get a proper band out here for these occasions."

VILLAGE OF NOVIDA
1100 HOURS LOCAL

THE First Assault Section, with Alpha Fire Team in the lead, walked across the field toward the village. The Odd Couple had already discovered the community and after an hour's observation, had determined it was safe to approach.

The first people to notice them was a small group of women drawing water from the well. They smiled and waved as the SEALs drew closer. Garth Redhawk was on the point, and he grinned and nodded to them, surprised and pleased by their amiable display. A couple of older men appeared on the scene, and they, too, were friendly. As the section walked into the village square, even more people, including some children, came out of their huts or left chores to join the small group. The women were barefoot, wearing blouses and skirts, while the men wore shirts, trousers and broad-brimmed hats. Several wore boots and carried short whips. It was at that time the SEALs noticed communal stables with horses.

A short, stocky man who seemed to be in his fifties stepped forward and spoke loudly, issuing sincerely happy salutations. Lieutenant Cruiser couldn't understand what he said, so he called for Chad Murchison to come forward. Chad had been a language major before enlisting in the Navy, and spoke French, German, Spanish and Italian fluently. He hurried to the front and offered his hand to the man.

"Buenos dias, señor," Chad said. *"Como esta usted?"*

The villager smiled and shook his head to indicate he couldn't understand. *"Bom dia,"* the man said. *"Muito prazer em conhecâ-lo."*

Chad looked back at Cruiser. "Sir, he's not speaking Spanish. I'm not sure, but I think it's Portuguese."

"Portuguese?" Cruiser said. "Why the hell would he be speaking in Portuguese? This is Bolivia. They speak Spanish here."

"Maybe he and these people came over here from Brazil," Chad suggested. "They speak Portuguese there."

"Shit!" Cruiser said. He turned to the section. "Do any of you guys speak Portuguese?"

Paulo Cinzento, one of the new men, stepped forward. "I speak Portuguese, sir."

"Oh, yeah?" Cruiser said, pleased. "How the hell did you learn to speak Portuguese?"

"I'm from San Diego, sir," Paulo replied. "My people came from Portugal and worked the tuna boats out of there for about three generations. I grew up with the language."

"Great," Cruiser said. "Go talk to the old guy there. Introduce us but don't mention that we're Americans. Just tell him we're patrolling this area and want to know how these nice folks are getting along."

"Aye, aye, sir!"

Paulo went over to the old man and began speaking. Within a moment they were going at it like they were long-lost brothers. A full ten minutes of conversation went by before the SEAL returned to the section commander. "There's a puzzling situation here, sir."

"What's going on?" Cruiser asked.

"Well, he thanked us for some rice and beans and said they came in handy," Paulo explained. "He asked about some guy by the name of Punzarrão, and I told him he was fine. He also said to give greetings to the other soldiers. Then he said no Bolivian troops have been around since the last time some weeks ago."

"Other soldiers and Bolivians, huh?" Cruiser mused. "Who is the old guy?"

"He's the *chefe*—the chief—and his name is João Cabeçinho," Paulo said. "It seems they're illegal squatters from Brazil, and they're raising cattle here. Old João said everyone was afraid of getting run out, but evidently the same guys who gave them the food also promised they would protect them from Bolivian police and soldiers."

"Okay," Cruiser said. "I get it. These are some of the people Alfredo was talking about. The Falangists have already gained a strong influence over them. Go tell the old guy that we have to go now. Tell him we hope to be back soon."

Paulo made the good-byes, and all the villagers waved as the SEALs formed up and headed back toward the creek where the boats were hidden. Chief Petty Officer Matt Gunnarson hurried forward along the column to walk with Lieutenant Cruiser. The chief was pessimistic. "What do you think, sir?"

"I think it's pretty obvious the Falangists have won the hearts and minds of those villagers," Cruiser said. "That means they've probably done the same thing to other civilians in the OA."

"That's bad news, sir," Gunnarson commented. "That means we'll be fighting on two fronts. We'll have to watch our backs."

"I'm afraid you're right," Cruiser said bitterly.

The column continued across the grasslands back toward the creek as it began to rain again.

CHAPTER 4

CAPITÁN Tomás Platas led his nine-man column across the savannah, moving at a steady pace as they followed their assigned patrol route. He was concerned about the physical conditioning of the men, and glanced back, noting that several walked along with heads bent, obviously struggling as they went through the grim, ancient military practice of putting one foot ahead of the other. These sweating Falangists had abandoned staff positions to join the revolution, and none had the stamina of younger soldiers. Many had not served in line outfits for years.

They were divided into two rifle teams and a machine gun crew, and all were veteran noncommissioned officers from the Chilean, Bolivian and Argentine armies. They were in full field gear, carrying rifles while the automatic weapons crew was further burdened with an Amali light machine gun. The second-in-command of the patrol was a scowling Portuguese who had served in the Spanish Foreign Legion for a decade. *Suboficial* Adolfo Punzarron—the last

name Spanishized from the original Punzarrão of his native country—was in excellent physical condition. This
large, muscular man with a shaven head had an enormous
mustache that curled out from beneath a nose battered flat
in innumerous brawls. Punzarron had fled into the *Legión*
to avoid a murder charge in Portugal.

The *suboficial*, with the staying power of a bull unable
to sense pain, scowled openly at the others in the patrol. He
had nothing but contempt for the headquarters types. At
least half of them were not truly devoted to the Falange.
They had fled into the sanctuary of the revolution because
of pending disciplinary actions, serious indebtedness,
shrewish wives, or other personal problems. Those were
the ones who found it so hard to readapt to field soldiering.

Here on the patrol, any slowing down or even a misstep
earned the faltering man a heavy slap across the back of
the head from the Portuguese's large hand. It didn't matter
if he was a *sargento* or *sargento-mayor*; Punzarron treated
the weakling like one of the pathetic wretches sent to his
regiment from recruiting stations to be brutalized into effectiveness for the ranks of the Foreign Legion.

Capitán Platas didn't like the man, but *Comandante*
Toledo, who had served with the *suboficial*, gave implicit
orders that none of the lieutenants or captains were to interfere with his methods. No one denied that Punzarron was a
brute, but he got instant results using his fists and boots.

The forty-year-old *sargento* carrying the thirteen-kilo
machine gun was having a particularly tough time of it.
The crew had been passing it among themselves to share
the load, but Punzarron quickly put a stop to that. Custom
dictated that the gunner was responsible for the weapon,
and by God, that meant he and he alone carried it! The
sargento-gunner had been supervising an ordnance repair
shop before leaving the Argentine armed forces, and it had
been years since he had served in a line combat outfit. He
finally stumbled and collapsed to the thick grass, near
exhaustion as the weapon fell to the ground.

Platas turned at the commotion and saw Punzarron pull the man to his feet, slapping his face hard. After the punch-up, the out-of-shape Argentine was forced to hold the weapon over his head and double-time around the column. Stark fear of the Portuguese ex-legionnaire gave him the strength to perform the punishment. Platas, who was from a crack Bolivian parachute battalion, appreciated the results of the punishment, but he disliked seeing a senior noncommissioned officer treated like a raw recruit.

After three circuits of the patrol, the gunner was allowed to stagger back into ranks to continue the trek.

THE VILLAGE OF NOVIDA
1330 HOURS LOCAL

CAPITÁN Platas and his patrol entered the village to find João Cabeçinho waiting to greet them. Some of the *vaqueiros* out with the communal cattle herd had spotted the Falangists and sent a boy riding in to tell the headman about the visitors moving across the savannah toward the community.

Suboficial Punzarron went up with Platas to speak to Cabeçinho while the men in the patrol sank to the ground to rest. Several women, noting the men's discomfort, brought them some rum to refresh themselves. As the exhausted men shared the liquor, Cabeçinho enthusiastically shook hands with the senior patrol members, speaking through Punzarron's translation since Platas spoke no Portuguese.

"We are surprised to see you so soon," Cabeçinho said. "Your other friends were here only a couple of days before."

Platas was puzzled. "What other friends?"

"They were soldiers like you," Cabeçinho explained, "but their uniforms were different. I also noticed they had rifles that were not exactly like the ones you carry. But they were *sujeitos agráveles*—nice guys. One of them spoke Portuguese in a strange way. Not like us and not like *Suboficial* Punzarrão. I thought it a little strange that none of them spoke Spanish."

"What did the men look like?" Platas asked. He was alarmed by the lack of Spanish speakers in the group and wanted to know more. "What were their nationalities? What race?"

"One of them looked like an *índio* from American western cinema," Cabeçinho replied. "And one was a *negro*. All the others were *europeus*. A couple were very light-skinned."

Punzarron looked at Platas and shrugged. "I am confused, *mi capitán*. The men of whom he speaks are obviously not Bolivian or even Chilean or Argentine if they did not speak Spanish."

"I think an unexpected situation has arisen here," Platas said. "Tell *Señor* Cabeçinho to keep a lookout for these strangers and any others that may show up. Tell him to notice how many of them there are, and to do his best to find out their nationality. Also instruct him to say nothing of us *Falangístas*. Impress upon him that there is a possibility of treachery in this situation."

Punzarron turned to the village headman and passed on the message in Portuguese. Cabeçinho asked, "Is there some sort of problem?"

"We don't know," Punzarron replied. "Just be careful."

"I shall do as requested," the village headman promised. *"Com todo o gusto."*

Platas ordered the *suboficial* to get the patrol back on their feet. "We're going straight back to headquarters," he said. "We must report this situation to *Comandante* Toledo immediately."

Punzarron barked the necessary orders, and the men struggled to their feet. The Portuguese noted the machine gunner would slow down the patrol, and he ordered one of the other members of the crew to take the heavy weapon from him. "You may now take turns with it." Sometimes discipline must come in second to expediency. To even things out, he would give the machine gun crew extra PT that evening.

Cabeçinho waved as the Falangists left the village.

SEAL BASE CAMP

THE detachment worked rapidly to prepare the bivouac to be temporarily abandoned during a long patrol out into the OA. Caches were closed while a minute inspection of the camp was made. All signs of the area having been occupied had to be obliterated, even though the SEALs eventually planned to return to the site. The slightest bit of carelessness could result in passing strangers inadvertently discovering something as small as a burnt match, a piece of an MRE packet or even a slight imprint of a boot in the soft soil. These seemingly insignificant objects would be like a neon light to a clever, vigilant enemy.

When the work was done, Brannigan led them a couple of hundred meters away, then sat everyone down for an oral OPORD of the coming operation. The men instinctively maintained team and section integrity as they settled into a semicircle to listen to the skipper's discourse.

"All right, my friends," Brannigan began, "here's the word. We're going to board the three rigid raider boats with the piraguas tied to the stern. We'll head down the Rio Ancho to that creek. By the way, we're now referring it to as Big Creek."

"Not a particularly colorful appellation, but aptly descriptive just the same," Chad Murchison remarked.

"Thank you, Petty Officer Murchison," Brannigan said. "We're so pleased you approve."

"Sorry, sir!" Chad uttered with a red face as the other SEALs grinned.

"To continue," Brannigan went on. "When we reach Big

Creek, we'll hold up there. All boats will be camouflaged and hidden, then the First Assault Section plus the Odd Couple will head cross-country to that village of Novida. The Second Assault Section will follow at a discreet distance with the Command Element right behind them. As soon as the First Section reaches the objective, they will halt and inform me. Meanwhile, our intrepid scouts will recon the area to see if any bad guys are in the vicinity."

Bruno Puglisi gave his SAW an affectionate pat on the receiver. "And if there are any around, can we kill 'em, sir?"

"From that point on we'll play it by ear, Puglisi," Brannigan said. "I'm sure you'll find some activity that will amuse you before it's all said and done on this operation." He gestured to Lieutenant (J.G.) Jim Cruiser and Senior Chief Buford Dawkins. "Let's move 'em out!"

The First Assault Section led the way to the boats on the river.

HEADQUARTERS, *BANDERA* 1
1800 HOURS

CAPITÁN Tomás Platas left the patrol hurriedly after their return to the garrison and reported to headquarters. He sought out *Generalísimo* Jose Maria de Castillo y Plato, *teniente-Coronel* Jeronimo Busch and *Comandante* Javier Toledo, to inform them of the strangers who had mysteriously appeared in the theater of war.

Meanwhile *Suboficial* Adolfo Punzarron kept the other members of the patrol back for a special inspection. The eight men were lined up in a single rank with their rifles slung. Each held his canteen in his right hand. Punzarron went to the first man and pointed to the water carrier, commanding, *"Derramelo!"*

The man turned the canteen upside down. A few drops spilled out. Punzarron moved to the next rifleman, giving the same order. Once more some drops of water dribbled from the container. However, when the third man obeyed the command, not a bit of water emerged. The *suboficial* punched him hard in the face, causing him to stumble back and fall to the ground.

Punzarron glared at the men. "I am trying to teach you water discipline! In the Spanish Foreign Legion in the Moroccan desert we learned the value of conserving our water. And you will learn it here, even if we are in the midst of a savannah that is crisscrossed with streams and creeks. Many of you have spent too many years in the luxury of garrison duty with plenty of water and beer available. You are on active field operations now, where only an *idiota* would guzzle down every drop in his canteen as if there is no tomorrow."

He went to the next two men, satisfied when they, too, had something left in their canteens. However, the next three NCOs had consumed all the water they had. They were treated to a hard clout each for their lack of self-control.

Meanwhile, as Punzarron administered his brand of discipline to the men of the patrol, Toledo, Castillo and Busch listened with great interest as Platas explained what had transpired in Novida. Castillo was worried. "Undoubtedly outsiders—and I mean foreigners—have moved into the Gran Chaco. The most disturbing element of the situation is that they could well be an international group brought in from the UN. Right now the last thing we need is a peace-keeping force traipsing around the future location of the DFF."

Busch snorted a laugh as he lit a cigar. "The UN, *mi generalísimo*? What is there to worry about from incompetent, badly led Third World soldiers trying to interfere with our plans?"

Toledo wasn't quite so optimistic. "Perhaps it isn't the United Nations, *Coronel* Busch. We cannot safely assume that is the case. If we are wrong, we will pay a terrible price for our arrogant complacency."

"Good thinking, *Comandante*," Castillo said. "I want you to send two of your combat sections out for a sweeping reconnaissance of the Grasslands in the vicinity of Novida."

"*Inmediatamente, mi generalísimo!*" Toledo said. "I shall dispatch Silber and Argento within the hour."

"Excellent," Castillo said. "And I think it is the time to bring in reinforcements." He looked at Busch. "How many men can we send for, *Coronel*?"

"*Bandera* 2 has approximately fifty men," Busch replied. "And it will only be a matter of weeks before we can transfer in enough personnel from Argentina and Chile to activate *Bandera* 3."

"*Pronto!*" Castillo said. "Do it!"

THE LOZANO GRASSLANDS
3 DECEMBER
0930 HOURS LOCAL

THE savannah offered little in the way of cover. Mike Assad and Dave Leibowitz knew they could easily be spotted by anyone within a short distance, and the duo moved cautiously and alertly, wanting to make sure they would see any strangers before they saw them. They had split off from the First Assault Section to investigate what lay ahead of them after the detachment left the boats and moved onto the grasslands. This was the Odd Couple's element, and the pair was used to operating alone in enemy territory.

The entire area was cut by little streams, and they could easily jump across most. Fortunately, the wider ones were shallow enough to be effortlessly waded. The two worked well together, able to conduct an excellent recon without one spoken word. Quick hand signals or gestures were all that was necessary for the team to exchange information on what was seen and heard as they moved along. If they

found themselves in a situation that required them to
speak, all they had to do was whisper into their LASH
headsets that amplified the sound in the earphones to make
it seem a normal tone of voice to the receiving party.

It was Dave who first came across the trail that had been
smashed down in the grass. He called Mike up to him, and
they dropped to their knees to study the spoor. "It looks like
maybe a dozen men, don't you think?" Mike whispered.

Dave nodded. "Right on. I'd say they're moving from
southwest to northeast."

"Wait a minute," Mike said. "They've come along here
in both directions." He leaned closer to the ground to study
the tracks. "Right! They came in from the northeast, and
went back in the exact opposite direction."

"Bad habit," Dave said. "You should never follow the
same path twice in enemy territory."

"What if they don't consider this enemy territory, ol'
buddy? This is prob'ly their stomping grounds."

"Good point," Dave said. "From where we are now, I
say they came from their base camp, and went down to that
village, then back to their own place again. I think we
ought to move slightly to the north and then turn east."

"You're right," Mike said. "That way we can take a
roundabout way to whatever destination those guys were
headed for."

The Odd Couple put the plan into action, moving through
the grass on the chosen azimuth. Both were glad it was too
early for the mosquitoes to come out. It was bad enough trying to conduct an efficient recon without having the little
bastards buzzing around. The insect repellent kept them off,
but they were still a nuisance. A half hour passed, then Dave
whispered into his LASH.

"Hold it!"

Mike looked up and saw what had alarmed him. A column of twelve men were coming their way. The strangers
seemed to be on the alert as if expecting trouble or looking

for someone. The Odd Couple decided it was the latter; and they moved back into some deeper grass to observe.

Mike and Dave used their binoculars for a closer look. The strangers were obviously military men garbed in camouflage uniforms, carrying weapons, and wearing web gear. "Hey," Dave whispered, "get a load of the insignia sewn on their arms."

Mike noted the red and black flash of the Falangists on the sleeves. "They're the bad guys all right."

"Well, why don't we follow 'em and see where they're going?" Dave suggested.

"May I lead?"

"Be my guest."

As they followed the patrol, they noted the professionalism of its members. Their physical conditioning seemed mixed, but they were obviously well-disciplined. As expected, they went straight to Novida.

The Odd Couple found a small knoll on the northwest side of the small community that offered good observation. The patrol was given warm greetings by the civilians, and the troops seemed familiar with the village. They went to the well where some women were drawing water, and carried on what seemed to be polite conversation with the females.

"Mmm," Mike mused. "They seem to have been told to be respectful to the local ladies. That means the value of good conduct with the indigenous personnel has been emphasized to them."

"Their leaders have prob'ly read Mao's *Little Red Book*."

"Yeah," Mike said. "It looks like the patrol is moving on. I'll bet half my next payday that the bastards are out looking for us."

"I'll bet *all* my next payday," Dave said. "C'mon! We got to get back to the detachment."

The two SEALs slid off the knoll, then turned toward Big Creek.

SEAL BIVOUAC
BIG CREEK
1400 HOURS LOCAL

THE Odd Couple, having rejoined the First Assault Section, led them back through the outlying defensive perimeter of the bivouac. The group hurried in the direction to Lieutenant Wild Bill Brannigan's CP. While the riflemen and the SAW gunner of the team dropped off, Lieutenant James Cruiser, Chief Matt Gunnarson and Connie Concord followed Mike and Dave. As the quintet strolled toward the creek, they were joined by Senior Chief Buford Dawkins, Milly Mills and Gutsy Olson of the Second Assault Section.

Brannigan was munching on a cereal bar when the eight men arrived. "Well!" he said. "And to what do I owe the honor of all these visitors?"

"Recon report, sir," Mike said. He quickly gave an oral presentation detailing the results of the scouting trip, telling about the Falangist patrol and its friendly reception at Novida.

"We'd pretty much figured the enemy had made friends with the locals," Brannigan said. "Not much surprise there. But I'd like to find out where those Falangists call home. And what sort of camp or garrison they might have."

"I volunteer the Second Assault Team for the mission, sir," the senior chief said.

"Accepted," Brannigan said. "I think you also better take another look at that village to see if there's any unusual activity there. The place could be an auxiliary headquarters of some kind." He looked at the Odd Couple and started to speak.

"We know, sir," Dave interrupted. "We'll be on point."

Brannigan smiled. "You'll leave at oh-five-hundred hours tomorrow."

THE LOZANO GRASSLANDS
VICINITY OF NOVIDA
4 DECEMBER
1030 HOURS LOCAL

THE Second Assault Section was sprawled in the thick grass, arranged in a defensive circle that offered protection from all sides. Senior Chief Petty Officer Buford Dawkins and his SAW gunner Petty Officer Second Class Joe Miskoski were in the middle of the formation. Joe lay on his back, snoozing through a light nap, while Dawkins sat cross-legged, glancing off in the direction of the small cattle-raising settlement.

The plucky, hardworking Odd Couple had been gone for close to an hour. Their mission was to run a recon of the village to check out the activity, keeping a special lookout for any Falangist units that might be in the vicinity. The senior chief reached over and roughly shook Joe awake at almost the same instant a whisper came over the LASH net from Lamar Taylor. "The recon team is coming in."

Buford raised himself just enough to see Mike Assad and Dave Leibowitz approaching the perimeter. Three minutes later the scouts joined him, sinking wearily into sitting positions at his side.

"The village is clear," Mike said. "Only the locals are there."

"But there's some cowboy types out with the cattle to the west," Dave added. "We can reach that track in the grass left by the Falangists if we go north, then turn back toward the southwest. From that point on, we can go straight to wherever it is they came from."

"It's a no-sweater," Mike assured the senior chief.

"Right," Dawkins said. He spoke into the LASH microphone. "Team leaders, get your guys up. We're moving out."

The section began a circuitous march, easing north to avoid the village and its cattle. The going was easy, but the need for intense alertness and continuous observation slowed the speed of the trek down to only a little faster than a crawl. The Falangists could be anywhere in the area, and they had already shown a disturbing propensity for sending out patrols. An hour and a half passed before the SEALs came across the trails left by the enemy. At that point, the distance between each man was increased, and the Odd Couple moved out on the point some twenty-five meters from the column.

OUTSIDE THE FALANGIST GARRISON
1400 HOURS LOCAL

MIKE Assad lay against the creek bank that sank a meter and a half into the terrain. He used the grass along the sides of the waterway for cover as he surveyed the enemy camp with his binoculars. Dave Leibowitz was on lookout on the other side of the creek, squatting down with his CAR-15 at the ready.

"Man!" Mike whispered as he watched the activity in the garrison. "Those guys are really chickenshit. I haven't seen so much saluting and drilling since we were up at Camp Pendleton last month."

"They've got a strong European tradition," Dave reminded him. "Remember what Alfredo said back in isolation." He looked behind to check out the area to the rear, then turned back toward the front. "How many guys do they have?"

"I'd say forty or so," Mike said. "That means they outnumber us about two to one."

"That's just this camp," Dave said. "They might have another."

"Hell!" Mike said. "They might have a dozen more. Who knows? Alfredo wasn't even sure." He put away his binoculars and crossed the creek, climbing up to join Dave.

"Mission accomplished! Let's get back to the senior chief and the section. We need to report to the Skipper before dark."

The two scouts moved in crouching positions as they hurried across the savannah toward the spot where Dawkins and the Second Assault Section waited for them.

CHAPTER 5

EVERYONE'S BDUs were sweat-soaked and grass-stained from days of wear. The high afternoon temperature was compounded by the heavy humidity, and while the SEALs perspired heavily, it did little to cool them since it couldn't evaporate in the steamy atmosphere. Some of the sweating might have come from nerves; this was a combat mission briefing. Apprehension is an emotional characteristic that affects both the mind and body even among the military elite.

The Odd Couple along with the section commanders, SAW gunners, and team leaders were sprawled on the grass in front of Lieutenant Wild Bill Brannigan. Chad Murchison, standing CP watch, stood off to one side listening. The rest of the detachment was out on security, enduring the discomfort of a bright, burning sun in the treeless and consequently shadeless terrain. Everyone was wishing for rain, even though it would offer no more than temporary relief before adding to the steamy discomfort.

Over at his briefing, the Skipper tipped his boonie hat onto the back of his head as he surveyed his subordinate leaders. He took a deep breath as if to make an important announcement, and the words he uttered, while not earth-shattering, were profound: "We came here to fight."

The SEALs looked at each other, shrugging as if to say, "So what else is new?"

"The situation we're in fits an old Chinese proverb I once heard," Brannigan continued. "The best way to test a tiger's courage and strength is to let him out of his cage." He grinned. "But in this case, the situation we have here today dictates that we go into the cage to get a rise out of the son of a bitch."

Connie Concord, leader of Bravo Fire Team, took the blade of grass he was chewing out of his mouth. "I hope we ain't gonna lock that cage door behind us once we're in there, sir."

"Oh, no," Brannigan assured him. "We'll have a way out in case those fangs and claws are stronger than we anticipated. This mission is to launch a sneak attack in the dark, shoot up the place, then make a quick withdrawal back into the cover of night."

Gutsy Olson, honcho of Delta Fire Team, looked up. "What if we start kicking their asses?"

"Then we'll continue the fight," Brannigan said. "If we inflict enough casualties, we'll break the back of this revolution. If that happens, we could easily be home by Christmas."

"There is one historical aspect of war that cannot be denied," Chad Murchison said. "There has never been one that ended in time for the troops to be home by Christmas." He glanced around. "I'm awfully sorry to be so pessimistic, fellows."

Bruno Puglisi chuckled. "Perfectly all right, old chum. Perhaps we'll be back in time for the polo season, hey, what?"

Chad's face reddened at the loud laughter of the others. He had tried to keep his privileged background a secret, but the longer a man serves in a unit, the more his buddies learn about him. They met his sweetheart, Penny Brubaker, when the unit was in Afghanistan. She was a UN relief worker, and it was obvious to the SEALs that the couple came from moneyed families.

"Oh, dear!" Joe Miskoski said. "I do miss driving about in my Rolls-Royce, chaps."

"Shut up!" Senior Chief Buford Dawkins bellowed. "This is a mission briefing not a bullshit session."

"Right you are, Senior Chief," Brannigan said, grinning to himself at Miskoski and Puglisi's affected upper-class accents. "So here's how it's going down. We'll leave the bivouac at twenty-four hours. Needless to say, make sure you have your night vision goggles with you. We'll go in a direct line to the position of the enemy garrison as was determined by the Odd Couple's GPS reading. When we arrive, the First Assault Section will form a line from east up to north. The Second Section will be from east around to the south. That will make a nice tight horseshoe formation. We don't want to completely surround the place or we'll be inflicting casualties on ourselves through friendly fire."

"Where is the Command Element gonna be, sir?" James Bradley asked.

"Right in the center," Brannigan replied. "The attack will be a fire mission only with automatic fire. There won't be much of a chance for sniping; and I want the two SAW gunners to pour a hell of a lot of quick bursts into the target area. You guys might not hit very many of 'em, but they'll sure as hell keep their heads down and not move around a lot. When I determine I've learned enough of about their capabilities, I'll order a withdrawal. We'll beat it back here, then hop aboard the boats for a trip back to the base camp."

"What about commo, sir?" Frank Gomez asked.

"All transmissions between myself and the section and team leaders will be over the AN/PRCs," Brannigan said.

"Team commo will be by LASH." He checked his watch. "We'll be leaving in approximately nine hours. Get back to your guys and brief them. I want everybody to take advantage of this opportunity to rest up."

The SEALs got slowly to their feet, then walked out toward the perimeter to find their teams.

HEADQUARTERS, *BANDERA* 1
1945 HOURS LOCAL

THE evening guard scheduled to take over the garrison's defensive perimeter had been drawn up on the parade ground in the vicinity of the headquarters hut. All wore freshly washed camouflage uniforms complete with Kevlar helmets, LASH headsets, night vision goggles and binoculars. Their web equipment held ammo pouches filled with magazines of 5.56-millimeter rounds for their CETME assault rifles. The only thing different from normal field attire were their boots; the footwear was spit-shined bright enough to pass inspection on any parade ground.

The officer of the guard for the night was *Suboficial* Adolfo Punzarron. He had dressed like the others with the exception of his headgear. Rather than a helmet, he wore the tasseled olive-green forage cap of the Spanish Foreign Legion. In place of the usual webbing, he sported a pistol belt holding a holstered Spanish Astra 7.63-millimeter automatic pistol.

Punzarron marched over to the far right man in the rank to begin his inspection. He went down the line from man to man, finding no fault with their collective appearance. These were veterans with years of military service and knew all the tricks of falling out sharp for guard mount. They were also aware of the *suboficial's* violent temper and wished to avoid a hard punch to the face. Everything looked good to Punzarron until he reached a Chilean paratrooper sergeant named Antonio Müller. There was no shine on his boots.

Punzarron snapped his eyes up to look straight into Müller's face. "Your boots look as if you rubbed melted chocolate all over them. Why did you not shine them?"

"My boots are for use in the field," Müller said calmly. He was also a large, muscular man who had spent his entire military career in parachute rifle companies. "I therefore applied waterproof dubbing for use on active operations, rather than polish to make them shiny and pretty."

Punzarron seemed to growl as he spoke. "I specifically issued orders that boots are to be highly shined for guard mount."

Müller sneered. "I'm no parade ground martinet. I'm a parachute infantryman, *por Dios,* and I'm going to look like one. I am ready for combat, not prancing about on a parade ground."

Punzarron threw a punch, but Müller deftly ducked it while handing off his rifle to the man next to him. The *suboficial* tried again, but Müller was faster, slamming his fist into the ex-legionnaire's jaw. Punzarron went down but quickly got back to his feet, charging his opponent. Müller was ready and responded with a combination of hooks and uppercuts that sent Punzarron to the dirt once more. This time when the Portuguese sprang to his feet, the had a knife in his right hand.

Müller stepped back, grabbing his rifle. "This is a *pelea entre soldados*—a soldier's fight—there is no place for a knife here. We are not thugs brawling in a tavern."

"There were no gentlemanly rules for fighting in the Spanish Foreign Legion," Punzarron said. "So you either continue to fight or give up."

"I am not going to fight like a street hoodlum," Müller said.

"So shoot me with your rifle," Punzarron challenged.

"I told you I am a soldier," Müller said. "I will not murder a superior officer."

"Then you give up?"

"I do not give up," Müller insisted. "I quit out of disgust!"

Punzarron laughed in triumph. "*Es el mismo*—it is the same." He slipped his knife back into its hiding place in his pistol belt, then called the guards to attention. After facing them to the left, he marched them off for posting.

Over on the thatched veranda of the headquarters hut *Generalísimo* Jose Maria de Castillo y Plato stood with *Teniente-Coronel* Jeronimo Busch. They had observed the altercation between Punzarron and Müller. Busch took the cigar out of his mouth. "I am not so sure the customs and traditions of the Spanish Foreign Legion should be applied in the Falangist forces, *mi generalísimo*. These men are all noncommissioned officers."

"Strict discipline for both soldiers and civilians will be the norm in the *Dictadura Fascista de Falangía, Coronel* Busch."

"I agree that many of our men are being put into excellent physical condition under *Suboficial* Punzarron," Busch said. "And they will set excellent examples when we begin filling the ranks with younger, inexperienced recruits. But such discipline could cause serious problems with South Americans." He turned and looked at Castillo. "Allow me to respectfully point out that we are not as compliant as Europeans."

"Compliance is an unpleasant word for obedience, *Coronel* Busch," Castillo said. "When used in its proper place, the expression puts the concept into a better light." He walked toward the door of the building. "Care to join me for a whiskey?"

"*Con mucho gusto, mi generalísimo!*"

5 DECEMBER
0200 HOURS LOCAL

BRANNIGAN'S Brigands came into the attack area in a double column, moving easily across the savannah with the darkness brightened to green hues in the night vision goggles. As they reached the point where the Odd Couple stood, the First Assault Section peeled off to the north to take up positions, while Senior Chief Buford Dawkins's Second Assault Section went south. Wild Bill Brannigan and his Command Element gathered around Mike Assad and Dave Leibowitz as the others continued on to the battle line.

Brannigan checked his watch, then spoke into the AN/PRC-126. "Brigand One and Brigand Two, this is Brigand. Move your teams forward to your firing positions. Make sure you place the SAW gunners where they can do the most good. Out."

The detachment began arranging itself for the coming firefight.

SARGENTO Antonio Müller sat cross-legged at his guard post, still seething over the knife-pulling by Punzarron. That *hijo de la chingada portugués* was going to have to be taught a severe lesson. He would learn the hard way that the Old World *mierda* of Europe wasn't going to work in South America; especially the ways of that goddamn Foreign Legion the son of a bitch served in over in Morocco.

Müller raised the Spanish-manufactured Vista-Nocturna binoculars to his eyes and used its night vision capability to survey his area of responsibility on the perimeter. Suddenly a trio of armed men rose out of the grass to his direct front, moving a few meters toward him before dropping back to the ground. Müller went directly to his LASH, raising Punzarron. "*Alarma!* Unknown armed men approaching the garrison limits."

Punzarron, who had been dozing in the adjutant's office of the headquarters hut, leaped to his feet and rushed out to the veranda where the alarm gong hung. Following Legion custom, he began banging it to call the camp to arms.

THE BATTLE

THE sounds of a banging gong and men shouting rolled across the savannah. Brannigan grabbed the AN/PRC-126 to contact the section and team leaders. He ignored proper radio transmission procedures as he ordered, "Open fire!"

Immediately salvos of automatic fire sparked from the SEALs' positions, slapping into the Falangist camp. The SAWs, employed by Bruno Puglisi and Joe Miskoski, sent out sweeping volleys at the rate of 725 rounds a minute. Even with a carefully applied delivery of fire bursts of six bullets at a time, the magazines emptied quickly. Puglisi and Joe, like the others, had no visual targets and were forced to keep their individual areas of fire covered by shooting blindly into the enemy camp.

TENIENTE-CORONEL Jeronimo Busch had slipped into his boots and grabbed both the Star 9-millimeter submachine gun and ammo harness at about the same instant that Punzarron hit that gong for the third time. He rushed outside, meeting Castillo on the veranda. Both realized they had absolutely no idea of where to go. But an agile *cabo* suddenly appeared to lead them to some slit trenches at the side of the building. Within moments a thoroughly terrified Ignacio Perez joined them. The little adjutant said nothing as he huddled into a fetal position in the dirt.

Toledo, his *capitánes* and noncommissioned officers were now at their positions as they had practiced during countless training drills. A good rate of rifle fire was pouring outward at the attackers, backed up by a trio of machine guns.

THE incoming hurricane of flying steel pounding into the SEAL positions grew with each passing moment. Bullets whined and cracked through the air around the Americans, some clipping the taller blades of grass. It was obvious to everyone that the enemy had night vision equipment and was well prepared to deal with sneak attacks, especially those that happened during the hours of darkness. But like the SEALs, this evening's violence made it impossible for them to deliver accurate fire.

Brannigan knew the tiger was now tested, and he was tough, efficient and professional. Now was the time to break contact. The Skipper thought quickly, almost instinctively reaching the decision to withdraw fire teams from the ends first to leave the center of his battle line as strong as possible. He once more grabbed the radio handset. "Fire Team Delta, this is Brigand. Break contact and withdraw a hundred meters to the rear. For God's sake keep you heads down! The incoming fire is as thick as swarms of hornets. Out!"

COMANDANTE Javier Toledo had been informed minutes before by *Capitán* Roberto Argento that there was no incoming on the east side of the camp. He ordered the Argentine officer to move his section over to the west side to add to the firepower in that area. Now Argento's men were interspaced with those of *Capitánes* Silber and Platas. The rate of outgoing fire was increasing dramatically, giving confidence to the Falangists.

Teniente-Coronel Jeronimo Busch didn't like lying in the slit trench. Cowering during a firefight wasn't part of his Prussian-Chilean heritage. He slipped into the harness with the extra forty-round magazines, pulling the night vision goggles out of their pouch on the shoulder strap. The Chilean gripped the submachine gun and leaped from the hole in the dirt. He rushed across the bullet-swept open space to join the fighters on the perimeter as he pulled the goggles down over his eyes.

Busch threw himself down between a pair of riflemen and began kicking off fire bursts at the muzzle flashes blinking rapidly from the attacker's side of the battle. After a few moments, the paratrooper officer noted a marked lessening of fire on the right flank. He immediately realized that the attackers were in the process of breaking contact. He scrambled to his feet and rushed to that side of the line, once more diving to the ground when he reached an advantageous spot for some serious shooting. This time he carefully regulated his pulls on the trigger, sending controlled fire bursts toward the enemy. Within a minute he was aware there was no one to his direct front. Now was the time to pull a one-man maneuver to outflank the *bastardos*. Busch jumped up yet again, rushing forward to seek combat.

BRANNIGAN ordered Bravo Fire Team to pull out of the fight. Connie Concord led his men toward the rear to join Cruiser and Bruno Puglisi. Cruiser yelled at the Bravos, "Hold up!"

Connie halted the men. "Aye, sir! What's the word?"

"Let's kick out some more salvos before we break contact," Cruiser said. "We don't want them to feel too confident about leaving the safety of their camp."

The Bravos, with Puglisi playing the SAW like a musical instrument, raked the area to the front with bullets. As they laid down the fire, the Command Element was heading off to join the others who had already pulled out of the line.

BUSCH was now crawling through the grass, paying no attention to the fact that he was headed into some of the Falangist fire as he worked his way down the line formerly held by the attackers. He finally spotted what appeared to be five men firing in the direction of the garrison. They suddenly leaped up to pull back.

Busch fired a long burst toward them, damning himself for not having arrived fifteen seconds earlier. He was rewarded with the sight of an attacker bowled over to the ground by the simultaneous strike of at least two of the 9-millimeter slugs. Suddenly a couple of the fallen man's pals turned on him, cutting loose with a wicked volley of return fire. Busch had to scamper backward to find cover as bullets plowed the grass and dirt around him.

LIEUTENANT Jim Cruiser was the man hit. At almost the exact moment he collapsed to the ground, Lamar Taylor and Paulo Cinzento each grabbed him by an arm. He cussed in pain as they dragged him back toward the rear. When they reached the rest of the detachment, he had gone numb.

Brannigan rushed over to his 2IC. "Can you walk, Jim?"

"Let me see," Cruiser said. "Maybe if—oh shit! I can't feel my legs, Bill!"

The hospital corpsman, James Bradley, joined them. He knelt down and gave the wounded officer an examination in the eerie illumination of the night vision goggles. As he applied a field compress to the wound, he asked, "Can you move your legs, sir?"

Cruiser shook his head. "No."

Brannigan turned to Lamar and Paulo. "Form for a chair carry. We've got to get the hell out of here."

The two SEALs slung their CAR-15s and reached out to grab each other's wrists to form a "chair" of their forearms. Brannigan and James picked Cruiser up and set him on the two SEALs' strong arms.

The unit formed up with Charlie Fire Team acting as rear guard, and headed for the boats.

"CESEN del fuego!"

Comandante Javier Toledo's voice boomed so loudly over the garrison area that he was heard above the shooting. The firing immediately ceased, leaving a buzzing silence in the men's battered eardrums. Castillo joined the *bandera* commander. "Are you going to pursue the enemy?"

"Only if I am ordered to do so, *mi generalísimo*."

"Why is that?" Castillo asked. He was used to the aggressive and risky tactics of the Spanish Foreign Legion.

"We do not know their numbers," Toledo explained. "The withdrawal could be a trap. An entire brigade of Bolivian infantry could be out there waiting for us to walk into an ambush."

Castillo was thoughtful for a moment. The *comandante* could be correct, and, of course, there weren't a lot of men in the *bandera*. One disaster could set the Falangist movement back as much as a year. "Very well, *comandante*. I agree with your choice of action."

Back on the firing line, *Sargento* Antonio Müller stood up and stretched. It had been one hell of a fight, though none of the Falangist subunits had sustained any casualties. The battle seemed to be more of fire than maneuver, and neither side had worked its way into an advantageous position. They simply exchanged shots.

Suboficial Adolfo Punzarron walked by, coming back from a front position where he'd been in the thick of the fight. His foreign legion forage cap was pushed forward cockily on his head, and his uniform was stained by mud and grass. He glanced over at Müller. "I'm going to put you in for a commendation, *Sargento*. Your timely warning of attackers probably saved the garrison."

Müller nodded. "It was a hell of a fight, eh, *Suboficial* Punzarron?"

Punzarron actually grinned. "It was a lot of fun, wasn't it?"

There would be peace now between the two. They were a couple of old soldiers who had cleared the air between them.

BIG CREEK
0500 HOURS

MILLY Mills brought Charlie Team in from its rear guard duties. He sought out Brannigan to report that there was no pursuit, then asked, "How's Lieutenant Cruiser?"

"He was hit twice in the right side," Brannigan answered. "Bradley said one of the bullets didn't exit. He's afraid it's in the spine. Cruiser can't feel or move his legs."

"Shit!" Milly exclaimed. "He ain't paralyzed, is he, sir?"

"Bradley can't tell," Brannigan said. He turned to Chief Matt Gunnarson. "You're commander of the First Assault Section for now. Take over."

"Aye, sir."

Bradley watched as Taylor and Cinzento gently placed Cruiser in one of the piragua boats. After the officer was made comfortable, the rest of the detachment boarded the other craft for the trip back up the Rio Ancho to the base camp.

CHAPTER 6

LIEUTENANT (J.G.) Jim Cruiser still had no feeling in his legs nor could he move them when he was placed aboard the Petroleo Colmo Company's Aérospatiale Gazelle helicopter for medical evacuation. Hospital Corpsman James Bradley supervised as Bruno Puglisi and Paulo Cinzento slid the stretcher into the aircraft's passenger compartment. Just before the cargo door was closed, Cruiser raised his right hand with the thumb extended to show his brother SEALs he still had a lot of fight left in him, even if it was mostly spiritual. He had taken a brutal physical battering from the almost simultaneous impact of the 9-millimeter slugs.

Brannigan and the others stood in silence as the chopper lifted into the air, then turned south toward civilization. No one moved for several long moments. The terrible potential consequences of the 2IC's injuries were foremost in their minds, along with that shameful personal thought of *I'm glad it wasn't me.*

Brannigan snapped them back to the present. "Listen up! We're going to have to reorganize a bit. Chief Gunnarson will take over the First Assault Section. Petty Officer Lamar Taylor will move into his place as leader of Alpha Fire Team." He looked around. "Where the hell is the Odd Couple?"

"Here, sir!" Mike Assad and Dave Leibowitz called out simultaneously.

"I'm going to give you guys a break," Brannigan said. "You've been running your asses off. You'll go to Alpha Fire Team as riflemen. Petty Officers Redhawk and Murchison will take your places as detachment scouts."

"We ain't tired, sir," Mike protested.

"I didn't ask if you were," Brannigan said, knowing that stubborn pride was behind the protest. A SEAL just naturally disliked being put in a position where he appeared as if he weren't up to the job. The Skipper soothed the hurt feelings by adding, "When we move back into high gear, I want you jumpy and eager. Now! All the section commanders and team leaders report to me at my CP, which is located at this exact spot where I'm standing. The rest of you get out on the perimeter except for Frank Gomez."

"You want me to do something, sir?" the commo man asked.

"Right," Brannigan replied. "Get on the Shadowfire and raise Alfredo. Tell him we need reinforcements yesterday."

"Aye, sir!" Frank replied. He got his entrenching tool and headed for the cache where the radio was hidden.

The unit leaders moved closer to the Skipper. He grinned at them. "I swear I'm having more staff meetings than Pentagon lieutenant commanders."

"Your office ain't quite as elegant as theirs, sir," Senior Chief Buford Dawkins commented, looking around the area next to the feted swamp.

"You ain't got a good-looking secretary either," Connie Concord added.

"At any rate, we're going to have to get into an aggressive

hit-and-run program," Brannigan said. "The Falangists outnumber us and undoubtedly will be sending out some serious recon and combat patrols to yank our chains. So we want to beat them to the punch. We're going to leave the base camp closed up and get the hell out of here for awhile. All detachmentsize operations will be curtailed for the time being. Sections and teams will operate separately on insurgency missions, but we'll stick as close together as possible to support each other when necessary. Moving around and biting at the enemy will keep him guessing and nervous. We'll also take advantage of the helicopter support we've got from Petroleo Colmo Company for resupply and to set up some scattered caches."

"Them bright red helicopters are like lit beacons flying through the sky," Gutsy Olson complained.

"They've been zipping around the area for months," Brannigan reminded him. "The Falangists and everybody else think they're exploring for oil in the Gran Chaco."

Frank Gomez came back from his commo chore and ripped off a page from his message pad, handing it to Brannigan. "Here's your answer, sir."

Brannigan read it, then shook his head. "No reinforcements available. It doesn't say if the situation is permanent or temporary. One thing I've learned in all my years of service is that the worst-case scenario is the one that's going to jump out and bite you. We're on our own."

"It's enough to piss off a saint," Chief Matt Gunnarson said.

"*We're* enough to piss off a saint," Milly Mills added.

HEADQUARTERS, *BANDERA* 1

GENERALÍSIMO Javier de Castillo y Plato had decided to give the headquarters garrison a name. The bucolic post would become larger as soon as *Bandera* 2 joined them. He had spent most of the previous night trying to decide which Spanish hero or heroic incident was good enough to be commemorated at this first official DFF military garrison.

Just before dawn, the decision was made. The *generalísimo* decided the camp would be dubbed *Campamento* Astray after one of Spain's most colorful military leaders. In fact, much of this inspiration for the twenty-first-century fascist organization came from that man.

MILLÁN Astray, the son of a lawyer, was born in La Coruña, Spain, in 1879. He began his military career at the Infantry Academy in Toledo in 1894 where he earned a commission as a *subalterno de infantería.* Two years later he was shipped to the Philippines to fight against the indigenous rebels seeking to overthrow their Spanish masters. It was in that vicious campaign that Astray earned his first decoration for bravery when he defeated two thousand rebels with only thirty men under his command in a battle at San Rafael.

He was subsequently transferred back to Spain as a *capitán,* where he served as a teacher of military science and tactics at his alma mater, the Infantry Academy. By 1912 he had tired of the peaceful existence and volunteered to return to combat. This time they shipped the gung ho officer out to Morocco to fight indigenous African rebels. Five years later, after he was once again posted to Spain, Astray put forth an idea of forming a foreign legion similar to that of France to campaign in the Dark Continent's desert area. After being sent for a close-up study of *la Légion Étrangère* of France he came back to Spain to form *la Legión Extranjera* of Spain. This earned him a promotion to the rank of *teniente-coronel* and command of the new foreign legion he had designed.

When the first recruits arrived in *la Legión,* Astray told them to forget their former lives, women and families. Everything they needed would be furnished by *la Legión* until they died in battle. And death would be their inevitable fate. They went into combat in a wild, reckless manner, giving no quarter and asking none in a series of bloody campaigns in which the *legionarios* earned a well-deserved reputation for cruelty and brutality.

Astray backed up his military philosophy and aims by risking his own life, insisting on personally leading his troops in battle. Consequently, he suffered three serious wounds in the process: the first in the leg; the second in the left arm, which had to be amputated; and the third in the face, which cost him his right eye.

He eventually was promoted to *general de brigada,* participating in the Spanish Civil War with his former subordinate Francisco Franco, who would rule Spain from 1939 to 1975. General Millán Astray, an extremist of right-wing causes, supported Nazi Germany during World War II.

He died of a heart attack in 1954, but his spirit lived on through successive generations of the *Legión Extranjero.* Now *Generalísimo* Jose Maria de Castillo y Plato saw to it that same élan had become the driving force in the modern Falange seeking to conquer the Gran Chaco.

1400 HOURS LOCAL

IT took the Piaggio turbojet four trips to transport *Bandera* 2 and all unit gear from their garrison in the north down to *Campamento* Astray. When the final ammo box and ration carton was off-loaded and carried to the new unit's recently constructed barracks, the commander, *Comandante* Gustavo Cappuzzo, formerly of the Argentine Marines, formed up his men and marched them to join *Bandera* 1 in a special formation on the small parade ground.

The *generalísimo* marched to the front of the two units and took the salutes of *Comandantes* Toledo and Cappuzzo. After giving the men permission to assume the more comfortable position of at ease, Castillo spoke to them in a loud voice.

"You have been brought together to meet a challenge thrown at us by an unidentified enemy who is skulking throughout the Gran Chaco. Their origins, numbers and exact weaponry are unknown, but that does not make them phantoms. They are foreigners, perhaps wretched mercenaries, sent in a desperate attempt to stop the Falangist Revolution. Thus, the *Dictadura Fascista de Falangía* faces its first serious threat from persons who wish to crush this new world order. Many officers and noncommissioned officers of the armed forces of Argentina, Bolivia and Chile have grown disgusted with the leftist softness of their countries. Consequently, these professional commanders and their subordinates stand with us, giving us support in personnel and matériel that allows us to grow stronger almost daily. There will also be volunteers from the civilian populations of South America as well as Spain, France, Portugal and Germany joining us soon. All these are good men who have recognized the growing threat within the insidious incursions of socialism and other fanatical philosophies of radical left politics."

Castillo began pacing back and forth, gazing at the *banderas*. They were not as large a force as an infantry company—totaling only ninety-two troops—but they were dedicated, professional soldiers ready to fight for the Falangist cause. He liked what he saw. This collective ferocity made up for the lack of numbers.

"You are being formed into a *Grupo de Batalla*—a battle group—of almost a hundred men," the *generalísimo* continued. "This *grupo* will be organized as current missions dictate. You will be broken down into rifle squads and machine gun crews along with special commando raiding teams. Additionally, a pair of Spanish Model L 60-millimeter mortars have been added to our arsenal."

A murmur of approval rumbled through the ranks.

Castillo smiled. "And, for the icing on the cake, we are

also receiving an EC-635 light utility helicopter that has been lately liberated from the Argentine Army. It will be invaluable for reconnaissance and the transport of troops and equipment. We expect much more growth in our capabilities of transport and support fire for infantry units." He turned, looking out at the side of the formation. "*Teniente-Coronel* Busch! Front and center, *marche*!"

Jeronimo Busch paraded onto the scene, going to the direct front of the *generalísimo*. After performing a faultless, snappy salute, he barked, "I report for duty, *mi generalísimo*." Busch made an about-face movement to face the two *banderas*.

"*Teniente-Coronel* Busch is hereby promoted to the rank of *coronel*," Castillo announced. "He will assume the direct field command of the *Grupo de Batalla*."

Busch marched two steps forward, as Castillo moved back to give him center stage. The Chilean paratrooper's voice boomed even louder than that of the supreme leader's.

"*Buenas tardes, soldados de fascismo!* I am honored to have been chosen to serve as your commanding officer during active campaigning. We shall fight together to firmly establish the nation of Falangia in a great first step toward establishing the global dominance of fascism. The glory will be great and the fight difficult. I do not promise you an easy time. What I do promise you is sweat, tears, blood and unending combat. You will know hunger and exhaustion as demands are placed upon you that will stretch your spiritual and physical strengths to the ultimate limits of human endurance. I expect each and every one of you to live by the creed of the *soldado Falangísta*! You must be brave! You must have the spirit of camaraderie! You must always go toward the sound of firing and seek out combat! You must make instant obedience a religion as you use the archangel Michael as your spiritual guide and mentor! Be brave and ferocious; fast and nimble; as tough as steel; and as alert as a hunting eagle! Our common destiny will be to have the *generalísimo* lead us to the magnificence and splendor of vanquishing the enemies of the way of life to which we are all dedicated."

Even as Busch made another about-face to turn toward Castillo, the two *banderas* broke into spontaneous cheers, ready for a fight.

THE CENTRAL PORTION OF THE OA
8 DECEMBER
0945 HOURS LOCAL

THE SEAL detachment moved twenty kilometers to the east along the Rio Ancho before coming to a halt. It had taken almost twenty-four hours of slow travel while they poled the piraguas as silently as possible with the raider craft tied on the sterns. Two men per boat labored at the task, changing off every hour on the hour. The new scout team of Garth Redhawk and Chad Murchison each took a side of the river, moving a kilometer ahead of the main group in the dual role of security and reconnaissance.

Now the detachment was set up on both banks of the waterway while Frank Gomez monitored the Shadowfire radio. As soon as the transmission they waited for came over the headphones, he called over to Lieutenant Wild Bill Brannigan.

"Sir! The chopper is on the way in."

"All right," Brannigan said. He took up his binoculars and scanned the western horizon. Within minutes the bright red of the Petroleo Colmo Dauphin helicopter came into view, flying directly toward the site. It approached rapidly, then slowed as it began to descend. When it was directly over the detachment, Senior Chief Buford Dawkins signaled it in for a landing. It came down to gentle contact with the grass.

The cargo door slid open, and Alfredo jumped out. "Goodies!" he called out.

The SEALs went to the aircraft, and Paul Cinzento and Wes Ferguson jumped in and immediately began passing out the bundles of supplies to the others. Ammunition and rations made up the bulk of the cargo, but one unidentified bundle tightly wrapped was also included. Alfredo noticed everyone looking at it. "Camouflage coverings," he said, identifying it. "I figured you guys would need extra if you were going to be hiding stuff all over the OA. There're also some individual capes you can throw over yourselves to hide in the grass. They're just the right motley color to allow you to blend in with your surroundings. I brought enough for everyone."

Brannigan unbuckled the straps and opened it up. He pulled one of the coverings out and checked it over. "Lightweight and compact," he remarked approvingly as he rolled it into a tight bundle to see how it would fit into a rucksack.

"I figured you would need 'em," Alfredo said. "The concealment on this savannah is as scarce as tenderness in a sergeant major's heart."

Brannigan laughed. "I've been wondering about you, Alfredo. I don't want to stick my nose where it doesn't belong, but you've had military service, haven't you?"

"I'm ex–Army Special Forces," Alfredo said, relenting. "Actually I was one of those mean sergeant majors before I retired."

"My confidence in you has blossomed, ex–Sergeant Major," Brannigan said.

"I have faith in you guys too," Alfredo said, moving toward the chopper. "Well! If you need anything else, let me know. You call. I haul. That's all." He waved as he got aboard the aircraft. The rotors kicked up, then the helicopter lifted skyward, turning back in the direction it came from.

Brannigan gestured to the section commanders. "Let's break this stuff out and distribute it. Put the leftovers in the boats. We'll cache it later."

Each man's load was increased by three days of MREs and four thirty-round magazines of 5.56-millimeter ammo. The SAW gunners' burdens were enlarged by a dozen magazines each, but some of these were distributed among the riflemen for portage purposes. Within ten minutes the job was done. Brannigan sent the men out to check the local area while he had a confab with the section and team leaders.

The senior members of the detachment settled down, lit cigarettes, chewed gum or bit into energy bars, while Brannigan strode to their front with his hands in his pockets, looking like a man about to take a peaceful walk through his neighborhood back home. He gazed at his men for a moment, then announced. "I'm ready to start a war."

"Aw, hell!" Connie Concord said, grinning. "I was fixing to put in for a thirty-day leave."

Chief Matt Gunnarson picked up a rock and lobbed it at him. "You'll get a leave all right, but it'll be restricted to the OA. Have fun. Don't forget your old buddies if you find any good-looking women."

"Okay, guys," Brannigan said. "The Second Assault Section is going to run a combo reconnaissance and combat patrol due north from here. Redhawk and Murchison will act as scouts. I want the area scoped out, but if an opportunity presents itself to make contact with the enemy, do so." He looked at Senior Chief Dawkins, the section commander. "But only if you have a distinct advantage in the situation. I'm talking about a win-win scenario, understood? This is not the time to take chances."

"Aye, sir," Dawkins said. "Understood. What time do we depart?"

"I was kind of hoping you were already gone," Brannigan said with a wink.

The senior chief got to his feet, tapping Milly Mills and Gutsy Olson. "You heard the Skipper." He gestured to Redhawk and Chad. "C'mon! Let's went!"

1315 HOURS LOCAL

GARTH Redhawk and Chad Murchison had set up an OP a hundred meters ahead of the section. The newly acquired camouflage capes allowed them to blend in perfectly with the surroundings. They used their binoculars to maintain a sharp lookout over the grassy plain that spread out all around them. They and the section were feeling the effects of the heavy, wet heat after long hours of hiking through the grass, and Dawkins had wisely called a break in their movement.

"Psst!" Chad said. "Take look out at two o'clock."

Redhawk swung his gaze in that direction. "Patrol. Four-man. I can't see any more."

"Neither can I," Chad said. He observed them for a few additional moments. "Look! They're displaying that Falangist insignia on their sleeves. We definitely have the enemy in sight."

Redhawk pulled out the AN/PRC-126 radio handset. "Brigand Two, this is scout. We've got a four-man enemy patrol about a hundred and fifty meters ahead, moving west to east. Over."

"Are they alone or part of a larger group?" replied Dawkins. "Over."

"They're definitely alone," Redhawk reported. "Over."

"We need an EPW," Dawkins said. "It'll be up to you guys. I can't get a fire team out there quick enough. What do you think about going after them? Can do? Over."

"Can do," Redhawk replied. "We're on our way. Out." He put away the handset, looking at Chad. "The senior chief wants an EPW."

"In my opinion, that is not an insurmountable undertaking," Chad said. "They're moving on a direct azimuth of two hundred and seventy degrees. If we stay low, we can hurry in a half-circuitous route and get ahead of them."

"They call that an end around in Oklahoma football," Redhawk said. "Let's do it!"

The scouts moved slightly south, then turned straight west, keeping as low on the horizon as possible. After ten minutes, they moved toward the target patrol, noting that the group continued in the same direction.

"Y'know," Redhawk remarked, "I think that patrol leader was told to follow a westward course. And that's exactly what he's doing. Two hundred and seventy degrees by the compass and straight as an arrow."

Chad grinned. "He isn't allowing for declension. Thus, it would appear that our antagonist is a young officer. Possibly the equivalent of an ensign."

For the next half hour the two SEALs dogged the enemy patrol, gradually moving ahead of them as the trek continued due west. When they had gone twenty meters ahead of the Falangists, the scouts turned inward until they reached a point where the bad guys would be well within rifle range when they moved across their front. Redhawk and Chad went to the ground, their camouflage capes over them with CAR-15s ready.

"There they are!" Chad exclaimed.

"It looks like the second guy is the one in charge," Redhawk said. As the senior ranking man of the pair, he would literally call the shots. "I'll take the point man while you hit the rear guy. Then we'll both go for the man right behind the leader. On my command."

He waited as the four Falangists pressed onward. They moved steadily, each one watching his field of fire, but unable to spot the hidden SEALs waiting in ambush.

Redhawk's voice was matter-of-fact when he spoke. "Fire."

The first round hit the lead man, who staggered sideways under the impact of the bullet before crumpling to the ground. At the same instant the last guy spun and dropped to the grass. A quick salvo got the third Falangist, and he buckled when two slugs jolted him. The patrol leader was on the ground by then, firing blindly in the direction of the incoming shots.

"Oiga!" Chad called out loudly in Spanish. *"Nosotros le mandamos a entregar!"*

"What'd you say?" Redhawk asked.

"I told him that we order him to surrender," Chad said.

"Well, tell him there's a hundred of us, and he's alone," Redhawk said. "Tell him to surrender or die."

Chad yelled, *"Estamos cien y usted está solo. Entrege o muere!"*

The Falangist stayed down without replying. Redhawk and Chad cut loose with some fire bursts that were low to the ground, obviously cracking the air just over the man's head.

"Esta es su ultima oportunidad para entregar!" Chad hollered. He spoke out of the side of his mouth to his companion. "I just told him this is his last chance to surrender."

"Tell the son of a bitch to stand up. Now!"

"Levantarse! Ahora!"

A moment later a figure emerged into sight from the grass. He raised his hands and waited. The two SEALs cautiously got to their feet and approached him. The Falangist appeared to be in his early twenties; he was slim and good-looking, with an aristocratic air about him.

"Keep an eye on him," Redhawk said. "I'll check out the casualties to make sure they're dead." He went from man to man, rolling them over before going through their pockets to search for identification or documents. He found nothing and went back to join Chad and their prisoner. "Tell him not to try any funny stuff."

"I speak English," the Falangist said. He was trying to put on a show of bravado, but the violent, unexpected deaths of his companions had obviously shaken him. "Who are you?"

"Hey!" Redhawk snapped. "We're the captur*ers* and you're the captur*ee,* understand? *We* ask the questions." He grabbed the man by the sleeve and pushed him toward the south. "Any smart-ass shit on your part, and you're as dead as your buddies. Got it? Let's go!"

SEAL BIVOUAC
RIO ANCHO
1715 HOURS LOCAL

THE EPW sat on the ground with his hands held behind his back in a plastic retainer. All the SEALs had been able to learn from him was that his name was Enrico Melendez and that his rank was *subalterno*. He refused to give his nationality, but Chad Murchison quickly cleared that up for Lieutenant Bill Brannigan.

"He's a Bolivian, sir."

"How can you tell, Murchison?"

"Those cloth wings sewn above his pocket are Bolivian," Chad said. "I collect parachutist badges for a hobby and have an extensive assortment. He is definitely a Bolivian paratrooper."

"Brannigan looked down at the prisoner. "All right, so you're a Bolivian. What is your position in this Falangist Revolution?"

"Under the rules of the Geneva Convention I am not required to answer any questions other than name, rank and service number," Melendez said defiantly.

"Don't give me that shit, kid," Brannigan said. "I think maybe you're a bandit. A goddamn felon. I'll just shoot you as a criminal."

"Bah!" Melendez said. "And you are American mercenaries! You will be the ones who are put against a wall and shot."

Frank Gomez came up on the bank from the boat where he kept the Shadowfire radio. "I transmitted the information on the EPW, sir. Alfredo is coming out personal to have a look at the guy."

"Well," Brannigan said, "then he can sort this shit out with his own interrogation methods."

Melendez winced and took a deep breath of resignation.

1830 HOURS LOCAL

SEAL security was particularly tight when the Petroleo Colmo chopper came in for a landing. Brannigan was worried about the bright red aircraft attracting unwanted attention if a bunch of pissed-off Falangists were out looking for whoever had shot up their patrol and captured its leader.

Alfredo stepped out of the passenger door and shook hands with Brannigan. He nodded to Frank Gomez, Chad Murchison and Garth Redhawk, who were the only SEALs in the immediate vicinity. He and the Skipper walked to where Melendez still sat with his hands behind his back.

Alfredo studied the young EPW for a few moments before speaking. "Your name is Enrico Melendez, eh?"

"I have already answered all the questions I intend to," Melendez said. "And I demand to have my hands released from these bonds."

"Your name is Enrico Melendez, and you are a *teniente* in the Bolivian Army."

"I demand my rights under the Geneva convention."

"You are listed as a deserter by the Bolivian Army and are wanted by the law," Alfredo said. "Your father's name is Bolivar Melendez, and he is the president of the *Banco Mercado* in La Paz. He lives with your mother Beatriz and your younger sister Mercedes at 12 Avenida de la Libertad in the exclusive suburb of Lujado."

Melendez's face paled.

"Do you wish for us to turn you over to the Bolivian federal authorities?" Alfredo asked. "Even your wealthy father and his political friends in the Chamber of Senators would be unable to save you. This situation with the *Falangístas* is serious enough that you will be shot as an example to other young turks in the Bolivian military." He paused long enough to light a *cigarillo*. After exhaling the smoke of the first drag, he said, "I am in a position to help you get out of this mess and back home. But you will have to cooperate with me."

The young prisoner moaned softly. "*Dios me ayuda*— God help me!"

2300 HOURS LOCAL

ALFREDO had brought in a couple of cases of French beer along with an assortment of sandwiches from the Petroleo Colmo mess kitchen. It was a cold camp for security reasons, and though the weather wasn't cool by any stretch of the imagination, it would have been nice if they could have had some smoky fires to keep the mosquitoes away. But at least they had their insect repellent.

Bill Brannigan and Alfredo sat on the riverbank eating ham-and-turkey sandwiches while knocking back cans of the imported beer. They were disappointed in the results of the interrogation of the young *Subalterno* Melendez. The young man couldn't tell them much except that both *banderas* in the OA had been brought together to concentrate their efforts against the invaders. The addition of the mortars to the machine guns as infantry support weapons was not good news, nor was the intelligence about additional troops scheduled to arrive. The stolen Argentine helicopter in the enemy's possession was also ominous. This all meant that as the Falangists grew stronger and more fluid, their combat effectiveness could reach alarming proportions.

Alfredo finished off his Kronenbourg beer. Under normal conditions out in a desolate wilderness he would have tossed the small bottle into the river. But security dictated that all the empty bottles and wrappers from the refreshments be taken back to the oil company for disposal. He belched contentedly, then took another bite of his sandwich. "The main thing we've learned from sweating out that EPW was that it's going to be a hell of a lot harder to defeat this Falangist rebellion than originally thought."

"I need more men," Brannigan flatly stated.

"We considered that from the get-go," Alfredo said. "Washington says that's a no-no. And the UN can't help unless Bolivia asks for aid. If the three countries involved were willing to do that, you guys wouldn't be here in the first place."

"Shit! This is a no-win situation."

"You've got permission to cut and run anytime you want to," Alfredo said. "Nobody is going to hold it against you." He reached for another beer. "We can have you out of here within twelve hours. What do you say?"

Brannigan gave the ex–Special Forces NCO the coldest stare he'd ever been given in his life.

"I thought not," Alfredo said, belching again.

CHAPTER 7

IGNACIO Perez sat on the chair in his small room in the far corner of the headquarters building, smoking nervously. The ashtray on the desk next to him was filled with cigarette butts. Beside it was a half-full bottle of cognac that had been opened less than an hour before. The little bald man was frightened out of his wits but not to the extent of trembling with fear or heavy, nervous sweating. His trepidation was the smothering type that weighed on his consciousness with a relentless pressure without bringing on noticeable physical reactions other than smoking and drinking too much.

One of the patrols sent out a couple of days before had gone missing, then was located earlier that morning. A reconnaissance party had radioed in that three men had been discovered dead, and a fourth was missing in action. This was the young *subalterno* named Enrico Melendez, and he had not be found anywhere in the vicinity. It was assumed he had been captured.

As far as Ignacio was concerned, this was a sign of things to come.

He was in an environment that was completely alien to his personality and temperament. The former accountant was the farthest thing from a soldier. He was not aggressive, brave nor physically robust. The little man had ended up in this frightening predicament after a conviction for embezzling money from the machine parts manufacturing firm where he was employed. And this trouble came about because of his wife Isabella.

She was a lot younger than he, and Ignacio had met her when she was a salesclerk in a small grocery he frequented in his Seville neighborhood. Isabella was pretty in a sort of cheap, second-rate way. Her hair was always arranged in a flamboyant manner, the blouses she chose emphasized the cleavage of her large breasts, and she wore miniskirts that showed off her well-shaped legs. She displayed a sort of tacky sensuality that drove Ignacio mad with lust and love.

She had a lot of boyfriends who were the types that worked irregularly, if at all, and were always in some sort of trouble with the police or creditors. When she began being friendly toward him, Ignacio knew it was because he had gainful employment with a regular paycheck. He certainly wasn't a handsome man. In fact, there was very little she found attractive in his appearance. It was ludicrous to think that a twenty-year-old girl found a bald, spindly yet potbellied middle-aged accountant good-looking. His inferiority complex made him tongue-tied in her presence, but eventually his romantic affections finally stifled his natural shyness. He had gasped with happiness when, after he finally got up the nerve to ask her out, she agreed to let him take her to a restaurant and the cinema one Saturday evening. After he escorted her home, she even agreed to go out with him again.

Thus began a courtship she dominated. He knew that

Isabella was seeing other men from time to time, but he loved her so much he forgave her indiscretions. He fooled himself into thinking that if she became his wife and saw his pure, loving devotion, she would lose interest in her paramours. He was frightened out of his wits when he proposed, expecting to be laughed at and sent away. But she accepted.

When they married, Isabella was able to quit her job, and Ignacio was now convinced that between the affection, support and security he provided, she would indeed be a faithful, happy wife. But after only six months she began complaining about the size of the apartment, her spending allowance, their few evenings out and the fact that she couldn't buy the best clothes or visit the most expensive beauty salons.

She left him once, coming back only after he promised to raise their standard of living. Ignacio was so helplessly and hopelessly in love that he began to cook the books at work just a bit for the cash to satisfy his self-centered, demanding wife. He was able to easily pull in an extra 50 euros a week. This was fine for awhile, but her insatiable desires for expensive things grew until he was desperately sifting out amounts that climbed upwards to 250 euros several times a month.

Then an unannounced audit occurred at the factory.

Actually, Ignacio wasn't surprised, since he figured that somewhere down the line someone was noticing the growing discrepancies in his books. The miscreant accountant was arrested at work and taken out by a pair of large policemen while his coworkers looked on in horror and revulsion. The news of his crime was in all the newspapers and on television. Ignacio Perez was disgraced and humiliated. He knew the moment he was roughly shoved into the jail cell that he had lost everything: his dignity, reputation, and Isabella.

The trial was conveniently short, since he admitted everything and threw himself on the mercy of the court.

The judge noted the circumstances that drove him to the crime as well as the fact he had never been in trouble with the law before. But embezzling 200,000 euros was a serious offense, even if it was a first one, and called for a sentence of ten to fifteen years. However, because of his clean prior record, Ignacio was given the choice between the penitentiary or three years in the Spanish Foreign Legion. He chose the *Legión.*

He should have taken prison.

Ignacio Perez simply could not adapt to a brutal military environment. Punches, kicks from the *cabos* and *sargentos,* along with weeks as an *arrestado* in the labor units, did nothing to help him become a better soldier. No matter how much Ignacio applied himself, he couldn't fire his rifle accurately, fold his clothes properly to be placed in his locker, shine his boots bright enough, or properly carry out the myriad other maddening tasks demanded of him. But finally, after enduring six months of hell, somebody took note of the fact that he was a former accountant and could read, write, and even type. These were rare qualities in the *Legión,* and he was taken away from line companies and field soldiering to be transferred to headquarters as an administrative clerk.

Ignacio's expertise in paperwork was so good that he was even made a *cabo* to give him some authority in dealing with problems that arose in the staff bureaucracy. The poor little fellow felt better now, sure that he could finish out his three-year enlistment, then go to the Canary Islands, where no one knew him, and begin a new life.

But *Coronel* Jose Maria Castillo y Plato, the regimental commander, pulled him out of headquarters to work in his office typing up his fascist manifesto. Ignacio thought the man mad, and the more he worked on the fascist philosophy, the more nervous he became in the *coronel's* presence. When Castillo left the legion, Ignacio was not asked if he wanted to go with him to become embroiled in an international military coup. Nor were any inquiries made regarding his opinion of fascism. Castillo simply appointed the diminutive clerk a personal adjutant, warranted him a *suboficial,* and dragged him off to South America. From that point on, he not only had a criminal record, he was a deserter from the Spanish Army.

Now Ignacio was alone and isolated in the wilds of the Gran Chaco, trying to figure out how to get out of this new trouble and find freedom and peace once again. The next time he saw a cheap slattern, he would know enough to avoid her like the boot of an angry *sargento.*

He downed the glass of brandy, refilled it and drank deeply again.

ABOVE THE LOZANO GRASSLANDS
PETROLEO COLMO AÉROSPATIALE GAZELLE HELICOPTER
1100 HOURS LOCAL

THE small red aircraft flew slowly across the savannah's expanse at an altitude of 750 meters. In the passenger seats behind the pilot, the CIA operative Alfredo sat with Dr. Carl Joplin of the U.S. State Department. The two, wearing intercom headsets, gazed pensively down at the flat terrain below them.

Joplin turned his eyes toward his companion. "So you're disappointed in the intelligence you gleaned from the young Bolivian officer, are you?"

"Disappointed is not the exact word, Dr. Joplin," Alfredo said. "Dissatisfied more aptly describes my reaction. The drug-induced interrogation only produced what we had already figured out. The basic problem with our young EPW was that he didn't know a lot. He had fallen under the influence of older officers back in his home unit, and he made some unwise political choices."

"What will become of him?"

"He'll be put under arrest in quarters by the Bolivian

Army," Alfredo explained. "When this Falangist revolution is broken up, he'll be allowed to resign his commission, provided he agrees to never divulge what he's done. The kid will more than likely go into the banking business with his father."

"Interesting," Joplin commented. "And how are the SEALs doing?"

"They located the Falangist headquarters a couple of weeks ago. They even made a brief raid on the place."

"That's encouraging," Joplin stated.

"They weren't strong enough to wipe it out or force a surrender," Alfredo said. "But it's good information for an air strike. How about sending a carrier down here?"

"That will *not* happen," Joplin said. "Could you arrange for one of the South American air forces to do the job?"

"If we could do that, we wouldn't need the SEALs," Alfredo said. "At any rate, the Falangist force in this area, while small, will be reinforced substantially before too much more time goes by."

"Could you be a bit more specific?"

"Early in the new year, they should be strongly established here on the Gran Chaco," Alfredo said. "And there has been no concerted effort to defeat them except for the insertion of twenty-one SEALs into the OA. And one of them, an officer, has been wounded and medevaced. So there're twenty of them now. Next week they might be down by another. Or two. Or a half dozen. Who knows?"

"I agree we must increase the size of the detachment," Joplin said. "What about the armed forces of Chile, Bolivia and Argentina? Have their internal situations improved?"

"I've nothing but discouraging news in those quarters," Alfredo said. "The lists of officers and noncommissioned officers going AWOL are growing on a daily basis. I realize some may be showing their support for the Falangists by staying away from their posts without actually joining in the fighting, but it is an indication of a problem that is becoming more threatening and complex."

"What are your chances of developing a mole in the Falangist movement?"

"You've heard of that proverbial snowball in hell, haven't you, Dr. Joplin?"

"I deal with it on an almost daily basis," Joplin said, smiling without humor. "In the meantime, what is the intrepid Wild Bill Brannigan planning on doing down there in the OA?"

"He's going into a hit-and-run fluid mode that depends heavily on resupply from Petroleo Colmo," Alfredo explained. "The SEALs are setting up caches around the area not only for normal resupply but to provide places to hunker down if they come under heavy attack."

"I hope we're not considering last stands."

"It could come to that if we leave them all by their lonesomes while their enemy grows stronger," Alfredo said glumly.

"Something must be done," Joplin said as much to himself as his companion.

"You mustn't forget that the loss of valuable people like a SEAL platoon would negatively affect morale within the special operations community," Alfredo said. "It wouldn't do a lot for confidence or trust in the State or Defense Departments."

Joplin made no comment as he gazed down at the grasslands, deep in thought.

HEADQUARTERS, *GRUPO DE BATALLA*
CAMPAMENTO ASTRAY
1600 HOURS LOCAL

SARGENTO Antonio Müller led his three men through the defensive perimeter around the garrison into its interior. They had just completed a daylong reconnaissance patrol and showed the fatigue brought on by physical exertion combined with high temperatures and humidity.

Their boots were caked with mud, and their camouflage
uniforms were sweat-soaked, but they marched smartly
into the cantonment area.

Müller brought the small column to a halt. Two of them
were *sargentos* and the other a *cabo* who had been broken
down from *sargento-mayor* for beating up an insubordinate
soldier while serving in the Argentine Army. That was his
basic motivation for deserting and joining the Falangist insurgency.

"Good job today," Müller told them. "Your physical
conditioning is now tops. When the new recruits arrive you
will be ready to give them hell. After you're dismissed
you're free to clean up and get ready for mess call. *Rompan
filas!*"

The men made about-faces, then broke ranks and ambled toward their barracks. Müller walked across the parade ground to headquarters, going in to report to the
intelligence officer. This was *Capitán* Diego Tippelskirch,
who had served in the same parachute infantry battalion in
the Chilean Army with the *sargento*. He had been sent
TDY from his battalion to a posting in a supersecret organization during President Antonio Penechet's notorious
reign. Like many such officers, the law was closing in on
Tippelskirch, and this was the basic reason why he opted
for the Falange. *Generalísimo* Castillo was glad to welcome him into the movement because of his many valuable
contacts in the military and naval intelligence services of
several South American countries.

"Reporting from patrol duty, *mi capitán*," *Sargento*
Müller said, saluting.

"How did it go, Müller?" Tippelskirch asked, looking
up from his paperwork.

"Nothing special to inform you about, sir," Müller said.
"But there was a lot of flying about by those red helicopters."

Tippelskirch nodded. "Those are the ones belonging to
that petroleum exploration firm. They've been in the Gran
Chaco for quite some time."

"Their activity seems to be increasing," Müller said. "I am used to seeing them from time to time, but I caught sight of them a total of four times today during our reconnaissance."

Tippelskirch was interested. "What were they doing?"

"Flying rapidly from place to place and landing," Müller said. "They would be out of sight over the far horizon for a short period of time, then suddenly take off and go to another location."

Tippelskirch shrugged. "Perhaps they've finally discovered oil. Since this area will soon be the DFF, the financial benefits will be most useful to our cause. At any rate, I will make a report about the activity at this evening's staff meeting. Anything else, Müller?"

"No, *mi capitán*."

The *sargento* saluted, made an about-face that would have done him credit on any parade ground, then marched smartly off to shower and change for mess call.

SEAL CACHE LISA
OA, WESTERN SECTION
11 DECEMBER
0745 HOURS LOCAL

GARTH Redhawk used hand signals to direct the Dauphin helicopter to the proper place for landing. As soon as its wheels touched down, all five men of the Command Element rushed forward to grab the bundles being handed out by the aircraft's two-man crew.

The equipment, 5.56-millimeter ammo and MREs, was to be stashed in the nearby cache dug the night before. This earthen storage area had been dubbed Lisa after Lieutenant Wild Bill Brannigan's wife. He had gotten the idea from studying the Battle of Dien Bien Phu, when the French made their last stand in their war in Vietnam. All the strongpoints in the fortified area had been named in the honor of the wives of several of the French officers. Brannigan decided to name this one after his spouse, giving permission to the assault teams to name their own caches after wives and sweethearts also.

When the unloading chore was done, the chopper took off without further delay, heading to another location with more cargo. Now, laboring in the growing heat of the morning, the entire Command Element began stacking the goods in the excavation. Brannigan helped with the fetching and carrying, carefully putting ammo boxes and MRE cartons on the tarpaulins laid down for them. As soon as everything was ready, more canvas covering was put over the goods.

At that point everyone scrambled out to begin the muscle-cramping task of shoveling dirt into the hole. As soon as that was finished, the careful camouflaging and masking of the location would be taken care of.

Frank Gomez, dirty and sweating, worked his shovel like an automaton, throwing earth into the shallow chasm. He looked up at Chad Murchison, who labored like a coolie at the task.

Chad winked at Frank. "I wonder what the poor people are doing today?"

OA, NORTHERN SECTION
0945 HOURS LOCAL

CHARLIE Fire Team—Milly Mills, Wes Ferguson and Pech Pecheur—moved cautiously across the savannah in a skirmish line as they approached a small village a hundred meters ahead. The bucolic community had been spotted during a flyover by the Dauphin chopper, and Senior Chief Buford Dawkins had detailed the Charlies to check the place out.

As they drew closer, the SEALs noted the site was made up of a half-dozen grass-thatched huts and one long one that appeared to be a dining or meeting center. A few plowed areas appearing to be vegetable gardens were located on the west side of the site. A closer look showed the cultivated areas weren't producing much in the way of food.

Some people came out of the larger building, indicating that a meal or meeting had been in progress. A tall, spindly, bearded man made his way through the small crowd. He stopped for a moment to gaze at the SEALs, then walked toward them in long strides. After going a few yards he stopped, waiting for them to come to him.

Milly warily eyed the other people, speaking to his men out of the corner of his mouth. "You guys get ready. If as much as a single weapon appears, open fire and start moving back."

However, the group of villagers did nothing more than watch them. When the SEALs walked up to the tall man, Milly nodded to him.

"Buenos días," the stranger said. *"Como puedo servirles?"*

Milly reached in his pocket for his Spanish phrase book. He pulled it out, thumbing through the pages.

The man noticed the book, his puzzlement evident by the expression on his face. "I speak English."

"Oh?" Milly said. "Good! How do you do?"

"I'm fine, thank you."

"You're an American, ain't you?" Milly commented.

"And evidently so are you," the man said pleasantly. "I am Reverend Walter Borden of the Christian Outreach Ministry. What can I do for you, sir? I assure you that we are on this land legally. I can produce all the permits and documentation issued us by the Bolivian government."

"I see," Milly said. "My name is Mills. I—that is my men and me—dropped by to, well, to see how things was going with you folks."

"What are you doing here?" Reverend Borden asked in unabashed curiosity.

"I can't discuss that right now," Milly said. "And I don't want to be impolite, but I'm afraid I'm going to have to ask you that same question. And I want an answer."

"You have the guns, sir," Borden said. "So I shall comply."

"Let me add the magic word to my question," Milly said, grinning slightly. "*Please* tell me what you're doing here."

"I am part of an international ministry of outreach to the poor," Borden said. "We are based in Dallas, Texas, and send missions out to various parts of the world to preach the Gospel and save souls. I had been working in the slums of La Paz. My work had gotten very frustrating, and I obtained permission from our church to move my flock away from the distractions of big city evil to the countryside. We have established this little village as a place to live and worship as Christians. We call it Caridad. That means *charity* in Spanish."

Milly looked past the man at the community. "Excuse me for saying so, Reverend, but you folks look a little worse for wear."

"We are having difficulties at this time," Borden admitted. "Our efforts in raising our own food have fallen far short of our hopes and expectations. These are people from the city, after all. We were just discussing the situation when you appeared in the distance."

"I can help you out," Milly said. "Foodstuffs like flour, rice and beans can be here within a couple of hours."

"We have no money, sir."

"You don't need none," Milly assured him. "The eats will be supplied for free. That includes tools and even medicine. Or medical treatment, if you need it."

"What would you require of us?" Borden asked suspiciously.

"There's some bad men around here," Milly said. "Soldiers that call theirselves Falangists. We came here to get rid of 'em. We would appreciate your help in what we're trying to do. I'm not talking about taking up arms. Just keep an eye out and give us information if you happen to see any of 'em. That's all we ask."

Borden shook his head. "I regret that I must refuse your kind offer of assistance after all, sir. We did not leave the turmoil of slum life to become embroiled in war."

"All right, sir," Milly said. He had already been fully briefed in the procedures for establishing friendly rapport with any indigenous people in the Gran Chaco. "We don't ask nothing of you then. But we still would like to help. I bet we could even get you some new seed for your crops."

"Your kindness seems like a sign from the Almighty," Borden said. "But I must reiterate that we will not become obligated to you in any way."

"Not to worry, sir," Milly said.

Borden swung his eyes to Wes Ferguson and Pech Pecheur. They seemed like a couple of tough guys, but there was an air of decency about them. He sighed and relented. "I must accept your help, sir. Frankly, we are desperate."

"Happy to oblige, sir," Milly said, reaching for the handset of the AN/PRC-126 radio.

CHAPTER 8

WHEN Carl Joplin, PhD, an undersecretary of state, left his office that morning, he carried no briefcase with him. He sauntered down the corridors of the building with his hands in his pockets, appearing like a man headed for the cafeteria to partake of a late breakfast. Wherever he might be going, he didn't seem to be in much of a hurry.

And that was the exact impression he wished to make.

Joplin was on his way to the bailiwick of no less a personage than United States Secretary of State Benjamin Bellingham. No prior arrangements had been made for the visit, and the undersecretary knew his unexpected arrival would not be met with pleasure by the boss man. The visit violated protocol in at least a dozen ways, but Joplin damned convention in order to take care of some vital business that morning.

Now, perusing a copy of the *Washington Post,* Joplin sat in Bellingham's anteroom in front of the receptionist. Even an undersecretary would have to cool his heels if he walked in unannounced "from the street." Twenty minutes passed before the receptionist's phone rang. She answered softly and hung up, glancing at the unanticipated visitor.

"The secretary will see you now, Dr. Joplin."

"Thank you!" he said brightly, laying the newspaper aside.

Joplin went through the door into the inner sanctum, walked down a short hallway to a massive portal and knocked on it. He entered after a gruff invitation was growled from inside.

"What the hell's going on, Carl?" the secretary of state asked irritably. He was a bear of a man with a thick shadow of beard across his jowls in spite of having been shaved by his barber less than an hour previously.

Joplin, completely at ease, walked up to the desk and plopped down in a handy chair. "I've a situation I need to speak to you about, Ben. It involves a little affair going on in the Gran Chaco area of Bolivia."

"Oh, yes," Bellingham said. "A packet came across my desk only yesterday. Just a moment." He reached into a box marked FILE, pulling out a red folder. He quickly perused the contents, then set it in front of him. "All right. A SEAL outfit is involved."

"It is no more than a slightly reinforced platoon," Joplin said. "They are badly in need of additional personnel." Then he quickly added, "*Fighting* personnel, that is."

Bellingham shrugged. "The information I have is that they're up against a right-wing guerrilla outfit not much more numerous than themselves. I wouldn't think that would be much of a problem for Navy SEALs. Besides, why isn't the local military doing anything about this?"

"The information you received must be rather sketchy," Joplin said. "The situation is a hell of a lot more complicated than that."

"Then please feel free to enlighten me, Carl."

"The Falangists have infiltrated the armed forces of Bolivia, Chile and Argentina," Joplin explained. "They have moles in key areas that have not yet been identified. This is one of those well-known secrets that exist in these situations. The spies and informers are undoubtedly making up lists of names of those who'll be eliminated when and if their revolution is successful."

"Blacklists are common among all conspirators," Beilingham pointed out. "Most shallow-minded zealots operate under the principle that other people are either with them or against them. There are no shades of gray in extremist political or religious movements."

"You must keep in mind that the Latin American military are not in close harmony with the populations of their countries," Joplin said. "Besides, many of the officers are uneasy because of the possibility this is the beginning of the biggest revolution in the history of South America. They don't want to be on the outside looking in if a continental fascist dictatorship is established. Such a government would dominate the southern portion of the continent very quickly, then eventually conquer the rest of it. Any participants would be guaranteed high rank in the resultant gigantic army, navy and air forces. Their strength and influence would rival that of the United States. An American Falangist movement would undoubtedly emerge as well. All this in perhaps less than a decade."

Bellingham shook his head, patting the folder. "My intelligence sources assure me this is a minor disturbance. In fact, it seems there's a CIA operative on the scene."

"The Falangists have won the hearts and minds of some of the locals," Joplin pointed out. "They now have a helicopter and heavy support weaponry. This is just a start of what could be a flood of aircraft, arms and personnel."

"What is the amount of this influx?"

"It can't be determined at this point," Joplin admitted. "I need your permission to go to the Department of Defense and request a buildup of our force down there. Initially, our special operations capabilities in the situation should be tripled."

"I don't feel that is necessary, Carl."

"Then let's save some American lives and abandon the project."

Bellingham frowned. "You know we can't do that! An agreement has already been made. It would be embarrassing if we pulled out. Hell! *You* were the one that worked out the deal."

"The SEALs stand a good chance of being wiped out, Ben!" Joplin snapped.

"I don't think so," Bellingham said. "Get back to me if there are any meaningful updates that radically change the situation."

"If that happens it will happen fast," Joplin warned him. "And it will be too late for our people involved in the mission."

"I appreciate your concern, really," Bellingham said. "But—"

"Thanks for your time, Ben," Carl said, standing up. "Just remember, this is a situation that could blow apart on us. Big time!" He walked to the door, his shoulders slumped.

VILLAGE OF CARIDAD
1100 HOURS LOCAL

ALFREDO the CIA operative and Charlie Fire Team, along with the reverend Walter Borden, stood beside the Dauphin helicopter as the bundles of goods for the villagers were unloaded and set in neat stacks on the ground. The cargo contained bags of rice, beans, dried fruit and vegetable seeds. Three small crates were included that had been packed with clothing, tools and basic medical supplies.

The relief organization supplying the items was a clandestine group tied closely to certain intelligence elements. The parcels they sent were generic in appearance, showing no indication of their origin. Any necessary instructions printed on the packages inside were in French, Spanish, Italian, English, German, Portuguese, Chinese Mandarin, Chinese Cantonese, Japanese, Vietnamese, Arabic, Hebrew and Filipino. No brand names or logos were in evidence, thus even the most determined investigator would not be able to trace them back to any particular country or source.

At a signal from Reverend Borden, several men came forward and began picking up the bundles, carrying them to the large meeting hall where the rest of the villagers happily waited. The people were ecstatic. After months of deprivation and the failed crops of the large vegetable gardens, they could now eat and replant. The clothing would replace their torn and worn garments, the tools would be used for the new planting, and the medical supplies, while rudimentary, would help with the treatment of minor injuries. The insect repellent was most welcome, as Borden's followers had been plagued mercilessly by mosquitoes since their first day in the Gran Chaco.

When all the cargo was neatly stacked under the thatched roof, Alfredo waited as the villagers gathered around them. When he had their undivided attention, he spoke to them in his fluent Spanish.

"Buena gente del pueblo de Caridad," he began. "We are happy to bring you these items to relieve your suffering and discomfort. We do this gladly but ask some favors of you in exchange for the gifts. You must never—*nunca*— reveal where these packages and boxes came from. *Comprenden?* You must not tell anyone of the presence of Americans in this area. They have come here to destroy a band of very bad men who wish to enslave not only you but a great part of South America under a very cruel leader they call *el generalísimo*. The Americans do not want you to have to fight these bad men. They do not want you to be in any sort of danger. What they ask is that you simply observe what is going on around here. If you see the bad men, make note of the date, time and what they were doing. The

Americans will come here now and then to gather this information as well as bring you more things that you need to make your village and farms grow. Also, if it is necessary, the Americans may ask you to temporarily take care of their wounded and sick. Or perhaps to offer them a hiding place under certain circumstances. They might even ask you to run errands for them in places were they cannot go."

Alfredo paused to light a cigarette, glancing at the crowd to judge their reception of his words. They seemed delighted to cooperate, and he felt the SEALs now had some good friends in the Gran Chaco.

"Ya!" he said, exhaling smoke. "Let us pass out these gifts to the people. *El reverendo* Borden will supervise the distribution."

Borden and a trio of his senior assistants formed the people by family groups into a long line to issue the food. Milly Mills stood beside Alfredo, watching as the rice and other staples were doled out. After a few minutes, a woman carrying a child in her arms came to Alfredo and spoke to him softly in a pleading voice. The CIA operative turned to Milly.

"This woman's child is sick with a bad fever," Alfredo explained. "She wants to know if there's anything you can do."

"There sure as hell is," Milly said. "The Navy's best hospital corpsman is back with our Command Element." He pulled out the handset of his AN/PRC-126 and pressed the transmit button. "Brigand, this is Charlie. Over."

HEADQUARTERS, *GRUPO DE BATALLA* *CAMPAMENTO* ASTRAY 1400 HOURS LOCAL

SUBOFICIAL Adolfo Punzarron stood by the door of the EC-635 light utility chopper as his patrol of six riflemen climbed aboard. The rotors of the aircraft were spinning, and when Punzarron pulled himself into the troop compartment, the pilot kicked up the engine to take off. As soon as he was at 300 meters' altitude, he turned toward the southwest.

Intelligence gathered from the cattlemen of Novida indicated that this was the area where the mysterious invaders had been appearing from time to time. These antagonists, who seemed phantomlike, had the uncanny ability to appear and disappear at will. The command and staff of the *Ejército Falangísta* had decided it was time for violent contact with the elusive foe. Thus, Punzarron was now on his way to accomplish that goal.

As the helicopter sped over the Gran Chaco, the *suboficial* studied his map, matching it with the features on the ground. The chart, like others of that area, was inaccurate with misjudged distances, missed topographical features, and out-of-date references in the legends on the map's outer edge. Punzarron angrily shoved it back into the side pocket of his uniform trousers.

The flight continued for twenty minutes before reaching its destination. The nose of the aircraft was raised, and it went into a hover for a moment before lowering until its skids touched the grassy terrain. Punzarron leaped out and sprinted a dozen meters away from the door with his men following. He waited until the chopper took off for the return flight to *Campamento* Astray before forming up his troops in a single rank facing him. These were some of the men he had whipped into shape using his methods of the Spanish Foreign Legion. Consequently, they were tough, confident and able to endure almost any situation they might encounter while campaigning in the field.

"Oigan!" he barked. "Listen up! I want you to remember that we are out here for one reason and one reason only. *Buscamos conflictos*—we're looking for trouble. If we run across any of those outsiders we are to engage them in combat at the first opportunity. The primary mission is to kill all of them. The secondary mission is to get some prisoners. I prefer the

primary. I will take the point, and you will form into a single file behind me. Even-numbered men will maintain watch on the right, odd numbers take the left. The last man will watch our rear. Any questions? Good. *Siguenme!*"

Punzarron turned and set up a fast pace across the savannah, his patrol eagerly falling in behind him.

VILLAGE OF CARIDAD
1800 HOURS LOCAL

WHEN the Petroleo Colmo helicopter dropped off Hospital Corpsman James Bradley, he was met by a concerned duo. Milly Mills, leader of Charlie Fire Team, and the Reverend Walter Borden greeted the African-American SEAL, wasting no time in escorting him toward a hut on the far side of the village. Milly introduced James and the minister as they hurried through the people who had gathered to see the appearance of the medical technician who would tend to the sick boy.

"Tell me about my patient," James said.

"He's a three-year-old boy," Milly explained. "I took a look at him myself, and even I could tell the kid is in real serious shape, James. Personally, I don't think the little guy is gonna make it."

"We don't know what's wrong with him," Reverend Borden said. "For the past three days he has had a high temperature that we have been unable to lower."

"What sort of medication have you given him?" James asked.

"We have no medicines," Reverend Borden said. "The mother has been bathing him with cool water."

James was shocked that anyone would bring a group of people out into the wilds without a good medicine chest but kept his thoughts to himself. He would have to take the time to give some rudimentary medical, sanitation and first aid instruction to the villagers as soon as possible.

When they reached the hut, they found the baby's father waiting for them. He took the three visitors inside where the little boy lay on a cot. The mother, a small, thin, dark woman, looked up hopefully as James set his medical kit down. He gave the child a cursory examination.

"Has the boy been urinating regularly?" James asked, reaching into his kit for an ear thermometer.

"No," Reverend Borden answered since the parents did not speak English. "Only a little, and it's been dark in color."

"Right," James said. He noted the dry skin and sunken eyeballs as he looked the boy over. "He's badly dehydrated." He pulled the thermometer from the ear, noting a temperature of 101 degrees. The first thing he had to do was to bring the fever under control as fast as possible. Since the boy was semiconscious and unable to take aspirin, the only alternative was alcohol baths. He pulled a bottle of alcohol from his kit along with some sterile cloths in sealed packets. As he opened up a couple, he gave instructions that the mother should dampen the cloths and gently bathe her son. The Reverend Borden translated the directions, and the woman eagerly began the treatment.

Since the little patient could not take fluids by mouth to treat the dehydration, James set up an IV to administer a saline solution. In order not to over rehydrate the boy and send him into shock, the SEAL decided to give him no more than 1.5 cubic centimeters of the solution over the next twenty-four hours.

Reverend Borden watched the proceedings. "Is there anything I can do to help?"

James inserted the needle into the boy's arm. "I could use a hand from the Lord, Reverend."

"I'll organize a prayer vigil right now," Borden said. He went outside to gather his flock.

Milly Mills looked down at the sick youngster, not liking what he saw. "What's his chances, James?"

James spoke in a low tone of voice. "Silm to none, Milly."

OA, SOUTHWEST SECTION
2300 HOURS LOCAL

SENIOR Chief Petty Officer Buford Dawkins had taken his SAW gunner Joe Miskoski along with Gutsy Olson's Delta Fire Team out to scour the savannah in that part of the OA. The mission was to search out any targets of opportunity. They left base camp early that morning just as the first light of dawn had glimmered over the eastern horizon. Each member of the patrol carried a couple of days' rations and plenty of ammunition.

Now, after hours of steady humping, they had settled down for the night. It was a cold camp with no fire or flashlights. If anyone really needed to look for something, he had to turn to his night vision goggles. All heating of MREs would be done via the FRHs. Gutsy organized the night's watch, setting up a two-hour-on and four-hour-off guard rotation that would take them to 0500 hours the next morning.

Senior Chief Dawkins hated to admit it, but there were times when he felt his advanced age of thirty-seven. Twinges from long-ago parachute jumps, muscles that had been pulled in training, and an old shrapnel wound in his left side bothered him with increasing frequency. It all made him wonder how much longer he would be able to go until the ability to lead men in the field faded away in a combination of age and growing physical disability. The thought of such a thing happening troubled him deeply. There were times in the middle of the night when he was in that twilight between wakefulness and slumber that the possibility of becoming a staff weenie brought him to full consciousness. The worst part of it was having to part company from the greatest guys in the world.

As he sat in the darkness, leaning against his rucksack, he studied the men around him there in the Gran Chaco. He knew Joe Miskoski and Gutsy Olson well from previous missions. Petty Officer Second Class Andy Malachenko and Petty Officer Guy Deveraux, while new acquaintances, were becoming more familiar to him.

Andy had been born in the Soviet Union, coming to America with his parents in 1994. The family settled into the Russian émigré community in Brighton Beach, New York, where he quickly learned English and adapted to his new country. The naturally rugged kid joined the Navy for adventure and travel and was attracted to the machismo of the SEALs. Guy Deveraux's French-Canadian great-grandparents came to the U.S. in the 1920s. He was born and raised in rural Maine, spending his boyhood fishing and hunting in the woods of the Pine Tree State. He always had a fascination for the sea from the rare glimpses he got of it when his family visited the coast. He enlisted in the Navy but found out he wasn't fond of shipboard life. The SEALs offered a rather challenging alternative, and he opted to take a chance.

Dawkins was more than just a little proud and approving of his Second Assault Section. The men in both fire teams had meshed into a damned fine outfit, and if the group were destined to be his last combat command, he would go out in a flash of glory.

VILLAGE OF CARIDAD
14 DECEMBER
0230 HOURS LOCAL

JAMES Bradley got up off the floor of the hut and walked over to examine his little patient in the lantern light. The boy's parents slept on cots on the far side of the dwelling. Both were exhausted from worry over their only child, and James had to gently demand that the woman get some rest after long periods of giving her son alcohol baths.

The boy fussed a little in his sleep when James inserted the ear thermometer. The temperature had dropped to ninety-nine degrees, but it was still much too high for a youngster. The hospital corpsman checked the physical appearance of the child, noting that he had shown no response to the saline solution. It would be better to catheterize him to make an accurate observation of his urine output, but James did not have a catheter in his medical kit. A noise from the door caught his attention, and James turned to see the entire Charlie Fire Team tiptoeing into the hut.

"How's the little feller doing?" Milly asked.

"So-so," James replied.

Pech Pecheur, a Cajun from Louisiana, peered down at the sleeping youngster. "He don't look too good, James."

"I have to tell you," James said, "I'm not too confident of a recovery. God only knows how long he's really been sick before anybody around here took note of it."

Wes Ferguson from Wichita, Kansas, had participated in Reverend Borden's prayer vigil. Although not outwardly religious, this private individual attended chapel regularly back in Coronado. "He's in God's hands, James. Just do your best to help things along."

The quartet of tough SEALs stood in silence, gazing down at the little boy who clung to life by that proverbial thread.

OA, SOUTHWEST SECTION
0500 HOURS LOCAL

GUY Devereaux checked his watch, noting the time. He took a final look at the sleeping figures of his teammates in the small bivouac, then walked over to Senior Chief Buford Dawkins and nudged him. Dawkins sat up immediately, wide-awake and ready to go. Guy continued on to the other SEALs, roughly shaking them awake.

"Drop your cocks and grab your socks," he growled at the group. He was a little cranky from having to listen to them peacefully sleep while he stood the last two hours of watch.

Chow that morning was granola energy bars and water from the canteens. Dawkins got on the AN/PRC-126 and raised Lieutenant Wild Bill Brannigan. The contact was expected, and Frank Gomez informed the senior chief that his orders for the day were to continue his patrol's mission until midafternoon before turning back.

Dawkins got to his feet as he shoved the handset back into its carrier. "All right, people. Off and on."

VILLAGE OF CARIDAD
0730 HOURS LOCAL

HOSPITAL Corpsman James Bradley learned that his small patient's name was Joselito and that he had been born and raised in the poorest slum of La Paz, Bolivia. The boy was now awake and fussing softly, showing a healthy displeasure about everything that was going on. The mother and father watched anxiously as James took his temperature one more time. The smile on the SEAL's face after reading the digital readout showed it was normal.

By the time Reverend Borden came in for his morning visit, James had determined that Joselito was recovering nicely from the dehydration. Spittle had formed around his mouth, and his tongue was bright pink and moist. James poured a little water from his canteen into a plastic cup given him by the boy's mother. Joselito took a couple of small gulps and easily swallowed them. The liquid did not come back up. Then he demonstrated one of the most solid evidences of being rehydrated; he suddenly peed a beautiful stream of clear liquid. It wasn't much, but it meant he was well on his way back to normal.

James glanced up at Borden. "Tell the parents that Joselito will be fine by tomorrow."

When Borden gave them the good news, the mother rushed forward and grabbed James's hand. She kissed him, weeping and exclaiming her unending gratitude in Spanish. The father embraced him, crying uncontrollably as he expressed how much he appreciated the African-American's kindness. James didn't understand a word, but he caught the meaning clearly and fully. He was actually embarrassed by their worshipful and emotional appreciation. As far as he was concerned, he had simply logically and properly administered a treatment according to what he had been taught in premed and corpsman's school.

He smiled awkwardly and cleared his throat, speaking to Reverend Borden. "Tell them to give the little guy small sips of water about every fifteen minutes for the rest of the day." Then he added, "But not too much at a time. He could get very sick if he drank a lot. If he gets hungry, he can have some soup. But no solid food for at least a couple of days. Okay?"

James quickly packed up his medical kit before he had to endure any more parental thankfulness for saving the toddler's life.

OA, SOUTHWEST SECTION
0900 HOURS LOCAL

GUY Deveraux was on point, moving steadily through the thick grass of the savannah, when he spotted the seven men in column a couple of hundred meters away. They were moving at an angle toward him. He suddenly dropped to his knees, whispering into his LASH, "Unknown formation.

Two hundred meters at two o'clock. Moving toward eight o'clock."

"Roger," came back Senior Chief Dawkins's voice. "Check 'em out careful. They might be Bolivian. We sure as hell don't want to piss off the local government by shooting up some of their soldiers."

Guy raised his binoculars to his eyes, immediately catching sight of the red, black, red insignia on their sleeves. "These are bad guys. They got that Falangist doo-dad sewn on their uniforms."

"Can you figure out a good point of contact?" Buford asked.

"Yeah," the point man answered. "I'll pull back and get with you guys."

He stayed down, turning to crawl back through what cover the grass offered.

FALANGIST PATROL

SUBOFICIAL Adolfo Punzarron still stayed on point like he had done the day before. He wanted to be the one to spot any potential enemies so that he could quickly organize an attack. The patrol followed a small creek that went less than a meter deep, running in a straight line across the grasslands. It would be a handy place to use for cover in case of attack.

The patrol moved at a steady pace, each man carefully maintaining vigilance in the direction of his field of fire. If this had been a couple of weeks earlier, they would have been panting and stumbling, but now they trekked on easily, sweating more from the heat than fatigue.

Suddenly incoming fire raked the formation, and one of the Falangists jerked violently before toppling to the ground.

"Ponense a cubierto!" Punzarron bellowed.

The men jumped down into the creek, using the banks

for cover as they returned fire toward the source of the attack.

THE FIREFIGHT

JOE Miskoski, working the SAW, pumped out heavy fire with instinctively regulated pulls on the trigger while Guy Deveraux and Andy Malachenko leaped up and charged toward the enemy. Bullets from the Falangists clipped the air around them, and they dove to the ground. The pair now fired three-round automatic bursts as the rest of the SEALs got to their feet and rapidly advanced forward to join them.

PUNZARRON and his men were able to stand up in the knee-deep water, leaning forward on the creek bank. They fired overlapping patterns of salvos at the enemy who appeared, disappeared and reappeared as they closed in.

"*Los hijos de chingadas* are using fire-and-maneuver!" Punzarron bellowed over the sound of the shooting, knowing the attackers were at a disadvantage because of being on open ground. "As soon as any show themselves, turn your fire on them!"

THE SEALs made two more attempts to close in, but the incoming was so heavy they were quickly pinned down. Dawkins growled into his LASH, "Press your bellies to the dirt! Any casualties?"

"Negative, Senior Chief!" Gutsy Olson, the fire team leader, reported.

"All right!" Dawkins said. "Now hear this! Don't fire, and don't make any sound. They'll think we all have been hit or hauled ass."

VILLAGE OF CARIDAD
1330 HOURS LOCAL

THE entire population of the small community watched the bright red Petroleo Colmo Gazelle helicopter come in for a landing. James Bradley, holding onto his medical kit, had now endured the everlasting gratitude of everybody in the village. He had never gotten so many friendly embraces in his life. He didn't mind the women so much, but the crushing bear hugs of the men were beginning to tell after he'd endured several dozen.

Little Joselito was in his mother's arms, completely bewildered by all the hullabaloo. He didn't realize he had even been sick, much less at death's door; all he knew was that he felt a lot better now than he had for the past few days. He also was unaware that the man everyone was giving so much attention to had saved his life.

When the chopper touched down, Lieutenant Wild Bill Brannigan stepped out. He walked up and took Milly Mills's salute, then was introduced to the Reverend Walter Borden. The minister gripped Brannigan's hand, shaking it with great feeling.

"You and your men are truly a blessing bestowed on us by the Good Lord above!" he cried. "You have brought us food and clothing and medicine, but above all, you brought us that most precious commodity: hope! The good doctor James saved a life, and all these grateful people look upon it as a sign that we will do more than simply survive. We shall grow and prosper in this community we have built for ourselves."

"I'm glad we could lend a hand," Brannigan said, having been apprised of James's good deed over the AN/PRC-126.

"We were in very bad shape," Borden admitted. "And we are all city folks, so none of us are expert in living off the land. Now, thanks to the seed you sent us, our gardens shall blossom properly and provide even more food for us."

"I'm real happy things are starting to pick up for you," Brannigan said, feeling awkward in the barrage of gratitude.

"We are more than happy to help you in your struggle," Borden said. "I abhor war, but you are such good men, I know your cause must be worthy and blessed by God."

"We appreciate your offer of help," Brannigan said. He turned to Milly. "Take your fire team off and do some patrolling. All around this village. Get back here within an hour, and we'll take you back to your assault section." He grabbed James's arm, pulling him toward the chopper. "Let's get the hell out of here."

The villagers cheered as the two climbed into the chopper, glad to escape all the disconcerting love being showered on them.

THE FIREFIGHT
1400 HOURS LOCAL

THE Falangist patrol had been waiting, silent and sweating, for four hours with no movement to their front. Punzarron, as patient in battle as he used to be when setting up an armed robbery in his native Portugal, had kept his men quiet. Now, although there had been no sign or sound of movement to the front, he was convinced the attackers were gone.

"We are going to advance," he called out to his five surviving men. "The skulking bastards have crawled away on their bellies like the *cobardes*—the cowards—that they are."

At his command, the patrol pulled themselves out of the creek and stood up on the bank. Bursts of fire swept across them, and two men tumbled to the grass. Cursing and snarling, the Falangists leaped back into the cover of the narrow waterway. Of the pair of casualties, one lay still in death while the other moaned softly with a belly wound.

* * *

"NOW hear this," Senior Chief Buford Dawkins whispered over the LASH. "Start easing back, but stay alert. I don't expect them to chance exposing themselves again, but they're prob'ly really pissed off at us."

Dawkins would have liked to stay and bring the fight to a more satisfying conclusion, but there was a strong possibility that the Falangists might have called for reinforcements. That was a luxury the Americans did not have.

The SEALs surreptitiously, quietly, slowly and stealthily hauled ass.

CHAPTER 9

CHIEF Petty Officer Matt Gunnarson, leader of the First Assault Section, walked through a pouring rain around the recently constructed cache that had been named after Connie Concord's wife. The earthen evacuation, now covered by carefully dug-up sod, was practically invisible, even to someone standing directly on top of it.

The assault section, recently reorganized since Lieutenant (J.G.) Jim Cruiser had been wounded nine days earlier, had already adapted to the new one-man command structure. Matt was an experienced leader, quickly able to turn things around to his own methods of leadership.

Mike Assad and Dave Leibowitz considered their assignment to the group as a sort of vacation after days of acting as the detachment's point men and scouts. They were well acquainted with the other old sweats in the section, having served with them in the platoon's first mission in Afghanistan. On the other hand, Petty Officer Second

Class Lamar Taylor and Petty Officer Third Class Paulo Cinzento were fresh assignees the original members were just beginning to know.

Lamar was a twenty-one-year-old African-American from Cincinnati, Ohio. This married man with two kids was at the beginning of his second four-year hitch after shipping over. His entrance into the SEALs had been through the inspiration of a high school teacher who had served in the outfit in Vietnam. Lamar still exchanged letters with the social studies instructor who had wielded such a positive influence in his life.

Paulo was from San Diego and had lived around the local naval facilities all his life. His family were tuna fishermen of Portuguese ancestry who had worked the seiners out of Southern California for three generations. The collapse of that industry kept the twenty-two-year-old from going to sea like the older men in his family, so he enlisted in the Navy to "ride the waves." However, the indoctrination in boot camp about SEALs attracted him to that challenging branch of the armed forces. His girlfriend Rosa was a court reporter in San Diego.

Matt was pleased with the condition of the hidden cache and now turned his attention to the men of the section. They all stood in the rain, their ponchos glistening with wetness, as they waited for the chief to get the day's real business rolling.

"All right," Matt said, "we're ready to go. We'll leave the raider boat and piragua hidden in the reeds there along the river. The Skipper wants us to recon this part of the OA. The mission is to gather what intelligence we can on local conditions. If we sight targets of opportunities, we're not to attack without an okay from the Command Element. Does everyone understand that? If we spot any bad guys, I'll get on the horn and describe the situation to Lieutenant Brannigan. He'll choose our course of action. Fight or flight. Got it? All right, Bravo Fire Team take the point."

The small column formed up and moved out onto the savannah that was getting a heavy soaking in the precipitation.

OA, SOUTHWEST SECTION
1000 HOURS LOCAL

THE rainstorm had passed through the area, and now the sun blazed down, boiling invisible clouds of humidity out of the soaked ground. Delta Fire Team along with Senior Chief Petty Officer Buford Dawkins and SAW gunner Joe Miskoski watched as the Petroleo Colmo helicopter came in for a windy landing that sent a rolling ripple across the grasslands. As soon as it touched down, Lieutenant Wild Bill Brannigan stepped out from the troop compartment and trotted over to his SEALs.

"Good morning, sir," Dawkins said, rendering a salute. "Anything special going on?"

"Same old shit mostly," Brannigan said. "But you're going to take a chopper ride over to the east to marry up with Charlie Fire Team. I want your entire section to be together."

"Right, sir. What're we gonna be doing?"

"The first thing is to set up a cache with the ammo and rations on board," Brannigan said. "You can name it after one of the guys' wives or sweethearts. The Command Element has Lisa, and Chief Gunnarson said they named theirs Maybelle after Petty Officer Concord's wife."

"Well, hell, I ain't married, sir," Dawkins said. He looked over at his men. "Hey, Gutsy! What's your old lady's name? We're gonna call our cache after her."

Gusty Olson laughed. "Krista. I'll have to take a picture of it to show her."

"Two reasons you ain't gonna be able to do that," Dawkins said. "First of all you ain't got a camera; and the second reason is that if a cache is done proper, you can't see the godamn thing anyhow."

Gutsy shrugged. "She'll be honored just the same. I guess."

"Now hear this," Brannigan said loudly to get everyone's attention. "Your mission after digging the cache is going to be pure reconnaissance, got it? Do not make any contact with the enemy unless I okay it first. Your mission will be to pinpoint Falangist movements and locations. The Petroleo Colmo outfit has acquired another Dauphin chopper so each of the assault sections will have one. The Command Element will play its transportation by ear. Let's go!"

"You heard the Skipper," Dawkins bellowed. "Start breaking ground on Krista."

Gutsy scowled. "I don't think I like the sound of that."

HEADQUARTERS, *GRUPO DE BATALLA* *CAMPAMENTO* ASTRAY NOON LOCAL

NINE new men had arrived in the garrison the day before after a flight from Argentina aboard the *generalísimo*'s Piaggio turbojet. Six were Spanish officers from both the Foreign Legion and parachute infantry units, and two were Portuguese noncommissioned officers from their nation's Marine Detachment for Special Duties. Additionally, one disaffected Spanish-speaking sergeant from the French *Gendarmerie Nationale* was also among the new men: He'd gotten into hot water for killing a stubborn and defiant Algerian terrorist suspect he had arrested; it looked like he was headed for a general court-martial. He made a critical decision to flee France to avoid prosecution.

The Frenchman's name was Arnaud Chaubere, and he was one of those individuals with cold eyes and a calm exterior not unlike that of a leopard preparing to attack. When the new men arrived, they were formed up for a quick inspection by *Generalísimo* Castillo. He looked at each one, but he stopped for a long moment in front of the former *gendarme*. "I've heard of you, Chaubere."

"Yes, *mi generalísimo*," he answered in French-accented Spanish.

"You had a bit of a problem with a terrorist prisoner, did you not?"

"Yes, *mi generalísimo*," Chaubere said. "I bent him a little too much, and he broke."

The *generalísimo* laughed aloud. "You're the type of man we're looking for. I hereby appoint you to the rank of *sargento-mayor*."

"Gracias, mi generalísimo!"

Coronel Jeronimo Busch, standing off to the side, was favorably impressed with all nine. They were obviously in top-notch physical condition, well-experienced and proven in combat, and had the right political attitudes to put forth the aims and goals of the Falangist movement.

After Castillo had finished his inspection, he turned the men over to *Capitán* Silber to be taken to an orientation. As he was walking back to headquarters, Busch hurried and caught up with him. *"Generalísimo,"* the *coronel* said. "I have a suggestion."

"And what might that be?" Castillo asked.

"I think we should team up that Frenchman Chaubere with Punzarron and Müller."

Castillo came to a halt and looked at him. He suddenly smiled. "That is an excellent suggestion, *Coronel*. I will have Ignacio take care of the paperwork for the assignment."

1400 HOURS LOCAL

WHEN *Generalísimo* Castillo walked into the staff meeting area of the thatched headquarters hut, he found everyone present and accounted for. *Coronel* Jeronimo Busch, *Comandantes* Javier Toledo and Gustavo Cappuzzo, and the intelligence officer *Capitán* Diego Tippelskirch were ready to conduct business. Even diminutive and edgy *Suboficial* Ignacio Perez was in his place with his pads of papers and folders.

"First things first," Castillo said, sitting down. "What are our latest strength figures, Ignacio?"

Ignacio quickly pulled out the correct folder. "With the nine new men who arrived today, we now have a total of ninety-four men, *mi generalísimo*. So far we have had six men killed and one is missing in action."

"They shall be avenged, *por Dios!*" Castillo said. "Anything else?"

"Our rations, ammunition and equipment inventory is more than adequate, *mi generalísimo,*" Ignacio said. "Also, we will soon receive another helicopter that has been— well—that is to say—*donated* to the *Ejército Falangísta* by members of the Argentine Air Force."

Everyone laughed loudly at the little man's understatement, and Castillo asked, "What sort of aircraft is it, Ignacio?"

"It is an SA-330 Puma, *mi generalísimo,*" Ignacio reported. He pulled out a descriptive document on the helicopters. "It is manufactured in Great Britain by Westland Helicopters and can travel at two hundred and seventy-eight kilometers an hour."

Busch didn't give a damn about the mechanical or technical features of the aircraft. "How many men can it carry, Perez?"

"Sixteen fully equipped soldiers can be transported in its troop compartment, *mi coronel,*" he said replacing the papers in the folder. "It should arrive here sometime within the next two days."

"That's good news!" Busch exclaimed. "Now we can get serious. Between the new helicopter and the EC-635, we will be able to carry twenty-four troops into battle."

"Things improve almost on a daily basis," Castillo stated happily. He nodded to Tippelskirch. "Anything going on in intelligence, *Capitán*?"

"*Si, mi generalísimo,*" Tippelskirch replied. "I have been very curious about this petroleum research company that flies constantly over the Gran Chaco. My usual sources have no information on them, but I have a contact in the Chilean Bureau of Security that can get me the information I need. However, it will take some time."

"Stay on that," Castillo ordered. "Anything else?"

"I visited the village of Novida and interrogated the headman there," Tippelskirch said. "*Suboficial* Punzarron acted as my interpreter, of course. I wanted to find out more about that enemy unit that passed through the area. After an hour of questioning, I have reached the conclusion the interlopers are Americans."

"Are you saying that the United States has dispatched armed forces into the Gran Chaco?" Castillo asked.

Tippelskirch shrugged. "I can't be sure of that. Perhaps they are from an American private military company. This is a new industry that has sprung out of the attack on New York City on *Nueve-Once*—Nine-Eleven."

"I believe such businesses only provide local security and bodyguards," Castillo said.

"Well, there is always the possibility they are CIA," Tippelskirch pointed out.

"Bah!" Castillo snarled. "They are *bandidos,* eh? And that's the way I want them to be referred to. Not as honorable soldiers or even guerrillas. Everyone make a note of that! They are *bandidos*! That will give our men more confidence when they go out to fight and kill them."

"I have a couple of suggestions, *mi generalísimo,*" Busch said. "I strongly suggest we move out of this garrison. The *bandidos* know this location and have even attacked us here. We should set up a fortified area with bunkers, barbed wire and mines."

"But we do not have the labor force necessary for such an undertaking," Castillo argued.

The Argentine *Capitán* Argento interjected, "I have an excellent solution to that problem, *mi generalísimo*. I can take care of it through contacts I have in the Argentine Federal Police."

"I'll leave that to you, Argento," Castillo said. He gestured to *Comandantes* Toledo and Cappuzzo. "You two will each detail men to search out a proper area where field fortifications can be constructed." Now his eyes snapped back to Busch. "Any more suggestions, *Coronel*?"

"Since the two helicopters give us the capability of setting up ambushes and sneak attacks, I think we should form up a special *equipo comando*—commando team," Busch said.

Once more Castillo approved. "And who are you considering for the team?"

"It's is a suggestion I made once before," Busch said. "*Suboficial* Punzarron, *Sargento-Mayor* Chaubere, and *Sargento* Müller."

Ignacio spoke up. "That has already been done, *mi generalísimo!*"

STATE DEPARTMENT
WASHINGTON, D.C.
16 DECEMBER
1845 HOURS LOCAL

THE cab pulled up in front of the State Department building, just outside the cement barricades put up to thwart suicide bomber vehicles. The passenger got out, turning to pay his fare, then walked up toward the building. After presenting an I.D. card at the door, he was admitted into the lobby. A quick exchange at the security desk between the man and the duty officer resulted in a phone call.

Moments later a balding young man in a white shirt, tan slacks and loafers appeared. He and the visitor recognized each other and shook hands, then the pair walked across the chamber to an empty elevator and got in. Eight seconds later they reached the third floor, stepping out into a hallway that led down to the office of Carl Joplin, PhD, Undersecretary of State. They walked into the reception area, and the young man turned the visitor over to the receptionist.

She smiled at him. "How are you today, Mr. Sanchez?"

"I am fine, thank you," Arturo Sanchez, special envoy from the government of Bolivia, replied. "I received a message to call on Dr. Joplin as quickly as possible."

"I'll let him know you're here," the receptionist said. She picked up her phone. "Mr. Sanchez has arrived, sir." She hung up. "You may go in."

Sanchez stepped through an unmarked door to find Joplin sitting at his desk. They shook hands, and the Chilean took an offered chair. Sanchez had a great deal of respect for the African-American undersecretary, and he waited patiently for him to initiate whatever proceedings he had in mind for the visit.

Joplin, as was his habit, cut to the chase. "There is a village of illegal alien Brazilians in Bolivia. They are engaged in raising cattle in the Gran Chaco area."

"I am not aware of them, Dr. Joplin, but I have no doubt that your information is correct," Sanchez said. "Would they have become involved in the unhappy circumstances in that part of my country?"

"They are not involved in the fighting," Joplin replied, "but they aid the Falangist movement as observers. They pass on information to them."

"That is intolerable," Sanchez stated, using a calm, diplomatic tone when speaking the angry words.

"Novida—that is their name for the village where they live—makes our men's mission down there more difficult," Joplin explained. "These are black people who view the local authorities with a marked amount of fear and mistrust. I have most reliable information that the fascists have offered them protection in exchange for serving them. Gifts of food are also involved in the exchanges."

"I can see that these villagers are dealt with right away," Sanchez said. "They are cooperating with enemies of the state."

"I would like to emphasize that these are decent people," Joplin cautioned him. "They are not involved in criminal activity, and they can't be blamed for accepting whatever help they can get. As undocumented foreigners, they have no place to turn when things go bad for them. Therefore, the United States government would prefer that they be peacefully and respectfully deported back to Brazil."

"I will see that the matter is handled with courtesy and consideration," Sanchez assured him.

"The United States government also requests that none of their belongings or money be taken from them," Joplin said. "And that includes their cattle. They are poor people."

"I cannot promise that," Sanchez said. "We have laws and procedures that must be followed. However, I will see what can be done. Is there anything else?"

"Not a this time, thank you," Joplin said. He visibly relaxed and smiled. "Now, Arturo, with our business taken care of, my wife and I would be pleased if you and Mrs. Sanchez came by for dinner tonight. Eight o'clock. It will be an intimate affair; just us four."

"I would be delighted, Carl," Sanchez said, standing up. "I must get back to my office and get this Novida village thing put in the pipeline. Until tonight at eight. Good afternoon, my friend."

"*Buenas tardes, amigo mio*," Joplin responded in Spanish.

OA, WESTERN SECTION
17 DECEMBER
1515 HOURS

THE Command Element acted as an independent unit when Lieutenant Wild Bill Brannigan took them to check out the area to the east of Cache Lisa. Garth Redhawk was on point, moving with the self-assuredness and silence of a Kiowa warrior. The camouflage paint on his face was applied in the old tribal manner, and his medicine bag was around his neck held by a rawhide thong. Back to the rear of the small column, Chad Murchison kept an eye to each side of their trek as well as the rear. Brannigan, Frank Gomez and James Bradley moved along between the two, covering the middle of the column.

Redhawk sighted the Falangist at the exact moment the man sighted him. They quickly exchanged shots, the reports of the CAR-15 and the CETME assault rifle cracking simultaneously. "Enemy front!" Redhawk said over the LASH. "Unknown number."

Brannigan immediately reacted to the situation and formed the element into a skirmish line with James and Chad going to Redhawk's left, while he and Frank went to the right. Everyone immediately went to the ground, since the encounter took place on an open, flat area with no cover other than the tall grass. The Falangists had wisely done the same, and now neither side could see the other.

"Redhawk," Brannigan said over the LASH, "move forward and check out the situation. If they haven't moved back, they could be just waiting for one of us to show ourselves. Be damn careful!"

"Aye, sir," Redhawk calmly replied in a whisper.

This descendant of the Kiowa and Comanche tribes eased silently toward the enemy, being careful to be as quiet as possible without causing undue movement of the grass. Being in combat took him deep into the culture of his people, and he felt that he was in his element. At that exact moment, Redhawk was performing the one thing he was on the earth to do; to kill as a warrior kills. It made no difference whether it was to close in on game such as elk or buffalo or to seek out the enemy of his people to slay them. He was a fighter, a hunter, and a plunderer. All his personal honor and purposes in life were wrapped up in those three endeavors. It was as if he had been pulled into a time warp.

Redhawk peered through the dense, waving vegetation, suddenly catching sight of an older man with gray hair. He was middle-aged but obviously in good physical condition. The Oklahoman aimed carefully, then slowly squeezed the trigger. The Falangist's head jerked violently as his skull exploded in a red shower of brains and blood.

Redhawk crawled off, turning in another direction for no other reason than he felt some sort of vibrations in that area. After going ten meters he discovered he had eased into a position behind another enemy soldier. A quick aim, and a pull on the trigger. The strike of the bullet hit the back of the man's head so hard that his face was slammed into the ground.

The SEAL now moved at a right angle, easing down into a shallow dip in the ground. When he reached the other side of the depression he was suddenly looking into the face of a wide-eyed Falangist. Redhawk, in an instinctive reflex, let off an unaimed round, and the guy's features caved inward with the bullet strike.

A gruff command was shouted in Spanish, and a sudden salvo of bullets whipped above The SEAL's head. He went as flat as he could as several volleys came so close he could feel the shock waves from the bullets as they whipped over him. Then the shooting stopped as quickly as it began. Redhawk remained plastered to the ground in the silence. Not even an insect buzzed.

Brannigan's voice came over the LASH. "They've pulled out. On your feet!"

The SEALs gathered together, going to each of the three corpses to check them for possible intelligence. But none bore documents of any kind, not even I.D. cards or tags.

Chad Murchison looked carefully at the second man Redhawk had killed. "I say! This fellow is rather mature, is he not?"

"All three of 'em are," Frank Gomez said. "Do you remember what they told us in Isolation? These guys are all noncommissioned officers and officers. They're veterans."

Brannigan checked the eastern horizon with his binoculars. "There could be more of them coming this way." He lowered the viewing device. "Redhawk, we'll head back to the cache. Follow a different azimuth than the one we used to get out here."

"Aye, sir!"

The patrol fell back into its march formation as the Native American took the lead.

ABOVE THE SAVANNAH
18 DECEMBER
0500 HOURS LOCAL

CORONEL Francisco Martinez sat in the copilot's seat of the old H-34 transport helicopter. He was the commander of the western sector of the *Policia Fronteriza*—the Border Police—and his men had nicknamed him El Garron—the Big Claw—after a well-known Bolivian wrestler who was always the bad guy in his matches.

Two more helicopters followed the colonel's, and both were filled with eight heavily armed policemen. They had traveled from their usual post on the Bolivian-Brazilian border to take care of a matter involving some squatters. The orders had come down outside of normal police channels, and as far as *Coronel* Martinez was concerned, that was a carte blanche to handle the situation any way he wanted.

And El Garron hated people of African ancestry.

When the choppers came in, each took a side of the village in a triangular formation. The well-trained policemen quickly leaped from the aircraft and formed up in skirmish lines, their Uzi 9-millimeter submachine guns holding fully loaded thirty-round magazines. Each agent also had four more attached to his shoulder harness.

El Garron knew the noise of the incoming helicopters would have awakened all the residents of the tiny community, and he strode toward the thatched huts to find the headman.

João Cabeçinho walked out into the countryside from the village. His people, who had stumbled out of their residences, stood around in a collective feeling of dread. The sight of armed police was a sure sign of immediate misery and disappointment in their lives.

El Garron stood with legs spread and his arms folded across his chest as he waited for the village chief to come up to him. The police officer sneered down at the small black man. *"Bom dia, preto,"* he said in Portuguese.

Cabeçinho knew there was nothing to gain with defiance. He noted the three stars on the rank patch held to the Bolivian's jacket by Velcro. "Good morning, *Coronel.* How may I serve you?"

"You may serve me by directing everyone who lives in your village to go out on the opposite side from here," El Garron said. "One of my men will be waiting to direct you to the exact spot."

Cabeçinho, with no choice but to obey, turned to his people, passing on the instructions in a low, sad tone of voice. This was the one thing they dreaded would happen from the first day they arrived on the Gran Chaco. All hope was gone now. The people moved slowly and hesitantly until the policemen charged in, shouting and gesturing angrily.

Ten minutes later the entire population of a hundred men, women and children stood close together some twenty meters from the village limits. The disappointment and frustration showed plainly on their faces as the knowledge their plans and hard work for starting a new life in the Gran Chaco had come to an end.

El Garron checked the positions of his men, gesturing

to move a squad a little closer. When all was ready, he allowed himself almost a full minute before getting down to business. After a deep breath, he bellowed out the order.

"*Tiren*—fire!"

CHAPTER 10

CAMPAMENTO Astray was completely abandoned and left to the mercies of the elements. Even as the last man got aboard for the final helicopter lift to the new garrison, the thatched buildings looked as if the process of rot and disintegration was already beginning.

The entire *Grupo de Batalla* took over four square acres of land ten kilometers to the southwest. The heavily jungled Selva Verde Mountains could easily be seen in the distance. This new stronghold was designed to have a linked series of bunkers and other field fortifications that would be covered by tiers of logs and earth under camouflaged netting. The construction had already begun, and the sounds of backhoes, picks and shovels filled the area.

However, none of the Falangists were involved in this toil except as supervisors. They were all officers and noncommissioned officers who by military tradition and regulations were above laboring like *peones*. The problem of a work crew had been solved two days earlier by the

Argentine *Capitán* Luis Bonicelli. He used Falangist members and fellow travelers in his country's Federal Police to arrange to have two dozen convicts flown in for the back-breaking work. These prisoners were under life sentences at a miserable penitentiary down in the wilds of Patagonia. They qualified for this dubious honor by being strong and robust for the grinding toil. Additionally, each of these men was picked for his lack of connections to the outside world. They were abandoned and forgotten men, already considered dead by family and friends.

After the chosen felons were culled from the general prison population, they were herded into the backs of trucks under tight security for the trip to the airport in Califate. Upon arrival they were hustled aboard an Argentine Air Force C-60 Transall already loaded with tools and a trio of backhoes for mechanical digging.

This was the first day of their labor, but remarkable progress was being made because of the brutal supervision of *Suboficial* Adolf Punzarron and *Sargento* Antonio Müller. The periodic appearance of *Coronel* Jeronimo Busch contributed greatly to the efficiency of the effort.

The first three bunkers constructed were those of the *estado mayor*—staff. The primary one was the *Centro de Mando*—the Command Bunker—where *Generalísimo* Jose Maria de Castillo y Plato maintained his headquarters. The *Centro de Inteligencia*—Intelligence Bunker—was used by *Capitán* Diego Tippelskirch, while *Suboficial* Ignacio Perez maintained his files and supplies in the *Centro de Administración*—the Administration Bunker. These facilities, with firing slits, were like the castle keeps in old medieval castles. They could also be the place to make a last stand in case of a massive attack. The bunkers were in a triangular arrangement on the high ground in the center of the fortress.

The construction of *Fuerte* Franco moved along rapidly and efficiently, well ahead of schedule.

CENTRO DE INTELIGENCIA

THIS was be the brain center of the *Grupo de Batalla*'s operations, where all incoming and outgoing information would be processed and logged by *Capitán*. Diego Tippelskirch and his staff of experienced *sargentos*.

Just prior to the move from the camp to the fortress, Tippelskirch had received some new radios through operatives the *generalísimo* had in the signals staff in the Spanish Foreign Legion. One RMAL (*Radio Militar Alcance Largo*) long-range radio was placed in the *Centro de Inteligencia*, while several medium-range RMAM (*Radio Militar Alcance Mediano*) radios were distributed among the subunits of the *Grupo de Batalla*. When the commo gear was installed, Tippelskirch wasted no time in making contact with his numerous agents within the ranks of the Argentine, Bolivian and Chilean armed forces. New call signs and procedures were quickly worked out, and the Falangists were now ready to operate as a fighting outfit with superb communications capabilities that were tuned in, net organized and oriented to the nth degree.

1000 HOURS LOCAL

THE *sargento* on the RMAL radio took down the transmission that came across in five-letter word groups. He recognized the "fist" of the other man through the dit and dah pattern of the transmission. The sender was an old pal from the *Infantería de Marina* where the two had served together for some ten years.

As soon as the other operator signed off, the *sargento* ripped the message from from the pad. He swiveled his chair to face *Capitán* Tippelskirch's desk just behind him. "*Mensaje apremiante, mi capitán,*" the *sargento* said. "An urgent message."

Tippelskirch took it, then worked the dial on the field

safe at his feet. After pulling out his code book, he set about deciphering the garbled missive. It took ten minutes to decode it, and when it was in plain Spanish he smiled to himself. It was just as he suspected. The intelligence officer slipped on his field cap and left the Communications Center.

He walked directly over to the *Centro de Mando* where a quartet of convicts worked at pulling a camouflage net over the top. Tippelskirch went down to the entrance and stepped inside, saluting the Falangist leader Castillo.

"I have received a most meaningful message, *mi generalísimo*," Tippelskirch reported.

"Congratulations," the *generalísimo* said. "It would appear your Intelligence Bunker is already up to speed."

"Indeed," Tippelskirch said proudly. "It comes through a mole I have inside the national security office in Santiago. He informs me he has solid proof that the Petroleo Colmo Company here on the Gran Chaco has strong American ties. Some messages to and from them have been relayed to a known CIA facility in Colombia."

"That is a most significant and useful thing to know," the *generalísimo* said. "I think there are many ways we can work this to our advantage."

"I smell the *Yanqui* influence all over this," Tippelskirch said. "No doubt of it!"

"Now we know for sure our *bandido* foe is an American force," the *generalísimo* said. "The more knowledge one has of the enemy, the more advantageous, no?"

"Such intelligence is worth a thousand men, *mi generalísimo*."

1600 HOURS LOCAL

THE helicopter landing pad was no more than a quickly cleared area of land twenty meters north of the headquarters bunkers. The pilot could easily discern the

unevenness of the ground, and he lowered the aircraft
slowly until its wheels gently touch down. The first man
off was *Capitán* Roberto Argento. He turned to his *sargento,* shouting over the noise of the engine. "Get over to
the *Centro de Inteligencia* and tell *Capitán* Tippelskirch to
meet me at headquarters immediately!"

As the noncommissioned officer rushed off, the five
men who made up the rest of the patrol disembarked, walking rapidly away from the helicopter. Casual observers
could see that something was wrong from the way they
stuck together, talking softly among themselves as they
made their way to their unit bunker.

Within a couple of minutes Tippelskirch joined Argento
at the entrance to the headquarters, and both went into the
fortification to speak with Castillo. The *generalísimo* was
concerned by the expression on Argento's face.

"Mi generalísimo," Argento said, saluting. "We have
come back from a visit to the village of Novida. We found
all the people dead. Men, women and children. All shot by
automatic fire. Some who had survived the preliminary
bursts had been dispatched by single shots to the head from
pistols."

Castillo was so shocked he quickly stood up, almost
bumping his head on the low bunker ceiling. "Who could
have done such a thing?"

Tippelskirch smiled. "I think perhaps the CIA."

"We could see where three helicopters had landed," Argento said. "The killers must have surrounded the place."

Castillo sat back down, looking at Tippelskirch. "So!
You think the CIA did it, eh?"

Tippelskirch shook his head. "Actually I doubt it," he admitted. "The villagers were illegal squatters. I imagine Bolivian police killed everyone, knowing nobody would really
care." He boldly leaned on the *generalísimo*'s desk in his
enthusiasm. "But we could make it look like Americans did
it. Or at least say that they did it. Of course, it would just be
our word against anyone who wished to contradict us."

Argento was puzzled. "What is all this about *norteamericanos*?"

"We have solid information," Tippelskirch said, "that the Petroleo Colmo Company is in league with the Americans. I think they are CIA operating in South America like their Air America did in Southeast Asia."

"Of course!" Castillo exclaimed. "It all fits."

"We need to get some photographs," Tippelskirch said. "Lots of photographs. I have a journalist friend who works for a right-wing newspaper here in Bolivia. He would be more than happy to write up articles favoring the Falangist movement and its aims. Especially when he can say that Americans massacred a village of innocents."

"I'll leave that up to you, *Capitán* Tippelskirch," Castillo said. "Meanwhile, I'm going to turn the problem of Petroleo Colmo over to *Coronel* Busch. He will know how to hunt down and destroy those damn helicopters of theirs."

"We are closing in on victory," Tippelskirch said confidently.

"I have more good news," Castillo said. "We are getting in twelve more men as reinforcements. It is still just a trickle, but when the time is right, it will become a flood."

Tippelskirch turned to Argento. "I'm getting a camera. Round up your patrol for a return trip to Novida."

STATE DEPARTMENT
WASHINGTON, D.C.
21 DECEMBER
0630 HOURS LOCAL

UNDERSECRETARY Carl Joplin yawned irritably as he strode down the hall. He was a creature of habit, and the early phone call that had gotten him out of bed an hour and a half early had already upset his day. He had received curt instructions to report ASAP to Secretary of State Benjamin Bellingham's office.

When he stepped into the receptionist's station, the lady generally on duty was not there. Instead Durwood Cooper, Bellingham's always uptight chief administrative assistant, was waiting for him.

"The secretary is inside," Cooper said, using the same brusque manner of the earlier phone call. He turned to lead Joplin back to the interior office.

When Joplin was ushered into Bellingham's presence, he was surprised to see the White House Chief of Staff Arlene Entienne also there. This Cajun-African-American was a beautiful green-eyed woman with dark brown hair. The features of both ethnicities blended well, giving her an exotic appearance. It was said that 90 percent of the men in Washington were love with her, while the other 10 percent were gays who nevertheless admired both her loveliness and taste in clothing.

Joplin gave her smile. "Hello, Arlene. I didn't expect to see you today. But it's a real pleasure, believe me."

"Always the diplomat, hey, Carl?"

Bellingham was impatient. "Sit down, Carl. We have a real bad situation down there in that South American operation you organized."

Joplin knew it meant big trouble when the current state of affairs was dropped in his lap. When things were going well, Bellingham claimed all responsibilities. They were his projects and his alone.

Bellingham continued. "The population of a small village of illegal Brazilian immigrants was massacred by persons unknown. The crime was discovered by Bolivian Federal Police. Their intelligence-gathering apparatus has informed them that these people were sympathetic toward the Falangists." He paused, giving Joplin a meaningful look. "Those are the antagonists of the special operations group you sent down there, are they not? What do you know about it?"

"Nothing," Joplin replied, disturbed. "This is the first I've heard of it."

Entienne interjected, "The White House has not been fully informed on this particular mission. Does it involve Army Special Forces?"

"They are a small Navy SEAL detachment," Joplin explained. "A total of twenty-one men. One of them was wounded in the fighting and is now in the Balboa Naval Hospital in San Diego."

"Would those SEALs be involved in the murders?" Bellingham asked straight out.

"Not at all!" Joplin replied testily. "That group is made up of some of the best of the best. They are not the type to go postal and turn their weapons on unarmed civilians."

Bellingham was not convinced. "God! I hope we don't have another My Lai as in Vietnam."

"I will bet my reputation on Lieutenant Brannigan and his men," Joplin said. "They did not commit that atrocity."

"I hope you're right," Bellingham said. "This story can't be held under wraps much longer."

A knock on the door interrupted the session, and Durwood Cooper stuck his head in. "Call for Ms. Entienne on line four."

She reached over and picked up the phone as Bellingham punched the corresponding button. "Hello," Entienne said. "Yes. This early, huh? All right, I'll inform the secretary of state." She hung up and glanced over at Bellingham. "That was the White House. The Bolivian ambassador has lodged a covert protest about the massacre. Reliable sources have informed them it was done by Americans."

Joplin gritted his teeth. "Did he say what Americans?"

Entienne shook her head. "Only that the perpetrators were American. We can be thankful that the crime is not yet out in the open."

"It's only a matter of time before some journalist is contacted by an unimpeachable source," Bellingham complained. He shot a glance at Joplin. "Call in your Bolivian connection. Find out what you can from him, then get back to me."

FUERTE FRANCO
0830 HOURS LOCAL

TWELVE more men arrived with the resupply chopper. They were evenly divided between Argentines and Chileans. All were noncommissioned officers from combat units, and their physical appearance gave stark evidence they were veteran field soldiers, not staff milquetoasts. *Sargento-Mayor* Arnaud Chaubere formed them up in front of the finished headquarters bunker. He called them to attention when *Generalísimo* Jose Maria de Castillo y Plato appeared.

Castillo gave the men an appraising gaze, liking what he saw. "*Hacan disminuir*—at ease! I welcome you to the *Ejército Falangísta*. We are at the beginning of our struggle to liberate the people of South America from their corrupt, uncaring leftist governments and bring them into a world of order, discipline and reward for hard work. There is no room for the indolent, inferior, cowardly and nonconformist under the Falangist philosophy. You men are showing you have the moral and physical courage to be in the vanguard of the greatest revolution in the history of mankind. Your names will be etched on a great memorial to be honored by countless generations to come. A man we all admire, Adolf Hitler, said that the German *Reich* would last for a thousand years. We Falangists will do much better than that. Our *Reich* will live on through eternity!

"Our strength grows continuously as more fighting men prepare to join us. Soon air force units will be added to our organizational charts along with ships of the Argentine and Chilean Navy. No one can stop us. We are invincible!

"Our spiritual leader is the Archangel Michael, who defeated Satan and hurled him into the pits of hell. He is also the patron of all paratroopers in the Western world. Pamphlets explaining this and how to seek spiritual encouragement from the archangel will be passed out to you along with weapons and ammunition. I will now turn you over to your instructors for some short training exercises to acquaint you with our methods of combat. *Arcángel Miguel vosotros bendiga*—may Archangel Michael bless you!"

Chaubere ordered them to attention and rendered a sharp salute to Castillo. As the *generalísimo* returned to his bunker, the new men were marched off to join their combat units.

STATE DEPARTMENT
WASHINGTON, D.C.
0930 HOURS

THE classified report from the Bolivian Federal Police on the massacre in the Gran Chaco was arranged in two neat piles in front of Carl Joplin, PhD. The larger stack was what he was still carefully reading, and the small were the pages he had already perused. A notebook off to the side contained the first draft of the official memo he planned to have properly typed up as a commentary on the document.

The task was interrupted by his desk phone buzzing. He picked up the receiver and was told that Arturo Sanchez, the envoy from Bolivia, had arrived as per Joplin's request.

"Send him in, please," the undersecretary said. He hung up the phone and waited a few seconds until Sanchez came into the office. "Sit down, Arturo. I've the official file from the report of the Bolivian police in regards to the killings at Novida."

"I am familiar with it," Sanchez remarked in a cold voice.

"The police don't name names of suspects or known murderers," Joplin said. "Do you have any views on the subject?"

"I can confidently state who did *not* do it," Sanchez said testily. "And that would be the Falangists. After all, those unfortunate people were being helpful to the fascists. It was a misguided kindness but understandable under the circumstances."

"I agree with you," Joplin said. "What about your Border Police?"

"If they had done it, the Federal Police would have found proof."

"Perhaps they did find proof but declined to reveal it to anyone," Joplin suggested.

"That seems a wild theory," Sanchez said. "There is no indication that the Border Police were anywhere in the vicinity of the village."

"I requested the illegals be expelled," Joplin said. "You said your Border Police would take care of it. Perhaps when they arrived to arrest the Brazilians, something untoward occurred that set off the mass executions."

Sanchez shook his head. "I think there is a good chance that your special operations people did it. After all, they would have been angry to have the Brazilians giving aid and encouragement to the Falangists."

"Our people are highly disciplined and well led," Joplin said. "It is not only preposterous but insulting to think they would commit so horrid a crime."

"I believe American troops committed such atrocities in Vietnam," Sanchez replied.

"There are atrocities committed by both sides in any conflict," Joplin said. "Certain people, including Americans, have made claims of war crimes by U.S. forces that have never been proven." Then he added, "And never will because the allegations are false."

"You and I are not going to get to the truth of this unfortunate matter this morning," Sanchez said. "So far Brazil has kept quiet about the murders, but eventually they will speak out in protest. This could cause Operation Falangist Fury to be compromised. That would be a great misfortune for all of us concerned when the story gets out. It will make it impossible to deal with future problems of that nature."

"Well, my friend," Joplin said, "you had better prepare yourself. This situation is going to get a lot worse before it gets better."

FUERTE FRANCO
CENTRO DE MANDO
1345 HOURS LOCAL

CAPITÁN Diego Tippelskirch went down the steps and through the doorway to where the *generalísimo* kept his desk. He walked into the earthen room and saluted Jose Maria de Castillo y Plato. *"Mi generalísimo,* I have just received yet another momentous report."

Castillo immediately forgot the ammunition inventory he had been studying. When Tippelskirch seemed happily excited, that meant good news. *"Que pasa, capitán?"*

"My source in La Paz tells me that it's been revealed to him that the massacre at Novida was carried out by the Bolivian Border Police."

"Por San Miguel!" Castillo exclaimed. "How can this be?"

"Evidently they were dispatched to the area to arrest the villagers for deportation," Tippelskirch explained. "The man in charge was *Coronel* Francisco Martinez, who is called El Garron by his men. He is an avowed racist who hates African people. The informer is one of the *coronel*'s men, and he said that everyone—men, women and children—were herded into a group outside the village then mowed down like stalks of corn."

"Mmm," Castillo mused. "He probably figured they would just rot out there on the Gran Chaco without ever being discovered."

"I think this Martinez is not worried one way or the other," Tippelskirch said. "He has friends in high places. A cover-up would be easy to arrange."

"That is quite an advantage to the gentleman," Castillo said.

"Not only for him, but for us as well," Tippelskirch said. "I could take *Suboficial* Punzarron to La Paz and meet with that journalist friend of mine. He works for the right-wing newspaper *El Conquistador.* Since Punzarron speaks

Portuguese, he could pose as a survivor. He can name the killers and describe the massacre. Be assured the information would be quickly published."

Castillo frowned. "What advantage is that to us?"

"He can tell them the crime was committed by *norteam-ericanos*," Tippelskirch said. "Men in uniforms speaking English and wearing green berets. American Special Forces."

Castillo's frown warped into a grin. "And he could say the people were killed because they supported the Falangists, no? It would be a great propaganda coup in our favor."

"*Por su puesto*—of course!" Tippelskirch said.

"Put your plan into action, *Capitán* Tippelskirch," Castillo said. "Wait! I should say *Comandante*. Tippelskirch. I am promoting you."

"*Gracias, mi generalísimo!*"

"And you should add the name of *Coronel* Martinez to the file of potential Falangists."

Tippelskirch smiled. "I already have, *mi generalísimo*."

1800 HOURS LOCAL

THE two dozen convicts were pleasantly surprised that their workday had been called off so early. There was still almost four hours of light left in the Southern Hemisphere summer day, and they generally were kept at their toil until the sun began to redden for its descent over the western horizon.

The prisoners marched in a column of twos from their latest machine gun emplacement work sites toward the barbed wire–encircled camp they called home. One thing that frustrated them as much as the hard labor was having no idea where in the world they were. One of the diehards said it didn't make much difference. Even if they escaped and became lost in the wilderness, it would be a faster and easier way to die than years of wasting away in prison.

When they got back to the camp they found the impressive and very tough-looking officer they had learned to fear, standing at the gate. They were marched up in front of him and brought to a halt. He waited until the group settled down before speaking to them. He displayed an uncustomary friendly smile.

"I remind you that I am *Coronel* Jeronimo Busch, the field commander of the *Grupo de Batalla* stationed here. One of our Argentine officers arranged for you to be taken from your prison cells and flown to this location to build field fortifications for our noble cause. You were chosen because you are all under life sentences, doomed to spend the rest of your days in prison until you are planted in the cemetery outside the walls. Nobody comes to visit you anymore, and you are lost and abandoned not only by society but by your families."

The convicts listened impassively to the words that simply repeated things they already knew and had accepted. This *coronel* was correct. They were the hopeless ones simply putting in time in the hell of confinement until their bodies gave up the ghost.

Busch continued, "But you now have a way out of this miserable existence to which your stupidity and evilness have condemned you. I am sure you have now figured out we are soldiers. In truth, we have a holy purpose for taking up arms. We call ourselves *Falangístas* and will one day rule all of South America. I am at this very moment offering you a chance to join our cause. The most obvious advantage to you is that you will not be returned to that penitentiary in Patagonia. You will be given new names, your pasts will be wiped out, and if you serve the Falangist cause faithfully, you will be given fine opportunities in the new order. You'll have money and women, be able to start families and raise children. And, best of all, you will be

honored and respected members of established society."
He paused as he watched them consider the proposition.
"Now! All who wish to join the *Ejército Falangísta* take
one step forward."

One man immediately stepped forward. Within an instant he was joined by the others. *Coronel* Jeronimo Busch
smiled to himself. Now the Falangist cause had cannon
fodder to throw at the enemy.

CHAPTER 11

THE cheap room seemed even smaller than it was with the five men crowded into it. They consisted of Dirk Wallenger, a reporter for the Global News Broadcasting television network of Washington, D.C.; the Chilean journalist Miguel Hennicke of the newspaper *El Conquistador;* a local TV cameraman; and a translator who was fluent in English, Spanish and Portuguese. All were gathered around the bed where *Suboficial* Adolfo Punzarron sat.

The Falangist wore a faded sports shirt, badly worn slacks, and cheap sandals that adorned his sockless feet. He was uncharacteristically unshaven, and his usually carefully tended mustache was shaggy and drooping. He had identified himself to his visitors as Maurício Castanho, a Brazilian cattleman and survivor of the massacre at Novida in the Gran Chaco of Bolivia.

Hennicke, speaking through the translator, said, "You

told us you had photographs of the atrocity in your village, *Señor* Castanho. May I see them?"

Punzarron aka Castanho walked over to the luggage stand in the corner of the room. He retrieved a large brown envelope from a battered suitcase and returned to the bed. "Here they are."

Hennicke began looking at the photos, passing them over one at a time to Wallenger. The images were disturbing. Dead men, women and children were strewn within a small area just outside a village. The corpses were bullet-torn and sprawled in grotesque positions from the violence of their deaths. It was obvious to the veteran journalists that these were real, not fakes.

Wallenger winced at the scenes. "Who took these photographs, sir?"

"A priest," Punzarron replied, using the cover story invented by Tippelskirch. "He is a traveling *padre* who visits settlements in the Gran Chaco. He performs marriages, baptisms, last rites and other such services for the people there. He always has a camera to record ceremonies. He used it to take those pictures of my poor, dead friends and neighbors." He sighed audibly and dramatically. "And my family who were all murdered."

Since Hennicke also spoke English, the translator had only to interpret in that language for the two journalists. After he told them what Punzarron said, he was confused. "This fellow speaks fluent Portuguese, but he does not speak in the Brazilian manner. I don't understand."

Hennicke shrugged. "What difference does his accent make? He was obviously there at that place. See? He's even in a couple of the photographs, standing among the corpses."

Wallenger agreed. "We don't care how he speaks. We're interested in the story of the slaughter." He turned to the cameraman. "Record all this. I'll edit it later myself."

Hennicke's attention was back on the subject. "*Señor* Castanho, tell us exactly what happened."

"We were all asleep," Punzarron said. "Then the sounds of helicopters woke us up. We all went outside our huts to see what was going on. We thought maybe it was our friends the *Falangístas*. But the visitors were somebody else in uniforms. I think maybe more than twenty of them. Their commander told us we were under arrest as illegal aliens. But our village chief João Cabeçinho said we had all the necessary visas and permits. He offered to go get them to show him. This made the commander angry, and he said we had to walk out of the village into the open country on the far side."

"Was he speaking Portuguese?" Wallenger asked.

"No," Punzarron said, shaking his head. "He spoke in Spanish. João Cabeçinho translated for us. And we obeyed the orders. As soon as we were gathered where they wanted us, the commander yelled something aloud. It sounded like an order to his men. They started shooting. Everybody was falling down, so I dove to the ground, and a couple of fellows fell on top of me. I lay still, acting as if I was dead. Then they walked among us, and if anyone twitched or moaned, they shot him in the head. They killed everybody. They killed men and women and little children. Everybody."

"Were these criminals soldiers?" Wallenger asked.

"Yes," Punzarron said. "They wore the type of uniforms that are spotted with different colors. And they wore green berets. But they did not speak Spanish among themselves. In fact the only one who spoke Spanish was the commander. And I heard words I recognized in English when the others talked. Like 'yes' and 'hurry' and 'kill babies.' And now I remember the leader said 'fire' before they shot us. All that I remember. I will never forget it as long as I live. It was horrible."

"Are you sure they weren't Bolivians?" Hennicke asked.

"Yes, I am sure," Punzarron said. "Some of them had blond hair and were very fair. There were some black men too, but most looked like American white men."

"Who are these *Falangístas* you spoke of before?" Hennicke asked.

"They are good men who are soldiers," Punzarron explained. "But they never hurt us. They brought us food and medical supplies. They visited our village many times and told us how they were the saviors of South America. They were fighting the men in the green berets, but they were not sure who they were." Punzarron paused for dramatic effect, then said, "I hope the Falangist liberators kill all those horrible Americans."

Wallenger signaled for the cameraman to stop shooting. He glanced at Hennicke. "What do you think, Miguel?"

"Who else could it be but Americans?" the Chilean said. "There are bandits in the area, but they are Bolivians with lots of Indians among them. None look like Europeans. And why would bandits use up a lot of bullets to kill people for no good reason? Most of those gangs are miserably poor. They even steal clothing. Let us also consider the helicopters. Those bastards were from an organized military force."

Wallenger turned to Punzarron. "Tell me, Mr. Castanho, did the killers steal anything? Did they loot the village?"

"No," Punzarron said. "After they were sure everybody was dead, they got back on their helicopters and flew away."

"May we have these photographs?" Hennicke asked.

"Yes, sir," Punzarron said. "I have other copies in my bag. There are plenty for both of you." He went back to the suitcase and pulled out another packet, handing it to Wallenger. "Do you have any more questions, sirs?"

"I don't," Wallenger replied. "At least not for the time being."

"Nor I," Hennicke said. "My friend and I will go now. We would like to see you again if possible."

"I will be here for three more days," Punzarron said. "Then the Falangists are going to help me get back to

Brazil." He showed what he hoped was a sad expression on his brutal face. "I never want to see the Gran Chaco again. I lost my wife and four children in that horrible criminal atrocity."

As the journalists, translator and cameraman left, *Capitán* Diego Tippelskirch in the room next door took the earphones off. They were attached to the recorder he had used to listen in on the conversation in Punzarron's room.

Un éxito grande de propaganda!

THE GRAN CHACO
SEAL BASE CAMP
24 DECEMBER
2200 HOURS LOCAL

BRANNIGAN'S Brigands were back together again, and it was Christmas Eve, but the detachment was not celebrating. A heavy rain fell, literally dampening the already subdued holiday spirits. Everyone was hunkered down in the base camp, listening to the deluge splattering heavily on the hootch roofs. Out in the countryside, the caches concealed in the grassy terrain of the Gran Chaco's savannah were ready and waiting when needed.

The reason for the reunification was that Lieutenant Wild Bill Brannigan was anxious to wrap up Operation Falangist Fury, and he wanted to launch a fresh campaign to destroy the Falangist enemy. At that moment, the Skipper was in his hootch, busy working out an OPLAN with Senior Chief Petty Officer Buford Dawkins and Chief Petty Officer Matt Gunnarson. Arrangements had already been made to have the Petroleo Colmo helicopters available for transport and resupply in the coming activities.

Out on the OP, James Bradley and Chad Murchison gazed into the drizzling darkness, feeling a bit sentimental and sad because of the Christmas season. They concentrated

on talking about anything but hearth and home as
the lonely hours on watch slowly passed. After a period of
subdued conversation, they had reached a point where neither had much to say, and they sank into a morose silence.
James finally eased out of the doldrums, asking, "What do
you think of Garth Redhawk? That guy's something else,
isn't he?"

"Assuredly," Chad said. "He killed three of the enemy
in a very short time, employing stealth in an area with little
cover. It would seem the genes of his warrior progenitors
have evidently been passed down to him intact."

"Right," James agreed. "He's the quintessential warrior."

"And even more dangerous than his forebears," Chad
said. "Along with the natural skills and endowment as a
fighting man, he has acquired modern military discipline.
He is also highly intelligent. The combination of all that is
bodacious."

James laughed. "That's the word! Bodacious! Redhawk
is like a natural boxer who instinctively dodges punches
thrown at him while seeing openings for his own attacks
without having to think about it. He just does it, y'know,
and it's the absolute correct thing to do at the times he un-
consciously reacts."

"You've described his attributes accurately," Chad said.
"In all veracity, I must say that I am glad to be teamed with
him on reconnaissance. I experience an intense feeling of
security knowing that Garth Redhawk is at my side."

"I can't blame you for that," James said.

As the two SEALs passed the time on the OP, Brannigan, Dawkins and Matt studied the map of the Gran Chaco
by flashlight within the confines of the hootch. Brannigan
took a sip of coffee. "The main thing we have to take under
consideration is the location of the new Falangist position.
It was discovered yesterday by one of the Petroleo Colmo
choppers. They got a fix and a good look. It appears to be
an earthen fort with fighting positions, trenches and
bunkers. Godamn formidable."

Dawkins growled deep in his throat. "A hard nut to crack, sir."

"Yeah," Brannigan said. "We'd never be able to take it by a frontal assault unless we get a lot of reinforcements."

"Which ain't gonna happen," Matt observed sourly. "I wish we could at least be issued a good satellite photograph of that place. Could you put in a request, sir?"

"Hell no," Brannigan said. "Haven't you figured it out yet, Chief? We're not really down here."

"Then if we ain't here, let's go over to the Fouled Anchor and have a beer with Salty," Dawkins said.

"Don't play with reality, Senior Chief," Brannigan advised. "It'll drive you crazy."

"I'm already halfway there, sir," Dawkins said, "And this fucking rain ain't helping anything."

"The only way we're going to get clear of this operation is to kick Falangist butt," Brannigan said. "And the only way we're going to be able to do that is to find their patrols or units out in the open away from the protection of that fortified area."

"You'll have to split us up again, sir," Dawkins argued. "We'll be right back to what we been doing all along."

"I'm taking a different approach," Brannigan said. "The idea is to have the Petroleo Colmo do our recon for us. As soon as one of 'em spots some Falangists, he'll alert us by broadcasting those famous words of Sherlock Holmes: 'The game is afoot.' Then he'll come straight here while the other chopper joins up. The whole detachment jumps aboard, and away we go to send the bastards to that great Nazi party meeting in the sky."

"I like that idea," Dawkins said. "We can come in from two different directions."

"Yeah," Matt said. "When it's feasible. But we still got this fucking savannah that's flat as a tablecloth and has no concealment or cover."

"It sucks," Brannigan agreed, "but at the moment it's the only battlefield we've got."

27 DECEMBER
0930 HOURS LOCAL

FRANK Gomez sprayed some insect repellent into his hand and rubbed it on his face. The rain had stopped, and although the mosquitoes were not yet out, some mysterious little gnats had made an appearance on the Gran Chaco. They didn't actually land on anybody, but they buzzed around faces, eyes and ears, annoying the hell out of the SEALs. Thankfully, the bug spray seemed to repel the little bastards.

The Shadowfire radio came to life, getting Frank's mind off the bugs. "Brigand, this is Petroleo. Over."

"Petroleo, this is Brigand. Over," Frank replied.

"Brigand, the game is afoot. Both choppers will be in for a pickup alpha-sierra-alpha-papa. Senior observer has the details. Out."

Frank crawled out of the commo hootch and raced over to Lieutenant Wild Bill Brannigan's earthen domicile. "The game is afoot, sir," the radio operator announced. "Choppers are on their way. They'll give you the poop when they get here."

The Skipper quickly broadcast the word to the section and team leaders via his AN/PRC-126. Then he grabbed his combat vest, CAR-15 and ammo, leaving the CP to stride over to the assembly area.

Within two minutes the entire detachment stood armed, equipped and ready for the coming mission. The silhouettes of the two helicopters appeared in the distance, and they closed in fast. As soon as they landed, the SEALs quickly got aboard in a prearranged order without a lot of fuss. The Command Element and the First Assault Section took the Dauphin, while the Second Assault Section crammed themselves into the limited space of the Gazelle. Takeoff was immediate, and the pilots quickly whirled the aircraft in the direction of the target.

Brannigan slipped the intercom headset on his head and went forward to confer with the senior observer who sat in the copilot's seat. It turned out to be Alfredo. "Hey, Bill," the CIA operative said. "Good target for you today." He pulled out a map to use as reference. "There is a Falangist patrol of eight men traveling on an azimuth of approximately two-eight-zero."

"Right," Brannigan said, checking the lay of the land as indicated on the chart. "Here's what I want you to do." He glanced over to make sure the pilot was listening in. "Fly directly over them on the line of march, and go far enough that you can set down over the horizon, out of their sight."

"Roger," the pilot said.

Brannigan stayed in the cockpit. Ten minutes later he could see the patrol column below. Alfredo leaned over toward him. "They don't pay us much mind. I guess they're used to these garish red helicopters buzzing around."

"I wonder how long we're going to have this advantage," Brannigan remarked.

Alfredo shrugged. "It's kind of like sex. Nothing good lasts forever."

OA, NORTH CENTRAL SECTOR
0950 HOURS LOCAL

THE choppers came in slow, barely creeping a meter or so above the ground as the SEALs unassed them with the rapidity of a parachute jump. As soon as the last man was out, the aircraft quickly soared higher, turning toward their home base.

"All right, people! Everybody gather round the Skipper!" Senior Chief Buford Dawkins said in the LASH.

"We're going to be a reception committee this morning," Brannigan said, taking out his compass, checking the angle of azimuth one-zero-zero. This was the exact opposite of the track followed by the Falangist patrol. "The Second Assault Section will set up in the grass to the direct front with Delta Fire Team on the left. Understood?"

"Aye, sir," Chief Matt Gunnarson replied.

"The First Assault Section will move down the right side of the enemy's line of march and prepare to launch the ambush," Brannigan said. He nodded to Dawkins. "You guys will start the proceedings. No one is to take any action until you open fire."

"Understood, sir," the senior chief said.

"I'll take the Command Element farther down to close up the rear," Brannigan said. "Delta Fire Team?"

"Yes, sir," team leader Gutsy Olson replied.

"You'll close in that left area where you'll be located."

"Any questions?" Brannigan asked. "Get into position. We've got about forty-five minutes."

THE FIREFIGHT
1040 HOURS

SENIOR Chief Buford Dawkins had positioned himself the farthest down in his First Assault Echelon. This gave him the responsibility of firing the first burst into the enemy column.

When the point man came into view, the senior chief began counting the Falangists as they walked past his place of concealment in the grass. One—two—three—. Moments later the eighth man appeared, and Dawkins squeezed off an automatic three-round burst. The unfortunate tail-end Charlie staggered sideways and crumpled to the grass.

Now the entire detachment opened up. Joe Miskoski and Bruno Puglisi worked their SAWs, sweeping salvos up and down the column. Brannigan led his four men of the Command Element to lock in the rear of the ambush. They kicked out a fusillade that prevented any escape in that direction.

Delta Fire Team, with the responsibility of holding in the left side of the fight, quickly came under heavy fire. Bullets whipped and whined among the trio of SEALs as the Falangists put pressure on that part of the line. Guy Devereaux grunted aloud as he took a hit in the shoulder. He rolled over onto his back, fumbling for his field dressing as he cursed his bad luck.

Then the shooting abruptly stopped.

Andy Malachenko now noticed Guy's predicament. "Corpsman! Delta Team!"

James Bradley rushed from the Command Element to sprint across the battlefield as the rest of the SEALs moved in to inspect the Falangists now sprawled on the ground. Guy sat up, wincing, as James knelt down beside him. After ripping the sleeve open, the corpsman was relieved. "You must've caught a ricochet, Guy. You got a friction burn from the bullet and a little skin was taken off."

"It don't hurt," Guy said. "It's numb. I don't think I'm gonna need any morphine."

"This baby is going to be plenty painful, buddy," James said as he began treating the wound. "It's going to hurt a lot worse than a direct hit. Let me know when it's really stinging, and I'll give you some relief."

"Shit!"

The rest of the detachment now stood among the fallen Falangists. Four were dead, and three dazed, wounded men looked up in numb dismay at the SEALs. Lamar Taylor was puzzled. "I thought there was eight of 'em. I only count seven."

"Hey! You're right," Wes Ferguson said after making his own count.

"Second Assault Section!" Brannigan yelled. "There's a missing bad guy. Search the area for him. Be careful! He may have some fight in him."

Matt Gunnarson formed his men for a careful search. With Guy Devereaux taken care of, James Bradley now came over to look after the wounded Falangists. None of them said anything as he began his examinations.

Ten minutes later, Matt brought his men back. "We couldn't find nothing, sir. If one of 'em is missing, he's got away."

"Damn it," Brannigan said, glancing out over the wide-open landscape. "The son of a bitch must be as slippery as an eel."

1130 HOURS

FRANK Gomez used hand signals to guide the Petroleo Colmo helicopters in to land at the ambush site. The three wounded Falangists were taken to the Dauphin for transport out of the area. Two could walk, but the third needed the help of his buddies to get aboard the aircraft. The EPWs would go on back with Alfredo for intense interrogation and further medical treatment.

Guy Devereaux seemed to be all right as he climbed aboard with his two Delta teammates. As soon as Dawkins crammed his section into the Gazelle, the rotors were revved for the flight back to the base camp.

WHEN the helicopters were only dots above the far horizon, *Sargento* Antonio Müller kicked off his camouflage cape and stood up. He spat in anger as he reached for his RMAM radio to contact *Fuerte* Franco.

CHAPTER 12

AS soon as the journalist Miguel Hennicke returned from Bolivia to Chile, he rushed to the offices of his newspaper, *El Conquistador.* His story of the massacre in the Gran Chaco was immediately put into production. His managing editor was almost giddy with delight when he saw the photos of the bloodied innocents. This situation would be a big score for all the anti-American movements in South America, whether they be rightists or leftists.

The images were prepared to be featured on a special page while a team of rewrite men were put to work scribbling provoking captions. Both the editorial department and pressroom worked late to print this special issue.

As soon as the edition hit the streets, they were bought up by the eager readership, and a second printing for local consumption had to be run off immediately. When that one was finished and headed for the streets, yet a third issue was printed that went to Valparalso, Talcahuano, Valdiva, Osorno and other urban centers of the Chilean Republic. From that point on the presses rolled for thirty-six straight hours as other issues were dispatched to all points of South America. By New Year's Day, the article and photographs had been widely read and circulated, enraging the entire Latin American public, no matter what their political views.

Crimen de "Green Berets"

!MATANZA HORROROSA DE PUEBLERINOS BRASILEÑOS EN EL GRAN CHACO!

Bolivian Federal Police officers have uncovered an unspeakable atrocity in which an entire village of people was massacred by members of the notorious American Green Berets. The crime was discovered during routine patrol duties in the Gran Chaco in the southeastern part of the nation. The investigation confirmed that more than a hundred Brazilian immigrants had been herded together and machine gunned in droves. Men, women and children died in the outrage. Nothing as horrible as this has been seen since the Stalinist era in the USSR.

One survivor was discovered hiding in a nearby gulley. His name was Maurício Castanho, a thirty-five-year-old cattleman who had lived in the village with his wife and five children. His entire family perished under the hails of bullets fired at them.

Señor Castanho stated that the killers wore United States Army uniforms and green berets. They came in a half-dozen helicopters and landed just at dawn while everyone was still asleep.

"They woke us all up and made everybody come outside," Castanho said. "They made us all stand with our hands over our heads. Even the women and children. Then they began taking some of the prettier girls aside, making them go back into the huts. We could hear their cries of pain and fear as the *norteamericanos* repeatedly raped them."

When the lecherous Green Berets had finished their sport, they dragged the shamed young women out naked and weeping, forcing them to join the others. Then the *norteamericanos* herded the entire population of the small community to a spot in an open field. At that point they began firing their submachine guns into the cringing crowd of innocents.

"Everyone was falling down," Castanho said. "I dove to the ground and two fellows fell on top of me. I lay still, acting as if I was dead. Then the Green Berets walked among the fallen people. If anyone moved or moaned, they put a pistol bullet in their heads.

"When they were sure there were no survivors they looted the village and got back on their helicopters and flew away. I got up and looked for my family. They were all dead. When the Bolivian Federal Police arrived I hid at first, but when I saw they were not Green Berets, I came out."

NOTE: Pictures of the massacre's victims can be found on page 2. See the Editorial Page for further commentary by the staff of *El Conquistador.*

Anti-American demonstrations broke out in all the major urban areas of South America. Leftist organizations marched in protest through Buenos Aires, Santiago, Bogotá, La Paz, Caracas and other capital cities. In some cases the police lost control of the demonstrators, and full-scale riots broke out in which American embassies and counselor offices were stoned. The members of the Falangist movement were highly amused that these left-wing radicals were unknowingly aiding a fascist cause.

Condemnations of the crime were voiced in the General Assembly of the United Nations and even some elements in Congress were calling for special hearings on Capitol Hill. Talk shows on both radio and television buzzed with opinions both in belief and disbelief of the killings. Both the left and right spectrums of American politics were all heard in full voice. Shock jocks, Hollywood stars, television personalities and journalists with agendas voiced their opinions and assessments of all aspects of who had killed the poor people of Novida so far away in the Gran Chaco region of Bolivia. During an interview, a well-known actress who supported radical causes spoke tearfully and passionately of the murdered people. However, when questioned further by the interviewer, she could not accurately give the locale of the Gran Chaco or even Bolivia.

FUERTE FRANCO
CONVICT CAMP
2200 HOURS LOCAL

THE convict bivouac behind the barbed wire enclosure was quiet. But all the men were wide-awake and gathered in a meeting in which business was conducted in low voices to avoid being overheard by the guards or passersby. The man presiding over the get-together was Gordo Pullini. He was the one who had stepped forward first when *Coronel* Jeronimo Busch called for volunteers to fight for the Falangist cause. The others had been watching him for his reaction, and as soon as he made a move, they did the same. Now these followers listened intently as Pullini explained some important matters to them.

"You *tipos* keep one thing in mind," he cautioned them. "These fucking *Falangístas* aren't to be trusted, *comprenden*? The main thing we must concentrate on is biding our time and make a careful study of what we must do to escape from these *locos*. The opportunity will depend on timing. But the first thing we must figure out is just where the hell this place is. Without that knowledge, we don't know which direction to go after we break out of here. Going the wrong way means ending up running straight back into the arms of the law. That is a one-way trip back to the penitentiary in Patagonia."

"For those who aren't executed," one man added bitterly.

* * *

WHEN *Capitán* Roberto Argento arranged to have the twenty-four convicts released into the custody of the Falangists, he was unaware that instead of a random selection being made from the overall prison population, all two dozen were members of a well-organized prison gang called the *Cofradía*. The name translated into English as "guild," a group of like persons or even a religious brotherhood. In a way, the *Cofredía* was all these things rolled into one.

They were one of a dozen gangs in the penitentiary. The great majority of convicts joined these organizations. A man alone would perish amid the convicts who were part of society's worst outcasts. None had anything to lose, and life was cheap. But when a prisoner was accepted into a gang, he had moral support, friends and a feeling of worth. Most of all, he had protection. In exchange for this he was expected to give his gang blind support even to the point of sacrificing his own life for the good of the others. If he found himself in such a situation, he might as well go ahead and take it all the way. If he failed or refused a suicide mission, his former pals would turn on him, and he would end up dead anyway. His mutilated body would be found in a remote corner of the penal facility by the guard staff.

The *Cofradía* gang had been extremely lucky when it came to their leaders. Throughout the twenty years of their existence three of their members had emerged from the ranks to take over and direct their activities. Through diligence, cunning and ruthlessness, they had gained control over drug trafficking, gambling and even a brothel in which prostitutes from the outside were brought in once or twice a month. It was true these unfortunate women were the lowest of the low in their professions, but for men without women they were virtual goddesses, examples of the utmost in feminine beauty, and sex with them was heavenly when compared with having to use another man to relieve one's passions.

All the initial investments made by the *Cofradía* in blood and money had paid off handsomely. In fact, the businesses were so successful that legal currency was used in all transactions rather than bartering of goods such as cigarettes and candy as is normally done in jails. The latest of these leaders, Gordo Pullini, had carried on the good work with customary success, and the gang had eventually amassed a million pesos—$330,000 American—that were waiting to be used when the right investment opportunities came along.

The *Cofradía* had excellent relationships with several high-ranking guards through blackmail, favors and a generous split of the take on the drugs, gaming and sex. When the word came down from the guard commander's office that a transfer to a labor camp was available, Pullini jumped at the chance to get his boys outside the walls. This was an opportunity to realize a very special dream. If they could get free, their treasury could be used for an escape to Colombia, where they could buy themselves into the lucrative business of smuggling drugs into the United States and Europe. When Pullini told the gang his plans and that they would live in luxurious mansions with beautiful women all under the protection of the drug cartels, they enthusiastically okayed the idea.

Pullini arranged to sell their business interests to a rival gang called the *Culebras*—the Snakes—for another million pesos. This brought their total treasury up to $660,000 American. After bribing the guard commander a measly $10,000 not to search their persons and belongings when they left the prison, the gang waited patiently for the trucks to show up to take them out to their great adventure.

NOW the *Cofradía* were in their camp within *Fuerte* Franco. Their money was still hidden away among their possessions. The Falangists were not properly trained or experienced in maintaining custody of convicts. Their search activities were pathetically inadequate when pitted against men who had lived for long years filled with subterfuge and secrecy in the bowels of confinement.

A sharp whistle from a lookout alerted the gang that someone was approaching the wire. The meeting quickly broke up as the convicts turned their attention back to normal camp life. *Suboficial* Adolfo Punzarron, recently back from his trip to Santiago, Chile, was at the gate with *Coronel* Jeronimo Busch.

"Oigan!" Punzarron yelled. "Listen up! All of you come over to the gate. *Coronel* Busch has something to say to you."

The prisoners dutifully walked from their rows of tents up to the camp entrance. Gordo Pullini pushed his way to the front. Busch looked them over, then spoke in a loud voice.

"Fellow fighters for Fascist freedom! We have learned that *norteamericanos* have committed a horrible crime at a nearby village. These were the notorious Green Berets who are well-known for their cruelty. They machine gunned every man, woman and child who lived in the little community of cattle herders. You will go with us to avenge these murders and kill the Americans. You will be given weapons and allowed the honor of participating in this act of sacred vengeance to be done in the name of *Falangísmo*."

"Vivan los Falangístas!" Pullini cried. *"Muerte a los Green Berets!"*

The other convicts echoed the cry. "Long live the Falangists! Death to the Green Berets!"

Busch smiled. "You are showing the right spirit. We have not erred in bringing you into our cause. Do not worry, *compañeros,* your time to fight is nigh."

"Soon you will have those weapons the *coronel* mentioned," Punzarron said. "You will be able to fight like men. Do you have any questions?" He looked at the convicts, who gazed back with blank expressions on their faces. "Very well. You are dismissed."

Pullini led his men back into the interior of the tent community as Busch and Punzarron watched. Bush frowned in puzzlement. "Have you noticed something, *Suboficial*? There are times when those convicts seem to be a well-organized group. It would seem they even have some form of discipline."

Punzarron shrugged and shook his head. "They are criminals, *mi coronel*. There are strong men among them who are the natural bosses. They have no leaders, only bullies."

"Of course," Busch agreed. "They are nothing but common thugs. I doubt if they really have the intellectual capacity to seriously coordinate their efforts into any meaningful organized activity."

WASHINGTON, D.C.
WHITE HOUSE PRESS CONFERENCE
3 JANUARY
1000 HOURS LOCAL

WHITE House Chief of Staff Arlene Entienne stood in front of Press Secretary Owen Peckham at the entrance to the short hallway that led down to the pressroom. She reached up and straightened his tie, smiling encouragement at him. "Are you ready to jump into the fray?"

"No," Peckham answered candidly. "I can think of ten thousand places I'd rather be today."

"Any special plans on dealing with the onslaught?" she asked.

"I'm going to come out swinging," Peckham said. "And from that point on, I'll duck and punch, punch and duck, until the bell rings."

"That's the way," Entienne said. "Go get 'em! I'll be here waiting when you've finished. Just keep in mind that you've been fully briefed. Information is ammunition."

Peckham went through the door into the hall and strode the few yards down to another door. He stepped through it and walked to the podium. "Good morning," he called out in what he hoped was a confident, solemn tone. He did not want to appear as if he were looking for friends among the journalists who sat in the seats to his front. "The first thing I wish to do before I take questions from you is to state that the news of the crime in Bolivia that is on all the prime-time telecasts and front pages of the nation's metropolitan newspapers is an insult to the honor and integrity of United States Army Special Forces. No American servicemen were involved in the outrage. The President of the United States categorically and emphatically denies that any armed forces of the U.S.A. had anything—directly or indirectly—to do with the crime." He paused and exhibited a stern look. "All right. Questions."

A young woman stood up. "Bennington of the *Boston World Journal.* Are there any American troops deployed in combat situations in South America at this time?"

"Yes," Peckham said. "But allow me to qualify that affirmative response. There is no secret that we have several units supporting specific Latin American drug operations with the cooperation and coordination of local police and military. Many times these activities result in gun battles."

"Fremont of *National Syndicated News Briefs,*" another reporter said. "Did the massacre mentioned in the news really happen?"

"Unfortunately, it did indeed occur," Peckham said. "The Bolivian government confirms the reports of the unfortunate incident and further acknowledges that the photographs of the victims are genuine."

Another man was called on. "Mackenzie of the *Ontario People's Advocate.* An eyewitness has been interviewed in the South American press. He said his wife and children were killed by the Green Berets. What is the United States government's reply to the man's charges?"

"No one from the U.S. government has had an opportunity to converse with the gentleman," Peckham said. "In fact, he has evidently disappeared from view. His veracity has not been properly challenged."

"Thompson of the *San Francisco Activist Informer*," a young woman said. "All the angry people in South America cannot be wrong. When the particular Green Berets who committed this atrocity are finally discovered, will the president make an apology to the world?"

"No American Special Forces troops were involved in those killings," Peckham said grimly. "We have issued that statement before, and at this point the United States government's denial of any participation or connection is final. That's it."

Dirk Wallenger of Global News Broadcasting stood up without bothering to identify himself, since both he and Peckham were old adversaries. "Was the CIA involved?"

"No," Peckham said, controlling his anger. "Did you not understand my opening statement nor the one I just this minute made?"

"I interviewed that only survivor of the murders when I was in Santiago, Chile, about a week ago," Wallenger said. "He was very convincing. The gentleman said that the killers wore U.S. Army uniforms and green berets. He also stated that they spoke English. How do you respond to those words from one of the victims?"

"A lot of people in the world speak English, Dirk," Peckham replied. "And anybody with the money can purchase a military-style green beret. Many wannabes order them out of catalogs along with camouflage uniforms and other military paraphernalia for weekends of reenactments or playing at war. I might add that the Royal Marines of Great Britain wear green berets. I believe they speak a bit of English, though I seriously doubt if the prime minister has dispatched any of them to South America to randomly travel around massacring entire villages of people. And the French Foreign Legion wears green berets too. And I'm sure there are many English-speaking legionnaires in their ranks. And one of their regiments is stationed in French Guiana in South America. But again, I have grave doubts they have been roaming the continent looking for little towns to wipe off the map."

"In that case will the president be dispatching any of the nation's armed forces to track down and capture the culprits?" Wallenger asked.

"There are no such plans now," Peckham said, "nor has Bolivia requested assistance in such an operation. And our present situation in the Middle East precludes responding to such an appeal."

Wallenger was stubborn. "But doesn't the president think this is important enough to make an effort to prove the accusations by this survivor false or at least mistaken?"

"The President of the United States is not going to dignify those ridiculous charges by addressing them in any official manner or form." He glanced around the room. "As I stated when I walked in here, no Americans were responsible for the incident."

"Anti-American demonstrations swept across South America," Wallenger said. "Our embassies have been stoned, the flag defiled, and effigies wearing green berets burned in the streets of the continent's major cities. Surely this is serious enough to—"

"Thank you for coming, ladies and gentleman, this is the end of the press conference," Peckham said.

He left the podium and exited the room, hurrying down the hall to where Arlene Entienne had been listening over the intercom to the session. "You did fine, Owen. To the point. Polite but firm. And you responded fully to each question."

"You know something, Arlene," Peckham said. "I just thought of an oxymoron: journalistic standards."

**FUERTE FRANCO
5 JANUARY
1000 HOURS LOCAL**

ALL the field fortifications and bunkers were completed. The convicts piled the final sandbags around the mortar position in the center of the garrison near the head-quarters complex. They stood back as the crews of the three Spanish Model L 60-millimeter mortars brought them in and set the weapons up.

The laborers had an easy time of it as they went around making final minor fixes and alterations. These were mostly done at the behest of various junior and warrant officers as they inspected the places where their units would be fighting. By midmorning the Argentine prisoners had nothing much to do but tend to the odd jobs that popped up. Consequently, they were dismissed from duty early and given permission to withdraw to their camp for a meal and a *siesta*.

1400 HOURS LOCAL

A surprise formation was called for the convicts, and they were rousted from their naps to form up. They obeyed the summons with the same dogged acceptance they demonstrated for surprise searches and rousting about from prison guards.

Suboficial Punzarron, *Sargento-Mayor* Chaubere and *Sargento* Müller had arrived with a box of used Spanish Army green fatigue uniforms complete with service caps. The type of military sandals worn in Morocco were included in the issue. The convicts were immediately ordered to strip off the blue prison overalls they usually wore and change into the replacement garments.

The uniforms actually raised the morale of the hard cases among the gang. This was a sign of even more change to come. Perhaps life would indeed become better for them. They horsed around and joked as the uniforms were pulled on. It took some time for everyone to sort through the clothing to find the proper fits. Even Punzarron showed good humor as he walked around, correcting the way they had put on the service caps. Most had the headgear tipped back on their heads and a half dozen were actually wearing them sideways. When they learned to keep them straight and tipped down toward their noses, they liked the swaggering look it gave them.

A half hour later when all were dressed properly, they formed up in their usual formation. Punzarron stood to their front. *"Ahora*—now," he said, "you are about to become men. Real men! We are going to turn you into soldiers. Before today we simply lined you up and ushered you from place to place for your work. It is time you learned what is called drill. We will take it a lesson at a time, and before you know it, you will look dignified and impressive as you march like soldiers when you go about the garrison." He turned to Müller. *"Sargento! Al frente y centro! Marche!"*

Müller marched up beside Punzarron and came to a halt, stamping his feet to the ground.

"Observe how the *sargento* is standing," Punzarron said. "He is at the position of attention. His chin is raised, shoulders back and squared, and his hands are straight and aligned with the seams of his trousers. His heels are together with his toes turned out at a forty-five-degree angle."

The convicts took careful note of how Müller stood.

"Now! Observe this!" Punzarron said. He looked at Müller. "At ease!"

The *sargento* smartly snapped his hands around behind his back, simultaneously grasping them together. At the same time, he moved his left foot to the left with another stamping of boots on the ground.

"Notice how *marcial*—soldierly—he is when he moves," Punzarron said. Once more he turned to the demonstrator. *"Pongase en posición de firmes!"*

Müller whipped into the position of attention.

"Pongase en posición de descanso!"

Müller assumed the position of at ease.

From that point on, the three Falangists ran the convicts

through the drill. It didn't take them long to catch on, and they moved from "attention" to "at ease" with military smartness. The only one having trouble was Gordo Pullini's main man Navajaso Coletti. He had always been a slow learner, and several times he reacted too late to the commands. Punzarron's good humor faded when Coletti had gotten a step behind and was standing at ease when he should have been standing at attention. The *suboficial* charged into the ranks and hit the convict as hard as he could. Coletti went to the ground but came up fighting.

"Calmate!" Pullini shouted at him. "Take it easy!"

Coletti pulled back his fists but glared at Punzarron. Then he brought himself to the right position. He took an additional hard slap across the face from the *suboficial* without reacting to it.

From that point on, the instructors put the students through the rudiments of marching. They went from "forward march" to "halt." Then "to the rear march" was introduced, and they began moving forward and back, keeping in step as Punzarron bellowed out the cadence, *"Uno, dos, tres, quatro!"*

Things began going better until they moved into the column and flanking movements. From that point on, all mistakes were dealt with punches and kicks from the trio of Falangist drill masters. But eventually, bruised and angry, the convicts responded quickly and correctly to the commands as the period of training continued.

1800 HOURS

GENERALÍSIMO Jose Maria de Castillo y Plato stood with *Coronel* Jeronimo Busch at the entrance to the convicts' camp. They watched as the prisoners marched back in a column of twos, eyes to the front, shoulders back, and in step with the cadence. Punzarron marched his charges inside, put them through a couple of "left flank,"

"right flank," "to the rear" and column movements, then
halted them, facing them toward him. He dismissed them,
and the tired men walked wearily to their tents to prepare
their evening meal.

Punzarron reported to the two officers while Chaubere
and Müller headed for the noncommissioned officers'
mess bunker. Castillo was pleased. "I congratulate you,
suboficial, you have shaped that scum into something re-
sembling soldiers."

Punzarron smiled at the compliment. But inside the
camp, Navajaso Coletti walked up to the gang leader,
Gordo Pullini. He spoke softly to his chief, saying, "If you
ever decide to have that Portuguese *hijo de puta* killed, I
would like the honor of sending him to hell."

"That I promise you, Nava," Pullini said. "Now let's eat
and get some rest after all this nonsense."

CHAPTER 13

THE EC-635 helicopter had landed five kilometers to the southwest of the field offices, out of sight and hearing of the site. Now, after a quick cross-country hike from the aircraft, *Coronel* Jeronimo Busch and his companion *Suboficial* Adolfo Punzarron peered at the facility through their binoculars. They were fifty meters away, well hidden under their camouflage capes as they observed the target of that morning's mission. Twenty meters farther behind the command duo, *Sargento-Mayor* Amaud Chaubere and *Sargento* Antonio Müller, along with four Falangist troops, were also concealed in the grass of the savannah.

The bright red Petroleo helicopters, tied down on their pads, were easily visible, but no guards were within sight. "They are careless with their security," Punzarron remarked.

"I do not think they want to give an outward impression that they are a tactical combat outfit," Busch said.

This mission was planned and put into execution the evening before. The Falangist intelligence officer, newly promoted *Comandante* Diego Tippelskirch, had been radioed a confirmation that the Petroleo Colmo Oil Company was a CIA front. This verification also contained the information that three missing Falangist fighters captured by the *bandidos* were being held in the firm's field office in the southeastern part of the Gran Chaco.

Now Busch turned toward Chaubere and Müller to signal them to move forward with the four troops. They approached with Star submachine guns locked and loaded to join Busch and Punzarron. The group moved *en masse* toward the building with Busch in the lead. When they reached the door, they paused only long enough to listen for any activity within the building. There was none. The *coronel* kicked the front door open, and they rushed inside.

The raiders found nothing but a small office, and they wasted no time in charging through another door that led farther into the interior of the building. This was a dormitory of sorts with four men lying in bunks. They had just awakened and opened their eyes in time for a quick glimpse of their killers. Eight submachine guns spurted bursts of 9-millimeter slugs that swept across the sleeping area. The oil company men were visibly pummeled by the bullet impacts, and a couple toppled out of their bunks onto the floor.

Müller noticed some keys hanging on a far wall by another door. He went over and took them off the wall. After unlocking the egress, he stepped into a short hallway that led to a cell at the end. He hurried to the barred gate and saw the three Falangists. Two were standing up grasping the bars, while the other looked up weakly from where he lay on his bunk.

One of the standing prisoners grinned widely. "*Por Dios!* We are glad to see you!"

The other man on his feet, a veteran *sargento* of the Chilean marines, was so happy he laughed aloud. "Those

hijos de chingadas were going to send us back to Santiago
for court-martial."

Müller quickly opened the cell, and the two shook
hands with them both, looking down at the man who still
lay on his bunk. "How's he doing?"

"Not too good," the first prisoner said. "He was given
some medical attention, but they said he would have to go
to a hospital for proper treatment. They were going to fly
us out this afternoon."

The second prisoner gestured at their badly injured
comrade. "He's not really fully conscious." He looked into
Müller's eyes. "We don't have the facilities to do anything
for him if we take the poor *tipo* back to *Fuerte* Franco. And
if we leave our poor *compañero* here, they will take him
away for treatment, but after that, he will go under intense
interrogation."

Müller walked over and sat down on the bunk. "Hello,
amigo," he said. "We can have you flown to an army hospital just over the Argentine border. They will have you on
your feet in no time." As he spoke, he pulled his Beretta automatic pistol from its holster on his web belt. He gently
placed the muzzle against the delirious man's temple. A
pull on the trigger sent brains and blood splattering over
the cell wall. Müller got to his feet. "Let's go, *compañeros!*"

The trio went back into the dormitory. When they
walked in they saw that an uninjured man had been found
under one of the bunks. He stood in his shorts and T-shirt
with his hands in the air. Busch stood in front of him,
scowling. *"Y tu nombre?"*

"Me llamo Roberto Torres-Martinez," Alfredo said, using a cover name. *"Soy de* Puerto Rico."

"A Puerto Rican, eh?" Busch remarked. "That means
you're an American citizen, does it not?"

"Wait a minute!" Müller exclaimed. "I've seen this fellow before!" He walked over and studied Alfredo's face.
"Seguro! He was on the helicopter that landed after that

patrol was ambushed. I found a good place for concealment in the grass." He laughed loudly. "The bastards were
looking all over for me."

The Chilean ex-marine confirmed it. "That is true. He
was there when they captured us."

Busch punched Alfredo once, causing him to stumble
backward. He hit him hard again, then a third time that sent
the CIA man to the floor. Chaubere walked over and
picked him up. He clipped him too, and Alfredo wisely
went down, feigning that he was badly dazed.

The punch-up was interrupted when Punzarron came in
from another side room. "There is a radio in there, and
somebody is calling over it."

Müller picked Alfredo up and frog-marched him into
the commo room with Busch and Chaubere following. A
voice came over the speaker. "Petrol, this is Brigand. Over.
I say again. Petrol, this is Brigand. Over."

Busch looked at Chaubere. "You speak English, do you
not?"

"Yes, sir," the Frenchman answered. "But I am afraid it
is like my Spanish. Heavily accented."

Busch reached out and yanked Alfredo from Müller's
grasp. "I know damn well that *you* speak English, *puertor-
riqueño!*"

"Yes," Alfredo said in English. "I speak the language
fluently."

"Then answer that transmission!" Busch ordered.

Alfredo picked up the microphone and waited. As soon
as the call was repeated, he pressed the TRANSMIT button.
"Brigand, this is Petrol. We are compromised. I say again.
We are compromised! We are—"

Chaubere knocked the microphone from Alfredo's
hand. The ex–Special Forces sergeant major reached over
and pulled Müller's pistol from the holster with the flap
still unfastened. But before he could fire, Busch swung up
his submachine gun and squeezed off a long burst.

Alfredo toppled to the floor, almost cut in half.

Busch looked from the mangled corpse over to his men. "Which of you brought the plastic explosives?"

"It is I, *mi coronel*," one answered as he snapped to attention.

"Take care of those damn red helicopters out there," Busch said. "I don't want to see another one of those in the sky over the Gran Chaco."

"*Si, mi coronel!*"

The Falangist pulled the white blocks of C4 from his haversack as he walked from the building to destroy the Petroleo Colmo aircraft.

SEAL BASE CAMP
COMMO HOOTCH
0545 HOURS LOCAL

FRANK Gomez looked up at Lieutenant Wild Bill Brannigan, who stood beside him. "That was Alfredo, sir."

"Shit!" Brannigan exclaimed. "What the hell could have happened?"

"He said he was compromised, sir."

"Godamn it, Gomez!" Brannigan snapped. "I know what he said. I'm wondering what went wrong."

"Yes, sir."

"This is a lost fucking cause," Brannigan said. "Our local support is completely wiped out. Get the SOI to see what we do in a case like this."

"Aye, sir." Frank reached over to a niche hacked in the dirt wall. The SOI, sealed in plastic with an AN-M14 incendiary thermite grenade standing on it, sat in the small excavation. He pulled it out, ripped off the covering, then handed it to the Skipper. Brannigan went through it, finding the information he was looking for. He showed it to Frank.

Frank tuned to the correct frequency, then began transmitting. "Matrix, this is Brigand. Over."

"This is Matrix," came an immediate reply. "Authentication kilo-papa-zulu-echo-tango. I say again. Authentication kilo-papa-zulu-echo-tango."

"This is Brigand," Frank replied. "Wait." He turned to the proper section of the SOI, reading through columns and rows of five-letter groups. "This is Brigand. Authentication follows. Uniform-whiskey-victor-zulu-mike." Then he added the day and month. "Zero-six-zero-one. Over."

"This is Matrix. Authentication verified. Over."

Frank handed the microphone to Brannigan. The Skipper spoke directly and plainly as he passed on the word of the disaster at the oil company's field office. "Petrol is compromised. Over."

A short pause followed before a reply was transmitted. "This is Matrix. You will move to map coordinates six zero—five one—two four—two two—three five—zero niner. I say again. Six zero—five one—two four—two two—three five—zero niner. Out."

Frank had copied down the coordinates. He ripped the page out of the pad and handed it to Brannigan. "There you are, sir."

"Yeah," Brannigan said, taking the piece of paper. "That's it. End of transmission. Period."

"They don't want to talk to us no more, sir," Frank said. "That's SOP."

"Yeah," Brannigan grumbled. He reached into his side trouser pocket and pulled out his map. He opened it up and read the grid lines right and up. "Well, hell! We've got a good ways to go."

"Where're we headed, sir? Frank asked.

"The Selva Verde Mountains," Brannigan replied. "That range is completely covered by jungle. The Rio Ancho will take us there, which means we can go by boat. But the contour lines on this fucking map are so close together a gnat couldn't piss between 'em. That means a steep, difficult climb up to our objective."

"Jesus," Frank said. He had already missed Thanksgiving

and Christmas with his family. Now it looked like it would still be a long time before he got home—if he made it. "What the hell are we gonna do up there?"

"Our best to fucking survive."

FUERTE FRANCO
HEADQUARTERS BUNKER
1430 HOURS LOCAL

GENERALÍSIMO Castillo called a conference with his senior field commander and intelligence officer. *Coronel* Jeronimo Busch and *Comandante* Diego Tippelskirch sat in the bunker with *Suboficial* Ignacio Perez off to one side at his little desk to take notes of the meeting.

Busch was in a good mood. "The *bandidos* are now without CIA assistance via the Petroleo Colmo Company. And we are the only ones with air support."

Castillo had a concern. "But what if another CIA cover unit moves into the area? Surely they would bring aircraft with them, no?

"That would create no difficulties for us, *mi generalísimo,*" Busch said. "If we see other aircraft in the Gran Chaco, we will shoot them down. Do not forget that the EC-635 has a twenty-millimeter cannon in the nose."

"You're right," Castillo said, relieved. "Well, in the meantime, I have been studying the map and putting myself in the place of the chief of the *bandidos*. As far as I can determine, he has but two choices. He can either give up the fight and withdraw from the Gran Chaco or carry out his campaign with a new source of support."

"I am not worried," *Comandante* Tippelskirch said. "Our intelligence net grows stronger at almost a daily rate. Nothing can be moved into the Gran Chaco without our operatives discovering it before it's done. We will be forewarned at every turn of the card in this game."

"Bueno," Castillo said, "what if the *bandidos* decide to carry out the fight with the resources they have?"

"I believe I've already come up with a plan to take care of that eventuality," *Coronel* Busch said. "We could send out hunter-killer teams to engage them in battle. Since the only helicopters in the campaign are ours, speed will be in our arsenal. We are the ones who can now move quickly from spot to spot to deal with trouble."

"And that is exactly what we shall do," Castillo said.

"Mi generalísimo," Busch said. "I would like to have Punzarron, Chaubere and Müller permanently assigned to me from this point on. I want those three men close by wherever I go."

"The four would be invincible," Tippelskirch said with a smile.

"Indeed!" Castillo said. "And I think you and *Coronel* Busch should get together to design some operational combat plans we can put into immediate effect."

Busch nodded. "I think the first thing we must do is switch over our basic tactical structure to become an immediate reaction force."

Castillo smiled his approval at the paratrooper. *"Coronel* Busch, when this great struggle of ours is won, you will be a *mariscal*! No, wait! You will be a *reichmariscal*!"

Ignacio, scribbling in his notebook, had recorded the minutes of the meeting almost word-for-word.

WASHINGTON, D.C.
THE PENTAGON
SPECIAL OPERATIONS LIAISON STAFF
7 JANUARY
0915 HOURS

THE office was in an isolated, little-used area of the Pentagon. After presenting his I.D. to the stern U.S. Army

Military Police guard at the entrance to the section, Carl Joplin, PhD, stepped through a door into a dingy portion of the big five-sided building. No buffer, mop or even a broom had touched the dusty floor for what looked like months or years. The only thing more isolated from the outside world would be a deep, abandoned coal mine.

Joplin had been in the place many times before. He went directly to the unmarked entrance of a nondescript office. He stepped inside to see the desks of Specialist Mary Kincaid, U.S. Army; and Senior Airman Lucille Zinkowski located in an outer office. Sometimes these stern and efficient young ladies were disturbed by Joplin's surprise appearances, but that morning they had been expecting him.

"Good morning, Dr. Joplin," Kincaid said.

"Colonel Turnbull is waiting to see you," Zinkowski said. "You can go right in."

Joplin walked into a conference room and crossed it to the office of Colonel John Turnbull, who served as the chief of staff of Special Operations liaison. The undersecretary rapped on the door and stepped inside.

"Hello, Carl," Turnbull said. "Grab a seat. This won't take long."

"All right, John," Joplin said, sitting down. "Fire away."

"The SEAL detachment you are dealing with is cut off and without support," Turnbull said, speaking rapidly. "The CIA facility that was backing them up is more than just compromised. It is wiped out."

Joplin leaped to his feet. "You've got to get those guys out of there!"

"I'm afraid they're going to have to stay and fight the good fight until the situation can be brought back under control," the colonel said. "Or maybe, to be more realistic, *if* the situation can be brought under control."

"What the hell are they supposed to do?"

"They will be moving east to the Selva Verde Mountains, where good cover and concealment is available," Turnbull said. "They only have access to equipment and ammunition in their base camp. They would never be able to get out to their auxiliary caches under the present circumstances."

"Then how the hell are they supposed to get over to those mountains?" Joplin asked.

"They'll be able to use a river down there for a straight shot to the place," Turnbull said. "At least that's what I'm told. I'm really not familiar with their OA. Hell! I don't even know what they're doing down there."

"We've got to pull them out," Joplin insisted.

"All I know is that orders are already issued telling them to go to the mountains," Turnbull said. "I was told to inform you. I've done that."

"Orders. Orders," Joplin mumbled.

"Those operational instructions are explicit and will be obeyed," Turnbull said.

"All right," Joplin said. "I suppose I should inform the secretary of state."

Turnbull shrugged. "What the hell can he do?"

Joplin turned and walked from the office, still mumbling to himself.

VILLAGE OF CARIDAD
THE GRAN CHACO
1530 HOURS LOCAL

A half-dozen people worked slowly down the rows of plants in the garden. Their hoes made clumping sounds in the soil as offending weeds were chopped out and cast aside. They were in a good mood. The crops were doing well and would soon augment the food brought in by the *norteamericanos*. During the various other activities in the community, some minor injuries, such as cuts and burns, had occurred as would be expected. The antiseptics and bandages in the medical kit given them by their American friends served well in those instances.

Truly, God had blessed this undertaking.

The sound of the helicopter engine in the distance caught their attention. Everyone stopped working and looked toward the southeast. Almost immediately a dot appeared just over the horizon, steadily growing larger as an aircraft approached. The gardeners looked at each other and smiled; their friends from the north were coming back for another visit. One of the men laughed and called out, "*Tal vez nos traen cerveza fria*—maybe they bring us cold beer!"

The reverend Walter Borden, working on an inventory in the food hut, stopped his task and walked outside. He looked up in time to see the helicopter make a wide circle of the village before coming in to land.

"*Nuestros amigos han regresado*—our friends have returned!"

Other joined him as he rushed over to greet the visitors. But as soon as four men jumped from the aircraft and strode rapidly toward the crowd, the happy mood plummeted to fearful uncertainty. These were not their friends; more than likely they were the soldiers they had been warned about.

Coronel Jeronimo Busch, followed by Punzarron, Chaubere and Müller, hurried to the village. The three lower-ranking men followed Busch as he walked toward Borden, who stood to the front of the crowd. The Chilean paratrooper immediately knew this was the headman. He held out his hand as he approached. "*Buenas tardes, señor,*" the colonel said. He introduced himself, then turned and indicated his subordinates, giving their ranks and names. "We are soldiers of the *Ejército Falangísta* and have come to inquire as to how you are."

"We are well, *gracias, coronel,*" Borden said. "I can get our papers for you, if you wish. We are here legally with the official permission of the Bolivian government."

"I am certain of that," Busch said, smiling. "The reason I inquire as to your well-being is that a tragedy has occurred some seventy-five kilometers south of here. The entire population of a village similar to this one was massacred."

"The Good Lord have mercy!" Borden cried. "Who committed the crime?"

"Americans," Busch said. "Green Berets, to be exact. Have you ever heard of that organization?"

"Yes, sir," Borden said. "I am an American missionary. We have established a religious community here to live in peace and observe God's laws."

"Most commendable, *señor clerigo*," Busch said. "Have you seen military men in this vicinity?"

"No, sir," Borden said, remembering the warning given him by the SEALs. "You are the first."

"I must warn you that if any appear, you should consider them hostile and dangerous. Take your people and flee!"

"I shall heed your advice, *señor el coronel*."

"I am going to have my men search your village," Busch announced. "We promise not to make a mess of things."

"I am distressed to hear that," Borden said. "I would rather you did not do this. We are not engaged in any underhanded activities."

"I am sorry," Busch said. "It is a necessity we are forced to observe. After all, we do not really know you, do we?"

"I understand," Borden said. "I assure you we are no more than peaceful farmers."

By then a half-dozen more men had come out of the helicopter. They stood by the aircraft in a formation of two ranks. Busch yelled over to them, *"Registran el pueblo. Pronto!"*

The detachment, broken down into two teams, rushed forward and began an efficient inspection of the huts. They spent forty minutes prowling the village under the joint command of Punzarron, Chaubere and Müller, while Busch stayed with Reverend Borden.

When the task was finished, Punzarron reported to Busch with a food carton. "We found a hut with boxes of food in it. Here is one for your inspection, *mi coronel*."

Busch took the container, noting the different languages printed on it. He raised his eyes and gazed suspiciously at Borden. "Where did you get this?"

"They are part of a delivery sent us through my mission," Borden explained. "It is the Christian Outreach Ministry."

"And where is this organization based?"

"In America," Borden replied. "Dallas, Texas, to be exact."

Busch was no longer smiling. "Many organizations from America are fronts for their Central Intelligence Agency."

"I swear to you, sir!" Borden said. "My mission group is not CIA."

"I want to believe you, of course," Busch said. "We are leaving now, but we will be back. Think of us as your friends. We can bring you things you need. Perhaps our food will be superior to what your mission sends you."

"We are not in need, *señor el coronel,*" Borden said.

"How fortunate for you," Busch remarked coldly. "Remember! We are the Falangists. The day is nigh when we will not only control the Gran Chaco but all of South America. Do not play coy or false with us. There would be dire consequences for you and your people."

"Yes, *señor el coronel,*" Borden acknowledged respectfully.

Busch shouted terse orders, and the Falangists made a hurried but orderly walk toward the helicopter. Borden watched as the aircraft lifted off to fly low over the grasslands.

"May the Good Lord save us from such friends!" he prayed aloud and fervently.

SEAL BASE CAMP

THE caches had been dug up and all the ammunition and rations pulled out for transportation down the Rio

Ancho. Brannigan would have liked to employ the rigid raider boats for the task by using their motors when noise wasn't a problem and poling them when silence was essential. But attempts to move the ungainly craft using the quieter method proved impossible. Even towing them behind the piraguas was impractical. It was obvious the craft were designed to be propelled rapidly through the water, not tediously pulled across it. On the other hand, there was no way to attach the motors to the sterns of the piraguas. A trial attempt almost sank one as its bow rose steeply out of the water under the weight.

Thus the piraguas were the boats of choice for the river trip across the savannah to the jungles of the Selva Verde Mountains.

Not all the caches had been excavated. Those that contained items not absolutely necessary for the mission such as extra clothing, web equipment, camouflage capes and netting were left in their earthen concealments. However, all of James Bradley's medical supplies and Frank Gomez's commo gear, including extra batteries, were placed in the little wooden boats.

2300 HOURS LOCAL

THE detachment stood in two ranks, observing section and team integrity. All were fully equipped for combat, including their night vision equipment. The knowledge that they were about to embark on an extremely dangerous trek through the heart of the enemy was foremost on everyone's mind, but none spoke any concerns aloud. This was a job to do—a rather hairy one—but still it was just another task in the dangerous lives they had volunteered for.

Brannigan went to the front of the formation and studied the detachment. It was at times like this that he missed Lieutenant (J.G.) Jim Cruiser. There was a quality of calm efficiency about him that gave Brannigan not only confidence in his men but in himself as well. At least it was comforting to have Senior Chief Petty Officer Buford Dawkins and Chief Petty Officer Matt Gunnarson around. Those old salts had smarts that could only be developed and nurtured over long years of military service.

Brannigan cleared his throat, speaking only loud enough to be heard. "Listen up," the Skipper said. "First thing. The Odd Couple is going to alternate point and re- connaissance duties with Redhawk and Murchison. Dev- ereaux is going to be pulled from the Second Assault Section and go with the Command Element. That way we'll have six men, while the assault sections will have seven each. During the run down the river we'll rotate three jobs in two-hour shifts. You will alternate poling the pi- raguas, acting as flankers on both sides of the river, and resting."

"Sir," Connie Concord said, raising his hand. "How in hell are we supposed to rest?"

"You'll just have to arrange yourselves as conveniently as possible among the three piraguas," Brannigan said. "Don't worry about being uncomfortable. Hell, you'll only be resting for a couple of hours anyway. But try to get as much sleep as possible. This is going to be a long trip."

Andy Malachenko asked, "Just how much time is it gonna take, sir?"

"If things go well," Brannigan said, "we'll be able to travel relatively fast—for a walking speed—and should reach our destination within forty-eight hours. When we get to our debarkation point, the boats will be hidden along the banks of the river, and we'll move from there up to the high ground and set up positions."

Bruno Puglisi frowned in puzzlement. "Then what, sir?"

"Then we'll await either further orders from home or organized assaults from the enemy," Brannigan said. "Whichever comes first. Any more questions? Good. Now hear this! First Section begins as flankers, the Second

Section poles the boats, and the Command Element will ride and rest."

Cries of derision rose from the assault sections, directed toward the Command Element. "Headquarters pukes! Staff weenies!"

Brannigan chuckled. "All right! Move out, you magnificent sons of bitches!"

CHAPTER 14

THE SEALs had managed to move twenty-six kilometers after eight hours of continuous travel from the base camp. Poling the piraguas down the river was the most difficult part of the journey. The men manning the boats were continuously working with their arms and shoulders, first placing the twenty-foot poles into the water until reaching bottom, then giving a hard push. That was bad enough, but it had to be done in cadence or the first boat would hardly move while those behind it banged into each other. This problem was eventually solved by having the man on the head boat speak softly over the LASH, saying, "Up! Down! Push! Up! Down! Push!" The first and third men poled on the starboard side while the second did his chores on the port side, all this done in time to the cadence. It was very monotonous and tiring. Lieutenant Wild Bill Brannigan took special note of the situation, and in the rotation of jobs, the SEALs went directly from poling to resting before going back to flanker duty.

It wasn't so bad to be a flanker. They simply walked along the riverbank, having to deal with uneven ground now and then as they strode down the Rio Ancho. The guys could gaze out over the panorama of deep grass around them, feeling the hot breeze off the savannah as they strolled rather slowly to keep from getting too far ahead of the piraguas. The only downside was that if the column was attacked, they would be the first casualties. Still, it was actually a rather pleasant walk in the country, though the heat was bothersome.

The guys resting after their poling duties were like any well-trained military men. A rookie might be restless and finicky about taking a nap, but all seasoned veterans have evolved into champion sleepers. Any experienced campaigner could sit down or lie down and fall asleep in an instant. In some cases, they would find no difficulty sleeping on their feet. They could even doze off for one or two minutes and come out of it a bit more refreshed than before they closed their eyes. The soft sounds of the first boat guy's voice were like a lullaby to those SEAL veterans as they recovered from their own muscle-cramping stints on the poles.

0830 HOURS LOCAL

"CHOPPER!"

Bruno Puglisi's voice alerted everyone, even those dozing in the bottoms of the piraguas. All eyes snapped northward to catch sight of a helicopter rapidly approaching. It was obvious the fliers had caught sight of them by the way the aircraft was rapidly climbing and swinging out to make a quick run past them.

Brannigan put his binoculars to his eyes, studying the growing image of the approaching helicopter. "Hold your fire! It has the light blue roundels of Argentina on the fuselage. We don't need to create an international incident here. There's already enough butt-wipes shooting at us."

"Shit, sir!" Puglisi said, hefting his SAW in his usual shoot-first-and-ask-questions-later attitude. "Nobody told us what kind of aircraft markings them Falangists have. If any."

"Patience, Puglisi," Brannigan counseled him.

The helicopter came boldly on, flying directly over them. Chad Murchison spoke over his LASH. "It's a Euro-copter EC-635. That's a twenty-millimeter cannon sticking out its nose, fellows. It's an efficacious aircraft employed by several nations for its qualities and attributes."

Joe Miskoski growled, "I don't have the slightest fucking idea of what you just said."

"Jesus, Chad!" Frank Gomez added. "Couldn't you just say it's a damn good chopper?"

The helicopter made one circle around them, then straightened up and sped off in the direction from where it had come.

Puglisi groused over his LASH, "I still think we shoulda shot the motherfucker down."

FUERTE FRANCO
0855 HOURS LOCAL

SUBALTERNO Ernesto Pizzaro was the first heli-copter pilot to desert his country's armed forces to become a permanent, active member of the *Ejército Falangísta*. Before cutting out, he had been doing the same as all the renegade pilots, going back and forth between his Argentine Air Force helicopter squadron and the Falangists when the opportunities presented themselves. His absences were misrepresented by his unit's adjutant, a Falangist sympathizer, who covered his ass by listing him as TDY when he wasn't present for duty. But now Pizzaro wanted to stay permanently at *Fuerte* Franco for the action and adventure when flying in the service of the *generalísimo*.

He had just returned from a mission with *Sargento* Antonio Müller as an observer. They had spotted the *bandidos* moving eastward on the Rio Ancho with three piraguas. Müller left the young pilot with the aircraft after landing, rushing over to the Command Bunker to report the crucial findings of the short reconnaissance patrol.

When Müller presented himself to Castillo, he found *Coronel* Jeronimo Busch also in the earthen office. The *sargento* gave an oral report, not wasting words as he quickly told them what he and Pizzaro had seen.

Castillo was pleased. "This is most interesting. It appears that the *bandidos* are making a major transfer of their command complete with bag and baggage, *verdad*?"

"Seguro, mi generalísimo," Busch agreed. "They are obviously withdrawing because their support from the Petroleo Colmo Company—or I should say the CIA—is gone. I wonder if they are trying to reach Paraguay. Perhaps they have aid available there."

Castillo nodded his head. "In that case, we must keep them from traveling that far." He swiveled in his chair and looked at the map of the Gran Chaco on the wall behind his desk. "Now, if I were the commander of the *bandidos,* what would motivate me to travel eastward whether I had support or not?" he mused.

"Ah!" Busch exclaimed. "The high country of the jungles. The Selva Verde Mountains! It would be a perfect place to set up defenses or link up with reinforcements."

"Of course," Castillo agreed. "A perfect place to hole up and hide until further help arrives, no?"

"You are absolutely correct when you say they must not be allowed to reach those mountains, *mi generalísimo,*" Busch said. "The *bastardos* have been ambushing our patrols almost at will. Now it is their turn to endure strikes from the unknown."

"Tiene razon!" Castillo exclaimed. "You are right! And let's take into consideration that we have two helicopters at our disposal, and they have none. Alert the garrison, *coronel,* we are going on the offensive. Now we shall mount a full-scale attack on those damned *bandidos*!"

1100 HOURS LOCAL

GENERALÍSIMO Castillo had been very precise as he dictated his operational orders to *Suboficial* Ignacio Perez. After writing down the combat directive word for word, the little man turned to his portable typewriter and carbon paper to make enough copies to pass out to the field officers who would lead the various echelons. In order to get out nine clear copies, he'd had to type the document three times. *Fuerte* Franco, without the power of generators, had no way to run word processors or photocopiers to ease the administrative burdens of the little adjutant and quartermaster.

Two lifts of twenty-four fully equipped men—each with eight on the EC-635 light utility helicopter and sixteen on the SA-330 utility helicopter—were organized for the trip to the battle site. *Coronel* Jeronimo Busch would be overall commander with *Suboficial* Punzarron, *Sargento-Mayor* Chaubere and *Sargento* Müller serving as his personal *equipo comando*. The three stalwarts would stick close to their field commander while he directed the operation to destroy the enemy in this one final effort.

Comandante Javier Toledo would command the first lift with *Capitánes* Francisco Silber and Roberto Argento as detachment leaders. *Comandante* Gustavo Cappuzzo was to lead the second lift, having as detachment commanders *Capitánes* Tomás Platas and Pablo Gonzales. The latter was a recently arrived infantry officer from the Bolivian Army.

The basic concept of the OPLAN was that after Busch and the *equipo comando* were set down in the EC-635, it would return to *Fuerte* Franco to join the SA-330 to begin the transport of the two main lifts. The first was to be taken to a point on both sides of the river ahead of the *bandidos*, while the second lift would be landed behind them. At a signal from Busch over the RMAM radio, the battle would commence with an all-out infantry attack supported by machine guns.

RIO ANCHO
THE SEALs
1245 HOURS LOCAL

THE sound of a single helicopter engine caught the immediate and collective attention of the detachment. Everyone went on the alert, including the men napping in the piraguas. They all sat up expectantly while the flankers scanned the skies for a sighting of the aircraft.

Joe Miskoski was on the left bank with his SAW, while Bruno Puglisi, who had been on break in the piragua, climbed up on the right bank to add his own SAW to the firepower on that side.

Brannigan spoke calmly into his LASH. "Command Element, get into the piraguas and be ready to lend a hand where and when necessary. Let's go, people! The shit's about to hit the fan!"

THE LOZANO GRASSLANDS
THE *EQUIPO COMANDO*

THE EC-635 came in slow about two meters off the deck with *Coronel* Busch and his *comandos* standing in the doors. As soon as Busch spoke *"Vamanos!"* into his LASH, all four leaped to the thick grass, hitting the ground at a run. They continued going until the chopper pulled up and away to return to *Fuerte* Franco.

Busch took the lead, heading toward the river with his picked men. They were stripped down lean and mean for light travel and quick attacks. They carried only weapons, ammunition, grenades, knives and canteens. The *equipo* kept a close watch in all directions as they hurried across the savannah. The only sounds from their rapid trek were the swishing noise made by the grass brushing against their uniform trousers. None of the superbly conditioned men breathed hard as they continued toward the *bandidos,* all eager to lock horns in this final *corrida.*

After a half hour of hard pushing, Busch suddenly signaled for them to hit the ground. All four dove into the grass. "Enemy sighted!" the *coronel* said softly. "*Ciento metres adelante*—a hundred meters ahead." He gave each man a chance to raise his head just enough to see the *bandidos.* "We will do nothing now but trail after them for the time being. When the two lifts arrive, the fight starts."

THE SEALS
1320 HOURS LOCAL

FOUR more helicopter flights had been heard on both sides of the river with only quick glances of the aircraft as they settled to the ground out of sight, then almost immediately took off again.

"Now hear this!" Wild Bill Brannigan said. "We're approximately thirty-plus hours away from where we climb out of this fucking river and start humping our asses up into the mountains. If we don't make it that far, this whole operation is shot down. And us with it."

"Sir," Senior Chief Buford Dawkins said, "we've had no sightings of the enemy other than a quick look at them choppers. I'm certain there's only two of 'em, but they both came in twice."

Chief Matt Gunnarson agreed. "And you can bet your asses they was bringing troops in with 'em."

"You're right about that," Brannigan said. "We're going to have to keep moving and fighting at the same time. If they pin us down even once, we're gone gooses. There's no way in hell we can start up again. It would just be a matter of slugging it out until all the ammo is expended."

Everyone listened over their LASH sets, knowing that a real possibility of sustaining high casualties existed in this predicament. The main objective now was to get to those distant Selva Verde Mountains.

"I'm going to have to pull three guys off the line to pole the piraguas," Brannigan continued. "I want Frank Gomez and Garth Redhawk to get up on the left bank with the First Assault Section. Chad Murchison and Guy Deveraux will go with the Second. James Bradley will stay with me in the piraguas to take care of the wounded." Brannigan waited until the detachment was organized. "That's it! Send me the guys for poling now. We'll trade 'em off when it seems necessary. Let's go, people."

THE *EQUIPO COMANDO*

CORONEL Busch and his men were formed in a skirmish line as they crawled through grass on their hands and knees, keeping as low as possible. Now and then they could hear one of the *bandidos* say something to a companion, and Busch estimated they were perhaps less than twenty meters away.

It was *Sargento* Müller who first sighted the enemy at close range. He quickly advised the others over the LASH. "They are no more than fifteen meters away."

"Escuchan!" Busch said. "On my command we will all fire a couple of six-round bursts in their direction. Then drop flat on your bellies and crawl away in the opposite direction." He raised his head and could see what appeared to be at least a half dozen of the enemy. *"Tiren!"*

The sudden eruptions of fire thundered twice, then the *comandos* went flat, turning to snake away into the grass.

* * *

CONNIE Concord jerked violently as two slugs slammed into his left arm, and he staggered sideways to tumble off the grassy bank into the water. James Bradley, in the second piragua, immediately dove in after him. He quickly found the wounded man in the muddy river and pulled him to the surface. Brannigan reached over the side of the boat and grabbed Connie under the arms, bodily hauling him aboard. James pulled himself from the river and wasted no time in examining the victim, who had slid into unconsciousness.

"He's hit bad, sir," James said. "The forearm is fractured, and he's got two massive soft tissue injuries."

"Christ!" Brannigan said. "They must've been really close."

"Yes, sir," Bradley said, digging into his medical kit. "Normally this could be handled easily, but I can't give him proper treatment for shock. That could kill him even if the wounds aren't necessarily fatal."

Now heavy firing broke out on the right side of the river, churning up clumps of grassy dirt and sending ricochets zinging off into the air.

THE BATTLE

CORONEL Busch's familiar voice sounded over *Comandante* Javier Toledo's RMAM radio. "Toledo, continue to fire, but move in closer! This is an attack not an exercise on the firing range! And use those machine guns for support!"

Toledo wasted no time in advancing his twenty-four men toward the enemy. The leading skirmish line of eight under the command *Capitán* Francisco Silber made first contact. Their fusillades swept back and forth into the enemy on the riverbank. Within sixty seconds the second rank under *Capitán* Roberto Argento joined them. Now sixteen assault weapons, skillfully employed and well-aimed, poured swarms of bullets at the *bandidos*. When the CETME Amali machine guns joined the assault, their accurate patterns of fire overlapped as timed volleys of the 5.56-millimeter slugs supported the riflemen ahead.

THE SEALs slid over the banks of the Rio Ancho to avoid the flying steel whipping around them. They returned fire in the obvious direction of the attack; unaimed but hitting close to the enemy. Joe Miskoski pumped out rounds from his SAW, trying to be as effective as possible as he swept the barrel up and down the line. Although they were unsure of the effects of their efforts, and bullets continued to crack and thud heavily around them, the SEALs suffered no further casualties. Over on the other side of the river, the First Assault Team was not taking fire after the initial attack that hit Connie.

"CAPPUZZO!" came Busch's angry voice over the RMAM. "Where the hell are you?"

"I am taking my command toward the sound of the fighting," *Comandante* Gustavo Cappuzzo radioed back. "But the battle seems to be moving eastward."

"Correcto!" Busch replied. "Forget about moving in to make contact until you're past the gunfire. Then make an abrupt move toward the river in skirmish lines. Keep going until you find the enemy. And don't forget your machine gun support!" He slipped the handset back onto his pistol belt, turning to Punzarron, Chaubere and Müller. "We are in a good position on the west of the enemy. We're going to move forward until we can fire at their rear guard. Punzarron, you and Chaubere take the south side of the river while Müller and I take the north."

The *Equipo Comando* split up, then began moving toward

the *bandidos* as soon as Punzarron and Chaubere had swum across to the other side.

THE SEALs continued the trek to the east, answering the salvos fired at them with bursts of their own. Neither side was able to deliver accurate fusillades, but the un-aimed fire kept both adversaries working in cautionary modes. Any rash attacks by anyone could be handily dealt with by the other side.

The piraguas were now tied together while Lieutenant Wild Bill Brannigan and Hospital Corpsman James Bradley both performed the poling chores in the front boat. They had piled a good amount of ammunition between them, and when some SEAL on the bank needed another bandoleer, it was a simple thing to reach down and toss him one. At this time they had plenty of the 5.56-millimeter bullets for both the CAR-15s and the SAWs.

Connie Concord was numbed by morphine as he lay in the second piragua. James had arranged him in a comfort-able position on his back with blankets over him and his feet elevated. This was all he could do in an attempt to keep Connie from going into shock. The hospital corpsman would have preferred to use an IV drip with epinephrine solution, but the present situation of kill or be killed did not offer the luxury of sophisticated medical treatments.

Brannigan had issued orders to knock off unnecessary chatter over the LASH systems. He had to use the devices to issue battle orders since he could not use the AN/PRC-126 handset. Both his hands were busy with the pole as he and James kept the piraguas moving as best they could. However, the Skipper could easily keep his eyes on the SEALs on both sides of the river as they continued to move in the eastward direction under fire. He wanted to keep them traveling the same distance and speed, and he made adjustments with terse comments. "Godamn it! Second Section slow down and First Section step it up."

The incoming fire, while still steady, was no longer so heavy. This was an ominous indication that the Falangists had figured out the situation and were concentrating on keeping pace with the SEALs as much as they were of blasting bullets in their direction.

AN hour had passed while Busch and his *comandos* trailed after the SEALs, and the *equipo* had stepped up the pace since they were not receiving fire. They listened carefully as they moved along both sides of the river, noting that the exchange of salvos was getting steadily louder.

Chaubere was the first one to catch sight of the *bandidos*. "*Voilà!* I can see the enemy, *mon colonel*," he said, slipping into French. "There is a man on each side of the river."

"*Atacen!*" Busch ordered.

The four Falangists rushed forward, their submachine guns spitting fiery salvos at the SEALs.

Up ahead, Chad Murchison on the north bank and Andy Malanchenko on the south, turned to meet the attack. They dropped to the ground, pumping the triggers of their CAR-15s. Bruno Puglisi immediately became aware of the situation and rushed back to join them. The squad automatic weapon added to the volleys of steel-jacketed slugs directed at the four attackers.

Busch immediately broke off the attack, and the *equipo* dropped to the grass as one man. They would bide their time, then once again make a charge on the rear of the *bandidos'* column.

1615 HOURS LOCAL

THE fighting went on all through the day. Neither side took casualties because of the nature of the fighting. No one could expose himself long enough to deliver accurate fire, so both sides more or less delivered independent firing in the blind. Many times the combatants simply raised their weapons without aiming, and squeezed off short fire bursts.

Busch's *Equipo Comando* kept the pressure on the rear of the SEALs with sporadic attacks before pulling back out of harm's way. While they didn't accomplish much in the way of inflicting casualties, they were able to keep an accurate measure of the enemy's rate of advance. Busch continually radioed *Comandantes* Toledo and Cappuzzo of the distance traveled by the *bandidos*. The information allowed the Falangist forces on both sides of the river to move along in the fluid battle.

Busch wanted to keep the pressure building until the *bandidos* could be pinned down in one spot. Then the Falangist force could hit them from two sides and quickly bring a victorious end to the day's fighting.

1930 HOURS LOCAL

BY now Wild Bill Brannigan and James Bradley poled the piraguas on pure adrenaline. They had passed the point of being able to assess their fatigue; instead they simply went through the process of pushing the boats along while poling like automatons.

"Ammo!" a voice came from the south bank. "Two bandoleers."

Brannigan reached down and grabbed the cloth holders, tossing them over to Gutsy Olson. The Skipper took a deep breath and shook his head to clear his mind. He opened his eyes wide and exhaled before breathing in again. Then he noticed that the incoming firing was lessening noticeably. "Hey, Chiefs!" he said, speaking to both Senior Chief Buford Dawkins and Chief Matt Gunnarson. "Is the enemy fire easing up?"

"Roger, sir," Dawkins replied. "I think them assholes may be needing an ammo resupply by now."

"Yeah," Matt agreed. "If we hear choppers again, you

can bet they'll be toting bullets into the combat area."

"Okay," Brannigan said. "I haven't heard any casualty reports from you guys."

"We ain't had any, sir," Dawkins said. "But on the other hand, I'm pretty sure we ain't inflicting any either."

"Then let's keep moving," Brannigan said. "Step up the pace if you can. Every meter closer we get to those mountains is an advantage to us."

"Aye, sir!" came back two simultaneous replies.

2030 HOURS LOCAL

THE sound of chopper engines eased in from the distance on both sides of the river. They stayed back out of range as they settled in to land with lights beaming down on the grassland beneath their skids.

The incoming fire on the SEALs dropped some more, indicating the Falangists were sending men back to pick up ammo for the line. Brannigan knew this would impede their fighting ability until darkness descended to end the long Southern Hemisphere summer day. He also was aware that the enemy had night vision capabilities, and this would add another problem to deal with. The longer the battle lasted, the more advantage the Falangists had. Brannigan had to come up with some sort of plan to stop the fighting or at least delay it for a few precious hours.

"Everybody," he said over the LASH, "keep moving!" He glanced back at James Bradley. "How's Connie doing?"

"He's still with us, sir."

2230 HOURS LOCAL

THE fighting now ceased as both sides went into a night combat mode. The Falangists would no doubt monitor the

SEALs' activities, waiting to see if an opening occurred where a grand slam could be dealt.

Brannigan's mind had been churning for the previous two hours, and he now had a tactical scheme. It was risky, probably could not succeed, and was a disaster waiting to happen, i.e., just the type of situation in which the United States Navy SEALs excelled.

Brannigan got on the LASH. "We're holding up right here. I want good solid defensive perimeters set up. Let the team leaders handle this. Meanwhile I want to see both section commanders along with the Odd Couple and Garth Redhawk. Let's go, people! We don't have a hell of a lot of time."

When the quintet of invited guests reported to the piraguas, they scrambled aboard the first one, settling down in the stern sheets. James Bradley now had time to get into the second boat to check Connie over. He found the injured man resting comfortably and not headed into shock. The wounds were serious, however, and the combination of broken bones and tissue damage was something to take seriously.

Brannigan took a swig of water from his canteen, then turned his full attention to the five men who had joined him. "We can't stay here," he said. "The only chance we have is to get the hell out of here and into the Selva Verde Mountains to set up and wait for whatever the high command has in store for us."

"I don't suppose you know what that might be, do you, sir?" Senior Chief Dawkins asked hopefully.

"I don't have clue," Brannigan admitted bitterly. "So here's what we're going to do. I want the Falangists to think we're camping out here. They'll pull back from the river and put out sentries, then wait for daylight to lower the boom on us. So! The Odd Couple and Redhawk strip down for action. By that, I mean no equipment, just pistols and knives. Get all the noise making crap out of your pockets like keys and coins. You guys are going to pussyfoot it onto the south bank of the river, taking out guards along the way. Just keep in mind that they have night vision goggles. You're going on a risky mission, but there's a good reason for it."

"I get it, sir," Mike Assad said. "We're going to clear a path to get down the river a ways."

"Exactly!" Brannigan said. "When you've done that, the whole detachment is going to get together on that bank. We'll put four men on each piragua and lift them out of the water. We'll carry them through the cleared area for about three-quarters or so of a kilometer. Then it's back in the river to pole like hell toward the mountains in the east."

Matt Gunnarson nodded his understanding. "So we'll stay up on the riverbanks until you call us in for the big move, right, sir?"

"That's it," Brannigan said.

Redhawk sniffed the air. "I smell rain, sir."

"I'll take your word for it," Brannigan said. "But I'd be surprised if the gods of war would give us a break like that."

The three men who would be operating with pistol and knife through the enemy lines began shedding unessential gear to leave in the piragua.

8 JANUARY
0200 HOURS LOCAL

THE rain fell heavily, beating an uneven staccato on both river and grass as Garth Redhawk signaled back to the Odd Couple bringing them to a halt. He was ten meters ahead of them as they lay prone in the grass. They had no ponchos, and their BDUs soaked up the water from the deluge and hung heavy on the SEALs' bodies. Three dead sentries were scattered between them and the spot where they had climbed from the river onto the south bank.

Dave Leibowitz looked past Redhawk and could see what had caught his attention. A Falangist guard sat cross-legged on the ground wrapped cozily in his rain gear while dozing with his night vision goggles pushed up on his forehead. They had noticed these were all older men as they moved stealthily through the enemy's picket line at the front of their main defensive perimeter. While these veterans were excellent noncommissioned officers, their age had caught up with them from the long hours of fighting that day. The heavily failing rain added to their fatigue. Most were inattentive and exhausted, with the vigor and alertness of youth badly faded, taking down their energy levels.

Redhawk had his K-Bar knife in his right hand as he got to his feet in a semierect position. He moved toward the sentry, glad the noise of the storm covered any inadvertent sound he might make. His boots seemed to tread nothingness as he approached his victim without disturbing even the heavily soaked knee-high grass. The SEAL struck suddenly and silently, putting a smothering hand over the guy's mouth and nose while making a deep cut completely across the throat. The wound from the razor-sharp blade went all the way down to the neck bone.

Mike Assad now spoke softly into his LASH. "All enemy sentries are cleared."

The word was passed through Wes Ferguson to Pech Pecheur. Pecheur, the last of the LASH link on the bank, now gave the welcome information to Wild Bill Brannigan, who waited back on the river with the rest of the detachment. When Brannigan spoke, the remaining men is the piraguas all heard him: "Drag 'em out of the river!"

Wes and Pech headed back to give a hand with the wooden boats.

THE FALANGIST FORCE
0715 HOURS LOCAL

CORONEL Jeronimo Busch was so furious that spittle flew from his mouth as he railed at all the *comandantes* and *capitánes*. He had called all six officers to come in from their units and report to him. "There are four dead pickets scattered up and down the line of battle! And now the *bandidos* are gone! They dragged their piraguas from the river and pulled them a kilometer! *Un kilómetro entero!* Then reentered the water and have now made good headway toward the Selva Verde Mountains!"

"No one heard anything, *mi coronel,*" *Comandante* Toledo said, shamefaced. "It was as if the *norteamericanos* or *europeos* or whatever they are, had turned to shadows and floated through us."

"Con permiso, mi coronel," *Comandante* Cappuzzo said, "but our men worked very late loading and carrying ammunition from the helicopters. This was done on both sides of the river. Our lines were not at full strength. Or even half. Two out of every three men were on the ammunition detail."

"We need to bring in younger men, *mi coronel,*" Toledo interjected. "Our older noncommissioned officers run out of steam eventually. It cannot be helped."

Busch knew Toledo was right, but he had to give everyone's fighting spirit another jump start. "That is no excuse! It is imperative that we defeat these *bandidos* as quickly as possible."

The new officer, *Capitán* Pablo Gonzales, was impressed by the enemy and didn't bother to hide it. "Those men we fight are not *bandidos, mi coronel!* Their skills and capabilities show that they are *militares profesionales* of an elite force. Mercenaries could not fight like that!"

"But we have two helicopters now," Toledo pointed out, "surely we can pursue them and catch them someplace on the river."

"Tonto—fool!" Busch bellowed. "There is every real possibility they were going to meet another group coming in from the east. That was why it was so important to pin them down here! If we go after them now, we could find ourselves drawn into a trap where we would be surrounded by an overwhelming force!"

Cappuzzo was in the mood for a fight. "I say we take a chance and go after them, *mi coronel!*"

Busch, liking the officer's fighting spirit, calmed down. "The *Ejército Falangísta* is not yet at full strength, *Comandante* Cappuzzo. At this time in our struggle we cannot afford to take undue risks." He paused and gripped his hands into fists. "This battle is over. But the war is not lost. As soon as we ascertain the exact situation of those *perros,* we will attack again!"

CHAPTER 15

THE Falangist headquarters bunker, *Centro de Administración,* had suddenly improved after the previous day's surprise delivery of up-to-date office machines. The misappropriated shipment came in via a rerouted Chilean Air Force CH-149 Cormorant transport helicopter. Two Honda generators, a Dell computer, a Lexmark Optra E312 printer, and a Spanish Duplicador-Extra copying machine were included in the cargo that arrived unexpectedly at the site.

All this was now being used by *Suboficial* Ignacio Perez in his job as adjutant and quartermaster. He worked feverishly inputting the old records into the new system so that everything was on the computer's hard drive. After printing hard copies of some of the more interesting documents as samples, everything was transferred to floppy disks.

In addition, the pallets the equipment arrived on had been broken apart and rebuilt into floorboards for the headquarters bunkers by three of the convicts detailed to the task. Ignacio's desk, filing cabinets and office machinery no longer sat on dirt.

These improvements came about from complicated arrangements that included three separate bribes and the blackmailing of an officer in the Chilean Air Force Intendance Department. *Comandante* Adolfo Tippelskirch arranged everything at the behest of *Generalísimo* Castillo. The Falangist leader wanted a detailed record kept of all activities and field operations during this founding period of the *Dictadura Fascista de Falangía.* This included the minutes of staff meetings, and he looked upon all this as good reference material for future historians. Castillo pictured a multivolume publication that would be a definitive and flattering history of the founding of the movement while concentrating particularly on the genius of its leader.

Castillo was also following in his idol Adolf Hitler's footsteps by writing a combination autobiography and manifesto he had titled *Mi Lucha.* This was based on Hitler's well-known publication, *Mein Kampf.* The Spanish and German names of these books translated into English as *My Struggle,* and Castillo thought the name of the book appropriate. Ignacio was expected to put the handwritten manuscript into the computer's Word 97 processing system as the work progressed.

The little man also received extra work from the intelligence officer, *Comandante* Tippelskirch. The Chilean's activities seemed to grow more complex with each passing week. Additional informants, operatives, reports and activities had begun to flood Tippelskirch's office in an unexpected abundance. He decided to take advantage of the word processing and copying capabilities now available in Ignacio's bailiwick. The diminutive accountant dutifully made all the necessary copies plus extras. These additional documents, of which Tippelskirch was unaware, went into a rucksack Ignacio kept concealed under his desk.

THE SEAL DEFENSIVE POSITION
SELVA VERDE MOUNTAINS
10 JANUARY

LIEUTENANT Wild Bill Brannigan had taken great care in the selection of the SEALs' mountaintop defensive perimeter. He had studied both maps and satellite photographs before leaving the base camp, determining that the best area to defend was at the apex of a small but steep mountain that rose nine hundred feet above the Lozano Grasslands. Thick jungle growth stretched from the top in a heavily treed forest that ran all the way into the lush savannah. After they hid the piraguas in the thick brush along the banks of the Rio Ancho, he led the detachment in a difficult forced march up the slopes to the chosen spot. No time was allowed for a breather to recover from the climb, as the SEALs immediately went to work setting up a compact defensive circle. The concealment and defensive capabilities of the site were superlative. This was the most important reasoning behind Brannigan's choice, since he realistically expected to come under attack by a numerically superior enemy.

When the perimeter was laid out properly, the Skipper reconfigured the detachment for the deadly task ahead. He decided to keep only James Bradley and Frank Gomez with him in the Command Element. All the riflemen would be needed on the defensive line.

James was tasked with organizing a central place to treat casualties as well as to take care of the patient he already had. Connie Concord's wound was bad enough that he was considered *hors de combat,* and needed to be monitored closely and often. Frank was close by where he could tend the AN/PSC-5 Shadowfire radio that kept them in touch with Special Operations Command through the CIA relay station in Colombia. However, in the event a sector of the perimeter became particularly hard-pressed during an attack, Frank would be sent to help out in that area.

All the fire teams were dissolved, and each Assault Section was reinstituted as one compact unit under the direct leadership of its commander. Chief Petty Officer Matt Gunnarson maintained control of the First, while the Second would continue operation under the leadership of Senior Chief Petty Officer Buford Dawkins. Garth Redhawk and Chad Murchison were sent to join Matt's outfit. The reorganization gave each section commander a SAW gunner and six riflemen. The First Section took the north and west sides of the perimeter, while the Second took the south and east. As soon as all this was announced, the men were personally assigned by Brannigan to their particular places in the line. The importance of excellent camouflage was prioritized in the defensive scheme.

The SAW gunners would stick close to the commanders to go to any part of the position where additional automatic fire was needed. Brannigan also picked out a couple of OP sites, giving each section the responsibility for manning one. These had to be placed in locations that allowed the occupants the ability to make a quick withdrawal back to the perimeter in the case of attack.

When all the shifting and settling in was finished, the detachment hunkered down. Bruno Puglisi and Joe Miskoski took the time to evenly divide the squad automatic weapon magazines between themselves. Puglisi slipped the bandoleers over his beefy shoulders and walked back through the thick brush and trees to join Chief Matt Gunnarson. As he sat down beside his section commander, the Italian-American from Philadelphia quipped, "Why do I keep thinking that we're fucked, forgotten and forsaken?"

Matt smiled wryly. "Don't forget dumped, deserted and desperate."

ABOVE THE SELVA VERDE MOUNTAINS
12 JANUARY
0115 HOURS LOCAL

SUBALTERNO Ernesto Pizzaro manned the controls of the EC-635 helicopter during the flight through the darkness over the mountain range. His copilot, *Suboficial* Manuel Obregon, monitored the newly acquired FLIR scope that had been installed during the last maintenance flight back to Argentina. The two aviators had been pals back in their old squadron of the *Fuerza Aerea Argentina,* and in spite of their wildly diverse family and social backgrounds, had developed a deep comradeship. Both were young and craved action, and this was their main motivation for joining the Falangist Revolution. The reconnaissance duty they performed that night was categorically not to their liking. There would be no strafing or rocketing involved.

The senior officers back at *Fuerte* Franco had concluded that the *bandidos* had escaped into the thick jungle that covered the Selva Verde Mountains and could hide there indefinitely without being found. The enemy needed to be accurately located to ascertain their location as well as to find out if they had linked up with any other forces. Now, with this newly acquired FLIR, a pattern search could be mounted at night to give the entire range a careful search. This was the second night of the monotonous activity, and the mission had worked a few kilometers farther south from the point of its beginning. Neither pilot talked as they continued the flight of going back and forth above the trees.

"Hay están!" Obregon suddenly cried out. "There they are!"

Pizzaro leaned over slightly to take a quick look at the scope. He could make out what appeared to be close to two dozen warm images arranged in a circular pattern. If this was not a defensive perimeter, then *putas* did not fuck. To make the situation even better, there was no sign of a larger force in the vicinity.

The young officer swung the chopper toward the northwest to head back to *Fuerte* Franco.

THE RIO ANCHO
0600 HOURS LOCAL

SARGENTO Antonio Müller leaped from the fuselage of the SA-330 helicopter to be quickly followed by the half-dozen men he had brought with him. Everyone wore basic webbing with ammo pouches and canteens. They carried Star 9-millimeter submachine guns. The morning's mission had come about from the previous night's FLIR reconnaissance in which the exact location of the *bandidos* had been determined. Müller and his men were charged with locating the enemy's boats and destroying them. That way, if the *bandidos* made another run for safety, they would go cross-country. No more boating on the river.

Logic dictated the piraguas had to be hidden somewhere in a direct line from the *bandidos'* defensive position down to the river. They obviously would have been unable to lug them all the way to the top of the mountain.

When they reached the river, two previously selected men from the Argentine *Infantería de Marina* quickly stripped down, then dove into the water to begin a search within the vegetation that grew thickly along the banks. The coolness felt good to the marines as they swam slowly in the Rio Ancho. They searched the far side, since that would be the most convenient place to conceal the small craft before ascending the jungle mountain. Müller and his men stood in the shadeless area, baked hard by the sun as the searchers swam from place to place, going into the brush hanging over in the water.

A half hour passed before a shout came from the Argentines. "*Tres* piraguas! Three!"

Müller was glad the task hadn't taken long. One of the generators back at *Fuerte* Franco was running the new ice machine. Cans of beer had already been set aside to cool down even before the detail left on the mission. By the time they got back, there would be plenty of cold beer.

"Push them out away from the bank," the *sargento* instructed, "then swim out of the way."

The order was quickly obeyed. The three piraguas were shoved into the middle of the slow-moving river, then the pair of marines paddled a few meters away. The rest of the detail joined Müller with their submachine guns. As soon as the *sargento* began firing, they joined in. Large splashes and chunks of wood flew upward as the slugs were sprayed at the boats. Within moments the craft were shot to pieces, the chunks floating on the water.

"Ya bastante!" Müller yelled. "That's enough!"

The swimmers came ashore to dress. As soon as they were ready to leave, the patrol headed to the helicopter for the quick flight back to *Fuerte* Franco for the cold beer. Back on the river, the pieces and splinters of the boats were already moving eastward on the sluggish current.

FUERTE FRANCO
1300 HOURS LOCAL

THE guard at the gate to the convicts' camp opened up the barbed wire portal to admit Gordo Pullini. He stepped inside and walked toward his gang, who stood in a group looking expectantly at him. An hour before he had been called to report directly to *Coronel* Jeronimo Busch. The fact that Pullini had been gone that much time was strong indication that something special was in the offing.

A tub of iced beer had been sent in earlier, and Pullini went directly to it and got a can. As the gang leader, he could expect that a lion's share would have been left for him. He popped it open, took a couple of deep swallows, then gestured to the others. *"Agruparsen alrededor de mi, tipos,"* he said. "Gather around me, guys."

The men moved closer, arranging themselves in their pecking order that had been established years before through fistfights, stabbings and bluffing. Those closest in sat down, while those less skilled in fighting and defending themselves in brawls had to stand in the rear.

"Coronel Busch has told me that they have the *bandidos* trapped on a mountaintop in the Selva Verde range," Pullini said. He glanced over at a man named Cortador Marconi. "You know that area well, *verdad,* Cortador?"

"Right, *jefe,*" the convict answered. "I was born and raised just south of there. Me and my *compinches* used to go there to lay low when things got too hot for us in Argentina."

Pullini smiled happily. "Then when we get there, we'll know exactly where we are."

Another convict, Cicatriz Bagni, raised his hand. "Why are we going there, *jefe*? Do they want us to fight the *bandidos*?"

"The guys they're calling *bandidos* are actually *norteamericanos,*" Pullini explained. "And, yes! They want us to fight them. Busch told me this is a chance for us to prove ourselves and become full-fledged citizens of a country these Falangists are going to establish here after they win their revolution."

Navajaso Coletti laughed. "We'll just eventually end up in another prison system."

"You are right," Pullini said. "So what we are going to do is go along with the game, see? Then, when the time is right, we'll make a run for it. Cortador can lead us out of there, and we can reach Colombia with all our money to buy into a drug cartel."

"Hold it!" a pessimistic gang member named Pancho DiPietro called out. "Do they expect us to fight those guys with our bare hands?"

"They are going to give us weapons," Pullini said, noting the instant expressions of happy surprise on his men's faces. "We will have Spanish Mauser rifles that hold five bullets."

"No es bueno!" Coletti said. "That isn't good! I am familiar with those Mausers. Those are real old rifles that are seven-millimeter. They are bolt action, and that means you got to work the bolt for each shot you make. And five bullets are not very many."

"Beggars can't be choosers," Pullini pronounced. "And they'll be good for providing food and protection on our way out of this cursed place."

A shrill warning whistle came from one of the lookouts. Everyone shut up and glanced toward the gate. A group of Falangists pushing a cart had just arrived. They had a crate with a small cardboard box sitting on top of it. The *sargento* yelled for six men to come forward. Pullini instantly picked out a half-dozen men who trotted over to see what was wanted. It took only a moment for the crate and box to be transferred from the cart to their hands. They carried them back, placing the load down in front of the gang leader.

One of the men, who had a stolen claw hammer, went to his tent to get it. Pullini opened the cardboard box on top, noting it had canvas bundles in it. When he unwrapped one of them, he found a rifle-cleaning kit complete with solvent, patches, oil and a ramrod. By that time the owner of the hammer was back. He immediately began taking off the top of the wooden container. Pullini looked inside and saw two dozen old rifles covered with a thick coating of Cosmoline.

"Are there any bullets in there, *jefe*?" Bagni asked.

Pullini shook his head. "No. But we're going to have a hell of a job cleaning up those rifles for use."

Coletti looked toward the gate. "I notice we're still locked down."

IGNACIO Perez made sure no one was near his door in the *Centro de Administración,* then he reached back under his desk and retrieved the rucksack he kept hidden there. He opened the main flap and pulled out the carefully arranged manila folders holding the documents he had sorted so precisely. He even had them neatly titled in his precise handwriting. All the floppy disks were stored in side pockets, concealed within socks and underwear.

He looked at each folder, counting them to make sure nothing was missing: "Roster of the *Ejército Falangísta*," "Operations Orders," "Radio Call Signs," "List of Operatives and Locations" "Intelligence Reports," "Minutes of Staff Meetings," and finally "Lists of Properties Stolen from the Armed Forces of Argentina, Bolivia and Chile." After carefully arranging them to avoid smudging or bending any, he placed a pair of uniform trousers and jacket on top to hide them from casual viewing. Next he checked his web gear that was hanging on the wall. He had never worn it because of his overwhelming staff duties, but it was ready for field work.

Ignacio stepped from his area and walked through the connecting tunnel to the office of *Generalísimo* Castillo. He rapped on the frame, waited for permission to enter, then walked in. "*Mi generalísimo,* I wish to respectfully request permission to go on the attack against the *bandidos.*"

Castillo suppressed a laugh. "*No me digas*—really, Ignacio. Do you crave action?"

"Yes, *mi generalísimo,*" Ignacio said.

"I am surprised by this unusual show of bravado," Castillo said. "But why do you suddenly wish to put yourself in harm's way?"

"I have heard some of the men speaking of me, *mi generalísimo,*" Ignacio said. "They laugh at me, saying I am a coward. I am humiliated by this. I thought perhaps if I just went out on an operation they would think more of me. I promise I would stay out of the way, *mi generalísimo!*"

Castillo was thoughtful for a moment. "I tell you what I will do, Ignacio. I will allow you to go, but I want you to stay with the fire support line. They will be the mortars and machine guns. I will place them on the south side of the mountain, and they will advance just far enough to bring the *bandidos* within range. Their mission will be to contain the enemy while the other lines make the actual attack."

"Yes, *mi generalísimo!*" Ignacio replied with apparent enthusiasm. "That will be fine. Then when we come back, everyone will say how I was in the fight."

"That's right, Ignacio," Castillo said in a condescending tone. "I think I will give you a medal. Would you like that?"

"Oh, yes, *mi generalísimo!*"

"Very well," Castillo said. "You report to *Capitán* Platas tomorrow morning. Tell him I have given you permission to accompany him during tomorrow's fighting."

"Muchas gracias, mi generalísimo!" Ignacio exclaimed. He affected a salute, then made a passable about-face movement, marching out of the office and back into the tunnel.

THE FOOTHILLS OF THE SELVA VERDE MOUNTAINS
14 JANUARY
0530 HOURS

THE EC-635 and SA-330 helicopters brought in the last lift of twenty-four men from *Fuerte* Franco. Now the entire attack force of seventy men and twenty-four convicts were assembled and ready to begin the assault on the mountain where the *bandidos* had holed up. Only twenty Falangists had been left behind in *Fuerte* Franco. These were men who were sick or recovering from injuries.

Every man in the operation—with the exception of the convicts—was fully briefed and knew what role he and his unit would play in the coming battle. These veterans did not have the bravado and optimism of young, unblooded rookies. They fully realized the dangers and difficulties of attacking uphill in thick vegetation and were prepared to conduct themselves as efficiently and bravely as possible under those conditions.

Generalísimo Castillo was in overall field command for what he hoped would be the last assault against the *bandidos*. *Coronel* Jeronimo Busch would take his *equipo comando* of Punzarron, Chaubere and Müller with him. This was what the Chilean paratrooper liked best. He was the type of soldiering officer who preferred the close-in, dirty and dangerous work in a small team to having overall command of a large force while standing back and directing the battle via radio and occasional helicopter flights. His three handpicked men were dedicated and fearless, perfectly matching their commander's qualities and mannerisms. He had been given *carte blanche* to do what he wanted during the battle.

Castillo planned on the first line of attack being the twenty-four convicts who would go into action on the east side. A special detachment of submachine gunners under the command of *Capitán* Pablo Gonzales would follow after them, ready to shoot down any of the criminals who hesitated or tried to run away. The convicts' equipment was basic, consisting of only canteens and ammo bandoleers while the rest of the Falangists carried full combat loads including Spanish M-5 hand grenades.

The second line of attack was under the overall command of *Comandante* Javier Toledo with *Capitán* Francisco Silber. The third line of attack would be led by *Comandante* Gustavo Cappuzzo and *Capitán* Roberto Argento. They would move out with the fire support line as a group. When they reached the south side of the *bandido* position, the machine guns and mortars would drop out to set up their weapons, while the third line of attack moved around to the east side to launch their assault from that direction. Everyone's eyes opened wide at the sight of Ignacio Perez wearing his rucksack and web gear as he joined *Capitán* Tomás Platas at the fire support line.

The *generalísimo* sent the larger SA-330 chopper back,

keeping the smaller EC-635 for observation flights during the battle. He made a commo check with his line commanders via the RMAM radios. All reported they were ready and in position, and Castillo gave the official order to begin the operation.

"*Lanzen el ataque!*"

CHAPTER 16

THE Argentine convicts were formed into two tight skirmish lines as they began their advance up the mountain toward the enemy on the west side of the battlefield. Each man had been given the opportunity to fire five rounds of his bolt-action Mauser rifle for familiarization. No instruction in proper aiming or the tactical employment of small arms in combat had been provided the amateur and reluctant soldiers.

Now, holding their old weapons at the ready with five rounds in the receiver and one in the chamber, they struggled up the steep terrain, already sweating heavily under the discomfort of the heat and humidity.

Gordo Pullini, in the middle of the front rank, glanced around at his gang, noting their expressions of uncertainty as they continued toward the objective. Some now carried the rifles in a way to push the clinging jungle plants aside that grasped at their clothing with nettles and vines.

Navajaso Coletti looked over at the gang chief. Nava was not a happy man. "This is some bad shit we've gotten into, *jefe*," he growled under his breath.

Capitán Pablo Gonzales, with a half-dozen men, followed the prisoners, keeping a close eye on them. Strict orders had been issued that any hesitancy or refusal to move would result in warning shots being fired over their heads. If that failed, offending men would be shot down without further comment. No more warnings, urgings or cursing; shoot to kill without mercy.

The higher the convicts climbed, the thicker the vegetation became until the two skirmish lines broke up as they labored through the briars and thorny jungle plants. Gonzales and his men were also having it tough, and the convicts disappeared and reappeared from sight as the assault continued through the trees and brush.

UP on the north side, the Second Echelon under *Comandante* Javier Toledo and *Capitán* Francisco Silber were also ascending the mountain toward the *norteamericanos*. The Falangists had stopped referring to their foe as *bandidos*. After the fight on the Rio Ancho, these Latin Americans recognized the enemy were also professional soldiers, and they were well equipped and armed. In spite of what the *generalísimo* said, this coming battle was going to be a tough fight with plenty of risk. There was no youthful arrogance among the noncommissioned officers.

The *equipo comando,* made up of *Coronel* Jeronimo Busch, Punzarron, Chaubere and Müller, was between the convicts and the Second Echelon, working their way into position from where they could launch independent raids on the enemy.

COMANDANTE Gustavo Cappuzzo, assisted by *Capitán* Roberto Argento, moved along the south side of the mountain, heading for their attack position over on the west side. They were trailed by the Fire Support Echelon of mortars and machine guns commanded by *Capitán* Tomás Platas. Platas and his men would drop out of the column at the midpoint of the march to set up the three mortars to shell the *norteamericanos* on the apex of the hill. The machine guns would be placed higher up to employ regulated grazing salvos into the enemy positions when the fighting started.

Back at the rear of the march, *Suboficial* Ignacio Perez worked hard to keep up with the column. His feet were already sore from so much unaccustomed walking in his boots, and the rucksack with its extra load of documents and floppy disks, pulled down on his shoulders with such weight that his arms had begun to fall asleep. He had to double-time for a few meters every few minutes, and the out-of-shape little headquarters weenie breathed hard as heavy rivulets of sweat seeped out from his cap and ran down his face.

0600 HOURS LOCAL

THE Fire Support Element reached its step-off point and split from the Third Echelon. The latter continued on its way to the eastern side of the mountains to launch its assault up that side.

Capitán Platas showed his men some mercy by allowing them a short break. After lugging machine guns, tripods, mortar tubes, base plates and ammunition, they were in bad need of a breather. Fifteen minutes later, at the time that Ignacio Perez finally caught up with them, the mortar crews began fixing up their firing position prior to hauling out the aiming stakes to get the heavy weapons all on the same azimuth for shelling the enemy.

Ignacio, his uniform soaked in sweat and his face beet red from exertion, let his rucksack fall to the ground before he sank to his knees. Platas gazed at him with amusement.

"You should have stayed back at *Fuerte* Franco with the sick, lame and lazy, Ignacio. You'd be a lot better off."

Before Ignacio replied, he took a mouthful of water from his canteen, held it, then swallowed the refreshing liquid, "I wish to see some action, *mi capitán.*"

"Most commendable," Platas said. "You will be able to take it easy back here with the mortars."

"Aren't the machine guns staying here too?" Ignacio asked.

Platas shook his head. "They must go farther up the mountain in order to be within range for enfilading and harassing fire on the *norteamericanos.*"

Ignacio forced himself to his feet. "I will go with the machine guns, *mi capitán.*"

"Then you better put on that rucksack," Platas advised him. "They're about to head out." He turned toward the machine gun squad. "You gunners! You've rested long enough. Move up into position. *Ahora!* Now!"

Ignacio grabbed his rucksack and stumbled after the machine gun crews who even now were lugging their weapons upward through the steep jungle terrain.

SEAL OP
EASTERN SLOPE

THE OP was well-concealed but uncomfortable as hell. Wes Ferguson and Gutsy Olson were crowded into the stand of palm brush that abounded with sharp needles on the leaves. Both had already received nasty cuts on their bare arms.

"We ought to get Purple Hearts for this," Wes complained in a whisper, dabbing at the deep scratches with a sanitary gauze pad.

"You better watch what you say," Gutsy cautioned him in a low voice. "You might end up really qualified for that medal before this is all over and done with."

"I suppose you're right," Wes said. "O' course most decorations earned on these secret missions ain't awarded until months or years after the fact." He sank into deep thought for a few moments before speaking again. "Have you ever thought about what you'll be doing after you retire from the SEALs?"

"Yeah," Gutsy said. "I've given it some thought. Krista and I both really like the San Diego area. After I retire we plan on staying there. Maybe I could get a civil service job at North Island or down in National City." He grinned. "Y'know what I mean? I'd be a double-dipper with a Navy pension and salary too."

"That sounds like a pretty good deal," Wes said. "As for me, I don't know yet if I'm going to make a career of the Navy. I keep thinking about going back to Wichita and going out to State to get a college degree. Then law school. I've always been interested in being a lawyer. My girlfriend is a receptionist in an attorney's office."

Gutsy chuckled. "Shit, Wes. You're gonna ship over. You got that crazy look in your eye. You couldn't make it on the outside."

Wes grinned. "You're prob'ly right. But the fact that we're going to be surrounded eventually is making civilian life look pretty godamn good right now."

"Hell!" Gutsy scoffed. "This ain't nothing. During our first mission in Afghanistan we was in a worse situation than this without long-range commo to the outside. The platoon was completely cut off, and we'd reached a point where it looked like we was gonna make a final stand and fight to the last man."

"Jesus!" Wes exclaimed. "I heard a little bit about that, but I didn't know it was that bad."

"Yeah," Gutsy said. "A chance patrol of Air Force F-16s picked up the automatic beacon from Frank's radio. They made commo and got us some air support."

A sharp crackling of a dead branch broke through the brush.

Wes grabbed the handset of the AN/PRC-126 and contacted Frank Gomez. "Brigand, this is the Oscar Papa East. It sounds like visitors are headed this way."

"Roger, Oscar Papa East," Frank replied. "Wait." A moment of radio silence followed before he spoke again. "Get your asses back to the perimeter. Out."

Gutsy and Wes eased out of the OP and began the short climb back up to the line.

THE SEAL PERIMETER
0610 HOURS

ALL positions along the perimeter were manned with every swinging dick on full alert. The SAW gunners Bruno Puglisi and Joe Miskoski were locked, loaded and ready to respond to any part of the line where extra automatic firepower would be needed.

Within the Command Element, Brannigan walked over to James Bradley's bucolic dispensary, noting that Connie Concord was heavily sedated and barely conscious. The Skipper knelt down and got a grin from the woozy petty officer. Brannigan grinned back and winked at him. "How're you doing, Connie?"

"Huh?"

"That's okay," Brannigan said. "You're doing fine."

James nodded his head. "He's out of danger now, sir. I'm still a little worried about shock, but he's beginning to heal nicely, and I don't think there's any serious danger of infection at this point."

"Right," Brannigan said. He patted Connie lightly on the shoulder. "We'll have you out of here before you know it, tiger."

"Huh?"

Brannigan walked back to Frank Gomez and his radio. "Get over to the Second Assault Section," the Skipper said. "The senior chief needs an extra hand."

"Aye, sir," Frank said. He grabbed his CAR-15 and hurried to the southeast side of the perimeter.

Brannigan slipped down into a sitting position, leaning against the Shadowfire radio. "Well, shit," he said aloud to himself. "Here we fucking go again."

THE SEAL PERIMETER
WESTERN SIDE
0630 HOURS LOCAL

THE loud sound of people crashing through the brush caught the combined attention of Andy Malachenko, Pech Pecheur and Guy Devereaux. Somebody was obviously charging toward them with little regard to noise discipline.

"Who the hell is that?" Pech asked. "The New Orleans Saints' defensive line?"

Guy laughed. "It sounds more like cattle stampede to me."

Figures suddenly appeared through the brush, obviously having a hell of a hard time making it up the hill. The three SEALs squeezed off a few three-round automatic fire bursts that kicked over a couple of the attackers. The others melted back out sight into the thick jungle growth.

Senior Chief Dawkins's voice came over the LASH. "It sounds like you guys are taking fire over there. Do you need any SAW support?"

Andy, as the senior man, responded. "Negative, Senior Chief. We received a half-dozen single shots, tops. We fired back and broke up the attack."

"That's odd as hell," Dawkins said. "Maybe they was snipers."

"If they are, they're the worst in the world," Andy said. "All their shots were high and wide."

"Okay," Dawkins said. "If things go bad over there, give me a holler."

THE BATTLE

THE Falangists' First Assault Echelon of the convicts was battered badly by the defenders' fire. Four of them were cut down in the fusillades that swept through the first rank. The rest of the prisoners instinctively turned and ran away from the murderous swarms of bullets smacking through the air around them.

Capitán Pablo Gonzales was infuriated when he perceived the former inmates charging through the trees toward him. "Fire at those *hijos de chingadas*!" he screamed at his men. "Give them some bursts over their heads!"

As soon as the bullets hit the tree trunks, sending down leaves and hunks of bark, the convicts came to a stop. They were in that very unique and unpleasant position of being damned if they do, and damned if they don't. The confused men looked at Gordo Pullini. He hesitated a moment, then another salvo splattered the trees above them. He knew the next one would be lower.

"All right, guys!" he yelled. "Turn around and go back up the hill!"

Now more frightened of the threat to their rear than the front, the convicts stumbled around and once again pushed through the brush toward the mountaintop. The angry, frightened men staggered fifteen meters before Pullini yelled at them again. "Halt! Halt! Start shooting at those guys ahead of us."

They worked triggers and bolts, sending a pitifully weak spattering of shots toward the defenders.

IGNACIO Perez sucked hot, humid air into his lungs as he toiled after the machine gunners ascending the mountain to his direct front. The rucksack crammed with documents and floppy disks of the intelligence information he had stolen felt like it was trying to pull him back down to level ground. He had a pistol for protection but gave it no thought in the overwhelming exhaustion and pain that made his legs feel as if they weighed a ton each.

The training and discipline he acquired in the Spanish Foreign Legion was proving helpful in the way he was being careful with his water. He took only occasional sips, holding them in his mouth a few moments before swallowing them. But his body, unaccustomed to hard physical activity after months in headquarters work, was beginning to rebel against the unkind treatment it was receiving. Cramps rippled through his legs, and his feet felt as if they were on fire in the heavy military leather boots.

Up ahead, the gunners were having their own troubles. The six-kilo weight of machine guns and the ten in the ammunition boxes of linked belts, made each step a separate agony, but they continued moving to higher ground to have the weapons within effective range of the enemy.

A Falangist skirmish line came into contact with the First Assault Section when the SEALs perceived movement a scant few meters to their front. Firing immediately broke out between the two groups, but no casualties were suffered by either side. After a few minutes of exchanging shots, the Falangists suddenly advanced forward, putting out a curtain of slugs from their CETME rifles on full automatic.

Bruno Puglisi increased the bursts from his SAW, swinging the bore from one end of the attack formation to other. Twigs, leaves and bark from trees were scattered by the intense salvos. The Odd Couple, coordinating their actions through ESP as usual, tossed out a couple M-67 hand grenades. They threw the explosives just above the brush but below the limbs of the trees. The detonations rocked the immediate area, and the Falangists broke off their attack.

From that point on, all the combatants stayed low, exchanging fire in a skirmish that had turned into a stalemate.

* * *

CORONEL Jeronimo Busch was in his element as he moved through the brush with the efficiency of a hunting tiger. His companions Punzarron, Chaubere and Müller were slightly to his rear in a V formation. The *equipo comando* counted on furtiveness and concealment more than speed as they made their way toward the *norteamericanos'* position to make contact on their own terms. They were on the northwest side of the battle, taking the precaution of stopping from time to time to simply listen to what was going on around them.

The next time they halted and sank down to kneeling positions, they perceived heavy firing on the north side and sporadic shots to the west. Punzarron chuckled and whispered into his LASH. "It would seem the convicts and their rifles are not making much of a show, eh?"

"They're out there simply to draw fire," Busch replied.

Müller wiped at the sweat on his face. "*Bueno,* they are making a damn good job of it."

"We are close to the front lines now," Busch said. "Chaubere and Müller, move to my right. Punzarron, take the left." He waited for them to get into position. "Now we go upward and make contact. The moment you sight the enemy, give them heavy bursts, and we will pull back. *Ya vamanos*—let's go!"

The quartet of veterans now eased forward, alert and ready with the knowledge they would find the *Yanquis* within a very short time. The brush was dense enough in the area that they could move without crouching over. After a couple of minutes, *Sargento-Mayor* Armand Chaubere sighted a figure in a camouflage uniform just to his right. The man was only partially visible, but the Frenchman saw enough to react.

He pumped a long burst, a short burst and a long burst from his submachine gun.

* * *

LAMAR Taylor took a hit in the shoulder, two in the chest, and fourth that plowed into his face, exiting out the back of his head in a spray of brains, bone fragments and blood.

Paulo Cinzento and Chad Murchison immediately shifted their fire toward the source of the incoming, pouring interlocking streams of bullets. When there was no return fire, Chad crawled rapidly toward Lamar to check him out. When he reached his buddy, he winced at the extent of the damage. At least Lamar died instantaneously without having to go through the hell of settling into shock before expiring. Chad's voice was low with grief when he spoke to Chief Petty Officer Matt Gunnarson over the LASH. "Lamar's KIA, Chief."

"Shit," Matt said. He grabbed the radio handset. "Brigand, this is Brigand One. Taylor is KIA."

A stab of anguish went through the Skipper's heart, but he maintained a tight lid on his emotions. "Brigand Two, this is Brigand. Send Gomez over to the First Section."

Senior Chief Buford Dawkins quickly obeyed, passing the word to the detachment's commo man. Frank left his firing position to sprint across the middle of the perimeter and report in to Matt for assignment.

"Taylor bought the farm," the chief petty officer said. "You can take his place with Murchison and Cinzento."

Frank wordlessly moved over to the position, finding Chad beside Lamar's body. Chad looked up at the new arrival. "Let's pull him back a ways, Frank. He's in the way here."

"Sure."

They each grabbed an arm and dragged Lamar five meters back into the brush, then Frank went up to the position the dead SEAL had occupied at the time of his death. The leaves of the nearby brush were splattered with blood.

* * *

CAPITÁN Tomás Platas studied the sketch map given him by the helicopter pilot *Subalterno* Ernesto Pizzaro. The young officer had assured him that the azimuths and distances shown were accurate. Platas took the trouble to make one more inspection of the three machine guns' positions, then he got on his RMAM radio. The Falangist commo net was simple enough. Each element commander was linked directly to *Generalísimo* Castillo, who used the call sign *Mando*.

"*Mando*," Platas said. "This is *Fuego*. The machine guns are in position now. The mortars are also ready. *A usted.*"

Castillo came back with short but explicit instructions. "*Tire*—fire!"

A sudden influx of incoming automatic fire swept across the south side of the SEAL perimeter. The heavy grazing salvos forced Milly Mills, Gutsy Olson and Wes Ferguson to hunker down in their fighting holes. The sweeping volleys crisscrossed as they pounded into the position.

"What the hell's going on over there?" Dawkins asked via the LASH.

"There's a machine gun squad down the mountain somewhere," Milly Mills replied. "They're sweeping the area with grazing fire. We're pinned down but good."

"Any assault?"

"Negative, Senior Chief," Milly said. "Just heavy incoming."

"Keep your heads down," Dawkins said. He got on the radio and informed Brannigan of the situation.

Brannigan quickly mulled over what was going on; lots of shooting but no assault. "They may not have enough manpower to launch an attack on that side," he said to

Dawkins. "But we can't tell for sure at this point. Tell your guys to stay undercover. Out."

Brannigan had no sooner replaced the handset in its carrier than the first mortar rounds rained down on the east side of the perimeter.

FALANGIST FIELD HEADQUARTERS
1900 HOURS LOCAL

THE battle had ground down to a struggle of attrition.

Whoever outlasted the other would win, and *Generalísimo* Castillo was confident the victor would be him and his Falangist forces. The enemy was both contained and outnumbered, and that always counted as 90 percent of a victory. The only thing he had to do from this point on was keep up the pressure without sustaining too many casualties.

Although the helicopter FLIR patrols confirmed the enemy strength at some nineteen men or so, and he outnumbered them by at least a four-to-one advantage, he had to fight a conservative and cautious battle. If he had more men he would damn the losses and overwhelm the *Yanquis* with one massive attack. But reinforcements were trickling in too slowly to risk losing men that might be needed in the near future.

The mortars were now zeroed in perfectly on the top of the mountain. Although the battery didn't have a plethora of ammunition, there were enough 60-millimeter shells that even with slow, steady barrages the enemy positions would be obliterated eventually.

That would force the *comandante Yanqui* to either be blown to hell, make an impossible attempt to break out, or wisely surrender.

Castillo wondered what choice his adversary would make.

CHAPTER 17

THE fighting had died down, and only occasional shots could be heard across the mountain battlefield. Each side showed patience and restraint, preferring to wait for the other guy to make a move, then respond to it. As is normal in such cases, a tension permeated the area in invisible vibrations that each combatant picked up. It was a time of nervousness and a strong sense of apprehension. Pessimism was a clear winner over optimism.

Suboficial Ignacio Perez had quietly moved off to a secluded spot east of the mortars. He had grown to like his bunker office at *Fuerte* Franco, and now he missed it. The heavy, fortified ceiling and the thick walls gave him a feeling of safety and security. Now he sat in a small clearing surrounded by thick brush. It was a poor substitute for the earthen protection he had in the *Centro de Administración*.

He had grown hungry and fixed a hurried meal of onion soup dissolved in cold water in his canteen cup. He drank the mixture slowly, not minding that it wasn't hot as he enjoyed the tangy taste. The food was from his French *ration de campagne,* and he thought it typical of that country to have special flavoring in food that was to be consumed in the primitive conditions of field operations.

Ignacio could hear the gunners talking, though he was too far away to discern what they were actually saying. The *generalísimo* seemed confident of a victory over the enemy he referred to as *bandidos.* Ignacio noted that the other Falangists were not so convinced of administering a nasty defeat, even though they outnumbered the *norteamericanos.* The experience on the Rio Ancho when the enemy made the escape during the rainstorm had shaken the morale of the troops. The enemy had gone right through their lines carrying boats! It was thought they might have other tricks up their sleeves. Perhaps they expected strong reinforcements at any time or air support from an aircraft carrier. Maybe an entire battalion of paratroopers would come in from the sky to help them in the battle.

Ignacio may have been an accountant by profession, but now he had been around the military long enough to be sure the Americans would not be defeated. The reports he had read and filed of the various ambushes they sprang on the Falangists showed an extremely skillful enemy who seemed to move at will anywhere they wished to go. For his own safety and well-being in life, he must somehow figure out a way to reach them. He knew it would be dangerous in this combat situation, but he had no choice; there was no opportunity for him to return to a peaceful life in his native land of Spain. His sentencing to the Foreign Legion in lieu of a prison sentence, then deserting to the Falangist cause, was a guarantee of never finding mercy or forgiveness within that justice system. He was sure the information he had in his rucksack would earn him a reward, perhaps permission to immigrate to the United States. He could speak a little English from studying the language during his school days. If he could—

The sudden firing of a barrage by the mortar battery interrupted his thoughts.

THE SEAL PERIMETER

THE incoming HE shells burst mostly in the trees, sending shrapnel and large steel splinters whirling downward toward the fighting positions. Now and then one of the 60-millimeter rounds would slip through small branches and hit the ground, throwing up dirt clods, smoke and chunks of white-hot metal. Each separate detonation let out a single brilliant flash of light that disappeared in an instant.

A nearby explosion rocked the Second Section, and Pech Pecheur felt a sharp blow to his thigh that was followed by a numbness going through his entire left leg. "Shit!" he said instinctively, "I been hit!" The words went through the LASH system.

Andy Malachenko damned the shelling as he rolled from his fighting hole to crawl rapidly over to Pech's position. "Pech needs a corpsman," he said, as he joined the wounded SEAL. Andy pulled Pech's field dressing from his combat vest and wasted no time in wrapping it around the injured leg. He pulled it as tight as he could. "How're you doing, Pech?"

Pech grimaced. "I guess I'm all right."

A moment later James Bradley raced up from his run across the perimeter in answer to Senior Chief Dawkins's radio message. Luckily, the barrage had halted, and he was able to help Andy drag the wounded man out of the hole where he would be easier to examine. James found a deep wound in the left thigh that could well include a broken bone.

"Give me a hand getting him back to my aid station, Andy," James said.

They were as gentle as they could be as they cradled

their buddy between them. It was awkward going during the short trek across the perimeter to the Command Element position, but they did their best not to shake their wounded buddy too much. When the pair arrived, they moved Pech in next to Connie Concord.

James wasted no time in getting to work on his newest patient. After getting Pech into a comfortable position, he put a tourniquet on the leg just above the wound, then removed the field dressing. A few deft snips with the scissors from the medical kit opened up the pant leg to allow access to the jagged gash from the shrapnel.

After administering fifty milligrams of tetracaine as a local anesthetic, James began the debridement procedure of removing foreign matter and dead tissue from the wound. He scraped and cut, cleaning out the injury as much possible under the crude, unsanitary conditions. He was glad to note there was no broken bone, thus no splinters left to complicate matters. With this done, he would leave the wound open for proper draining.

After the injection of a tetanus shot, James turned to preventive treatment for infection. Pech would be immobile for quite awhile before it was time for a redebridement and the closing of the wound.

Brannigan came over when he noted that James had finished with the preliminary work. Pech looked up with an apologetic look. "Sorry about this, sir."

"You just concentrate on healing up," Brannigan said. He walked back to his bare-bones CP and picked up the handset of the AN/PRC-126. "Brigand Two, this is Brigand. How many mortars do you estimate are shelling us? Over."

"Three or four," Senior Chief Dawkins replied. "They don't seem to be overly supplied with ammo. I came to that conclusion from their short barrages. But they can still fuck us up. Over."

"Send Redhawk over to me. Out."

Garth Redhawk came in out of the dark, squatting down

beside Brannigan. "The senior chief says you want to see me, sir."

"Right," Brannigan said. "These mortars are going to start taking us out steadily one at a time. As long as they maintain even this slow rate, they're not going to need much more than another twelve hours before we'll all be casualties."

Redhawk showed a rare grin. "Somebody ought to go down the mountain and knock them fuckers out, sir."

Brannigan grinned back. "Do you think you can take the time to tend to that little matter?"

"My social calendar is completely cleared for the next few hours."

"Okay," Brannigan said, turning businesslike. "The best way is to drop thermite grenades down the tubes. You'll have to avoid sentries, get in there undetected and do the job. Then you make a quick exit and get the hell out before they realize their heavy weapons are melting."

"Aye, sir," Redhawk said. "How many of them grenades do I need?"

"Take four," Brannigan said. "And nothing else except your CAR-15 and whatever you can carry in your vest. You got to be a lean, mean, mortar-destroying machine."

"I understand, sir," Redhawk said. "I'll be ready to go as soon as I shuck most of this shit I got strapped on me."

Brannigan walked over to the ammunition hole to get the grenades while Redhawk stripped for action.

FALANGIST FIRE SUPPORT ECHELON
15 JANUARY
0001 HOURS LOCAL

IGNACIO Perez had spent the entire evening concealed in the small clearing he had discovered. All his gear was ready for a quick exit. His pistol belt and holster were fastened around his potbelly, his Foreign Legion garrison cap was on his head, and he sat on the rucksack that had only to be picked up and slipped over his bony shoulders.

After several long moments of listening to determine no one was in the near vicinity, Ignacio got to his feet. He stood motionless for a final short period of tuning his ear into the near environment, then slipped his night vision goggles on. Now he looked out through the brush and could see that the entire mortar group was asleep. There wasn't even a guard posted. He quietly struggled into his rucksack and stepped out into the jungle, immediately heading east.

After pushing his way through the vegetation for three hundred or so meters, he abruptly turned north to head directly for the American positions.

BETWEEN THE LINES
0200 HOURS LOCAL

GARTH Redhawk moved carefully down the jungle mountain, watching his step not only for the purposes of stealth but to be careful of the four thermite grenades he had attached to his combat vest. The environment of thick vegetation looked strange through his night vision goggles, at times becoming a muddled view of green and white spots and splotches.

He eased down a small gulley and just reached the bottom when a nearby noise startled him. The Native American immediately dropped into a crouch. The noise repeated, and the sound of someone breathing hard could now be heard. Redhawk raised up just enough to be able to peer over the palm brush to his front. To his surprise he saw the figure of a diminutive man struggling under the weight of a rucksack. The fellow wore a night vision device yet seemed to be having trouble with his footing. After a few more moments of observing him, the SEAL saw the man's problem was that he was near exhaustion.

Even more strange was the fact the little guy was stumbling toward the Brigands' defensive perimeter. Redhawk was out of LASH range and couldn't warn the guys up on the line. However, the infiltrator or whatever he was made enough noise to wake the dead. He'd be blasted to mincemeat before he got within fifteen meters of the SEALs' positions. Either that or he'd drop dead from a heart attack first.

After Shorty passed on by, Redhawk rose to continue on his way.

FALANGIST FIRE SUPPORT ECHELON
0330 HOURS LOCAL

THE edge of the clearing offered an excellent view of the mortar positions just a short distance away. Garth Redhawk noted the three heavy weapons with the covers over the tubes, all aligned on the same azimuth. Behind them were three stacks of ammunition boxes, aiming stakes, and other gear neatly arranged in exactly the same manner to the rear of the firing positions. It was all very soldierly and very professional.

The SEAL spent a few moments checking out the situation. Some shelter halves were pitched a ways from the battery, and the glowing embers of fires that had been used during the day could still be easily discerned. That, and the fact that there was no sentry posted, gave a very strong indication that here was an outfit that felt they were completely out of harm's way.

Not! the SEAL thought to himself with a grin.

Redhawk slung his CAR-15 and eased out of the jungle, treading lightly over to the mortars. The first thing he did was go to each one and remove the muzzle covers. When the last one was off, he took a thermite grenade off his vest, pulled the pin and dropped it down the tube. He quickly went to the next two, performing the same action in a swift, sure manner. With that done, he left the clearing, slipping back into the jungle for the trek back to the perimeter.

Inside the tubes the grenades' thermite fillers began their forty-second burns. The resulting temperature of 4,300 degrees Fahrenheit changed the filler into molten iron that flowed from the canister. The innards of the mortar tubes ignited and fused, turning into liquid metal.

CAPITÁN Tomás Platas slept soundly in his tent. He dreamed of his hometown of Trinidad in Bolivia, and he was walking down the street going to his parents' house. As he plodded along *La Avenida de la Revolución,* he heard a strange hissing sound. It began to grow louder and louder until he suddenly woke up.

He sat up, noticing an acrid smell, then saw a glow so bright it showed through the canvas of the tent. The officer crawled out into the open and stood up. The bright light, now casting a daylight quality over the area, was coming from the mortars. By now others were climbing from their shelters to see what the hell was happening.

Everyone rushed to the weapons to see them slumping down like melting candle wax. One doubled over and fell on its base plate. The two parts were immediately welded together.

Platas turned to the senior *sargento,* screaming at him. "What did you do? Why are our mortars on fire?"

The *sargento* could only shrug. "I have no idea what is going on, *mi capitán!*"

An older *cabo,* who had been broken in rank in the Argentine Army for getting drunk and driving a truck into the front of the officers' club, sniffed the air. "That is thermite, *mi capitán.*"

"How the hell did thermite get down in those *chingaderas* mortars?" Platas roared.

"We don't even have white phosphorous shells in our inventory," the *sargento* pointed out. "I cannot see how anything untoward like this could have happened."

No one said anything for a moment as they all realized that one or more of the phantom *norteamericanos* had entered their bivouac while all were asleep. Platas hung his head in abject misery.

"I must radio the *generalísimo* and tell him we have no more mortar support."

BETWEEN THE LINES
0430 HOURS LOCAL

A mountain seems twice as steep going up it than comning down, and Redhawk's thigh muscles burned with the effort as he ascended the slope back toward the detachment perimeter. He moved diagonally across the high ground, changing to the opposite direction now and then as he planted his feet firmly before stepping upward.

Then, as before, another rustling of vegetation caught his attention. He wondered if it was the little guy he had seen earlier. This disturbance however, was not quite so loud. It was more like a whisk sound of somebody brushing up against a low-hanging branch of a tree. He ducked down and waited. Within moments four Falangists, stripped down for action, appeared to his direct front. They moved efficiently through the undergrowth, showing no signs of fatigue.

Redhawk could see them well. They were hard-core dudes toting submachine guns. He surmised they were a small patrol that could either be out for reconnaissance or combat purposes. The badass quartet looked like they could do some serious damage if they set their minds to it.

The SEAL waited until they passed, then he moved on.

THE SEAL PERIMETER
0450 HOURS LOCAL

THE dawn of the long summer day was beginning to turn the night's blackness into a misty grayness when Redhawk approached the south side of the perimeter. He spoke in a whisper into his LASH. "Hey, you Second Section guys, this is Redhawk. I'm approaching the perimeter."

Gutsy Olson's voice came over the system. "Okay, Redhawk. Did you bring any coffee and doughnuts with you?"

"Sorry," Redhawk said, moving toward the perimeter. "The take-out places around here suck." He reached the apex of the mountain and walked between the positions manned by Gutsy and Wes Ferguson. "You don't have to sweat the mortars anymore."

"Thank God for small favors," Wes said.

Redhawk crossed the middle of the defensive area going straight to Lieutenant Wild Bill Brannigan's CP. The Skipper was cooking some MRE chili con carne in an FRH as the Brigand walked up. Redhawk pulled the leftover thermite grenade off his vest and set it down. "I got one left over."

"Your efficiency boggles the mind," Brannigan remarked.

"There was only three of 'em, sir," Redhawk said. "I didn't stick around to do any more damage, although it was a piece of cake. They didn't even have a sentry posted. I could've put this final grenade in the ammo, but the explosions would have alerted anyone within a hundred kilometers. Anyhow, it was certain them guys weren't expecting any unwanted visitors."

"Complacency will always fuck you up in a combat situation," Brannigan said. He dug his spoon into the chili. "Did you see anything interesting while you were out and about?"

"Yes, sir," Redhawk answered. "On the way down I saw this little bitty guy carrying a big rucksack. He was a Falangist for sure, but I can't quite figure out what he was doing wandering around in the jungle in the dead of night. On the way back there was a four-man patrol that crossed my path. These guys looked like they knew what they were doing. But they weren't moving toward the perimeter. Instead, they headed to the west."

"Probably a recon patrol," Brannigan surmised. "Did you find the enemy machine guns?"

"Negative, sir. They must be farther up the mountain somewhere."

"No doubt," Brannigan said. "Okay, Redhawk. Well done. You can report back to Chief Gunnarson."

"Is it okay if I look in on Pech, sir?"

"Sure."

It began to rain as Redhawk walked toward James Bradley's treatment area.

0600 HOURS LOCAL

THE rain fell heavily, splattering off leaves and dripping down toward the ground as *Coronel* Jeronimo Busch led his *equipo comando* through the brush. All four men were soaking wet, more from the water on the trees and brush than from the downpour, as they slowly worked their way upward toward the enemy position in the southwest portion of the battlefield.

The unexpected storm gave them a perfect opportunity to launch a quick daylight surprise attack without having problems with sound. After inflicting casualties on the enemy's line, they could quickly withdraw farther down the mountain before turning to set up an impromptu defense.

The Falangists were in a close-packed skirmish line with Chaubere in the lead. He suddenly came to a halt, whispering a warning over the LASH to the others. He had caught a fleeting glimpse of one of the *Yanquis* through the brush ahead. Busch quickly worked his way over to take a look. "*Escuchen*—listen!" he said. "Close in on Chaubere and me. Hurry!"

Punzarron and Müller quickly complied, crowding

together with the other two. Busch pointed ahead. They all glanced in that direction for a moment, then saw the *Yanqui* appear momentarily. He disappeared from view, but it was obvious he had not moved from the position.

"Fire on my command," the *coronel* said. "One long burst each."

Now four submachine guns were aimed at the exact spot they had sighted the *norteamericano*.

"*Tiren*—Fire!"

WES Ferguson shook under the impact of the automatic fire, twisting in his fighting position before slumping to the ground. Guy Devereaux and Joe Miskoski quickly returned a salvo in the direction of the incoming. After a couple of beats it was obvious the attackers had headed back down the mountain in the rain.

Guy hurried over to Wes, rolling him over for an examination. Most of his face was shot away, and his right arm was almost blown off between the shoulder and elbow. Joe and Senior Chief Buford Dawkins joined him.

"Oh, man," Joe said softly.

"Let's put him on his poncho and wrap him up," Dawkins said in a low voice. He spoke into the LASH. "Mills, Olson, Malachenko! You guys stick to your positions."

Brannigan came over from the CP and looked down at the dead SEAL. "Godamn it! You've got to be doubly alert when it's raining. That's when those bastards are going to launch these sneak attacks. Pass the word, Senior Chief!"

"Aye, sir," Dawkins replied.

"Put him in the ground," Brannigan ordered.

The Skipper walked back toward the CP as Guy and Joe began digging a grave with their entrenching tools. Joe worked methodically with the small shovel. "Wild Bill must think we're gonna be here for awhile."

"Maybe he figures we ain't ever getting off this fucking mountain," Guy remarked.

CHAPTER 18

THE SELVA VERDE MOUNTAINS
THE BATTLE
16 JANUARY

GENERALÍSIMO Jose Maria de Castillo y Plato began the violent proceedings by ordering a coordinated attack on all sides of the mountain defenses held by the *Yanquis*. The Falangists moved from their attack positions, holding their skirmish formations as well as they could while struggling against both the steepness of the mountain and the heavy vegetation that seemed to reach out and grab at them.

Less than a quarter of an hour later, the first contacts were made, and numerous firefights broke out all over the mountain. The detonation of hand grenades blasted within the rat-tat-tat sounds of rifle and machine gun fire. At this preliminary portion of the battle, no casualties were suffered by either side, but the combatants moved around a bit to find more advantageous positions to inflict punishment on each other.

* * *

THE fighting flared up heavier first on the east side of the battlefield. *Comandante* Gustavo Cappuzzo and *Capitán* Roberto Argento led the attack by example, going to the front of their men, pumping out fire bursts with their submachine guns. The Falangists cheered, and a footrace of sorts broke out as they all attempted to catch up with their senior officers.

The Second Assault Section under Senior Chief Petty Officer Buford Dawkins bitterly resisted the assault. Joe Miskoski's SAW spat streams of rounds that swept along the entire front while the riflemen of the team used three-round automatic bursts between tossing grenades down on the attackers. A couple of Falangists who managed to run past Cappuzzo and Argento paid with their lives for their recklessness. Now the enemy formation tightened up, getting low in the brush to exchange shots with the *norteamericanos*.

Andy Malachenko spotted an opportunity for a one-man assault when a Falangist to his front pulled back. Andy bounded from his fighting hole and ran a few paces down the mountain before throwing himself into a thick tangle of shrubs. He'd no sooner began pumping rounds at the enemy to the front when Joe and Guy Devereaux joined him. All three put out heavy overlapping salvos that finally broke the back of the enemy attack. As the Falangists withdrew to regroup, the three SEALs quickly returned to the perimeter. They found Milly Mills putting a compress on a slight wound from a shrapnel fragment in his right deltoid muscle. Milly was more pissed off than hurt. "I'd've been out there with you fuckers, but one of those bastards tossed a grenade at me."

"Well, ol' buddy," Joe said. "The next time the son of a bitches come this way, you just toss one right back at 'em."

"Yeah?" Milly said sarcastically. "I was already planning on doing that very thing."

CHIEF Petty Officer Matt Gunnarson, the Odd Couple and Garth Redhawk were having a hell of a time on the north side of the perimeter. *Comandante* Javier Toledo and *Capitán* Francisco Silber were using a closely coordinated tactic of basic fire-and-maneuver to get in close to the SEAL position. After laying down a final fusillade, the Falangists leaped to their feet and charged into the perimeter with wild yells.

Hand-to-hand fighting broke out as the two lines collided. All the combatants were wielding rifle butts and bayonets while bellowing at the top of their lungs. Garth Redhawk even threw a wild left cross that sent a Falangist to the ground. Nobody was shooting during the melee of trying to club, kick, punch and stab each other until Mike Assad caught a nasty butt stroke to his chest from a burly Chilean *sargento*. He staggered backward, firing instinctively just as he hit the ground. This stimulated fresh bursts of shooting until the Falangists, still in the direct front of the perimeter, had to break off and pull back. They left the body of one comrade behind as the SEALs settled back into their fighting holes, cutting loose several salvos at the fleeing enemy. These mostly smacked into tree trunks.

GORDO Pullini and his gang stumbled uncertainly forward with the submachine guns of *Capitán* Pablo Gonzales at their backs. Their firing was miserably inadequate as they worked the bolts of the old Mauser rifles with each shot. After twenty minutes of the frustrating work, the firing from above suddenly increased. With bullets zinging around their heads and knocking spinning chunks of bark off the trees, the convicts turned and ran until they once again came upon Gonzales.

"You miserable scum!" the *capitán* screamed at them. "Turn around and get back up that hill, or you'll die here this moment!"

The convicts slowly turned around but did not move until the submachine guns were fired over their heads as warning shots. *"Ya vamanos, muchachos!"* Pullini yelled. "Let's go, boys!"

They stumbled over their dead as they once again scrambled up the slope. Now the original two dozen were down to eighteen.

PETTY Officer First Class Gutsy Olson was the only SEAL on the south side of the perimeter. He had been stationed there to give the alarm in case the Falangists launched an attack from that direction. Although this had not happened, incoming machine gun fire splattered all around him as the enemy crews farther down the mountain sent numerous grazing fusillades onto the apex.

Suddenly a spent round struck Gutsy just above his right eye, cutting a gash. The wound immediately began swelling, and his vision blurred as he wrapped a field compress around his head. After tying it off as tight as possible, he settled down to hang in tough, wishing he had an ice pack to put on his eye.

1400 HOURS LOCAL

GUTSY'S vision was cleared, but his right eye was swollen completely shut. He had an old-fashioned shiner, looking like somebody had delivered a haymaker to his head during a barroom brawl. By then the machine gun fire had come to a stop, and no more rounds zapped into the immediate area, but he had to stay in his fighting hole since he didn't want to be caught in the open if the automatic weapons renewed their plunging salvos.

He kept his CAR-15 ready to fire as he peered into the jungle to make sure no attackers or infiltrators tried to penetrate the perimeter on that side. He was aware of the mysterious hit-and-run tactics that had occurred on the lines during the fighting, but the raiders seemed to be avoiding the south side. Gutsy yawned with nervous boredom as the shooting and detonations went off around the other parts of the defensive position. He had never felt so lonely in his life.

A figure suddenly emerged into view at his direct front.

A small man, walking unsteadily, moved through the jungle from west to east. The guy had a rucksack on his back, looking as if he were out for no more than a hike. However, the Falangist insignia was visible on his sleeve, so Gutsy took his weapon to his shoulder and carefully aimed.

Then Shorty changed direction and went from east to west.

Gutsy decided the guy had to be either looking for something or was lost. And he wasn't carrying a rifle. The SEAL watched for a moment more, then yelled, "Halt!"

Shorty stopped and turned toward him, raising his hands. "I quit! I no fight! I quit!"

"Come up here real slow, Shorty," Gutsy said. He waited as the guy moved up toward the perimeter, then the SEAL spoke into his LASH. "Hey, Senior Chief! I got an EPW!"

1430 HOURS LOCAL

LIEUTENANT Wild Bill Brannigan paid scant attention to the sounds of scattered shots as he gazed down at the little guy sitting on the ground in front of him. The EPW had military equipment and wore a uniform, but it was obvious as hell he wasn't a soldier. Or if he was a member of some armed forces, he had been misassigned to a combat unit instead an outfit like a mess kit repair battalion where he should have been.

Brannigan glared at him. "I'm think you're a spy."

"I don't unnerstan'," Ignacio Perez said with a hopeful smile. "No more fight. I quit. Oh, yes!"

"We found a lot of papers and computer disks in your rucksack," Brannigan said. "What are they all about?"

"I quit. No more fight."

"Shit!" Brannigan said. He spoke into the LASH. "Chief Gunnarson, send Gomez back here to the Command Element."

Frank Gomez came trotting up less than a minute later. He started to report to Brannigan but caught sight of the prisoner. "Who the hell is he?"

"He's somebody that Olson captured," Brannigan said. "He doesn't speak English, so ask him who the hell he is and where he comes from. I also want to know about the stuff in his rucksack."

"Aye, sir," Frank said. He knelt down beside the EPW and began talking to him. After an exchange that went on for five minutes, Frank stood up. "Sir, he says his name is Ignacio Perez, and he's a warrant officer in the Falangist Army. The guy wants to defect and says that he worked as the adjutant for the *generalísimo*."

"That must be that Castillo guy they told us about in Isolation," Brannigan said.

"Yes, sir," Frank replied. "And he says the papers and computer disks in his rucksack are secret intelligence and operational documents of the Falangists. They include the names of special contacts those guys have in the Bolivian, Argentine and Chilean armies."

"Jesus!" Brannigan exclaimed, having trouble believing that such good luck had occurred. "Find out why he defected."

After another conversation with Ignacio, Frank said, "He wants to get the hell away from the Falangists. He was hijacked out of the Spanish Foreign Legion where he was serving in lieu of a prison sentence. He is hoping he will be allowed to go to America."

"Give one of those documents a read and tell me what it says," Brannigan ordered.

Frank reached in Ignacio's rucksack and pulled out a folder. He flipped it open and read the top page. "This one here lists the names of Chilean intelligence officers that are either sympathetic or belong to the Falangist movement."

"Gomez," Brannigan said in a steady voice in spite of his excitement, "get on that fucking Shadowfire radio and raise Matrix. Tell them what's come stumbling up the mountains to us."

"Aye, sir!"

Frank went to the radio and flipped it on. After getting Matrix and going through the authentication procedure, he informed the CIA operator of what had unexpectedly transpired in the Selva Verde Mountains.

Ignacio, now sure that things were going his way, smiled.

FALANGIST LINES
EASTERN SIDE
1830 HOURS LOCAL

THE original convict contingent from the penitentiary in Patagonia were now down to thirteen from the original twenty-four. The poorly armed men had made constant attacks with submachine guns at their backs and were now so desperate some considered simply getting it over with quicker by refusing to move up the mountain again. It seemed better to die without further fear and exhaustion.

Capitán Pablo Gonzales recognized that they were almost at a breaking point. It would do nothing for the Falangist cause to shoot them down below the mountaintop rather than forcing them to die at the enemy's line of defense. He ordered a stand down, pulling them farther back and giving them a chance to rest, eat and get their emotions under control. The convicts were taken to a glade and allowed to get off their feet. Their wardens, however, still kept the muzzles of their submachine guns on them. Several of the prisoners thought they would be shot down at this point but saw no hope in resistance. They simply sank to the soft jungle ground to wait whatever fate had destined for them.

Gordo Pullini recognized the fatalistic attitude that was fast developing among his gang. It was now time for him to take over and get them back under his personal control. The one thing that *Capitán* Gonzales didn't know about convicts was that after long years behind walls, they had developed efficient albeit simple ways of communication. These could be codes tapped on cell walls, passing notes via twine and paper clip hooks, or speaking in secret ways to convey special meanings or instructions.

As the gang leader sat in the clearing, his leading lieutenants gathered around him, looking as if they had settled down in the locale casually, without any special purpose. Cortador Marconi, Cicatriz Bagni, Pancho DiPietro and Navajaso Coletti seemed to be daydreaming as Pullini spoke softly in a patois of prison slang. Although their gazes and attention seemed to be directed elsewhere, each man received and completely understood the instructions. When Pullini stopped speaking, the subchiefs casually got to their feet and stretched, then walked around the group, stopping to get a light for a cigarette or exchange a word or two. The guards with the submachine guns did not notice anything unusual, unaware that each of the wandering convicts had passed on orders to two men each.

The guards, now wanting to eat and grab *siestas,* moved away to organize themselves into three shifts to watch over their charges. *Capitán* Gonzales was lying on his back, fast asleep.

Each convict slowly worked the bolt of his rifle, chambering one round. Pullini watched, then stood up and walked over to the side like he had to urinate. His men watched him carefully for a few moments. He suddenly turned, and his gang leaped to their feet and aimed at the individual submachine gunners they had been assigned to kill.

Thirteen Mauser rifles barked and spat death.

Now the convicts looked back to Pullini. "Get the submachine guns and bullets," he said. "Take all the rations they carry."

As soon as the task was completed, the convicts hurried from the clearing, entering the jungle to begin a trek upward into the mountains, leaving the corpses of Gonzales and his men to rot in the high jungle terrain.

CAMPO DE AVIAÇÃO CABRAL
ARREDORES, BRAZIL
17 JANUARY

THE preliminary examinations of the intelligence turned over by Ignacio Perez proved to be absolutely accurate. The problem was having to wade through all the names in the documents to eliminate trusted officers who had not joined the Falangists. Because of that, it was still too risky to call in the armed forces of Argentina, Bolivia or Chile to fight against the *generalísimo*'s men. This left Wild Bill Brannigan and his SEALs twisting in the wind.

It was the time for dirty tricks to be played, and nobody knew that game better that a United States undersecretary of state by the name of Dr. Carl Joplin.

He made contact with his counterpart Bernardo Spinola from the Brazilian embassy in Washington, and the pair met in an upscale restaurant in Silver Springs, Maryland. The two statesmen spoke low over the wine and dinners with Joplin doing most of the talking. He glibly informed Spinola that there was irrefutable proof that the massacre of the Brazilian settlers in the Gran Chaco had been done by the Falangists. Spinola listened intently as Joplin explained why the armed forces of Argentina, Bolivia and Chile could not be brought in to deal a death blow to the murderers, even though they were now contained in the Selva Verde Mountains. It would be helpful if Brazil could furnish gun helicopters to make an aerial assault to back up the Americans who even now were locked in battle with the fascists. This, of course, was top secret and not for public consumption, but it would be sweet revenge for the Brazilians.

Now, in that airfield in Brazil, four Defender 500 Scout multi-mission helicopters of the *Força Aérea do Brasil* were warming up for a combat mission. These small aircraft were armed with 40-millimeter grenade launchers that spewed out the little explosive devices in deadly salvos. Although they would have been at a disadvantage against heavily armed troops with anti-aircraft capabilities, they would do fine against the Falangists.

At a signal from the operations officer, the choppers' rotors were engaged, and they took off, turning in a westward direction for the fifty-kilometer flight to the Selva Verde Mountains of Bolivia.

THE SEAL POSITION
SELVA VERDE MOUNTAINS

BRANNIGAN had received specific orders via the CIA communications station Matrix. He pulled in his perimeter so tight that all sides were in visible contact with each other. They were to hunker down and keep low because of a helicopter assault that would be coming in from the east. Although the nationality of the aircraft were not identified over the net, the SEALs were told they were on his side and would not be fired on under any circumstances. If friendly fire had to be inadvertently endured, then endure it. When the aerial attack was over, Brannigan would then contact Matrix for further instructions.

The Skipper used the pause in operations to take stock of his casualties; sadly, he had two KIA and four WIA on that godamned mountaintop. He hoped like hell the attacking choppers wouldn't add to that count.

COMANDANTE Gustavo Cappuzzo knelt down just behind the third skirmish line of his attack force. He had turned them out early to be ready when the order came from the *generalísimo* to once again storm the enemy positions above them.

Capitán Roberto Argento walked up after relieving himself behind a stand of razor palms. He joined the *comandante,* standing beside him to wait for the orders to renew combat. The battle had drained everyone's energy, badly sapping their morale and determination to carry on the fight. The *norteamericanos* showed no signs of crumbling under the numerous attacks.

"*Que es eso*—what is that?" Argento asked. "Listen, *mi comandante.*"

Cappuzzo stood up, then heard the sound of several aircraft engines gradually approaching. "Ah!" he exclaimed happily. "Reinforcements!"

Argento looked around. "Too bad they can't land near here. There are no suitable spots to set down."

"They will land down by the *generalísimo*'s field headquarters," Cappuzzo said. "The new men will be sent up; don't worry. Perhaps the *generalísimo* will delay the battle to reorganize our lines."

Now a quartet of helicopters suddenly appeared, coming in low and fast. Immediately small, deadly detonations sprang up in rows along the ground to their front, working their way through the ranks of the Falangist troops. A half dozen were ripped apart in the explosives, while shrapnel slapped through the trees, cutting down vegetation and blowing holes into more men who happened to be in the wrong place at the wrong time.

SOUTHERN SIDE
0525 HOURS LOCAL

THE Falangist machine gun crews had heard what sounded like an aerial attack, rejoicing that they now had support from helicopter gunships. This would make their job of providing covering fire much easier. But when the aircraft appeared, they were not headed toward the enemy positions up on the hill. Instead they came straight down on them.

Knee-high explosions swept through the area, blowing the machine guns over while pummeling the gunners and ammo bearers into hunks of meat.

FALANGIST FIELD HEADQUARTERS
0530 HOURS LOCAL

GENERALÍSIMO Castillo responded to the call from *Comandante* Cappuzzo. Cappuzzo's voice was wild with fear and shock. "We are under aerial attack, *mi generalísimo*! Helicopters have strafed us with small air-to-ground missiles! I have sixty-five percent casualties. We have been rendered incapable of continuing the attack!"

Castillo flipped to another frequency and raised *Comandante* Diego Tippelskirch, who was in the *Centro de Inteligencia* bunker back at *Fuerte* Franco. "Tippelskirch!" Castillo yelled. "We are under helicopter attack! Who the hell is it?"

"I know nothing of about enemy aerial potential," Tippelskirch replied, the panic in his voice evident over the handset. "I have received no warning of such a possibility from my contacts."

"This is not a *possibility*!" Castillo bellowed in rage. "It is a *reality* that is inflicting heavy casualties on us. Check this out immediately." He switched back to the tactical frequency in time to receive a call from *Comandante* Javier Toledo on the north side. He reported 50 percent casualties. Castillo had to calm himself as the truth of the catastrophe swept over him. There was nothing left to do but request their own helicopters to come to the Selva Verde Mountains and evacuate them back to *Fuerte* Franco. But first he would give the word to his combat elements to make their way back to field headquarters as best they could.

WESTERN SIDE
0550 HOURS LOCAL

GORDO Pullini and his convict gang had drawn off deep into the jungle to remain out of sight of any Falangists who might come hunting them down. Now they had submachine guns and could reasonably expect to put up a spirited defense in case they were attacked by vengeful men of the hated *generalísimo*.

The strain of what they had been through after being forced to attack an enemy who possessed modern automatic weapons while they lugged along antiquated bolt-action rifles had finally caught up with them. The full realization of their situation now pulled their emotions into a tumble, leaving them confused, with a feeling of spiritual exhaustion.

"What the hell is that, Chief?" someone asked as the noise of heavy firing and aircraft reached them.

"*Ay Dios de me vida!*" one man moaned. "They are sending airplanes to bomb us now."

Nimble Pancho DiPietro suddenly leaped up and scampered to a tree. He worked his way up to the top branches, then peered in the direction of the noise. "Helicopters!" he shouted down to his buddies. "And they are diving down on the Falangists!"

Everyone cheered and laughed, but Pullini was in no mood to celebrate. "Let's move farther away, guys! They may come this way."

Now thoroughly frightened about this new potential danger, the convicts obeyed their chief and began hurriedly trekking through the jungle in a northeast direction.

FALANGIST FIELD HEADQUARTERS
0610 HOURS LOCAL

THE *generalísimo* and the headquarters guards looked up in alarm at the sudden rustling of brush to the north. *Coronel* Jeronimo Busch, *Suboficial* Adolfo Punzarron, along with Chaubere and Müller, came into view, hurrying into the clearing. Busch wasted no time in reporting in to the commander-in-chief.

"*Mi generalísimo,* four helicopters have strafed our entire force," the *coronel* said grimly. "Casualties are high. We were lucky to be able to move southeast out of harm's way. We found Gonzales and his men shot up along with some of those cursed convicts. But there were only a dozen or so corpses of the miserable criminals. We could not find the others."

"A new, unexpected development has been thrown at us by the enemy," Castillo said. "Perhaps we were drawn into a trap from the outset. I don't know. I wanted to order the machine guns brought down here, but I could not raise Platas."

"They are all dead, *mi generalísimo,*" Busch said. "And the machine guns destroyed."

"What about Ignacio Perez?" Castillo asked.

Busch shrugged. "We saw nothing of him up there. The miserable little bastard was probably hiding in the woods like a trembling rabbit."

Punzarron, Chaubere and Müller went over to the ammunition dump to refill their magazines.

CHAPTER 19

A slight wind blew across the open area where Senior Chief Buford Dawkins, the Odd Couple and Garth Redhawk waited with Ignacio Perez. Dawkins had Ignacio's rucksack in hand, and it had been taped shut in accordance with strict instructions given by the man who was to pick it up. Ignacio was in a good mood, knowing that he had just come out of one of the worst stages of his life. Although the SEALs were not able to guarantee him any good deals like immigration to the U.S.A., he knew there would be some sort of reward for him because of the valuable information he had provided. Ignacio at least had a realistic hope he would be turned over to the Americans. The worst-case scenario dictated that he would be given a fresh start someplace where no one knew about him or his background.

A Brazilian Army CH-146 chopper appeared in the eastern sky and made a careful circle around the landing area before coming in. As soon as it touched down, a lone man wearing a nondescript military fatigue uniform stepped out. He walked over to the SEALs and spoke to Dawkins. "Haul ass."

"Damn quick," Dawkins replied as the countersign. "Here's the guy, and here's his goodies."

The stranger took the rucksack without another word, gesturing to Ignacio to come with him. They walked over to the helicopter and got in. It immediately took off, turning toward Brazil.

Dave Leibowitz scratched his armpit. "Where do you think they're taking him, Senior Chief?"

"To Langley, Virginia, no doubt," Dawkins replied. "The CIA is gonna wring him dry. And you can bet intelligence reps from a half-dozen countries on both sides of the Atlantic will want to talk at him too."

Mike Assad hefted his CAR-15 up on his shoulder. "The little guy will get something out of this."

"It depends on his prior record," Dawkins said. "If he's clean-cut, he might even be given a new I.D. and a resident visa for the States."

"He's not going to be able to settle in South America or Europe," Redhawk opined. "He's got to go somewhere them Falangists can't get to him. Once they figure he ratted 'em out, he's gonna be on a shit list."

"He's gonna be on a *hit* list," Dawkins said, correcting him. "Let's go. The Skipper's waiting for us."

The SEALs turned and walked toward the jungle to go back up the mountain.

GRAN CHACO
FUERTE FRANCO
1200 HOURS LOCAL

WHEN the Falangists who had participated in the battle returned to *Fuerte* Franco to join the rear echelon party, the entire group numbered 60 men. This was down from the 110 they had when at peak strength. These survivors expected an attack at any time and had been spread thinly among the bunkers and other fortifications.

Morale was decidedly bad. A dark feeling of hopelessness permeated the collective mood of the Falangists, and their responses to shoring up defenses were listless. It seemed a probability rather than a possibility that a much larger force would be sent against them. The senior officers quickly picked up on the growing emotional depression, and *Generalísimo* Castillo called a staff meeting of his ranking commanders to discuss an issue that was growing more serious by the hour.

Coronel Jeronimo Busch and *Comandantes* Javier Toledo and Gustavo Cappuzzo took seats in front of the *generalísimo*'s desk in the *Centro de Mando* bunker. The mood was glum, but the officers held out hope for the situation to turn around. And this was the one thing emphasized by *Coronel* Busch.

"We still have reinforcements that can be sent us," he said in an optimistic tone. "It is only a matter of time. Have we not had additional men coming in here from time to time? There is no reason why that should stop. There will be more weapons, supplies and ammunition as well. Even helicopters. Perhaps several jet fighters will be able to fly support sorties for us."

Toledo caught the enthusiasm. "*Por su puesto*—of course! We have no reason to despair. Time is on our side."

"You need to speak to the men of all this potential, *mi generalísimo*," Cappuzzo said.

"Yes," Busch agreed. "But speak to them as if all this is on a schedule that is already in the administrative mill. Even if we must endure an assault before things improve, the men will fight heroically, even desperately, if they have hope."

"*Muy bien*—very well!" Castillo said, banging his fist on the desk. "We will parade the men this afternoon, and I will deliver a speech of inspiration to them."

1400 HOURS LOCAL

THE formation was a mass one without regard to sub-unit integrity. The Falangists, with their *capitánes* and *co-mandantes* at their head, faced *Generalísimo* Castillo with *Coronel* Jeronimo Busch standing to his left rear. The men were called to attention, then put at ease. Castillo took a half-dozen steps toward them.

"*Guerreros Falangístas*—Falangist warriors!" he spoke loudly. "You stand now in the vanguard of our movement; your courage and devotion to the fascist cause undaunted and unswerving. Although we have lost many men and are forced back into *Fuerte* Franco, we are far from defeated. Even now there are several lifts of jet attack-fighters waiting to be brought out to aid us. Two extra SA-330 helicopters are waiting in Argentina to be ferried here. A recent purchase of 82-millimeter heavy mortars and 12.7-millimeter heavy machine guns has been made from the Russian Federation."

Busch carefully studied the men to their front, happy to note that many were beginning to stand straighter with their shoulders back. This was the sure sign of professional soldiers whose morale had begun an upswing.

Castillo continued, "All our supporters and sources in Europe are working full-time to get reinforcements out to us from across the Atlantic Ocean. Meanwhile, brave soldiers, marines and airmen of Argentina, Bolivia and Chile are standing by to be funneled into our replacement program. They will be followed within a short time by Spaniards, Frenchmen, Portuguese and Germans. The result of these precise personnel actions is that we will be stronger than ever. Now what we ask of you is to maintain the faith! Stay brave! Remember that any setbacks, like this one, are only temporary. Consider it an opportunity to grow in the spiritual and physical strength that make us truly worthy of the victory that will be ours." He paused and raised his hands, shouting, "*Arcángel Miguel, nos bendiga*—Archangel Michael, bless us! With your divine protection and guidance we shall prevail and cast the devils of communism and socialism into hell with Satan."

The resultant cheers were not orchestrated as the Falangist fighters exploded into spontaneous shouting, their fighting ardor completely restored.

WASHINGTON, D.C.
THE STATE DEPARTMENT
20 JANUARY
1030 HOURS LOCAL

THE conference room was set aside for particularly sensitive sessions. It was located adjacent to the secretary of state's office and could be accessed from there or by a special corridor that was manned twenty-four/seven by a special detail of the Capitol Police. It was not a large place, and it seemed crowded with the half-dozen people seated around the one table in the small chamber.

The American contingent consisted of Secretary of State Benjamin Bellingham, White House Chief of Staff Arlene Entienne and Undersecretary Carl Joplin, PhD. The other three seats were taken up by Arturo Sanchez of Bolivia, Luis Bonicelli of Argentina and Patricio Ludendorff of Chile. This trio of gentlemen were special envoys from their Latin American nations who had first appeared in the United States to seek help in fighting the Falangists. The agenda for that morning consisted of two subjects.

The first was the revelations of intelligence brought out of the Gran Chaco by a Falangist defector identified as Ignacio Perez. *Señor* Perez's veracity was wholly accepted, even though he had been positively identified as a convicted embezzler, a deserter from the Spanish Foreign Legion and a member of a fanatical fascist organization. Investigations and interrogations had fully explained the unusual circumstances of his life, thus offering satisfactory clarifications as to his past conduct and associations.

The South Americans reported that there was an ongoing process in their armed forces of culling a great number of loyal officers out of lists of fascist revolutionaries furnished by Perez. For Chile, however, the split between loyalists and rebels was almost 50 percent, though many of the suspects were no more than fellow travelers who had done nothing but express sympathy for the fascist movement. These latter want-to-be revolutionaries would be reprimanded then scattered throughout the army and navy to less desirable postings.

The second item on the agenda concerned the presence of Americans participating in the armed conflict directed against the Falangist Army. It was no longer possible to credibly deny that *norteamericanos* were fighting in the Gran Chaco territory of the Republic of Bolivia. But it was workable to identify them as employees of private military companies as well as freebooting mercenaries who hired on as temporary operatives.

With everyone in agreement and putting up a united front, the session was brought to a satisfactory adjournment. However, Dr. Carl Joplin had another matter that only he could discuss with the Bolivian gentleman, Arturo Sanchez. As every one got up to leave, Joplin invited Sanchez to accompany him to his office for a rather sensitive tête-à-tête.

CARL JOPLIN'S OFFICE
1400 HOURS LOCAL

WHEN Joplin and Sanchez settled down in the former's private office, the Chilean knew exactly what they would be discussing. He saved a lot of time by saying, "We must address the problem of that unfortunate incident at Novida."

"The massacre of the Brazilian squatters received a lot of publicity," Joplin acknowledged. "The fact that some behind-the-scenes chicanery on my part convinced the Brazilian government that the Falangists were the culprits does not clear those muddy waters."

"Not to worry," Sanchez said confidently. "I have been informed that the removal of one man involved in the crime will silence any others with knowledge of the truth."

Joplin wasn't convinced. "How can getting rid of a single individual accomplish that much?"

"The individual in question has power and influence," Sanchez said. "All the less-ranking people involved will know that any unwise revelations or statements on their part will result in them also being dealt with in a manner of extreme prejudice."

Joplin thought a moment, then smiled at his Chilean friend. "It works for me, Arturo."

THE LOZANO GRASSLANDS
1630 HOURS LOCAL

THE fourteen SEALs left in the OA trudged along the Rio Ancho in the direction of their base camp. The two KIAs Lamar Taylor and Wes Ferguson had been evacuated through the efforts of the same CIA guy who had picked up Ignacio Perez. The seriously wounded Pech Pecheur and Connie Concord had also been taken out. Milly Mills and Gutsy Olson were last-minute additions to the list of evacuees. They protested bitterly that their wounds were minor, but Hospital Corpsman James Bradley stated that their injuries needed proper examination. The chance for serious infection in the Gran Chaco was high enough to warrant them being taken away.

It took a stern direct order from Lieutenant Wild Bill Brannigan to make the two SEALs get aboard the helicopter for the trip out of the OA.

Brannigan's realignment had put him, Frank Gomez and James Bradley in the Command Element. The First Assault Section was commanded by Chief Matt Gunnarson with five riflemen, and the Second Assault Section had four riflemen led by Senior Chief Buford Dawkins. However, the Odd Couple was back on scouting duty, and that would cut the First Section down to three riflemen from time to time.

Now Mike Assad and Dave Leibowitz kept the pace slow as the trek continued down the river. There hadn't been any rain for awhile, and a dusty heat hung over the savannah, sapping the strengths of men who hadn't chowed down on Class A rations for the past fifty-two days.

"Drop!" Mike said. He and Dave hit the dirt in instincts developed over periods of intense training and combat.

"What the hell did you see?"

"There's a guy out there waving at us," Mike said.

"Hey! Maybe you're wrong. Could it be a girl? Hopefully good-looking."

"What are you? Crazy?" Mike said. He raised his eyes and looked. "He's obviously trying to get our attention."

Dave spoke into the LASH, informing Brannigan of the situation. Within moments, Frank Gomez showed up. "The Skipper wants me to speak to him in Spanish. It could be a trap or a Falangist straggler who wants to surrender. The guy could end up being a valuable EPW with plenty of information."

"We'll cover you," Mike said. "Do your thing, Frank."

Frank crawled forward a dozen meters, then stopped. "Who are you?" he yelled in Spanish.

"*Estuvimos prisioneros de los Falangístas,*" came back the shouted answer. "*Estamos trece.*"

"Shit," Frank said under his breath, then turned to the LASH. "Sir. The guy says they were prisoners of the Falangists and that there are thirteen of 'em."

"You guys stay where you are," Brannigan said, then addressed the rest of the detachment. "All right, now hear this!

We're forming as skirmishers. Command Element in the middle, First Section to the left and Second Section to the right. Let's go!"

The SEALs quickly got into formation, then moved slowly forward. The SAW gunners were especially watchful, keeping a lookout for any sudden attack. But nothing happened as they continued toward Frank and the Odd Couple. When they reached them, Brannigan ordered Frank to tell the man to have all his people stand up with their hands in the air. Frank complied.

Immediately thirteen men stood to the front with their hands raised. At Frank's direction they came forward slowly, well spread out until they were within fifteen meters of the Brigands. At that point the SEALs moved forward and surrounded the group.

Gordo Pullini immediately identified himself as the leader. Frank brought him over to Brannigan, who questioned him, learning that he and his twelve men were virtual slaves of the Falangists. Pullini insisted on surrendering, and Brannigan had no choice but to take them in as EPWs.

"This fucking situation is just getting stranger and stranger," the Skipper complained.

PUERTO ALEGRE, BOLIVIA
2350 HOURS LOCAL

ALL good things come to an end, and this was the case for *Coronel* Francisco "El Garron" Martinez of the Bolivian *Policia Fronteriza,* who was now in the last hours of a fourteen-day furlough in this city on the Paraguá River in eastern Bolivia.

He had already seen to having his luggage sent aboard the riverboat that would carry him back to his duty station. But before he left for the trip up to the police barracks on the Brazilian border, he had wanted to have one final

rendezvous with his favorite whore in the Bordello el
Baron. It had been a satisfying session, since she was the
only *puta* in the place who could stand his rough brand of
sex. He left her bruised but soothed her feelings with a
large tip of 200 bolivianos.

Now, completely satiated, El Garron headed for the
dock to get aboard the boat. He had a bottle of rum to help
him slip into sleep to get through the rest of the night. He
caught up with a drunken riverboat crewman who was pre-
ceding him down the narrow walk between warehouses.
The guy was weaving and singing under his breath, and
Martinez grabbed the fellow and shoved him aside with a
curse, then continued on his way.

The drunkard eased a .38 Colt revolver with a silencer
from his waistband and pumped five shots into the police
officer's back. Martinez hit the concrete to begin the double process of going into shock and bleeding to death as
his assassin rushed down an alley where a car waited for
him.

SEAL BASE CAMP
21 JANUARY
1140 HOURS LOCAL

BRANNIGAN had radioed a full disclosure on
Gordo Pullini and his motley group to Matrix in Colombia.
Because of the intelligence provided by Ignacio Perez,
Brannigan was informed the thirteen were convicts and not
slave laborers as Pullini had claimed. Under some rough
interrogation, the head prisoner finally came clean about
being a prison gang from Patagonia known as the
Cofradía, who had volunteered to go to the Gran Chaco. He
also pointed out that they had built the fortified area
known as *Fuerte* Franco and knew every single bunker and
emplacement in the place. Pullini wanted to make a deal;
in exchange for the inside intelligence on the defenses, he

wanted permission to bring his gang to America. And he wanted all the money back the SEALs had discovered in their packs. He explained this was hard-earned currency necessary to finance their future enterprises.

Now the Skipper had his instructions from higher headquarters through Matrix, and he had the Odd Couple bring Pullini over to him. Following the established procedures, Brannigan had Pullini pushed down to a kneeling position while he stood to his direct front. This put the professional criminal at a psychological disadvantage. Frank Gomez was behind the gang leader to act as the interpreter.

"All right," Brannigan began, "your story has been verified, and we know you were taken from a penitentiary in Argentina and performed construction work for the Falangists. An investigation of the battlefield in the Selva Verde Mountains has also revealed you were poorly armed with old rifles and forced to attack our positions."

"You see, *jefe*," Pullini said. "I have been most truthful with you."

"And I have been authorized to tell you that for providing me with inside information on the layout of Fort Franco, you will not only be allowed to keep the money you had in your packs, but will be given an additional twenty-five thousand American dollars."

"Oh, thank you, *jefe*!" Pullini cried happily. "Such generosity reflects what great people you *norteamericanos* are."

"And," Brannigan continued, "you and your men will be taken to an undisclosed place where you will be able to live any lifestyle that suits you; whether it be criminal or law-abiding."

"We wish to go to America, *jefe*!" Pullini said hopefully.

"Forget it!" Brannigan barked.

"Then to Colombia," Pullini said. "That would please us very much."

"I was told you would go to an undisclosed location that

will suit you fine," Brannigan said. "That's all you're being offered."

Pullini frowned. "In that case, we will tell you nothing of *Fuerte* Franco."

"Now hear this," Brannigan said coldly. "I am going to make this offer to you one more time. One more fucking time, understand? Not twice more. Once more."

Pullini took the hint, realizing that the alternative was a summary execution out there in the wilds of the Gran Chaco. "*Jefe,* if you have some paper and a pencil, I will draw you a sketch map of the place and describe every bunker."

FUERTE FRANCO
2000 HOURS LOCAL

MORALE was high in the now depleted but unbowed *Ejército Falangista*. The units gathered in their individual bunkers to discuss not *if* reinforcements and supplies would arrive, but *when*. They had been rationing the beer but now began freely passing the valued brew out with no limits. Even if they ran out, it would only be a matter of days before a hundred or so replacement cases would come in via helicopter.

At this time in the evening it had become a custom to turn on their radios to listen to the powerful *Voc de las Americas* radio station that broadcast news, sports and lots of music. The men in the fortress guzzled their beer while tapping their toes and singing to the old tango and conga music that most preferred over the modern *rock y roll*. A break came in the entertainment for a news bulletin. The announcer's voice was tense with excitement.

"*El noticario mas reciente*—breaking news! The governments of Argentina, Bolivia and Chile have announced dozens of arrests of rebel officers of their armed forces. More apprehensions are scheduled and will continue for the next day or two. These dissidents were members of the Falangist movement who had been conducting armed insurrection in the Gran Chaco of Bolivia. The officers who remained back in their home countries organized a grand scheme to funnel personnel, ammunition, supplies and other necessities for the waging of war to the field headquarters of a colonel of the Spanish Foreign Legion. This man, *Coronel* Jose Maria de Castillo y Plato, proclaimed himself a self-styled generalissimo who advanced a mad scheme to conquer all of South America and put the entire continent under his fascist dictatorship."

Mouths opened in stunned surprise in all the bunkers, and the Falangists looked at each other in alarm. Their revolution was coming unraveled.

The broadcast continued with even more disturbing news. "Some of those officers arrested include *Comandante* Manuel Valdez of the Bolivian Air Force Intelligence Service, *Coronel* Guillermo Kraus of the Chilean Air Force, *Capitán de Fragata* Carlos Maggiore of Argentine Naval Intelligence . . ."

The list went on, and the Falangists recognized comrades in the movement who would now be in military prisons going through intense interrogation to give up all they knew. Now stark fear swept through the bunkers with the realization there was no place they could go. But an additional message following the reading of names brought relief and hope to them.

"The affected governments have announced that an amnesty will be offered to those rebels who turn themselves in within the next seventy-two hours. They will be expected to reveal all names and information demanded of them. In return, though they will be summarily dismissed from their country's armed forces, they will face no prison time or other judicial punishment."

22 JANUARY
0400 HOURS LOCAL

SARGENTO-MAYOR Gustavo Kreiling was the chief of the night guard. Just before the sentries were posted that evening, another special formation was announced by the *generalísimo*. Castillo loudly and angrily attacked the news broadcast as nothing but lies. He described it as a poor attempt to lower the morale and determination of the Falangist fighters. "But we are made of sterner stuff!" he bellowed. "Now our anger and thirst for revenge is tripled! When our new men and arms arrive, this continent will be knee deep in the blood of communists and socialists!" The men seemed heartened and encouraged all over again, and the event was closed with wild cheering.

But secretly, each man was wondering how the hell the three nations obtained the names of men they knew were actual agents and operatives for the movement. Castillo had made no mention of that.

Now Kreiling checked his watch. He walked over to where the chief of the relief on duty sat drinking a cup of coffee. The *sargento-mayor* touched his shoulder. "It is time."

The man got up and went out to bring in his sentries from their posts. Kreiling went to the sleeping guards, shaking each awake. He picked out a half dozen. "You men go to the bunkers and wake the others. Remember! No *chingaderos* officers, eh? Tell the guys it is time."

As the chosen men filed out, another special detail came in with the two helicopter pilots, *Subalterno* Ernesto Pizzaro and *Suboficial* Manuel Obregon. The two airmen were sleepy and confused. "*Que pasa*—what's going on?" Pizzaro asked.

"There is a special mission laid on," Kreiling explained. "Both helicopters will be involved."

"I don't know anything about a special mission," Pizzaro insisted. "We haven't been briefed about it."

"Look, kid," Kreiling said. "You do exactly as you are told—*exactamente*—and you won't get hurt! Understood?"

Both pilots nodded their heads in affirmative manners.

Over at the officers' bunker a half-dozen men rushed down the entrances and began grabbing weapons while, at that same moment, a quartet invaded the quarters of *Suboficial* Punzarron, *Sargento-Mayor* Chaubere and *Sargento* Müller. In both places the inhabitants were told to say quiet and remain inside. If any of them so much as showed their heads in a firing slit, they would be blasted by submachine gun fire.

"*Oigan!*" came a call from among the officers. "I am *Comandante* Tippelskirch. I wish to go with you. I know you are seeking amnesty."

"I will see," a *sargento* said.

When Kreiling heard of Tippelskirch's request, he gave in. It might be a good idea if all the *sargento-mayores* and *sargentos* had at least one officer with them when they surrendered to the authorities.

0500 HOURS

THE choppers were warmed up and ready to go. *Sargento-Mayor* Kreiling blew several sharp blasts on his thunder whistle. The men watching the officers' bunker turned and sprinted across the fortress garrison to the helipads. They joined the others cramming aboard the two helicopters. The aircraft were so overloaded they had to fight to get airborne as their rotors bit air in the struggle to climb into the sky.

It took a quarter of an hour, then the noses of the choppers dropped, and the pair headed toward the western horizon.

* * *

THE officers and *comandos* emerged from their bunkers. The sound of the departing aircraft was evidence enough that all the men were now gone. At least the weapons and ammunition taken from their quarters had been left in a neat stack.

"Müller!" Busch barked. "Check the command bunkers to see if they've been damaged."

The *sargento* rushed off to make the inspection. Punzarron and Chaubere kept quiet as the *generalísimo* conferred with Busch, the *comandantes* and the *capitánes*. When Müller returned, he had good news. "The command bunker system is undamaged, *mi generalísimo*," he reported. "None of the ammunition or rations have been taken away. It is fully stocked."

"A blessing of the *arcángel*," Castillo remarked. "Now listen to me all of you. We are going to be attacked, and I intend to stay here and fight to the death. Anything you do is your own choice. If you seek to escape through the Gran Chaco or the Selva Verde Mountains, I will not censure you. The battle here will be the *batalla última*—a last stand for fascism. I am going to the command bunkers."

The *generalísimo* walked toward the fortifications. There was no hesitation among the others. They all followed him.

PETROLEO COLMO FIELD OFFICE
23 JANUARY
1045 HOURS LOCAL

THE building had been cleaned up as well as possible since the massacre, but faded splotches of blood still showed on the floor slats. All the furniture had been removed, and the SEALs were seated on the floor with their backs resting against the walls.

At the front of the room, far from their regular haunts at the Naval Amphibious Base in Coronado, California,

Commander Thomas Carey, N3, and Lieutenant Commander Ernest Berringer, N2, stood ready to deliver an almost impromptu OPORD. The asset for this latest operation was waiting by the door to be called. Some satellite photographs had been mounted on the wall to the briefing team's rear. These images showed a fortified area identified as Fort Franco. These confirmed the sketches made by the convict chief Gordo Pullini.

Carey stepped forward to begin his presentation. "You may consider what I am about to tell you as a modified operation order. The attack phase of this mission will be planned by Lieutenant Brannigan. Now! You are tasked with attacking the ten fanatical Falangists who are making a last stand in this area they call Fort Franco. They have gotten on the radio and sent out calls that they will fight to the death."

Bruno Puglisi raised his hand. "Why don't you just send some aircraft over there and bomb the shit out of 'em, sir?"

"We need prisoners, Petty Officer," Carey replied. "These are the guys who know the true extent of the Falangist organization in France, Germany, Portugal and Spain. They'll have to be taken by basic fire and maneuver. Without being able to interrogate them, the sleeper cells in the capital cities of those countries will remain unknown. That means the fascist movement will continue."

"Sir, I ain't trying to get out of anything," Senior Chief Buford Dawkins said, "but why ain't the Argentines and all them making the attack? They know the bad guys in their own armed forces now, right?"

"Wrong, Senior Chief," Carey said. "They're still in the process of weeding them out. It is hoped the amnesty will bring more in. But it has been decided that since you guys are already here and primed to go, that the honors will be yours."

"Let's do it!" Paulo Cinzento blurted out. "We got some KIAs to get even for."

"There's something to keep in mind," Carey said. He

turned to the map, indicating an area of Fort Franco with his laser pointer. "Those three bunkers arranged in a triangular shape is the location you'll attack. They are connected by short tunnels, so the defenders will be able to easily shift from one to the other. Lieutenant Brannigan has already been apprised of the site's defensive capabilities. You will go by chopper from this location to Fort Franco to execute the OPORD. Any questions? In that case, Commander Berringer will carry on the intelligence portion of this briefing."

Berringer came to the front. "I won't be saying anything today. I brought an asset who is intimately familiar with the men you'll be fighting as well as the physical aspects of the bunkers they occupy." He looked at the man standing by the door, gesturing to him to join him.

Diego Tippelskirch walked up, speaking in excellent English. "I am a former intelligence officer of the Falangists. The three bunkers you will attack consist of the Command Bunker that the leader of the Falangist Army used as his headquarters. There is also an Administration Bunker, and lastly an Intelligence Bunker. All these were in effect offices and storage areas, but they are still bunkers with firing slits. They were designed for defense, thus you must keep in mind you will be under their weapons' sights as you advance toward them."

Joe Miskoski spoke up. "What about support weapons? Do them guys have any machine guns or mortars?"

"They have only submachine guns and assault rifles that can be fired in both semi- and automatic modes," Tippelskirch replied. "There is one special thing I must tell you. Four of those men are what you would describe as real badasses. They formed a commando team that carried on independently within the combat operations of the Falangists. Those men are responsible for the deaths of your comrades who gave their lives in battle."

There were no questions for the defector, and Carey took the floor once again. "There you have it. Because you will have no air or heavy weapons support, your job will be dangerous. It's going to be like the gunfight at the OK Corral in Tombstone, Arizona. You guys have one hell of a bloody row to hoe. Be careful! Be skillful! Be ready!"

The briefing ended on that note.

CHAPTER 20

THE two Argentine Army SA-330s set down out of rifle range of the three-bunker command complex. Noise discipline wasn't a factor at this time of the assault since the noise of the choppers announced the arrival of the attackers.

Brannigan's Brigands unassed the aircraft, moving away from the LZ to form up within the abandoned bunkers on the outskirts of the fortress. Brannigan, as usual, kept Frank Gomez and James Bradley with him. Both would act as riflemen, but if James had to go into his hospital corpsman role, Frank would cover him and give a hand moving the wounded to a safe location.

Chief Matt Gunnarson's First Assault Section had Bruno Puglisi as its SAW gunner. He stuck close to Matt to add firepower where and when necessary. The riflemen were Mike Assad, Dave Leibowitz, Garth Redhawk and Paul Cinzento. Now they moved to the right, spreading out in a skirmish formation.

Over on the left Senior Chief Dawkins honchoed his Second Assault Section into position. Joe Miskoski stuck close to the section commander, as per detachment SOP. The rest of the section, Andy Malachenko, Guy Devereaux and Chad Murchison, were in their usual roles toting their CAR-15s.

Brannigan knew that potential casualties could cause impromptu changes of personnel assignments, but he figured he could keep that to a minimum by concentrating the attacks on one bunker at a time. The battlefield was so limited in scope and size that to attempt a complete envelopment would result in casualties from friendly fire.

The detachment moved closer to the objective, keeping low and using the other bunkers for cover. When they reached a point where the target bunkers were within range, the SEALs settled down to launch the assault. Brannigan had already chosen the Command Bunker as the initial target of the attack.

But first things first as demanded by protocol and special orders.

Frank Gomez, with a bullhorn hanging on his belt, picked up the sound device and pressed the SPEAK button. "Attention inside the bunkers," he said in Spanish. "Your situation is hopeless. Save your lives and avoid bloodshed. Come out now with your hands up. You will be treated as EPWs under the provisions of the Geneva convention."

THE COMMAND BUNKER

JOSE Maria de Castillo y Plato laughed as soon as the bullhorn address came to an end. "Those *Yanquis* must think this is going to be easy for them."

"Con su permiso, mi generalísimo," said *Coronel* Jeronimo Busch. "I speak excellent English. I have even attended several courses at the United States Army's Command and

General Staff College at Fort Leavenworth, Kansas. I request the pleasure of replying to our visitors."

"Please do the honors, *Coronel*," Castillo said.

Busch moved up close to the firing slit and took a deep breath, then shouted, "Go fuck yourselves!"

SEAL DETACHMENT

"I'M going to take that as a no," Brannigan said. He spoke into the LASH. "Second Section move forward. First Section lay down covering fire. Now!"

Joe Miskoski immediately put out heavy fire bursts from the SAW, sweeping the muzzle to spray the firing slit from one side to the other. Andy, Guy and Chad crawled forward as that salvo was joined by fusillades from Chief Gunnarson's men.

Dirt and splinters flew off the bunker, but the Falangists returned a heavy staccato of fire bursts that clipped the dirt between the individual SEALs while whipping the air just above their heads. Brannigan ordered the advance stopped. "Keep the fire on the objective! Make 'em duck their heads! First section move left and hit the next bunker!"

THE FIRST ASSAULT SECTION

CHIEF Matt Gunnarson pulled his men around toward the Intelligence Bunker. When they got into position, Bruno Puglisi's SAW spat rounds at the target while the riflemen scampered forward, then threw themselves down in the grass. The section continued to spray heavy volleys, all directed at the viewing slit. The Falangists inside replied with regulated salvos of automatic bursts, trying to get sight pictures of the flitting images of advancing attackers.

INTELLIGENCE BUNKER

COMANDANTE Gustavo Cappucco, along with *Capitánes* Francisco Silber and Tomás Platas, had done their best to return the incoming, but the Americans maintained uncoordinated but steady volleys. The Falangists were driven to the floor as more slugs cracked through the firing slit. The incoming intensified quickly, then *Coronel* Busch came into the bunker through the tunnel. He went straight to the slit, shoving his submachine gun through and sending long streams of slugs outward.

Cappucco, Silber and Platas got back to their feet to join him. Now all four men had gained the advantage as their combined return fire slowed the attackers down. Platas's skull suddenly exploded out the back in an eruption of bone splinters, blood and brains. He was knocked against the rear wall, sliding down to the floor to an undignified sitting position. Busch turned away, yelling down the tunnel for *Capitán* Roberto Argento to join them in the bunker.

THE SEALS

"FIRST section!" Brannigan ordered into the LASH. "Renew your assault on the Command Bunker."

Matt Gunnarson and his guys began advancing on their bellies, pausing to lay down their own covering fire in the slow but steady assault. It was an orchestrated operation in spite of the noisy, blasting chaos over the scene as the men alternated their advances and salvos. Suddenly Paulo Cinzento's head rocked back violently, and he collapsed to his belly. Dave Leibowitz crawled over to check him out. He'd taken a hit just above the left eye, leaving a gaping exit wound. "Paulo is KIA," Dave said over the LASH.

The belly-crawling, shoot-and-rush assault continued. Meanwhile Brannigan made his way around to the other side of the fight, joining the Second Assault Section to check out things at the Intelligence Bunker. He threw himself down beside Senior Chief Dawkins, who kept working the trigger as he spoke. "Sir, they're firing out of there like there's no tomorrow," the senior chief said.

"We need those mortars those headquarters pukes didn't want to give us," Brannigan said angrily.

"It's the same old shit, sir," Dawkins said. "Orders is orders."

Over on the far right of the line, Garth Redhawk was making a rapid belly crawl through some higher grass, moving at an oblique direction from the bunker. After going ten meters, he moved back in the opposite way, continuing on until he reached a corner of the firing slit. The Native American rolled over on his back and pulled a grenade off his combat vest. After a yank on the pin, he went back on his belly and tossed the M-67 through the firing slit. He scurried backward just as the detonation went off, sending a cloud of dust outward.

The section took advantage of this unexpected turn of events, jumping to their feet to charge forward with all weapons aimed at the slit. As soon as they reached the bunker, three more grenades were tossed in. The trio of explosives heralded the end of the defensive emplacement as Cappucco, Silber and Argento died together, their bodies shredded by steel fragments.

THE BUNKERS

THE explosions from the grenades sent a deafening concussion and flying metal splinters through the entire bunker complex. Over in the Administrative Bunker, *Comandante* Javier Toledo was ripped to pieces along with *Suboficial* Adolfo Punzarron. The only casualty in the Command Bunker was the Frenchman Arnaud Chaubere.

Castillo, Busch and Müller, though knocked down, were able to struggle back to their feet. Choking clouds of dust swirled around the trio of survivors, and blood flowed from their concussion-battered ears.

Castillo wept bitterly and heavily, having drawn into himself. He ignored his two companions as he staggered over to his splintered desk. He kicked a bottom drawer out, then reached in to pull out the special presentation pistol given him by the officers of his old Foreign Legion regiment. It had been given him in recognition of his promotion from *teniente-coronel* to *coronel*.

He took the prized Campo-Giro Model 1913 automatic pistol and without hesitation stuck the muzzle in his mouth and pulled the trigger. He fell backward, bouncing off the earthen wall to fall face-first over what was left of the office furniture.

Busch turned to Müller. "You and I have served for years together as paratroopers. Although in other units we would be separated by rank, as airborne soldiers we are brothers. You must trust what I am going to do. I have a serious purpose, and it will benefit us and the cause we have embraced with all our souls."

Müller snapped to the position of attention. "*Seguro, mi coronel!* I obey without question."

Busch limped over to the firing slit. He yelled loudly, "There are only two of us left. We wish to surrender."

OUTSIDE THE BUNKER

THE SEALs watched dispassionately as the two Falangists crawled through the firing slit, then slowly got to their feet with their hands over their heads. Both were covered in dust and the blood of their dead comrades.

The Odd Couple hurried forward and roughly searched them, then pulled their hands down and behind their backs.

Plastic constraints were quickly placed around their wrists. Mike and Dave then each grabbed one by the collar and hauled him over to Brannigan.

The Skipper made no comments as he reached for the handset of the AN/PRC-126 radio to call in the choppers. A few meters away, Bruno Puglisi and Garth Redhawk stood beside Paulo's body as James Bradley checked him over. KIA.

The war in the Gran Chaco was over.

CHAPTER 21

THE arrival of the C-130 Hercules caused no ripple of interest as it touched down and began its taxi run to an isolated area of the base. A pair of M1078A1 2.5-ton cargo trucks were waiting as the big transport approached the end of the runway. The aircraft turned, then the pilot shut down its inboard port engine as the passenger door opened. Thirteen men in extremely filthy BDUs disembarked, stepping unsteadily down to the concrete after the long air trip. All carried rucksacks and weapons. They seemed extremely tired and downcast, but the appearance of one individual from behind the truck brought smiles to their faces when he stepped out and hollered at them.

"What the hell took you so long?"

Lieutenant (J.G.) Jim Cruiser, using a cane but moving along confidently and steadily, walked over to them. He shook hands with Lieutenant Wild Bill Brannigan, then turned to endure the poundings and rough greetings of the others.

"I'm doing fine," Cruiser said, answering all the inquiries. "I'll be back to duty within a couple of months." His mood sobered a bit. "The other aircraft got in a couple of days ago bringing in the wounded and KIAs. I knew Ferguson and Taylor, but I'd never met Cinzento. Milly and Gutsy were in great shape, and are due to be released from Balboa tomorrow. But Pecheur and Connie are going to be gone for awhile. Both had pretty serious injuries. They might even be facing disability separations from the Navy."

"Shit happens," Brannigan said. He turned to the detachment. "Get on the trucks, guys. You've still got a debriefing before you're turned loose."

"Well, anyway, welcome home," Cruiser said. He walked over to join Brannigan in the truck's cab.

CIA SAFE HOUSE
GEORGETOWN, VIRGINIA

A Spanish citizen by the name of Ignacio Perez had gotten into the habit of selecting Big Macs, extra large fries and chocolate milkshakes when it was time for his mentors to go out for his sustenance. He was consuming the menu three times a day and loving it. The thinness he had developed on French rations down in the Gran Chaco was rounding out to a quite noticeable plumpness.

Ignacio had been through the grilling mill since his arrival back in the States. Agents from the CIA and FBI had combed through his papers as the little man explained the setup of the Falangists. Other agencies as well as intelligence officials from South America and Europe still waited to have their turn at him. While he waited for their arrival, he spent his time studying English and watching TV programs to pick up a bit more of the idiom. His favorite shows were reruns of *Cheers* after he figured out the character Norm was an accountant.

A place in the Federal Witness Protection Program had been arranged for Ignacio, and he would eventually be given a complete new identity and sent to an area where he could begin that new life he wanted so badly.

THE REPUBLICS OF ARGENTINA, BOLIVIA AND CHILE

THE newspapers and magazines of all three countries ran a special feature that had two photos of a dead Falangist fighter. He was identified both as Adolfo Punzarron, a deserter from the Spanish Foreign Legion, and Adolfo Punzarrão, a fugitive murderer from Portugal.

One of the photographs had been published in the Chilean newspaper *El Conquistador* when, under the alias of Maurício Castanho, he testified he was a Brazilian squatter who had lost his family during a massacre he claimed was done by American Green Berets. The other picture showed his shrapnel-torn corpse that had been pulled out of a bunker at a Falangist stronghold. This was all offered as proof that the outrage committed against the Brazilian squatters was done by the fascists, and Punzarrão aka Punzarron had been one of the killers.

A related story also appeared with the one about the Portuguese murderer. This one reported that two Falangist prisoners who were listed as deserters from the Chilean Army—*Teniente-Coronal* Jeronimo Busch and *Sargento* Antonio Müller—had escaped from a military prison near San Bernardo, Chile. There were strong suspicions that the breakout was the result of both inside and outside collusion. A military police official stated that the men had undoubtedly been taken into the Falangist underground, where they would be inserted into an escape-and-evasion net. They would eventually end up at a hideout somewhere in Europe.

**CORONADO, CALIFORNIA
THE BRANNIGAN RESIDENCE
5 FEBRUARY
1300 HOURS LOCAL**

LIEUTENANT Bill Brannigan's wife Lisa sat at the table on the patio, sipping a glass of Chardonnay as she watched her husband turning the steaks on the barbecue. She was used to him being somewhat taciturn after coming back from a mission, but this latest operation had left him almost completely uncommunicative.

The official word was that he and his detachment had been on a highly classified training operation in which some new infiltration and exfiltration techniques had been tested. Some things had gone terribly wrong in which three men were killed in accidents and four injured, two of them quite seriously.

Lisa was a naval pilot stationed at North Island NAS in an EA-6B Prowler squadron, and she could read between the lines of the report. She quickly figured out there had been a supersecret mission of some sort that had taken place under some very heavy wraps. Whether it was a success or not would not be known for years if ever. Meanwhile, families might never be informed that their relatives were killed in action, nor would any medals be issued, and any acts of heroism would be hidden forever in files marked TOP SECRET. Only when the operation was officially declassified would the dead be properly honored and the brave receive the medals due them.

Now, in the peaceful atmosphere of the patio, Brannigan used tongs to grasp the steaks, slipping them on the plates. He walked over to the table and set one steak down for Lisa and the other for himself. She spooned out the salad and green beans as he took a chair and started to eat. Brannigan stopped with his fork halfway between the meat and his mouth. He looked at his wife in a special, meaningful way.

"Ain't this some shit?"

She smiled sadly but proudly, knowing exactly what he was referring to.

OFF THE SOUTHEAST COAST OF CUBA
PRESIDENTS' DAY

BACK when Jimmy Carter was the President of the United States, floods of refugees from Cuba braved the dangerous crossing to Florida in attempts to get to America to start new lives under the blessings of freedom. Many people perished in vessels that were sometimes no more than inflated tractor inner tubes. President Carter was disturbed by these tragedies and made a deal to let the defectors into the U.S.A. if the Cuban leader Fidel Castro would lift the ban on their fleeing his autocratic government.

This became known as the Mariel Boat Lift, and 125,000 people left Cuba under its provisions. Unfortunately, Castro emptied prisons and insane asylums, inserting these undesirables into the flow of authentic refugees. This created a nightmare for everyone concerned when the truth was discovered. Undesirable Cubans ended up spending years in custody while decent Marielitos, as they were known, suffered the stigma of being associated with criminals and lunatics.

For Fidel Castro this was one big joke he had played on the American president.

0330 HOURS

OFF in the darkness, the Cuban shore was shadowy and indistinct as a nondescript fishing boat stood by. A group of thirteen men slipped over the side into two rubber rafts for a very short boat trip. These individuals making ready to row to the beach were Gordo Pullini and his gang

members. They had been issued handguns, clothing, and
carried knapsacks with over $100,000 American packed in
them. In this reverse of the Mariel Boat Lift, they planned
to set up whatever illegal activities were available to
Spanish-speaking, ruthless professional criminals within
Cuban society.

Payback time, Fidel!

GLOSSARY

2IC: Second in command
AA: Anti-aircraft
AFSOC: Air Force Special Operations Command
AGL: Above ground level
aka: Also known as
ARG: Amphibious ready group
ASAP: As soon as possible
ASL: Above sea level
AT-4: Antiarmor rocket launchers
Attack board (also compass board): A board with a compass, watch and depth gauge used by subsurface swimmers
AWOL: Away without leave, i.e., absent from one's unit without permission, aka French leave
BOQ: Bachelor officers' quarters
Briefback: A briefing given to staff by a SEAL platoon regarding their assigned mission. This must be approved before it is implemented.
BDU: Battle dress uniform
BUD/S: Basic underwater demolition SEAL training course
C4: Plastic explosive

CAR-15: Compact model of the M-16 rifle
CATF: Commander, Amphibious Task Force
CNO: Chief of naval operations
CO: Commanding officer
Cover: Hat, headgear
CP: Command post
CPU: Computer processing unit
CPX: Command post exercise
CRRC: Combat rubber raiding craft
CS: Tear gas
CSAR: Combat search and rescue
CVBG: Carrier battle group
DPV: Desert patrol vehicle
Det Cord: Detonating cord
Draeger Mk V: Underwater air supply equipment
DZ: Drop zone
E&E: Escape and evasion
EPW: Enemy prisoner of war
ESP: Extrasensory perception
FLIR: Forward-looking infrared radar
French leave: See AWOL
FRH: Flameless ration heater
FTX: Field training exercise
GPS: Global Positioning System
H&K MP-5: Heckler & Koch MP-5 submachine gun
HAHO: High altitude high opening parachute jump
HALO: High altitude low opening parachute jump
HE: High explosive
Head: Navy and Marine Corps term for toilet; called a latrine in the Army
Hors de combat: Out of the battle (expression in French)
HSB: High-speed boat
JSOC: Joint Special Operation Command
K-Bar: A brand of knives manufactured for military and camping purposes
KIA: Killed in action
LBE: Load-bearing equipment

LSSC: Light SEAL support craft

Light sticks: Flexible plastic tubes that illuminate

Limpet mine: An explosive mine that is attached to the hulls of vessels

LZ: Landing zone

M-18 claymore mine: A mine fired electrically with a blasting cap

M-60 E3: A compact model of the M-60 machine gun

M-67: An antipersonnel grenade

M-203: A single-shot 40 millimeter grenade launcher

MATC: A fast river support craft

MCPO: Master chief petty officer

Medevac: Medical evacuation

Mk 138 satchel charge: Canvas container filled with explosive

MRE: Meal ready to eat

MSSC: Medium SEAL support craft

N2: Intelligence staff

N3: Operations and plans staff

NAS: Naval air station

NAVSPECWAR: Naval Special Warfare

NCO: Noncommissioned officer, i.e., a corporal or sergeant

NCP: Navy College Program

NFL: National Football League

NVG: Night vision goggles

OA: Operational area

OCONUS: Outside the continental United States

OER: Officer evaluation report

OP: Observation post

OPLAN: Operations plan. This is the preliminary form of an OPORD.

OPORD: Operations order. This is the directive derived from the OPLAN of how an operation is to be carried out. It's pretty much etched in stone.

PBL: Patrol boat, light

PC: Patrol coastal vessel

PDQ: Pretty damn quick

PLF: Parachute landing fall

PO: Petty officer (e.g., PO1C is petty officer first class)

POV: Privately owned vehicle

PT: Physical training

RIB: Rigid inflatable boat

RPG: Rocket propelled grenade

RPM: Revolutions per minute

RTO: Radio telephone operator

SAW: Squad automatic weapon—M249 5.56-millimeter magazine or clip-fed machine gun

SCPO: Senior chief petty officer

SDV: Seal delivery vehicle

SERE: Survival, Evasion, Resistance and Escape

SITREP: Situation report

SOCOM: Special operations command

SOF: Special Operations Forces•

SOI: Signal operating instructions

SOLS: Special operations liaison staff

SOP: Standard operating procedures

SPECOPS: Special operations

Special boat squadrons: Units that participate in SEAL missions

SPECWARCOM: Special Warfare Command

TDY: Temporary duty

UN: United Nations

Unass: To jump out of or off of something

Watch bill: A list of personnel and stations for the watch

WIA: Wounded in action

The explosive, all-new military action series.

SEALS

JACK TERRAL

They go where other warriors fear to tread.

In Afghanistan, a native CIA contact wants to defect with detailed knowledge of anti-American insurgent operations. But time is short, and the risk is high. William "Wild Bill" Brannigan and his SEAL platoon are called in for the difficult and dangerous mission. According to plan, they night-jump into the lawless Afghan desert and make their way to the rendezvous point.

Then things stop going according to plan.

0-515-14041-4

Available wherever books are sold or at penguin.com